"Sasha Lord's intensely romantic voice is a gift to the genre." —Lisa Kleypas

Praise for the Novels of Sasha Lord

Beyond the Wild Wind

"Intriguing. . . . The story line never slows down . . . a delightful romance." —*Midwest Book Review*

"*Beyond the Wild Wind* is another bold adventure in Ms. Lord's Wild series . . . action-packed [and] emotionally charged." —Romance Reviews Today

"Intense emotions and searing sensuality flow from Lord's powerful prose. The author has the ability to create characters whose passions ignite the imagination, and her talent for vivid storytelling increases with each new tantalizing tale."
—*Romantic Times* (4½ stars, Top Pick)

Across a Wild Sea

"Lord is a grand mistress at blending the reality of a medieval romance with magic and myth to create a story with the essence of a fairy tale and the drama of a grand epic. Those who love Mary Stewart will savor Lord's latest."
—*Romantic Times* (4 stars)

"Ms. Lord's richly woven historical draws readers into a vivid world of court politics, hatred, jealousy, greed, and erotic passion. With multidimensional characters and a stunning love story, you can't help but be thoroughly captivated by this reading pleasure." —*Rendezvous*

continued . . .

"A superb historical romantic fantasy that combines medieval elements with a fine adult-fairy-tale-like atmosphere. . . . The exciting story line blends the fantasy elements inside a well-written historical tale that showcases Sasha Lord's ability to provide a wild read for her fans."   —The Best Reviews

In a Wild Wood

"Dark and filled with potent sensuality and rough sex (á la early Johanna Lindsey), Lord's latest pushes the boundaries with an emotionally intense, sexually charged tale."   —*Romantic Times* (4½ stars, Top Pick)

"This exciting medieval romance is an intriguing historical relationship drama. . . . a cleverly developed support cast."   —*Midwest Book Review*

Under a Wild Sky

"Sasha Lord weaves a most imaginative tale."
                                        —Bertrice Small

"Stunningly imaginative and compelling."
                                        —Virginia Henley

"Lord's debut is a powerful, highly romantic adventure with marvelous mystical overtones. Like a lush fairy tale, the story unfolds against a backdrop brimming with fascinating characters, a legend of grand proportions, and magical animals."   —*Romantic Times* (4½ stars)

"Ms. Lord's debut novel was a surefire hit with this reader, and I eagerly look forward to the next book of hers featuring characters from *Under a Wild Sky*."
                                        —*Rendezvous*

IN MY
WILD DREAM

SASHA LORD

A SIGNET ECLIPSE BOOK

SIGNET ECLIPSE
Published by New American Library, a division of
Penguin Group (USA) Inc., 375 Hudson Street,
New York, New York 10014, USA
Penguin Group (Canada), 90 Eglinton Avenue East, Suite 700, Toronto,
Ontario M4P 2Y3, Canada (a division of Pearson Penguin Canada Inc.)
Penguin Books Ltd., 80 Strand, London WC2R 0RL, England
Penguin Ireland, 25 St. Stephen's Green, Dublin 2,
Ireland (a division of Penguin Books Ltd.)
Penguin Group (Australia), 250 Camberwell Road, Camberwell, Victoria 3124,
Australia (a division of Pearson Australia Group Pty. Ltd.)
Penguin Books India Pvt. Ltd., 11 Community Centre, Panchsheel Park,
New Delhi - 110 017, India
Penguin Group (NZ), 67 Apollo Drive, Mairangi Bay, Auckland 1310,
New Zealand (a division of Pearson New Zealand Ltd.)
Penguin Books (South Africa) (Pty.) Ltd., 24 Sturdee Avenue,
Rosebank, Johannesburg 2196, South Africa

Penguin Books Ltd., Registered Offices:
80 Strand, London WC2R 0RL, England

First published by Signet Eclipse, an imprint of New American Library,
a division of Penguin Group (USA) Inc.

First Printing, February 2007
10 9 8 7 6 5 4 3 2 1

SIGNET ECLIPSE and logo are trademarks of Penguin Group (USA) Inc.

Printed in the United States of America

PUBLISHER'S NOTE
This is a work of fiction. Names, characters, places, and incidents either are
the product of the author's imagination or are used fictitiously, and any resemblance to actual persons, living or dead, business establishments, events, or
locales is entirely coincidental.
   The publisher does not have any control over and does not assume any
responsibility for author or third-party Web sites or their content.

To Avalon . . . follow your dreams.

DAGDA

Gender: Masculine
Usage: Irish Mythology
Pronounced: DAHG-dah

Means powerful god of the earth, knowledge, magic, abundance and treaties. He was skilled in combat and possessed a huge club, the handle of which could revive the dead.

DANU

Gender: Feminine
Usage: Irish Mythology
Pronounced: DAH-new

Means mother of all gods.

Prologue

Aberdour Castle, in the Highlands of Scotland
1066

Liam Caenmore spread his arms wide, clenched his fists and screamed. Wave after wave of heart-wrenching sorrow and intense fury erupted from his powerful chest and reverberated through the shadowed forest, sending birds and rodents scrambling in fear. His wizened face twisted as rivulets of salty tears poured from his eyes and soaked his graying beard.

"Sarah!" he bellowed.

Pain shot through his chest and rippled through his blood. He fell to one knee as he struggled to draw breath.

"Sarah," he cried, his voice filled with misery. "I miss you. Come back to me. I need you. . . ."

The emotional agony radiated through his body, making him weak and disoriented. Flashes of light danced across his vision. He clasped his hands over his heart, feeling it shatter. So much had happened . . . so many people had been hurt. It was only fitting that this pain now enveloped him, sending tentacles of wretched despair through his soul.

A horse thundered out of the trees and skidded to a stop only feet from his crumpled form. A young man leapt from the stallion and raced to Liam's side.

"Father!"

"Sarah . . ." Liam whispered. "I miss her." He glanced up and touched the younger man's concerned face. "I miss your mother. She loved you, Cadedryn. You were the moon and stars to her. It is my fault . . . She always knew what to do."

"I miss her, too, Father, but her death was an accident. How could you have known the rocks were unstable? They had remained strong and secure for centuries. 'Tis only by chance she was sitting in the very spot where the boulder crashed."

"You are so young," Liam said quietly as he took a deep breath.

"I am no longer a boy," Cadedryn reminded him. "I am five years past my tenth birthday. I am a man."

Liam smiled. "Sarah thinks you are growing up too—" He broke off abruptly, aware he was speaking of her as if she still lived. Tears welled up in his eyes, and his face clenched in pain. "I want her back," he cried. "We are lost without her!"

"What about me?" Cadedryn shouted. "You languish in grief and forget that your son also sorrows. Would she want this? Would she want you to live in eternal torment? She loved life and sunshine, yet you wallow in shadows."

"You do not understand my loss. I lost my love, my precious wife."

"I lost my mother." Cadedryn paced around his father, his green eyes glimmering with pain and loneliness. "And now I am losing you, too. The castle is barren and the halls are silent without her laughter. I miss her encouragement and her comforting words. I have had nothing to ease the pain, either. No one else to call for solace. No other family."

Liam rose to his feet. A strange light entered his

eyes and he placed both hands on Cadedryn's shoulders. "You should have family. Sarah and I have been selfish. We thought only of ourselves. You should be with other boys, perhaps even one you could call brother. But you must find your own way. There is nothing I can offer you here."

"You are my father!" Cadedryn shouted, gripping Liam's arms. "I will stay with you!"

"There are things you do not know. I have already asked McCafferty to foster you. Your swordsmanship is unparalleled, yet you have not been tested in battle. McCafferty will guide you, act as a second father to you. He will teach you, then send you to fight for Scotland. It is best this way. It is the way of the titled families."

"We have no title," Cadedryn snarled, his youthful face twisted in anger. "The king stripped our family of our title when you married my mother. You always told me that the title meant nothing compared to your happiness with her."

Liam closed his eyes against Cadedryn's furry, then opened them and stared at him with resolution. "You will go to the McCafferty laird and foster with him. The way will be hard, but you must learn more than what you have learned here at Aberdour Castle. You must have knowledge of the world. You cannot stay secluded with an old man like me."

"No! I do not want to go. Why do you cast me out? What have I done wrong?"

Another shaft of pain rippled through Liam's chest. "It is I who has done wrong. I want the best for you, Cadedryn." He pulled away from his stunned son. "Let me give you some advice; heed me well." He gripped Cadedryn's hand. "You will endure much ridicule for what I have done. Other lords will treat you with disdain despite your blue blood, for they will not see you as an earl's son but rather as the son of a man who lost his title. Yet remember, Sarah was a wonderful mother. You have nothing to be ashamed of."

Cadedryn flung his father's hand off his own then shoved Liam in the chest, sending him stumbling against a tree. "Your warning comes too late! Already I hear the villagers whispering about my tainted heritage. You intend to send me into a household where everyone will despise me? So you can wallow alone in your sorrow?" He paced away, then spun back to face Liam. "Love did this to you and to me," he growled. "Everything happened because of love. You married a woman against the king's will and rejected another who was selected for you. You lost your title, and then you lost your wife."

Liam tried to interrupt, but Cadedryn shook his head in angry denial. "I have seen the truth!" Cadedryn shouted. "You cast me aside only days after my mother's death. If this is what love does to a grown man, then I will never succumb to its strangling grip. I will never let myself become a hollow shell, dependent upon another's presence. This is one lesson you have taught me well. No woman shall ever claim my heart."

Liam's pain-filled eyes focused on his enraged son. "You have her green eyes, as green as the emerald hills behind Aberdour Castle," he whispered. "Don't let my pain strip you of happiness. Love is not to blame."

"You want me to become battle hardened, Father? A true warrior does not succumb to love." Cadedryn's gaze grew hooded and he turned away. "I will go to McCafferty, and I will ignore any who dare insult me, but I will not return to Aberdour Castle. Not until your body lies deep within the earth and a tombstone marks your grave."

Liam took a step forward. "Do not say such things." He clutched his chest. "I am not casting you out. I am trying to help you."

Cadedryn lifted a brow in a sardonic expression as his youthful face turned cold. "Good-bye."

Liam's face crumpled and he reached out toward Cadedryn. "My son . . . Don't leave me like this. . . ."

Cadedryn leapt upon his horse and reined the stallion around to stare down at his weakened father. "You are the one who wants to send me away. Why don't you follow Mother into the world of darkness?" he snarled. "Your soul is already dead." Spinning the horse, he thrummed his heels against the stallion's sides and sent him galloping out of the clearing.

Liam took a step forward, his hand outstretched and his palm turned upward in supplication. "Son!" he called. "Wait!" A sound to his right caused him to turn. A figure cloaked in a hooded red cape stepped out of the shadows. "Who goes there?" Liam whispered. "Ah . . . 'Tis you. How long have you been standing there? What do you want?"

The hooded figure picked up a knife from under a tree where Liam had tossed it moments ago. "I want retribution. Your dirk, my revenge," the person hissed.

Liam gasped and staggered backward. "No," he whispered, seeing his own knife in the hands of the attacker.

The red cape flared as the person rushed forward and plunged the dirk deep into Liam's chest, then twisted it cruelly before yanking it free.

Blood poured from the wound and drenched Liam's

clothing, spreading a crismon stain down his white shirt and over his brown leggings. Liam fell to his knees as he clutched his wound and gasped for breath. His heart raced, pumping blood with increasing pressure. Then, as his life force drained away, his heart slowed to a chaotic, irregular rhythm.

The hooded figure nudged him with a booted foot. Liam's glazed eyes looked up into the attacker's face. "Why?" he whispered. "Why now? Did I anger you so much?"

"One day your son will share your fate, and I will have completed my revenge."

Fear snaked through Liam's dying heart. "Not Cadedryn. He is innocent . . . I am doing as you asked. I am sending him away."

Deep in the woods, Cadedryn pulled his stallion to a stop. Something felt wrong. His father had begged him to wait, and he had always been a good son. He should not have left his father. He should not have said those terrible words. He should return and face Liam, man-to-man, and listen to his explanation. Perhaps there was a reason Liam wanted him to foster with McCafferty.

Cadedryn spun around and sent his horse galloping back toward the meadow.

The sound of his horse returning made the hooded figure move away from Liam and slink deeper into the shadows. "First Sarah . . ." the person snarled. "Then you . . . and finally *him*."

"You did not need to suffer," Liam whispered, coughing on his own blood.

Without answering, the figure melted away.

Cadedryn cantered his horse through the forest, then spied his father lying on the ground. "No!" he shouted as he beheld his father's blood-soaked tunic and nearly lifeless form. He leapt off his horse and raced to his father's side. "I did not mean my last words! Do not go to her. Do not kill yourself only to be with her again!" Cadedryn yanked the dirk free and flung it into the bushes.

Liam struggled to draw breath. It was important . . . He had to tell Cadedryn. He had to protect him. "Not . . . suicide . . ." he whispered.

Cadedryn pressed his hand against the wound, desperately trying to stop the flow of life's blood. "You loved her so much," he accused as tears pricked his eyelids.

"That . . . is . . . what . . . they . . . will . . . say . . ."

His brow knit in confusion, Cadedryn peered down at his dying father. "What happened?"

Liam tried to answer, but his lips would not move. Suddenly, he saw a shimmering form float down from the sky and reach for him.

"Sarah . . ." Liam whispered as he stretched his hand toward her. Then his heart stilled.

Chapter 1

Loch Nidean Forest, just off the coast of Scotland . . . 1076

The deep forest lay silent as its fey mistress lay in uneasy sleep beneath the sheltering arms of an old ash tree. Long strands of grandfather moss dripped from the tree branches, and dense undergrowth carpeted the ground, creating a spongy forest floor that absorbed the sounds of evening insects and nocturnal creatures, all sounds, that is, except the moans of the red-haired woman who tossed back and forth in her bed of ferns, caught in the throes of her nighttime world.

A night owl swiveled its head, looking down at the woman as a young weasel scampered along the limb of a Scots pine and sniffed her bright tresses.

Kassandra twisted restlessly as sweat rolled down her delicate forehead. She gasped, her eyes closed, and flung her hand outward as if reaching for something.

The weasel chattered and backed away, his intelligent eyes watching her with concern.

"Who are you?" Kassandra moaned aloud while her eyes flickered beneath closed lids. Her breathing quickened and her legs twitched. The light blanket covering her body was tossed aside as her motions grew increasingly agitated. "Where did you go? Take care," she cried. "Danger stalks close by!"

Within the dream, she raced through the dark woods, tears streaming down her face. A flash of metal in moonlight drew her forward, but the ring of steel against steel made her hesitate. "Is that you?" she whispered, unable to see clearly through the dream mist.

She stumbled against a tree and hugged it closely, feeling the scrape of bark against her soft skin. "What is happening? This is not my normal dream . . . Where is the sun? The flowers? My friend laughing in the meadow?"

A man bellowed with pain as another shouted in victory. The sounds reverberated in Kassandra's dream world, coming from every direction. She peered through the forest, desperate to locate the fighters. "I know you need me," she whimpered. "I need you, too. We are wed. You are my mate, yet there is something so different about you this time. Something so—"

Suddenly, the nimble weasel bent down from the dark branches and dangled in front of her, holding on to the branch with his hind feet. His tiny front paws waved in the air, exposing his white belly as his black eyes glimmered in the darkness.

"I must find him soon," she told the weasel, still asleep but communicating with him from her dream world.

You've been dreaming of him for a long time, he answered her silently.

"For the last ten years . . . Ever since I was six. But I want to see him. I want to feel his hand pressed against my cheek. I feel a longing that I have not felt before, as if I must find him in the flesh, for knowing him only in my dreams is no longer enough."

Mayhap he does not exist.

"Don't you hear him, hear the swords? He is in danger. As much as I want him, he needs me. We are meant to be together. I thought he would come to me, but mayhap I must go find him. He is calling for me."

The weasel blinked his huge rust-rimmed eyes and cocked his head to listen carefully. *I hear only the wind in the trees.*

Kassandra flinched as swords clashed and sparks flickered in the shadows, and although the clash was in her dream, her sleeping form twitched in reaction.

Mist swirled as she pushed away from the tree and began running once again. After tripping on her night rail, she gathered the front of it in her hands, but it was like smoke and slipped through her fingers. She struggled, her fear escalating as the smoke filled her throat and she began to choke. As she became faint, she fell first to her knees, then toppled forward, striking her head against a rock.

You're dreaming, the weasel reminded her as he leapt from the branches and scurried close.

Her eyes flickered as the dream mellowed. The smoke was gone and the forest enclosed her with a sense of security. She stared at the weasel across the dream mist.

"I am dreaming," she repeated. "But I know this dream. My mate is in danger and I must find him. I must awaken and search for him."

The weasel tilted his head. *You are not married to a real man. He is only in your dreams.*

"I will unite with him," she insisted. "We are destined for each other. I know it. I have always known it." She rose and the folds of her gown swirled around her form, molding to her lush body. The smoke drifted away. Boldly now, with sure and steady steps, she strode through the dream forest, nimbly stepping over logs and avoiding stones.

She knew the weasel followed her through the woods; she felt his reassuring presence. He was always with her in these dreams. He understood her like others did not, but even he was becoming frustrated with her need to find her spiritual mate.

She knew she was dreaming. She was familiar with the smoke, the different landscapes, the strange sounds that only she could hear, yet this particular dream frightened her. It was changing. It was stirring her in new ways and a sense of urgency rippled through her body.

She paused and listened carefully as goose bumps rose along her bare arms . . .

The dream used to be so lovely—set in a forest flooded with golden sunrays, leaves fluttering beneath the wind's subtle breath. He had first appeared in her dream on her sixth birthday, and although she never saw his face, he became her dearest friend. They had danced through the dream mist and chased dragonflies together; he was forever her gentle playmate.

But in recent dreams, he had matured into a man. The difference made her shiver with trepidation, afraid of her own aching need for something she could not define. His young muscles were hard and his hair was almost black. Odd vibrations drew her deeper into her dream as her blood began to pulse with recognition. He was no longer just a friend; he was her mate. She knew him. She wanted to find him.

The clash of swords rang once more, but as she finally spied the combatants, she sensed another presence. Its malevolent spirit swept through the forest and blocked her path.

Kassandra gasped. "What do you want?" she cried. "Are you the one who seeks to harm him?"

Cold winds swirled around her feet and the weasel clambered upon her shoulders.

Kassandra narrowed her eyes in anger. "Cease this!" she shouted. "You are not welcome here! Nothing shall rip us asunder!"

The spirit shrank back and shadows folded around it like the fabric of a black velvet gown. Other faces flashed before her, some friend, some foe, but Kassandra strode boldly forward—ignoring them until the darkness gave way to a verdant, moonlit meadow.

In the center knelt her dream man.

Just beyond him lay another man who was unfamiliar to her. The fallen one's blood soaked the ground and death hung over him in a seething cloud. The two were connected yet disjoined as if present in different times. Kassanda's dream wavered and she could not make out what was real and what was symbolic.

Her man rose and turned his back on both her and the dead man, seemingly unaware of their presence. He spread his arms wide. "God of all gods, father of mine," he called out. "You gave me battle skills! I have become your warrior!"

Kassandra approached slowly. "Dagda," she said softly. "My Celtic battle king. See me. Hear me. 'Tis your Danu, mother of the gods. I know you even though you have changed. I sense your spirit."

Her man closed his eyes and turned in a full circle, his arms spread wide to the stars. Blood dripped down his left arm. He held a small, intricately engraved dirk. "My family gave you its blood and I will have my victory! My father lies buried in an unsanctified grave," he shouted. "Killed with this blade!" A jagged wound ran from his wrist to his shoulder, then swept across his chest, appearing like a streak of lightning followed by his roar of thunder. "I will avenge him!"

Kassandra covered her mouth to stifle her cry of distress. "What happened to you? You are bleeding so much! Your wounds are so deep!" She looked at the fallen man, at his lifeless eyes. His soul was reaching for a sweet spirit, but an ugly cloud oozed between them, thick and impenetrable.

Her Dagda stumbled as blood loss made him weak, but he stubbornly remained standing. He shook his right fist at the moon. "Why did you take my father? They say he thrust this blade deep within his own heart. Did I send him to the underworld? Did I cause his death?"

Kassandra reached for him, but her hands swept through empty air. "Dagda," she whispered. "Let me help you."

He is in another dream world, the weasel cautioned her, finally seeing the man she had insisted existed. He scampered closer, his beady eyes flickering with concern. *Those who do not accept the dream world cannot hear you. He is no longer your playmate. He is a man, and men outside Loch Nidean do not follow their hearts. Let go of this dream. You have lost him.*

"You must hear me!" she cried to Dagda, ignoring the weasel. "We are meant to be together! We need each other. I yearn for you so much, I tremble inside."

Dagda fell to his knees. "Mother goddess," he murmured. "Bless me. Give me victory against my enemies. I am ready to come home."

Kassandra knelt beside him, her white nightdress fluttering around them both. "I am here," she said quietly.

He lifted his blade. "My sword sings a sorrowful song. The beauty is gone. I will never be whole again."

Kassandra swept the air above his hand, comforting and healing him. "I will take care of you," she promised. "I will make you whole."

His eyes snapped open and he gazed directly at her. "Who are you?" he demanded. His face shimmered in the mist, incomplete and partially obscured. He appeared confused and dazed.

Her heart raced. "I am Danu, your dream friend. We have known each other for many years. We are life mates."

The forest melted, leaving them on the still surface of an endless blue lake. No land existed beneath their knees, yet they did not sink. Hazy mist drifted around them and faint moonlight illuminated the water as if from below.

"Do I know you?" he asked. His gaze flickered over her visage and he cautiously touched her face. "Warm. Everything else is so cold, but you are warm." He cupped her cheek and drew her forward.

"I can feel you," she murmured. "You can feel me."

He pulled her close. "Your eyes are like the ocean." With his right hand, he touched the lake and wet his finger, then stroked the corner of her eyebrow. "Dark blue. Tumultuous. Passionate." He dug his fingers into her hair and tilted her head back.

She arched her neck and his rough lips brushed against the hollow of her throat. His hand wrapped around her back and held her as his other palm caressed her breast. "Not warm," he corrected huskily. "Hot. Like fire. A fire faery."

She quivered beneath his caress.

Suddenly, a wind vortex erupted between them,

flinging them backward, and a hooded figure rose between them.

"No!" Kassandra screamed. "I can't lose you!" She pushed forward and gripped Dagda's belt, but the power driving them apart was too great and her hands slipped. She stretched, trying to catch him, but her hands raked through the shadowed figure standing amid the wind tunnel and she was flung backward. Her hair whipped across her face, blinding her, but she flailed, trying to find him, to hold him, when her hands snagged on something sharp. A dirk. A beautiful, hand-engraved knife.

As she fell backward with only the dirk in her hand, her man crashed through the water and immediately began sinking. "Danu!" he shouted at her.

"Dagda! Reach for me! Take my hand!" She reached for him, but the distance between them grew too quickly.

"I can't hear you," he shouted. "Where did you go? I want to feel your heat! My heart is cold, but you ignite me!"

The wind tunnel broadened, its tentacles spreading through the mist, destroying the fragile water droplets and splintering the peace. Kassandra struggled against the forces. "I will not lose you again!"

The man stared at her as the lake water enfolded him in its embrace. "Find me," he commanded from a great distance. "Find me in my world. You have part of me. Use it to find me." Then the water swept over his head and he disappeared.

The wind died as suddenly as it had risen and Kassandra was left standing alone in the vast, watery expanse of her lonely dream world, holding only the glowing dirk in her hand.

*   *   *

"No!" Kassandra screamed as she sat up. Sweat dripped down her face and her woodland clothing was plastered against her moist skin. She plucked the loose blouse away from her throat and pulled her skirt down over her bare knees. She blinked rapidly, startled by the bright sunshine streaming through the tree branches. Nearby, her friend the weasel peeked over a log and fixed his gaze upon her.

Kassandra's heart beat crazily and she fell back against the leaves. "It was him, but something is different." She turned to her side and stared at the weasel. "Triu-cair, he's changed. He is no longer a boy." An intimate heat flooded her body and she wrapped her arms around her chest. Her flesh rubbed against the fabric, tingling with a new sensation. She swallowed and pulled the gown away from her body.

The weasel leapt over the log, dove into a pile of leaves and then poked his head up through the debris.

Kassandra smiled and stroked his nose. "He bade me to find him." She glanced through the trees toward the east. A nervous shudder racked her body. She sighed as she rose gracefully to her feet and shook the leaves from her hair. Her face was delicately defined with high cheekbones and a sweetly curved chin, but unlike the others in her blond family, her hair was streaked with blazing red and burnished copper, and her nose was finely dusted with freckles.

The other members of the village had teased her about her looks, but never cruelly, for her compassionate nature made her a loving friend and a kind companion. She was half sister to Princess Kalial, born of Kalial's mother and an unknown father. It was the way of the royal family. They mated in the dark, producing children of mixed heritage, until one was pronounced the new princess. The others, like Kassandra, lived in freedom, unfettered by conventional rules or duties.

As she rose, an engraved knife tumbled to the ground.

She picked it up and scrutinized it. A delicate inscription was carved on the back, and the tip was stained with rust-colored dust. Closing her eyes, she recalled the moment in her dream when the shadowed figure had ripped Dagda from her arms. Her heart thundered and she opened her eyes and stared at the dirk once again.

The dirk had followed her out of the dream and into this world. *He* had sent it to her. She knew it was his. She could feel his essence beating within it.

She began to tremble.

"His knife . . ." she whispered. "Elegant . . . Highlander design . . ." She stroked the surface with her thumb. "Wealthy . . . You are a gentleman. A gentleman of the court, with a connection to this knife that runs deep." She caressed the blade and a shiver of excitement rippled through her. In a crossing of dream and reality, the knife had materialized from the mists of her mind and was now here, solid and true. He had insisted that she must find him, and this dirk would lead her to him.

Kassandra started toward the village, smiling as she recalled her half sister. Kalial was mild in temperament and strong in heart. She communicated with animals and had a powerful McCat, a black jaguar that acted as her familiar. Her marriage to an outsider had ensured the safety of Loch Nidean, and due to her actions, the once-destroyed forest was growing back, becoming once again a verdant and peaceful home to the forest people.

A butterfly fluttered past Kassandra and landed on her hair. She gently lifted it with her finger and blew on its brilliant blue wings until it fluttered away. "Mayhap Kalial will understand my dream. She knows the outsiders and their world. She will know if my sense of danger is misplaced." She glanced down at the weasel scampering behind her as the creature wriggled his nose in agreement. Again she shivered. She had always listened to her dreams, feeling it was her duty to help those she saw in danger, but this time the danger involved her life mate.

The weasel stopped, rose on his hind legs and narrowed his eyes. *You cannot call him your mate when you have never met him in the flesh. He is only a figment in your imagination. I have never even seen him until now and you have never seen his face. He is not real.*

"No. I don't believe that. He *is* real and we have a bond that goes as deep as the bond between Princess Kalial and her husband, Ronin McTaver." She abruptly changed direction, avoiding the village in favor of a small clearing where several woodland ponies were grazing. She gripped the mane of one and swung astride, then patted the mare's neck in fond affection.

The pony nickered and began walking east as Kassandra guided the creature with her knees. "You don't understand. The dream has changed. I have delayed too long. I must go to him. Immediately. My sister will help me. I know she will."

"No! Absolutely not!" Kalial declared. Her baby half sister had arrived at the McTaver castle in the middle of the night and insisted upon speaking with her immediately, but her proposal was beyond prepos-

terous! "Do you have any idea how different the outside world is from your sheltered forest? The men live
for war. They fight in huge battles and kill each other
just to claim large castles and fly their colored flags
from the ramparts. They treat women as chattel, not
permitting them any of the freedoms you take for
granted. The women sew and embroider and learn to
manage servants. They ride sidesaddle and speak in
lowered tones. They—"

"I must go!" Kassandra argued fiercely. "He is my
life mate and he told me to find him." Triu-cair leapt
on top of Kassandra's head and burrowed underneath
her tresses. "Augh!" she cried as she tried to extricate
him. "Get down! You will tangle my hair and I will
have to brush it out again. Blasted red mess that it
is already . . ."

"You see. That is another problem," Kalial pointed
out as patiently as she could. "Your hair. It is too
uncommon. People will think you bewitched. And you
cannot have animals like a polecat following you
around like a pet. It just isn't acceptable."

Kassandra dragged Triu-cair down and dropped him
on the floor. She leaned forward and spoke earnestly.
"It is not just that I wish to find him. He is in my
dreams and I have been content with that. Until now.
I did not need any physical contact, but now there is
something new. It is as if I am being drawn to him in
a strange way and my blood is pounding for want of
his presence."

Kalial stood up and took a deep breath. "Your
words make me only more leery of helping you. You
are ten and six and innocent to the ways of men."

Kassandra jumped to her feet, shaking her head.
"That is not true! I know all about mates. I do not

desire a physical mating. I want only a spiritual bonding. He is my dream friend and . . . and . . ." She cast about, trying to come up with a word that Kalial would understand. "He is my husband."

Kalial laughed shortly, although amusement did not reach her eyes. "What will you do if I say no?"

Kassandra lifted her chin and pressed her lips together. "I will go anyway. I will find him."

"And then what?"

"Then what?" Kassandra repeated, perplexed by the question.

"What will you do once you find him? *If* you find him?"

Kassandra titled her head, her eyes crinkled in confusion. "I will tell him," she answered. "I will tell him that he is my dream man and we are destined to be together for eternity."

"Oh, Kassandra, my little sister. You know nothing of this world."

"That is not true. I have dined with you and Ronin many times. You taught me the manners and rules of your society and I have even learned how to dance your dances."

"Yes, you have many of those superficial skills, but you are still a fey child of the forest. I cannot bring you to court unless you agree to several additional codes of conduct. For your own protection."

"Like what? I'll do anything!"

"We must hide your hair under a wig and an elaborate mantle, and you must never show your red locks to anyone. We must powder your golden skin and hide your freckles, for no woman would allow her skin to be so touched by the sun. You must wear concealing, demure clothing and act mild mannered so as not to draw attention to yourself." She glanced at Triu-cair. "And you must not show your weasel to anyone!"

Kassandra laughed and spun around in a circle, her red hair streaming out behind her and her blue eyes sparkling with pleasure. "Done!" she cried happily. "Done and done again!"

Late through the night, the two ladies worked hard on Kassandra's transformation, agreeing that she would masquerade as a distant relative who was acting as companion to Princess Kalial. They created a black wig that looked acceptable underneath a flowing head-dress and elegant coronet, and managed to find just the right combination of tinted cream and white face powder to completely obscure Kassandra's freckles. With a modest gown and a concealing shawl, she looked completely changed. Even Kalial nodded in satisfaction.

"You look like a perfect lady," she said wryly. "I only hope you act like one. One more thing," she warned. "I advise you not to talk about your dreams. The lords and ladies will not understand them and will find them frightening."

Kassandra nodded absently as she stroked the coarse wig and wriggled her nose to halt a fit of sneezing. "Of course, Kalial. Anything you say."

Dubious about Kassandra's ability to follow through with the disguise, but grudgingly impressed with the transformation, Kalial ushered her into a bedroom and bade her sleep for the few hours before dawn. "I had planned on leaving tomorrow, so all is ready. If you had arrived a day later, I would have already been gone."

Kassandra grinned and sat on the edge of the bed. She had slept on a straw-filled mattress twice before and had found it to be comfortable enough, although she preferred sleeping in the crook of a tree branch. "The fates are smiling upon me," she answered.

"Or frowning upon me," Kalial grumbled as she shut the door behind her and left her little sister alone. She had a lot of explaining to her husband to do!

Chapter 2

Kassandra woke with a pounding pulse the next morning. She stared up at the unfamiliar ceiling and twitched beneath the unaccustomed coverlet. She had had the same dream again, and felt the same desperate urgency to find her Dagda. Goose bumps rippled along her arms and her belly ached with a new hunger. She took a slow breath, trying to calm her racing heart, but images of his faceless spirit drifted in and out of her mind until she flung the blanket to the floor and sat up to glare out the window.

"I will find him," she said out loud. "I will find him and we will unite in harmony. It is simple. He will be delighted to see me and we will be wed immediately." She rose, gathered the coverlet from the floor and draped it over the kickboard.

He had mentioned her blue eyes, but he had said nothing about her hair.

Kassandra touched her long mane. Mountains of red curls poured down her face like a river of red maple leaves. Kalial had thought that it would be a hardship for Kassandra to hide her hair, but she did not know how much Kassandra despised it. Even in the village, the vibrant red color had made her stand apart, destroying any chance she had of blending in with the other girls and obliterating her attempts to feel pretty and ordinary.

Her red hair was the bane of her existence, the outward manifestation of some inner curse. Anyone who saw the flame-red tendrils knew she was odd, yet all she wanted was to feel part of the village. This disguise Kalial had created was exactly what she wanted. She could pretend to be just like any other girl searching for her eternal mate.

Kassandra rose abruptly and paced around the room. Maybe she could even pretend she didn't have prophetic dreams. She paused and picked up the weasel sunning himself in the window. Rubbing her face against his soft fur, she mentally shook her head. No, she could not hide her dreams. They had been part of her for years. It was true that sometimes her dreams were disturbing, particularly when they foretold of sorrowful events, but often she was able to change the outcome. If she dreamed that a warren of rabbits was going to be buried under a collapsing den, she sought to move them before the earth fell. At times, the responsibility of knowing the future was difficult, yet when she was able to save some creature, it was deeply gratifying.

The people of her village understood her dreams, but outsiders did not. Ronin, her sister's husband, gave her guarded looks when she spoke of her prophecies. Kalial could speak to animals, but she could not see the future and often looked at Kassandra askance when she talked of events to come. However, Kalial had remained faithful and caring and was the one person Kassandra trusted completely.

After returning to the vanity table, Kassandra picked up several pins and bound her hair, then anchored the wig firmly. She set the mantle atop the wig and secured it with her coronet. With Kalial's help, she was certain she would find her man. Not only did her dreams urge her to help him, she *wanted* to find him. She wanted to feel his earthly hands stroke her cheek and, dare she admit it, she wanted to feel his true flesh press against hers.

She smiled into the polished metal. The false hairpiece and the concealing mantle transformed her from a wild and bizarre red-haired forest nymph into an elegant, black-haired woman. As long as no one knew about her true coloring, she could pretend to be something she was not.

You cannot hide forever.

"This is not your concern," Kassandra snapped back at her weasel. "I am going to court and Kalial insists I wear this disguise. Besides, what if I find my Dagda, my true love? I do not want to frighten him away by looking hideous."

Your true love will care for you as you are, not as you want to be.

"You are not an odd-looking woman with strange tendencies, whereas I am. Anyone from the outside world will think I am strange."

Not strange. Unusual.

"They are not my Dagda. He is the man I seek."

Triu-cair scampered off the ledge and landed on the tumbled bed. His wise eyes peered up at her with a mixture of concern and worry. *Perhaps he is not real. He may be only an image your mind has created.*

"You saw him last time."

But only in the dream. You cannot know for certain that he truly exists.

"You sound like the others." Kassandra walked over to the window seat and stared out at the glorious day. Princess Kalial stood in the courtyard below completing her preparations while Laird Ronin McTaver watched. Turning with a smile, Kassandra motioned to Triu-cair. "Come along," she said. "It is time to seek my destiny."

Ronin faced his wife in the courtyard. "How long do you intend to stay?" he asked her.

"A fortnight, maybe two. Kassandra will doubtless want to return as soon as she realizes the impossibility of her task. Men are much harder to comprehend than she realizes, and as soon as she is confronted with their inflated sense of self"—she poked her husband playfully—"then she will give up on her search. She belongs in the forest, not in this outside world."

"Why do you allow her to accompany you? She does not like socializing with strangers and has never before expressed an inclination to travel from home."

Kalial sighed and glanced up toward Kassandra's window. "She must. If I don't take her, she will go on her own."

"I don't see why. She should be content in Loch Nidean. She is such an interesting child and always welcome to visit here. She knows so much about the land, she is a big help to me."

"She has always been your favorite of my relatives, but it is time for her to seek her mate. She is ten and six! She wants her own husband and children, her own family."

Ronin shook his head. "The man she wants lives only in her dreams. I doubt such a man will be dancing at the king's feet."

"You do not believe in her dream man, do you?" Kalial accused softly.

Ronin cast his gaze across the fields to where a herd of horses gamboled. His eyes grew sad. "No. If he had been a true prophecy, he would have arrived many years ago when she first started talking about him. I want her to forget him and find a mate within her village. Then I would not have to worry about her choice."

Kalial walked closer to her husband, pulled his face toward her and kissed him on the lips. "Will you miss me?"

He grunted and clasped her close. "More than you can imagine. There will be many men there. Should I be jealous?"

Kalial playfully slapped his chest. "Don't be ridiculous. There is not a man in this kingdom who could compare with you."

"What if someone from another kingdom is there? Some strong, handsome youngster who has an eye for a golden beauty like you?"

"I love you and only you," she whispered.

Kassandra strode around the corner of the courtyard, her weasel scampering behind her. "I'm sorry I'm late," she called. "I was caught in my dream and I found it hard to awaken."

Ronin glanced at her disguise in surprise, and Kalial blushed at being caught snuggling with her husband in broad daylight. She stepped back but Ronin grabbed her hand and would not let her retreat far.

Sighing, Kalial looked at her half sister. "Are you ready?" she asked. "Are you sure you want to go?"

Kassandra hesitated for a moment as she touched her wig. She could stay home where she was comfortable and accepted and avoid the outside world. She could wait for her dream man to arrive in the forest and never have to confront the shocked stares of the lords and ladies of the court if they happened to see through her ruse.

She touched the dirk where it rested in the folds of her skirt. It was her connection to him. He had reached across the dream world and asked for her. "I want to go to court," Kassandra replied firmly. "I . . . I must search for him, even if I cannot find him."

"Are you certain?" Kalial questioned. "You have always been so adamantly against traveling from home."

Gripping the hilt of the hidden dagger, Kassandra nodded. "I'm certain. I want to go to court."

Kalial and Ronin looked at each other quizzically; then Ronin pointed to the elaborate mantle and wig. "Kassandra, what are you wearing on your head? And why is your face so pasty white?"

Kassandra touched a false curl self-consciously. "We thought I ought to look more acceptable if I was going to be near so many strangers."

"No—"

Kalial interrupted her husband with a quick lift of her hand. "We both believe that Kassandra will feel more comfortable wearing a mantle. It will make her less shocking to the members of court."

"Why do you suddenly want to go to court? What has changed? You always said that your dream man would come to you," Ronin said.

Kassandra averted her gaze and shifted her weight back and forth.

Ronin tilted her chin up. "What is different?"

"My dream changed."

He pursed his lips and looked at Kalial. "I don't understand these dreams," he said gruffly. "Talk to your sister."

Kassandra looked up at her older sister with a pleading look. "I thought he would come to me, but he hasn't. It is as if something is holding him away. Look"—she held up the engraved dirk—"this is his."

Ronin shook his head angrily. "Kassandra, there is no

possible way that is his. You must have found it after
some soldier lost it while trying to cross Loch Nidean."

Kalial placed a restraining hand on her husband's
arm.

"At least keep her sheltered from the politics," he
said. Then, still grumbling, he turned and walked up
to his wife's horse, leaving the two of them alone.

"You have had this obsession for a very long time,"
Kalial chided. "Because of your dream, you have refused to allow any others to touch your heart."

"I know he is supposed to be my husband," Kassandra replied. "I will not marry anyone else. This dirk
is of a unique, Highland design. Perhaps he will be at
court, and I have not met him because I have never
gone before. You promised to let me attend. Give me
one fortnight. It is time I searched for him instead of
waiting for him to come and find me. You know my
dreams often show the future. Why should you doubt
this one?"

"It is not that I want you to ignore your fey dreams.
You have used your gift wisely and helped many with
your warnings. 'Tis just that I wonder if you are misin-
terpreting this particular dream."

"I am not."

"Didn't you think that you were supposed to meet
each other ten years ago when you were six? You
waited by the edge of the forest every day for three
weeks, but he never came. Then you waited for ten
years, never venturing far in case he should appear.
Your love is a childish fantasy. Life mates are . . ."
She looked over at her husband, remembering the way
he had touched her that morning. "Life mates are
more than just friends. They have a connection that
is physical as well as spiritual."

Kassandra's eyes hardened with determination. "That is why I must find him."

"Do you understand what I mean?" Kalial asked gently.

Her little sister shrugged. "I know everything I need to know."

Kalial shook her head, unsure how to explain. "Kassandra, if you do not find him, will you consider that the dream may mean something other than what you think it does? Will you finally open your thoughts to include others?"

"I know what it means," she replied stubbornly.

Kalial sighed and looked helplessly toward where her husband was leaning against her horse. He raised an eyebrow.

"Promise me that you will think about what I have said," she insisted.

Kassandra glanced back and forth between the two. Her brother-in-law appeared irritated and her half sister concerned. She did not want to upset either of them. "I promise," she said reluctantly.

Kalial smiled and gathered her in a warm embrace. "We have prepared a horse for you and packed a valise with clothes, which has been loaded onto the wagon."

As Kassandra pulled away from Kalial, she motioned for the weasel. He sprang into her arms and climbed atop her head.

"Do you intend to bring Triu-cair?" Kalial asked dubiously.

"Yes. I could not fathom being apart from him, but I will not let anyone see him."

"He is not a pet the ladies of court would find acceptable," Kalial repeated her warning.

"I know," Kassandra answered, her eyes sparkling. "That is exactly why I care for him as much as I do."

Ronin grinned. "Ever since you were a babe, you have gone against convention. 'Tis no surprise you two are sisters."

"I will keep my hair covered," Kassandra promised. "I will try my best to be amiable and polite. I will not ride astride. I will not speak of the forest. I will wear dresses and keep my freckles concealed. I will hide Triu-cair and I will endeavor to make friends with some of the other ladies. And I promise to be pleasant to the gentlemen—all of them."

Ronin harrumphed, then opened his arms. "I doubt you can do all that, my dear. You have never been able to mind your manners completely. 'Tis a fault of the red hair. All temper and flash, but I love you nonetheless. Now hurry and don't delay my wife."

Kassandra smiled and gave him a warm hug. "Don't let the brown stud at the mares," she reminded him. "Their foal will not reach maturity. I saw it in my dreams."

He grinned and hugged her back. "I know. Not until next year. Take care, both of you. You two ladies are precious to me."

Kalial smiled and blew him a kiss as she and Kassandra, along with the wagon and ten men-at-arms, rode out of the yard and headed to court.

Chapter 3

Curtis McCafferty, only son of Laird McCafferty, and Cadedryn Caenmore, displaced earl of the neighboring Aberdour Castle, rode their horses to the top of the hill and stared down the slopes toward the royal castle. The King of Scotland, Malcolm III, and his wife, Queen Margaret, were in residence.

Curtis glanced over at his companion. They were foster brothers and Cadedryn's quest to regain his family's title had become as important to Curtis as it was to Cadedryn. Their familial lands lay side by side and their castles were within a day's ride of each other, although neither had been home for over a decade. After Cadedryn's father's death, he had gone to live with the McCaffertys until war had sent them both into foreign lands to fight in the name of their country. Their personal bond had strengthened with time, and nothing, Curtis swore silently as he stared at the castle below—no war, no king and no woman—would ever come between them. They were as close as if blood itself bound them together.

"The king sent for you," Curtis reminded Cadedryn. "You should be joyous, but instead you appear solemn."

Cadedryn smiled grimly. He was tired. For years, he had battled in the front lines, always seeking the most dangerous and daring missions in an effort to make his name known to the king. Curtis had followed him faithfully even though he had nothing to prove. Unlike Cadedryn, Curtis had a well-respected father. He had a home and a title. He needed nothing from the king.

But Cadedryn did. And now, after years of living with a bloodied sword in his hand, his name had been noticed. The king had sent a letter commending him for his bravery and service to the crown, then bidding him to come to the royal court.

"The letter may mean nothing," Cadedryn said. "He may not even listen to my petition."

"It is a beginning," Curtis encouraged. "You know that my fondest desire is to see the Aberdour and Fergus lands united, for then you will be the largest property owner in Scotland. As your best friend, I will share your success. Since my lands abut yours and Fergus's, it will assure me of two safe borders. It is the culmination of all our dreams."

"Have you written to Lord Fergus? Will he and his daughter, Corine, be at court?"

Curtis nodded. "Lord Fergus has agreed to hear your marriage proposal to Corine, but the lady herself has cautioned that she will not agree to wed you until after your meeting with the king. She hopes to learn that you have been successful in your desire to have your title reinstated."

"As do I," Cadedryn answered wryly.

"I will speak to her personally," Curtis offered. "I knew her as a child. Perhaps she will be more receptive to your proposal if I explain the importance of joining your lands with hers."

A flicker of unease raced down Cadedryn's spine. He glanced left and right, his sense of danger well honed from years of war, but he saw nothing to cause his trepidation. "Come," he said abruptly. "Let's race to the castle!"

Curtis whooped aloud, then kicked his stallion, sending him careening down the slope.

Cadedryn grinned and allowed his foster brother a several-length lead. Then he leaned forward and clucked to his own stud, which exploded in a burst of tautly controlled speed. Cadedryn bent low as the thundering hooves shook the ground and the wind stung his face. Soon both horses became lathered with sweat and Cadedryn's stallion swept past Curtis's with unflagging power while Curtis's horse struggled to keep from falling farther behind.

"Cadedryn!" Curtis shouted as he kicked and pushed his stallion for more speed. "You lily-livered son of a whore!"

Cadedryn ducked his head under his arm to assess Curtis's position and laughed. "I thought you had more stamina!" he shouted. "Wait until I tell the housemaids how soon you lose your strength!"

Curtis bent low and whipped his steed as he flung a string of curses at his friend.

Again Cadedryn twisted in the saddle, and this time he saw the flash of a caravan plodding through the trees below. "Slow down," he called out, but Curtis ignored him as he swept past, intent on winning.

"Curtis!" Cadedryn shouted.

Curtis raced his stallion down the slope, his speed unchecked as he burst through the thin row of trees at full speed and crashed into the caravan. Instant chaos erupted as the horses whinnied in fear, a woman screamed and the guards shouted in anger, trying to control their panicked mounts. The horses pulling a wagon reared and bucked and the wagon listed to the side as a strut snapped. The driver and a maid were flung to the ground and rolled for several feet before coming to an ungainly stop.

Cadedryn sent his own horse racing forward to assist the hapless travelers, even as Curtis managed to extricate his horse from the melee.

A finely bred chestnut mare carrying a young woman squealed and reared, her ears laced back in fury. Spying Cadedryn's stallion, she lunged and bit his neck. The stallion skidded to a stop, nearly falling to his knees, and the mare spun and landed a punishing kick on his haunch. As both horses flailed to keep their balance, their riders frantically struggled to maintain theirs.

"You idiot!" the woman screamed as she gripped the mare's mane and desperately pitched her weight forward to stay in the awkward sidesaddle.

Cadedryn yanked his stallion back and managed to break free of the churning hooves when one of the panicked wagon horses crashed into his backside, pushing him directly into the mare once again. This time the woman's dress caught on the rivet of his saddle and she was dragged partially off her steed. She tottered precariously for a moment before Cadedryn hauled her up onto his own horse for safety.

"Bloody bastard!" she shouted as she was crushed against his chest.

"Stop wiggling," he yelled back as he struggled to control his plunging steed and keep her from tumbling to the ground. "Stay still!"

"You blasted idiot!"

"You already cursed at me," he grumbled as he finally managed to extricate them from the disaster. "My apologies, ma'am."

"Your recklessness has put many in danger! Have you no care for living creatures? Look at the horses. . . . My mare is injured. And the servants riding the wagon are—"

He narrowed his eyes in anger and deliberately loosened his grip.

Starting to fall, she gasped and wrapped her arms around his neck.

"I recommend ceasing this tirade at once," he commanded. "I did not cause this accident."

She craned her neck and glared back at him. "Did not cause it?" she cried incredulously. "Your horse crashed into mine!"

His breath caught. The incident momentarily forgotten, he stared into her blazing eyes. They were bluer than anything he had ever seen, bluer than the most beautiful Highland loch or the most brilliant royal sapphire.

"Did you hear me?" she insisted as she managed to pull one leg free and swing it over his horse's withers. Unfortunately, it resulted in her facing him squarely. She flushed and tried to lean back, but the motion sent the unfamiliar mantle fluttering, thereby upsetting the stallion. He trotted forward and tossed his head.

"Augh!" she grunted as she fell against the man.

He pulled her close in an effort to stabilize her, but the press of her breasts made him flinch.

The horse whinnied in reaction and half reared, forcing her body to lie flush against his.

A strange sensation trickled through her belly and she shoved backward, trying to see the man's face as the stallion's front hooves struck the ground and the man managed to rein him in.

Kassandra's head spun and her senses came alive. She smelled the lathered horseflesh intermixed with the man's intense, masculine scent. She felt his strong muscles bunching under her hands and beneath her thighs. "Let go of me," she whispered, fear of her own reaction making her suddenly nervous.

He pulled back, as if surprised by his own response to her. The action toppled both of them sideways and sent him teetering while Kassandra had to grip the saddle cantle to keep from falling. Then the horse scuttled sideways, making things worse.

Kassandra struggled to turn around, trying to right herself. She unwound her legs and accidentally struck him in the jaw with a closed fist. "Oh!" She reached for him, attempting to help him but managed to unseat him instead.

He fell heavily to the ground with a grunt of anger.

The horse's head swung around and he pranced nervously in place.

She clung to the saddle, facing the horse's tail. "Easy boy," she whispered, abruptly realizing her predicament. "No need to run again. Easy now."

Cadedryn rose to unsteady feet. "No woman unseats me," he growled.

She glanced down at him in surprise. "It appears you are incorrect. You are on the ground whereas I am on your horse." Her mantle blew across her face and she tried to shove it aside.

He lifted a brow in amusement. "Perhaps you should remove the mantle. You seem to be having difficulty with it."

Her face flushed with anger and embarrassment. "And you should attend your plow horse with more care!"

"My plow horse?" he thundered. "You little brat! I'll have you know he is a master stallion!"

The horse leapt forward, startled by the man's anger, then spun in a circle and swished his tail, making Kassandra shriek. "Stop frightening the horse," she cried as she squeezed her legs to keep atop the nervous creature. *"Shush,"* she murmured. Her brow knit and she looked at the broken wagon and a weeping servant with consternation. Why hadn't she dreamed this? Why hadn't she been forewarned?

He stepped back and placed his hands on his hips. "It seems that you are the one frightening my horse. Why don't you just slip off and be done with these ridiculous antics?" When she tossed him an angry glare, he picked up a stick and waved it in the air. "Would you like some assistance? I could slap his flanks. Isn't that what *plow horses* respond to?"

"That kind of assistance would be no favor!" she snapped as she struggled to swing her leg around. Her skirts tangled around her waist, exposing her boots and calves, and he smiled.

" 'Tis a shame such a lovely miss has such an acid tongue," he called out, but his grin turned to a frown when she managed to swing completely around and face the proper direction on his stallion. Her look turned triumphant as she gathered the reins and calmed the great beast.

"And 'tis a poor day that one meets a horse ridden by an unskilled flunkey." She walked the horse over to the crying maid and swung down next to her, completely ignoring the man's furious glare.

"Miss?" Kassandra said softly. "Where does it hurt?"

The servant burst into fresh tears and pointed to her skinned knee and bleeding leg just as Kalial and the stranger's companion reached them.

"There now," Kassandra soothed. "It is only a scratch. All will be well once we wash the dirt from the wound. I will even give you a poultice that will ensure you receive no scars."

"I'm cold." The maid shivered, wrapping her arms around her shoulders.

Kassandra glanced up and scowled at the man who had assaulted her. "I am sure one of these arrogant, reckless men will offer their jackets for your use."

"Ma'am," the companion gasped. "She is but a servant!"

Kassandra rose and put her hands on her hips, swinging her gaze to encompass them both. "She is a creature that feels pain and knows discomfort, no matter what her standing in your society."

Kalial stepped in and handed the servant her shawl, then gripped Kassandra's arm and yanked her away. "This is not acceptable," she hissed. "No lady would talk to a man the way you have, nor demand that he relinquish his clothes for a servant's chill."

Kassandra lifted her chin toward the man who had run into her. Their gazes collided, blue into green, like two ocean waves crashing against each other. She sucked in her breath, unable to read the impenetrable expression on his face.

Cadedryn saw her eyes widen and heard her breath catch. For one moment, he saw nothing else—the broken wagon, the heaving horses, even his grumbling companion faded away. He had never seen a lady tend a serf, yet she had done so as if it were natural and right. She had spoken to the woman kindly and had touched her without shuddering in disgust.

Kassandra dragged her gaze away and pressed a hand over her mouth. This was not an auspicious beginning. She had promised to follow society's dictates and customs, but her blasted temper was already causing problems. She swallowed and forced a tremulous smile.

She clasped her sister's hand. "I apologize for my

temper," she murmured. "Are you hurt anywhere? Are all the animals safe? Where is Triu-cair?"

Kalial shook her head and touched Kassandra's face, tucking away a tiny red curl that had escaped her pins. "Yes, we are fine. I worried that you would be trampled. Thank the gods that gentleman was here to help you."

Kassandra frowned. "He did nothing of the sort. I offer him no thanks, and place the blame for the mishap squarely on his shoulders, but"—she held up her hand to stop Kalial's caution—"I will be polite and not berate him any more for it."

Casting one last glance over her shoulder at the two men, she stalked away, her mantle fluttering as she began gathering the scattered items.

Kalial frowned after her, then turned to the man. "My apologies. She is a distant relative who has never traveled far from home and the last few days have placed a strain upon her. She is acting as my companion. Please forgive her harsh words and unusual actions."

The larger man raised an eyebrow. "Mayhap she should return home," he replied caustically.

Kalial shook her head but did not explain. "Are you unhurt?"

"Aye," he grumbled. "Please accept *our* apologies," he said with a short bow. "We did not expect to encounter anyone traveling upon this road so late in the day. We have recently returned from abroad and are on our way to the king's court."

"Our start was delayed," Kalial informed him. "I am Kalial McTaver and that is Lady Kassandra."

He bowed briefly once again. "McTaver. I am familiar with your husband, the laird, and I know your son by marriage, the Earl of Kirkcaldy. May I present Curtis McCafferty, son of the McCafferty laird, and I am Cadedryn Caenmore."

"Caenmore? Are you the son of the late Earl of Aberdour?"

Cadedryn flushed. "My family has not had the privilege of reclaiming that title," he said through clenched teeth. "It is my fondest desire that soon it will be mine again."

Kalial smiled and placed her hand in his to curtsy. "Yes, I remember the tale of your father and his bride. I spoke unthinkingly. Please accept *my* apologies."

"Of course," he answered smoothly. "I am pleased to make your acquaintance." He swept his hand in a courtly flourish even though his gaze strayed to Kassandra as she strode through the area, checking on the horses and gathering far-flung items. "My pleasure knows no bounds."

After Cadedryn and Curtis left, the men-at-arms repaired the wagon and the women's entourage entered the streets of the village surrounding the king's summer castle. Of the many royal castles, this one was less a fortress and more a place for gentle relaxation and summertime enjoyment. A large tourney field was lined with colorful tents, and an enormous, well-tended garden was filled with flowers and blossoming trees. A bustling stable was clustered among several other outbuildings, but even as Kassandra craned her neck, she was unable to see them all.

As they rode their horses at a sedate pace through the narrow streets, a shiver of unease tickled the back of her neck at all the activity around her. She looked at Kalial with trepidation. "I don't feel comfortable among all these people," she murmured. "It is not like your home."

Kalial reached over and patted her hand. "You are a fine young lady with a caring heart, but after the way you acted on the road, I am not sure you should attend formal court functions. You can't defy convention so completely. You should remain discreet and keep to the sidelines. Don't do anything that will bring undue attention to you."

Kassandra grimaced. "You should be scolding Cadedryn Caenmore, not me," she answered. "He is the one who crashed into our caravan, destroyed the wagon and hurt your servant." She stroked her weasel's head and clucked to him. "And he looked at me so strangely. It made me feel uneasy."

" 'Tis just what Ronin was concerned about. You do not understand the ways of outsider men. Caenmore was actually behaving quite politely. 'Twas not his actions that caused the accident."

Kassandra glanced up. "He was in a horse race that plowed into our entourage; thus he is as much to blame as anyone. I don't like him. He acts like he is an important personage and I dislike such arrogance."

"He *is* someone important," Kalial said wryly. "He is the son of an earl and closely related to King Malcolm."

Kassandra shrugged and turned away. "If he is not my dream mate, then he is not important to me." She shivered once again, this time in memory of his intent gaze. She did not like talking about him, for he was already distracting her. She needed to stay focused on locating her dream man. As her gaze swept the busy streets, she was beset by doubt. How was she ever to find him?

They rode up to the castle in silence, each mulling over her own thoughts. Kassandra stayed close beside Kalial as the groomsmen took their horses and led them away, then followed quietly as they were escorted through the halls until they reached their rooms.

Kalial smiled pleasantly. "We are honored to be given such spacious quarters. My husband must have sent a messenger ahead."

Kassandra scratched her head underneath the itchy wig and rubbed her cheeks. "I am thankful to have my own room," she agreed. "Otherwise I would have had to maintain my disguise day *and* night." She turned toward her half sister. "Are we ready to venture out? I want to start my search right away."

"Do you know what he looks like?" Kalial asked.

Kassandra adjusted her mantle and shook her head. "No. I have never seen his visage, but I am certain I will *feel* him when I meet him. He is the man I am destined to find, the man who will touch my deepest soul and make me complete. I am certain I will know him immediately."

Kalial sighed and gave her sister a half smile. "Very well."

"Besides, I know he has a scar on his left hand and I have the dirk that links us." She checked her hairline. "Is my hair fully concealed?"

Kalial picked up a brush and fixed a few stray curls. "Such lovely hair," she murmured. "I wish you could display it proudly."

"I am pleased to keep it covered," Kassandra replied. "If I had soft blond hair like yours, I would be much happier, but instead I have this bright, unsightly color. It pleases me to hide it underneath the wig and mantle. I do not want to frighten away my dream man before I even meet him."

Kalial sighed again and slid another pin in Kassandra's mass of curls and secured the wig as Triu-cair scrambled up on the wardrobe and chattered at the ladies. He grasped a red feather in his tiny hands and waved it over his head, mimicking Kassandra.

"You beast!" she cried as she sprang up and chased him around the room. The weasel jumped from the tops of the furniture to the floor, then scurried under the bed and shrieked. Kassandra dropped to the floor and peered under the mattress. "If you want food, you'll have to come out eventually," she called. "Then I'll get my revenge." She fished under the bed, but Triu-cair scurried beyond her reach.

"Kassandra!" Kalial snapped, her patience running thin. "I told you that he would cause trouble. There are events starting on the field, which is an appropriate place to begin your introductions, but the weasel must stay in your chambers. Leave him be and brush your gown off so we can attend the joust. We are already much delayed."

Kassandra sat back on her heels. "Joust? Will the Highland lords be attending?"

"Presumably. If we are not too late already. But, Kassandra, please mind your manners. No more disastrous meetings like today, all right?"

Kassandra peeked under the bed again and shook her finger at Triu-cair. "Stay here," she admonished. "I don't want Kalial to get angry with us."

Triu-cair sulked in a corner and covered his nose with his tail.

Hoping he would remain there, Kassandra rose and wiped the dust from her gown. She felt nervous and anxious now that the moment was at hand. Who would her dream man turn out to be? What would he look like? For a brief moment, she recalled the sensation of Cadedryn Caenmore's hard chest as she was flung against him. He had felt firm and powerful, very much in control of the heaving stallion. The feeling had upset her and she had lashed out at him, wanting to see his calm disrupted.

She smiled privately, remembering him tumbling to the ground and glaring up at her. She had managed to take him down a peg or two!

They left their chambers and made their way to the courtyard. Two men-at-arms fell in behind them as they walked over to the festival. The event was half over and a large scoreboard with the lists was partially filled out. The lesser lords were entered first, and the winner of each of their matches was paired with the next contestant. It was a system that gave the higher lords a considerable advantage for they could relax for the first part of the day and be rested and ready for their event, while the underlings were tired and exhausted before the sun was high in the sky. But fairness was not considered a critical aspect of the event.

Kassandra surreptitiously pulled the dirk from the folds of her skirt and gazed at the board where familial insignias were hung. Nothing there even remotely resembled the design on the knife and Kassandra frowned in discouragement.

"Come along, Kassandra," Kalial admonished her. "We have seats in the yellow tent."

"I'd like to look around, if you don't mind," Kassandra replied.

"Kassandra!" Kalial said sharply. "You cannot wander about unescorted."

"One of the men will come with me," she said, glancing at the soldiers.

One stepped forward. "I will accompany the young miss," he agreed.

Sighing with resignation, Kalial nodded. "Find me when you give up searching for your mystery man. Remember, this is the king's court. You cannot wander about into unpopulated areas and it is highly inappropriate to address anyone to whom you have not been properly introduced."

"I know, sister . . ." Kassandra answered as she waved her hand, but her attention was already focused on a shaded area where many men had gathered to share cups of warm ale. She fully intended to wander at will in search of her dream man, despite her sister's warning.

She just hoped she would not encounter Cadedryn Caenmore again.

Chapter 4

Kassandra walked through the throng for much of the afternoon, searching every man's face with hopeful determination, but as the hours passed, she became discouraged. Several times she felt drawn in a certain direction, only to come across Cadedryn Caenmore. Each time, she turned quickly away, unwilling to talk with him, yet feeling oddly disturbed by his presence.

At last, she sat on a bench and propped her chin in her hands. This was going to be much more difficult than she had imagined.

"Milady?" the soldier asked respectfully. "I see the garderobe. Will you be fine if I step aside for a moment?"

Kassandra waved him away with a smile. "I am well able to be alone for a few minutes," she replied. "In fact, I would enjoy some peaceful solitude."

He nodded thankfully and left to relieve himself.

Kassandra spied an open field, barren of the exhausting mass of people. She rose and, after glancing about to ensure her guard was not near, headed over to the empty area, passing a group of men lounging in the shadows of a tent. As she began walking, tremors fluttered up and down her arms and her heart started pounding. She caught her breath, certain her dream man must be near.

Inside the tent, Cadedryn, Curtis and three other

lords were preparing their equipment for the tourney. "Who is that?" one lord asked another as they watched her walk past. "I've never seen her before."

His companion shook his head. "Don't know her, but I wouldn't mind meeting her. Fair skin, fine figure . . . must be some lady's companion."

Cadedryn felt the hairs on his arms rise, and an unfamiliar tingling rippled though his body. He glanced around, trying to find the cause of his sudden unease as well as the source of the other men's comments. Then he spied Kassandra. All day long he had caught glimpses of her. It seemed that no matter where he went, she was already there, and each time he saw her, he was reminded of her unusual behavior on the road.

Dragging his gaze away and looking back down at the leather strap he was inspecting, he forced an uninterested grunt. "That, my lords, is the ill-mannered relative of Lady McTaver. I advise you to stay well clear of her shrewish tongue and easily roused temper."

The men fell silent, each weighing his warning against the woman's obvious appeal. "It would take an awfully nasty witch to turn me away from such a comely prospect," one said.

"I'll admit she has some physical virtues," Cadedryn said grudgingly, remembering the feel of her body pressed against his. He turned to Curtis and motioned to his gauntlets. He had to escape. Immediately. The memory of her did things to his body she shouldn't be able to do. He needed to escape to where no woman was allowed so he would not risk seeing her before the event. He wanted to do well so that the king would take notice of his presence and his intended bride would find favor with his skills.

"I'll leave you to your perusing. My name is about to be called," Cadedryn mumbled, then left the ale tent and, accompanied by Curtis, entered the tent where the rest of his armor was being polished. Just before the flap closed, he shot a look over his shoulder. Kassandra had paused and was gazing around with uncertainty. A faint breeze flirted with her skirts and pressed them briefly against her legs.

He turned away as he felt an unexpected flicker of compassion for her obvious discomfort. She did not seem at ease and was already bearing the brunt of several dubious looks from strolling ladies and their escorts. She looked out of place and apprehensive. He understood her feelings. He, too, was feeling uneasy.

Shaking his head, he tried to forget about her and focus on what was at hand. Her worries were not his. He had earned the right to attend this joust and was finally in a position to confront the king and ask for the return of his rightful title. He had no time for naive misses.

Curtis followed him into the tent and helped him don his armor; then they both walked outside toward the mounting block. Cadedryn motioned to the groomsman to bring his stallion forward.

"Good luck," Curtis said. "I confirmed that Lady Corine and her mother, Lady Morgana, are in attendance. Lady Corine bade me give this to you." He held a yellow scarf out to Cadedryn.

Cadedryn looked at it curiously.

"Tie it upon your lance. It will announce your courtship of Lady Corine."

"You have spoken with her already," Cadedryn commented.

Curtis smiled. "She is a lovely lass, witty and sharp.

She reminded me of the frog I put in her soup when we were children."

Cadedryn tied the scarf, his thoughts drifting. Curtis's reminiscences of childhood pranks were hardly important at this time. Instead, he needed to concentrate on impressing the court with his expertise. "I am still awaiting her formal acceptance of my proposal. Perhaps this joust will encourage her to a speedy decision."

Curtis lowered his eyes as a frown flickered across his face. Corine had not sounded as receptive as they had hoped. She had insisted that she would do as her mother wished her to do. Only after much cajoling had Curtis been able to convince her to give him a favor to place upon Cadedryn's lance. "Fight as you always do," Curtis advised. "She will be suitably awed."

"As long as she gives me the answer I desire. I am tired of waiting upon her leisure."

"It is a game all women play. She is like a finely feathered hawk taking its time returning to its master. The bird may fly about for the moment but knows it must eventually heed its master's call."

"Aptly put, Curtis. Once she learns her place, she will make a fine wife. Especially with her dower lands lying adjacent to mine."

Curtis nodded. "Aye. A wise political choice indeed. The king is pleased, evidenced by his invitation to court. As long as there are no complications, your father's disgrace will be erased by the union of the Fergus and Caenmore properties." He laughed, although his eyes held no humor. "Once your lands are joined, my property will be only a small valley snuggled next to your vast holdings."

Cadedryn slid his helmet over his head, muffling his voice. "My family's disgrace will be erased," he confirmed. "Liam was supposed to marry Morgana, and in jilting her, he infuriated many important families. When I marry Corine Fergus, I will be completing the union that was supposed to be formed a generation ago. My father was a fool to throw away his name and position. He suffered greatly and thrust that disgrace upon his only son. I will regain my title and lift my family into favor. My children will not be subject to the same ridicule I have had to endure."

Cadedryn clambered onto the mounting block and settled into his saddle. "Go and make sure she is in the tents. I will limber up in the exercise yard." Cadedryn reined his horse and rode away.

Curtis stared after him, scowling at the dismissive tone in Cadedryn's command. This invitation to court was exactly what Cadedryn had been waiting for. Although Curtis wanted what was best for his friend, he also felt a twinge of jealousy for Cadedryn's good fortune. Like brothers, they had always battled for supremacy. Cadedryn often won, but Curtis always had the superiority of a title. If Cadedryn regained his earldom, Curtis's lesser lordship would be negligible and even that contest would be lost.

Curtis shrugged, chuckling to himself. His father always said that their conflict made them stronger men. They were each forced to be better and reach higher. Their competitiveness had created an unbreakable bond between them and they could not love each other more than if they were truly brothers. In fact, Laird McCafferty had ofttimes commented that Curtis appeared to love his foster brother more than his own father.

"McCafferty!" Lord Dunbar called out to Curtis from where he was lounging against a tent pole. "You should place your allegiance with more care. Caenmore is nothing more than a peasant bastard."

Curtis smiled amiably, but a warning light entered his eye. "You are the one who should mind your friends and allies, for the king has called Caenmore home. I would not speak of him in such words, for to do so may result in your own disfavor."

"The king grows soft. Caenmore should not be allowed at court. He should be banished to a hovel and set to rut with pigs."

Curtis threw back his head and laughed. "You dare say such things when his back is turned, but I challenge you to say them once you are facing the point of his sword."

Dunbar shuffled and glanced over his shoulder toward where Cadedryn had ridden away.

Curtis took a step forward and cocked his head. "Aye, watch your back, for his swordsmanship is unparalleled. I daresay even someone as fat and lazy as you has heard tales of his prowess."

"It does not erase his breeding. Even peasants can fight, but it takes a well-born man to lead."

"And how many armies have you led? I thought not. If I had a choice to follow you or him, I would not hesitate to choose Caenmore."

The lord huffed and crossed his arms as he narrowed his gaze. "You speak with great loyalty."

"As I should. He saved my life in battle many a time. I owe much to him."

"I advise you to take care, McCafferty. His family has been known to betray an oath; thus I would not place much weight upon his word."

Cadedryn smiled with satisfaction as his horse cantered around the warming ring. Everything was finally coming to fruition. As soon as he wed Corine Fergus, all would be settled and he would regain his title. His father's disgrace would be erased at last, and he could resume his social and political standing.

Cadedryn had fought for years on foreign soil before the king had sent for his return, but it had finally come. He would not allow anything to disrupt his plans.

His horse snorted and tossed his head, disturbing Cadedryn from his musings. From the corner of his eye, he saw a piece of silk fluttering in the breeze, causing his horse to look over in interest. Irritated, Cadedryn peered through the slits in his helmet to locate the source and saw Kassandra leaning against the railing, her hand outstretched toward an untamed mare. He frowned and sent his horse cantering toward her. The woman was not supposed to be in this area! Did she have no common sense at all?

"Lady Kassandra!" he called out as his stallion pranced over toward her. "You are not allowed behind the tents. Please depart immediately!"

Kassandra twisted to face him. Her mantle blew across her cheeks and her skirts tangled, making her trip and fall. "Must you always cause trouble wherever you go?" she grumbled as she picked herself up and brushed at the dirt on her skirt. "I came here to be alone."

Cadedryn stared at her in amazement, his green eyes boring into hers through the slits in his visor. "Milady, you are the one causing difficulty. Ladies are not allowed in the exercise ring, especially without an escort. Begone, and rejoin the others."

"You are an ill-mannered horse's ass," Kassandra snapped. "You have no right to order me about."

Cadedryn sat back, stunned by her response. "Ladies do not speak such curses. You would do well to learn some manners."

"Bastard!" Kassandra spat.

Cadedryn froze. "You have used the one word that I have heard all too often. Why not add 'peasant' in front and you will be like every other person at court."

Kassandra frowned, sensing the real pain behind his words. "It seems that we have reached an impasse," she said softly. "We have both struck a sensitive area without intending to. Shall we call a truce?"

He stared down at her beautiful eyes. They seemed familiar, yet he had never seen such brilliance before. They shone with sincerity and his anger eased. He nodded. "Truce, but you must take care at court. Even small mistakes can brand you with a soiled reputation and make your life untenable."

She smiled, her coral lips curling in a gentle smile. "I am back here because I was getting discouraged. Please don't tell Kalial."

Unable to refuse her smile, Cadedryn relented. "Can I be of assistance?"

"Perhaps," she replied. "I am searching for someone."

"Of course. Anything to oblige."

Kassandra pulled the dirk from her pocket and held it up in the sunlight. "I have been searching for the owner of this weapon, but have not seen one with similar engraving anywhere. Do you perchance recognize it?"

Cadedryn stared at the dirk in shock. He clenched his thighs together convulsively, causing his stallion to rear.

Kassandra scrambled back. "Take care!" she admonished as he struggled to calm the beast.

Cadedryn forced his horse to stand still, then

reached for the knife. "How did you come by this?" he questioned harshly, his gauntleted hand open to receive it.

Kassandra pulled back just out of his reach. "You sound angry. Why?"

"How—did—you—come—by—it?" he repeated carefully.

Kassandra's gaze widened and she stepped closer. "Do you recognize it?"

"It does not belong to you. Where did you find it?" He reached out again and twitched his fingers, indicating that she should hand it over immediately.

"I did not find it exactly. I—"

"Did you steal it?" he interrupted.

"Of course not!" Kassandra cried.

"Then how did you come to have such a valuable talisman in your possession? It is a very important weapon. How much do you want for it?"

"I have no intention of selling it," Kassandra replied, affronted. "I want to return it to its rightful owner."

"Then give it to me. It belongs to a member of my family."

Kassandra's heart raced. "Truly?" she cried. "Who? Your cousin? Your brother? Where is he?" She spun around as if she could spot the person immediately. "I should have known. That is why I thought you disturbed me. You must be related to him. Is he courageous? Is he hàndsome? Is he caring and loving?"

He grunted and nudged his horse close to her. "The real owner of that knife was feckless, careless and irresponsible, and now he is dead."

"Dead!"

"Dead. Most say he committed suicide by that very blade."

She shook her head violently, causing her headdress to wobble. "No! That is not possible! I know he is alive and you are just being rude and . . . and despicable!"

"Nevertheless, the dirk is now mine, so be a sweetling and give it to me." He waved his fingers once again.

Kassandra stared past him, her mind spinning. She felt faint and tiny spots of light flickered in her vision. "I know he is alive. He . . ." An image from her dream flashed before her. He was bleeding from his left hand as he stared up at the lonely moon. He was reaching for her, asking for her help.

"I do not have any more time," Cadedryn snapped. "The next joust is about to begin."

She closed her hand around the knife. "You must provide proof, sir. Either convince me that the man I am seeking is dead, or I will continue to search for him."

Cadedryn took several steadying breaths. "You are behaving ridiculously. It was my father's knife because I say it was. My word is enough."

"Proof," Kassandra repeated as she took a step backward, unease whispering through her. It was as if she felt compelled to obey him and had to physically fight to remain several feet away. His green eyes were commanding yet filled with a buried pain that plucked at her heart. She hesitated, almost willing to forego her search for the moment just to comfort him.

"What proof do you require?"

"Was your father wounded on the hand?" she asked, seeing his flare of anger as she held the dirk close to her breast.

Cadedryn sat back, his manner turning icy. "You insult me," he said coldly. "From the moment we met you have shown a childish lack of manners. Suggesting that my father was a cripple is both poor etiquette and incorrect. Our conversation is over, but I hereby warn you that I will obtain what is rightfully mine, with or without your compliance." He spun his horse around and galloped toward the lists.

"She has the dirk my mother gave my father," Cadedryn hissed to Curtis. "She might have the proof I need to convince the king that my father's death was not a suicide."

"You must forget your notion that it was murder," Curtis answered. "He was distraught after the death of his wife, and the only person to gain by his death was you. May I remind you that you were also the last person to see him alive? It would be wiser to leave those events buried in the past."

"He did not commit suicide. He was too strong for that," Cadedryn insisted. "He missed her, yes, but he would not commit a sin that would cast him in hell when my mother was in heaven. As much as I despise his decisions, we both loved my mother. He wanted to be with her for eternity."

Curtis placed a hand on Cadedryn's shoulder. "Remember how distraught your father was after your mother's death? Do you recall his desire to be with her? It is time to forget. Your father killed himself ten years ago."

Cadedryn shook his head. "I have never believed that, Curtis. You know my convictions."

Curtis's face flushed and he glared at his longtime companion. "Is it a good time to stir the rumors again? You are near to achieving your goals. If you create controversy, the king might reconsider his forgiveness. Even if something *did* happen, and someone *did* harm him, 'twas long ago. Situations change. People change."

Cadedryn checked his sword, mulling over Curtis's advice. He knew that his friend spoke true, but seeing the dirk had reminded him of many things he had forgotten. "Still, perhaps she knows some details I have not yet learned."

"I doubt it," Curtis commented as he patted Cadedryn's horse and checked the mount's girth. "How could she? She would have been in the schoolroom when your father died."

"My father was frail with grief. Someone young could have taken him unaware."

Curtis laughed uncomfortably and averted his gaze. "You would suspect a young girl? Upon whom else would you cast the blame? Am I next?"

Cadedryn looked down curiously. "Of course not, Curtis. I would never suspect you of anything so nefarious."

"We did not begin as friends," Curtis reminded him. "In fact, I was at Aberdour Castle the day your father died. I did not want you to come to my home to foster and I told you so that very afternoon."

Cadedryn shook his head. "What purpose do you have in saying these things? We were only boys. Much time has past since those days and our mutual distrust is long gone."

"I just want to be assured of your loyalty. Should anyone speak ill of me, I want to know that you would dispute it, just as I would defend you."

"Indeed. Have no concerns."

Curtis nodded, his face relaxing into a smile. "How did Lady Kassandra present the dirk? Was she asking for coin?"

"She asked who owned it."

Curtis lifted a jousting lance to Cadedryn. "What does she intend to do with it now?"

"She said she wants to return it to its rightful owner."

"Then that is the end of it. Tell her it is yours and be done with the issue."

"She demanded proof that it is mine."

Curtis shook his head in confusion. "What kind proof would she require? Surely your name is adequate."

Cadedryn closed his fist. "She must have other plans," he murmured. "If she was as pure as she portrays herself to be, then I would have the dirk in my belt at this very moment. Instead, she is playing some game. We may be underestimating her." He lifted the lance high in the air and stared across the field at his opponent. "I have suffered enough shame by far crueler adversaries. She will regret crossing my path."

Curtis jumped back as a page snapped the flag down and Cadedryn's horse leapt forward. "Good luck!" he called, but Cadedryn had already galloped halfway down the jousting ropes with his lance lowered to attack.

Chapter 5

"There!" Kassandra cried as she pointed to the man. "That is the one who says he knows my life mate. The same man who crashed his horse into us earlier today." She had returned to the bench and found a frantic man-at-arms. After soothing him and promising not to tell anyone that he had misplaced her, they had found their way to the spectator tents. After finding the yellow one where her sister was sitting, the man-at-arms had bowed away and left Kassandra in her sister's safekeeping. "I am certain he knows the identity of my husband," Kassandra insisted.

Kalial sighed. "Kassandra, stop saying that this dream man is your husband. You don't even know who he is."

"My *future* husband," Kassandra clarified. "Caenmore knows the owner of the dirk my dream mate gave me to assist my search."

Kalial tilted her head and looked into her sister's earnest face. "Do you feel him nearby?"

Kassandra shuffled her feet and snuck a quick glance at Cadedryn from underneath her lashes as he thundered past. "I'm not entirely certain I can trust my senses," she mumbled.

Two women sitting behind them glanced at each other. The older one frowned and nudged the younger one, who narrowed her eyes with distrust. "They are speaking of Cadedryn," the older one whispered. "We cannot wait any longer. You must stake your claim or we risk losing him."

The younger woman glanced at the far end of the field where the men assisting the jousters were watching the event. Curtis, her childhood playmate, was leaning against a pole. He had grown far more handsome during his years abroad than she had ever thought he could become.

"Corine!" the older woman hissed. "Attend my words or you will make my heart race . . ." The older woman fluttered her eyelashes and swayed in her seat.

Corine's attention immediately swung away from the men and she touched the woman's hand with concern. "Don't fret, Mother," she whispered. "I am listening. I intend to wed Caenmore and no one will interfere. I will make sure of that." She leaned forward toward the two in front and cleared her throat to attract their attention.

"How are you faring, Princess Kalial?" she inquired. "Do you know Laird Caenmore?"

Kalial and Kassandra glanced back. The woman behind them was beautiful, her elegant face framed by perfect, sleek black hair and her clothing expensively tailored, as was the older woman beside her. The family resemblance was clear. Kalial answered with a guarded tone. "Lady Corine. It is a pleasure to see you again. Lady Morgana," Kalial said, acknowledging to Corine's mother.

Morgana nodded but rose and excused herself, apparently exhausted by the proceedings. Her unpredictable health was well known, and Kalial watched her depart with some concern.

Corine looked pointedly at the two remaining women. "May I have the honor of an introduction?"

Kalial motioned to her sister. "Please make the acquaintance of my companion, Lady Kassandra."

"And to whom are you married, Kassandra?" Lady Corine asked. "I heard you mention a husband."

Kassandra shrank back. This woman was angry . . . She had underlying jealousies that tormented her soul. Guilt seemed to hover around her like a thundercloud about to erupt. Shuddering, Kassandra lowered her eyes and shook her head. "I'm not married," she murmured.

"No? What a shame. Yet so hopeful. Don't worry about looks, my dear," she said as she glanced pointedly at Kassandra's coarse black hair. "Eventually there will be someone for you, as long as you don't aim too high."

Kalial started to rise in anger, but Kassandra touched her on the sleeve. "Pay no attention," she pleaded. "I do not want to disturb anyone. Her words mean nothing to me."

Kalial settled back down, but she glared at Corine with distaste.

A horn blew and the crier announced that Cadedryn Caenmore had won the match. He bowed to the king and queen, then rode along the rope of flags until he reached the spectator tent. "Lady Corine," he stated as he bowed again from atop his horse.

She smoothed her frowning brow and smiled with false warmth. "Caenmore," she acknowledged. "Many congratulations on your victory. Your prowess with a lance is proving equal to your swordsmanship."

"Your token gave me strength and courage, milady." Dismounting with the aid of a squire, he pulled off his gauntlets and untied the silk scarf from his lance. "I was honored to receive it from Curtis McCafferty. It seems that we have a friend in common. In the future, I hope to find many other things we may share together."

Lady Corine rose and leaned over the barrier separating the jousting field from the seats. "I am pleased it served you well. Have you met Princess Kalial and her companion, Lady Kassandra?"

"Several times," Cadedryn said wryly. "It seems that fate continues to place us in each other's path." He held out his left hand and politely grasped Kalial's extended hand as she curtsied. Bowing over it, he nodded, then turned to take Kassandra's.

Kassandra gasped. "Your hand! It is scarred!"

Cadedryn's cheek muscles twitched as he struggled to contain his anger. "I assure you, the injury is not contagious."

"No! I only meant that the man I am seeking has a wounded hand. You said nothing about it when I asked you moments ago."

Withdrawing his proffered hand, he glared at her. "You asked about my father, not about me."

"Kassandra!" Kalial said warningly.

Ignoring her, Kassandra leaned forward and gripped Cadedryn's hand. "I should have known. You made me feel so strange and unsettled because you are my eternal life mate." She drew his hand to her lips and kissed it. "Neither of us realized the truth, but now I see with open eyes. Surely you see it, too?"

Cadedryn yanked his hand away. "Milady, restrain yourself!"

"How could I have been so blind? You are my Dagda. Did you recognize me, your Danu?"

Cadedryn frowned. "What are you chattering about?"

Kalial desperately attempted to pull Kassandra back, but the excited woman shook off her restraining hand. "From our dreams?" she explained to him. "Do you remember me? I am to be your lifelong love and your dearest friend. I am to be your wife!"

"You are mad," Cadedryn stated with finality. "Be silent and no one will speak of this. I warned you about acting so strangley."

Kassandra scrambled between the stools, slipped underneath the barrier and pressed close to him and his horse. She looked up with sparkling eyes. "Don't you feel it when I am near? Does not your body tingle and your blood pound?"

His heart thundered and he had an insane desire to nod. Her blue eyes pulled at him, demanding his response, yet he could not answer her. He felt the hairs on his forearm quiver and his gut clench. There was too much at stake . . . too many plans already set in motion. Shaking his head in denial, he stepped away from her.

She followed. "Oh yes, you do! I know it, for I have seen it in my dreams. We are destined to come together. We will fall deeply in love and nothing shall tear us asunder. I will be beside you forever, acting as your greatest ally. Together we will be invincible. Our love will be immeasurable! We are everything we need, everything we search for in another. We need no castle, no riches or gold. We will have a love most others only dream of!"

For one instant, his heart caught. Her eyes shone with such fervor that for a single deep breath he was entranced. Then Lady Corine laughed. "What a poor child! She is so desperate to find a husband, she will latch onto any hapless gentleman and try to claim him as her own. Sadly, you have chosen the wrong man, Kassandra. Caenmore is no more moved by declarations of love than a castle is shaken by a summer breeze. His father was a fool for love, but Curtis assures me he is far wiser."

"You don't know anything about him!" Kassandra cried as she spun to confront the woman's mockery. "He knows I am his true love and he will marry me!" She turned back to Cadedryn and smiled with delight. "I found you, just like you asked me. I always knew we would come together. Everyone else doubted, but I never did. I—"

"Lady Kassandra, cease embarrassing yourself," he murmured. "We have never met before today, and only hours ago you were casting aspersions upon me."

"And I do so apologize. I was so intent on finding you, I was thoughtless and blind. But now that I have found you, we can—"

"We will do nothing."

"We will get married! We will fall in love!"

He shook his head. "No. I will not fall in love with anyone. I have duties and responsibilities that I will not cast aside as my father did before me."

"But—"

"I am sorry, milady, but you are mistaken. I am not the man you are seeking. Please, stop this. Soon everyone will hear and you will be taunted mercilessly."

Kassandra's lips trembled. "Your wound . . ."

"Many swordsmen have wounds."

"The dirk . . . You gave it to me in my dream."

" 'Twas my father's, not mine. He carried it on the night he died, and it is your obligation to return it to me."

"You were there, weren't you?" Kassandra gasped. "You found his body and saw his blood soak the earth!"

Cadedryn's face turned cold and he started to turn away from her.

"There was someone else," she continued. "Someone else there that night."

He spun back and stared at her, his green eyes blazing. "What do you know?" he demanded. "What do you know of his death?"

She fell silent, confused by his infuriated tone, as Lady Corine turned white and placed her hand across her own chest.

He shuddered. "You say things you could not know. Unless you have proof that there was another man in the meadow, I suggest you hold your tongue."

"Our love . . ."

"We have no love. Not now, not ever."

Lady Corine's color returned with a rush and she strode over to Cadedryn and placed a proprietary hand on his arm. "You are acting foolish, Lady Kassandra. 'Tis no wonder you have not found a husband." She leaned toward her. "Take my advice, woman to woman. Leave this one alone. Don't chase. Let them come to you."

Kassandra fell back, bewildered and distressed. "You don't believe that, do you?" she asked Cadedryn tearfully. "In my dream you told me to come find you."

"Lady Corine speaks the truth, milady." Cadedryn replied. "This is not the place for ill-mannered lasses. 'Tis clear you have not been raised to survive at the king's court. This may not be the best place for you. I don't want to see you hurt by the insensitivity of others. I am the last person you should set your sights upon, for I have goals that go far beyond simply finding a wife. You should search for someone more like youself, someone kind and unassuming. Seek a young knight who will lay his heart at your feet."

Kalial reached out to Kassandra once again, and this time her hands were not restraining but comforting.

Kassandra's gaze swung back and forth between Corine and Cadedryn, then swept toward her sister.

"Kassandra," Kalial murmured as she held out her arms.

Kassandra shook her head, rejecting comfort. She dashed the welling tears from her face, then with a haunted glance toward Cadedryn, she raced out of the spectator tent.

"Such a silly child," Corine criticized as Kalial exited the tent and set out after Kassandra. "She obviously has no experience with men or she would know that her declarations only annoy the harder sex. She should be more discreet and reserved or she will attract no one's interest."

Cadedryn watched Kassandra as well. His hooded expression did not reveal his thoughts, but inside he trembled. She spoke of another person in the meadow. What did she know and how did she know it?

"And her hair and face!" Lady Corine continued. "She is probably pockmarked beneath all that paste."

"She is simply young and unaware of political machinations," Cadedryn replied. "She is harmless. Leave her be."

"It sounds like you are defending the child," Corine snapped. "I would take it amiss if you allowed her to continue her ridiculous campaign to win you."

"Just because I do not want to besmirch her does not mean I want to wed her. As I stated in my initial letter to you, my attachments will be formed based upon more important matters. Speaking of which, you have yet to give me a formal answer, Lady Corine."

Corine arched her brows. "Have you reconciled with the king? Have you heard anything about the title?"

Cadedryn plucked her hand from his arm and turned toward the stables.

"Don't sulk," Lady Corine called after him as he stalked away. "I will say yes when you have proven your worth and status. When the king declares his favor publicly, then I will agree to the union. You must understand my hesitancy, Cadedryn. Your father jilted my mother and I refuse to undergo a similar humiliation. Once you have your title, I will be secure in knowing you will not put it in jeopardy again and I will say yes. It is merely a political maneuver. Besides," she exclaimed, "it is not as if we are marrying for love."

Cadedryn led his horse out of the tourney field and walked back to the preparation yard. Corine's parting comments echoed in his mind and he forced himself to take a deep breath. She was absolutely correct. They were not marrying for love, which was exactly as he wanted it. He desired a political alliance, not a clinging bride.

He acknowledged that his mother and father had found something special with each other, but that same love had made many others unhappy. It was his duty to avoid his father's mistakes and restore his familial reputation.

He divested himself of his heavy armor and rinsed his face in the horse trough. He rubbed his forehead and closed his eyes against the sun. Things were getting more complicated and he was emotionally exhausted.

The king was acting polite but hardly welcoming and Cadedryn was not certain he would rebestow the earldom, even if to do so would thereby allow Cadedryn to wed Lady Corine. Without a title, however, she would never agree to a marriage that would lower her own family's status.

He must impress upon all that joining the two families would not only add greatly to the stability of the Highlands, it would also right his father's wrong.

Cadedryn rubbed his forehead again, then pressed his thumbs to his temples. He needed to get away, if only for an hour or so. A small grin flitted over his face. Lady Kassandra would not be tortured by his numerous political concerns. She seemed more concerned about servants and dreams than estates and titles.

He walked away from the jousting area and entered the cool gardens. The normally busy place was now empty and peaceful, the flowered paths deserted. Many years ago, before his mother died, he had played in gardens like these. His mother had tended the flowers while his tiny wooden men had fought mock battles among the prickly thorns.

He paused to lean against a blossoming tree, and bowed his head.

A woman rose from the shadowed bench where she had been sitting. "Caenmore?"

Cadedryn's eyes snapped open and he stiffened. It was Kassandra. Again!

"I'm sorry to bother you, but I still have your dirk . . ."

"Yes. My father's knife." He took several steps toward her.

Kassandra held the piece out to him, but instead of taking it, he stroked her wet cheek where a tear lingered. She was soft and warm. "I did not intend to make you cry, milady," he murmured.

Kassandra tilted her face into his palm and closed her eyes.

"You should have fabricated a more plausible story. Carrying on about dreams only makes you appear touched in the head. I know the value of an unsullied reputation. Once damaged, it is difficult to repair. You are too sweet to suffer at the hands of the court ladies."

She nodded and pulled away from his hand.

"You should tell me the truth," Cadedryn said quietly. "Who gave you the dirk? If there is something you know about my father's death, you need to tell me."

"I wish I could say I am not plagued by dreams, yet I cannot pretend they are false. I have known you from my earliest days. I know your love of water and your distaste for apples. I know that your hair was blond as an infant and only darkened to its current color after your fifth birthday."

He shook his head. "Any gypsy could determine those things from a few well-placed questions and a small investment of coin."

"Do you think I am trying to trick you?"

"It has crossed my mind."

"Why? Why would I do such a thing?"

"For political gain. I may soon be an earl. Or perhaps you have been sent by an unknown enemy to distract me from my goals."

Kassandra smiled and placed her finger across his lips. "You know you are wrong. I have no ambitions to gain a meaningless title and I have no need to cause you distress."

He inhaled her scent. She was fresh and light and

he was tempted to capture her finger in his mouth and taste her, but she shifted away before he could act on his impulse. "All women have ambitions."

Kassandra laughed, her musical tones gently teasing him. "As all men wish to be earls? Is that what you really want?"

"I would accept my duty, but only if it is God's will."

"So you *do* believe in destiny?"

He could not suppress a grin. "You are more clever than I thought. You have surprised me, Lady Kassandra, but you have not convinced me."

"Then I challenge you to a contest. You have already proven your competitive nature by winning the joust, and I hear you are skilled with a sword."

"You want to claim that I will fall in love with you and ask for your hand in marriage? That would be a most unwise proposition, for it will never happen."

"No, I am not saying that, although your suggestion is intriguing." She held the dirk out once more. "If you find it, it is yours and you may go along your way with nothing owed to me. If I find it, then I get to keep it and you may not demand it back."

His gaze narrowed. "Milady, the knife is not a toy."

Kassandra shrugged and placed her hand across his eyes as she closed her own. "You can choose to play or not. Let us allow destiny to decide." Then, without warning, she flung the dirk deep into the greenery.

He yanked her hand off his face and shouted at her. "Once again you prove your foolish nature! That piece of steel is priceless! Do you have any idea of its worth?"

She dashed into the bed of pansies and ducked under the carefully manicured bushes, calling over her shoulder, "Then I suggest you start searching!"

He darted after her, attempting to grab her ankle,

but she crawled rapidly out of his reach. "You minx," he growled under his breath and he followed her into the shadows. He scanned the ground, searching for the dirk. "I'll find it and stop this madness." He was forced down on his hands and knees in the moist soil and he chuckled at the feel of dirt squishing between his fingers.

"I hear you!" she called from his right.

"If I catch you, you will sorely regret this!" he answered as he searched to the left. He swept the ground quickly, rummaging through piles of leaves and prodding through tangled branches. "How deep does this hedge go?" he grumbled as a stray branch scratched his neck.

"Oh!" she gasped just out of his sight as another branch caught her mantle and threatened to pull it off. She yanked the mantle more firmly in place and shoved a stray lock of red hair back under her wig. "Blasted hair," she muttered. "If only I could cut it all off."

Suddenly Cadedryn saw a flash of light reflecting off something on the far side of the hedge. "Yes!" he shouted as he scrambled forward.

"Yes!" she cried as she, too, saw the gleam.

Without regard to their clothing, they both scurried through the last row of branches and raced toward the object lying in a bed of pink petals underneath a flowering tree. Cadedryn took the lead and was reaching for it when Kassandra shoved him, knocking him sideways.

"What?" he gasped as he fell over. "That is not fair!"

She laughed and stood over him, panting for breath. "I never said we were fighting fair," she declared, then turned to collect her trophy, but Cadedryn sprang up and swept her off her feet.

"Put me down!" she commanded.

"Not a chance," he replied as he scanned the tree branches and spotted one strong enough to support her weight. He plopped her on it and grinned at her affronted look. Stepping back, he sauntered over to the glittering object half buried in the petals.

Desperate to stop him, Kassandra leapt off the branch and toppled to the ground. "Augh!" she cried. "My leg!"

Cadedryn spun around and knelt to assist her. "Is it broken?" he asked with concern.

She sprang up and dashed around him, laughing. "I've climbed more trees than any child, and I can climb them faster and higher!"

"You cheat!" He swiped at her, but she eluded his grasp and raced to capture the prize. "What kind of female are you?" Not to be outdone, he lunged after her.

They both tumbled in the flowers, but she managed to grip the dirk a mere second before his hand wrapped around hers. He yanked her toward him and she rolled atop his form, struggling to maintain possession of the knife.

"I found it first," she shouted.

"I saw it first," he growled back as he flung her off and rolled over her, pinning her hand over her head.

She smiled up at him, teasing him with a saucy look. She was utterly defenseless yet completely unaware of her vulnerability, but Cadedryn was acutely conscious of their intimate position. He squeezed her hand. "It is mine," he commanded. "Drop it."

"Make me," she whispered. She tilted her head, unconsciously exposing her throat.

He caught his breath as desire surged through him. She was sweet, innocent and fresh. She was wild and untamed and completely unrestrained. She acted more like a child playmate than a courtly woman, yet her actions woke something deep inside him that had long slumbered. Something youthful and exciting . . . something free and liberating. A sense of life beyond the struggle for power.

He lowered his head and softly brushed his lips against hers.

She froze, her eyes wide in surprise.

"Where is your playful spirit now?" he taunted her. He shifted slightly and gently kissed the corner of her mouth.

She turned her head to meet his lips. "You see?" she whispered. "I was right. We are meant to be together. I feel it and you feel it."

This time *he* froze. He shook his head. "What are you talking about?"

"Us," she smiled. "Our love."

"Bloody hell!" he shouted as he scrambled up and staggered back several steps. "You are an enchantress!"

Kassandra blinked rapidly and rose up on one elbow. "Dagda?" she asked, confused by his changed attitude.

"What? By whose name do you keep calling me?"

"By your true name. You are Dagda and I am Danu. You kissed me like a man kisses a woman. You cannot deny it."

"Like a man kisses a woman?" he shouted, outraged by her innocent expression. "You know nothing of men and women. You are . . . are . . ." he sputtered. Gripping her arm, he yanked her to her feet, then took a deep breath before continuing. "You listen well," he commanded. "I am here to regain my title. I am going to do that, then marry Lady Corine and unite two families that would have been joined long ago except for the foolishness of my father. I will be an earl and will be highly respected. What I will not do is wed a minx like you."

"But we kissed!"

"Corine is right; you know nothing of men."

Kassandra pulled her arm free and glared at him. "What of passion and love? Are you willing to forego all in your insane quest for power? If you wed Lady Corine, you will have a cold bed and a colder heart!"

"Men do not forego passion after they marry. I will find a woman—a woman of experience who will satisfy my urges while my wife stands by to bear my children. That is the way of all high-born men."

"Not true!"

His mouth gaped open at her heartfelt denial.

She stood akimbo, her eyes glittering with anger. "Ronin McTaver is not like that. He loves Kalial and would never keep another."

"Are you truly as naive as you appear? All good men are governed by the same rules. We are lustful creatures and expend our lust on appreciative whores, but we do not *love*, not if we want to keep our titles and lands intact!"

"What about your parents? They did not have mere lust."

"And look what it did to them. Do not speak of love! I will not fall in love!" he thundered. "You know nothing about my life. My parents are not to be discussed. Not now, not ever!"

"No," she cried. "You are capable of love. I know it. I know you from my dreams!"

He leaned close and peered into her frightened eyes. "You think you know me? Then follow me and see what you think of the man you claim to love."

Chapter 6

He dragged her back under the hedge and through the flowers, carelessly trampling the blossoms.

"Stop!" Kassandra cried. "Where are you taking me?"

"You think one kiss is proof of love? You think I *want* to fall in love? I am a man of war, a man of power and politics. I value strength and conquest, not sweetness and romance."

"You can be strong and still embrace another," Kassandra defended.

"Not me." He pulled her out the side door of the garden and dragged her through the servant's alley, where various peasants leapt out of their way and gaped at them in astonishment.

"I am not supposed to be back here," Kassandra stammered as she struggled to keep her balance. "Kalial told me to have an escort—"

"I doubt you listen to much of what Kalial tells you, and you certainly don't listen to me. You have already escaped your guard once and I daresay you will again. I was clear in my rejection of your proposal, yet you still sought to change my mind with your playful antics. Well, I played *your* game and now you will see what activities *I* enjoy." He pointed to a wooden house with boarded windows and a scarlet door. "That is one of my playgrounds. Do you know what lies beyond the red door? No? It is a prostitute's hut. Does the man of your dreams frequent such places?"

"No," Kassandra whispered.

"Ah, and look over here." He smirked as he yanked her away from the brothel and pointed to a row of kennels. Dogs lunged at the fence, each one snarling and growling. One dog bit the edge of a wooden bar and snapped a splinter off, then shoved his snarling muzzle into the gap.

Kassandra shrank back, feeling the beast's rage. "Why are they so angry?"

"They are fighting dogs, trained from birth to maim and kill. Have you ever watched such a sport? I have. In fact, I own three of them and one is a champion contender. Does the man of your dreams enjoy watching helpless animals rip each other apart?"

She shook her head.

"This is who I am, Lady Kassandra. I am not a man who welcomes the softer side of life, and I do not want you or your ridiculous claims of eternal love."

"It can't be true," she whimpered. "You are not like that . . . You love dogs. I dreamed of a hound you tended as a child."

Cadedryn's face went white, then flushed with fury. "Your informant has seriously miscalculated me." He captured her hand and pulled her past the dogs to a closed courtyard. Lifting a heavy metal latch, he shoved the door open and yanked her inside.

The stench of sweat and unwashed bodies made her gag.

"This is my favorite place. This yard where men fight men and blood runs freely. This is not the jousting field where gentlemen don fancy armor and gallop pretty ponies past rows of lovely ladies. Here is where I spend most of my time. If I were to say I loved at all, I would declare myself wed to this field. I am an expert swordsman and I live and breathe with a sword in my hand." He yanked off his embroidered vest and flung his silken shirt into the mud, then spread his arms and clenched his fists. "I am not your man!"

Kassandra cowered back against the wooden stockade, revolted by his disclosures yet fascinated by his intensity. He radiated strength and his muscles bulged as he shook his arms. Pulsing veins wound up his forearms and snaked across his bare chest, diving underneath black curls.

"Have you ever seen this side of the man you think you love?" he shouted.

Terrified, she shook her head again.

He turned away and grabbed the shoulder of a man practicing maneuvers with a long stick. Spinning him around, Cadedryn slammed his fist into the man's jaw. The man staggered back, stunned by the unprovoked attack, but he quickly recovered and swung back, nearly smashing Cadedryn's head with the stick.

Kassandra screamed.

Cadedryn tackled the man, using his superior strength to pin him to the ground, but the man bucked upward and managed to wedge the stick between them. With a mighty shove, he heaved Cadedryn off and kicked him in the thigh.

Cadedryn rolled twice, then sprang to his feet with a feral growl. The two men circled each other warily, waiting for the other's defense to crack.

Kassandra covered her mouth with her hands. Cadedryn's black hair was wildly tousled and his body was coated with sweat and dirt. He glanced at her, his eyes wickedly excited. "Care to join us?" he mocked. "Are you up for a bit of rough and tumble?"

The man lunged and crashed the stick against Cadedryn's side, splitting the skin. Cadedryn roared in pain.

Blood splattered Kassandra's face. In horror, she wiped her cheek and stared at the red mark. Suddenly, Cadedryn stood in front of her, his chest heaving with exertion. He waved a double-bladed sword in front of her face.

"Fear me," he warned her. "I am not who you want me to be." He lifted the blade above his head and slammed it into the wood.

Kassandra shrieked and clenched her eyes shut, certain he was about to behead her. She gasped when he pressed his body flush against hers. He exuded blazing heat and she felt his bare flesh burn through her silk dress.

"Feel me? Feel this? This is the kind of love I understand." He ground his hips against hers. "Physical . . ." He leaned down and nibbled her neck. "Intimate . . ."

His hot breath sent tremors through her. She became light-headed and felt herself begin to slide down the wall.

He gripped her waist and held her upright. His hand spread wide and his fingers stroked the underside of her breast. "Are you this kind of woman? Do you want this kind of man?"

She shook uncontrollably, unable to understand his vehemence yet magnetically drawn to him.

He pushed her against the wall as he stood back. "This is who I am," he said softly, almost apologetically. He touched a frayed thread that dangled from her mantle. "You and I are nothing alike. Even if it were possible for me to love, I would not choose you. I vowed not to love on the day my father died, for I never wanted to experience his agony. I want a woman with whom I have no emotional commitments. I want a woman who comprehends my base nature, who accepts my wooden heart. You are a lovely girl, but you could never understand me."

"And Lady Corine can?" she asked tremulously.

"Not even her. Now go, and we will never speak of this again. I"—he wiped the blood from her cheek with his thumb—"I wish . . . I wish it could have been otherwise. For your sake."

She nodded, her eyes shimmering with unshed tears. "I'm sorry," she whispered.

"Do you accept that I am not your dream man now?"

She nodded again.

"Then go."

She turned, struggled briefly with the heavy latch, then fled out of the courtyard.

With a heavy heart, he watched her escape. "For my sake, as well," he added softly.

Lost in the depths of her dream, she found herself sinking . . . sinking in a deep bog and each time she struggled, she sank deeper. "Triu-cair!" she cried.

The weasel chattered at the edge of the sinkhole, speaking to her in this ephemeral dream state. *Stop fighting,* he advised.

Kassandra flailed her arms and tried to shake her leg free, but the other foot immediately sank several inches deeper. "Help!"

Triu-cair scampered toward her, his light weight floating on top of the treacherous terrain. He sprang up on her shoulder and tugged on her hair. *The more you fight, the deeper you sink.*

"I have to fight or I will lose everything. I will lose him, my life . . . everything!"

You lose only yourself when you lose sight of the truth.

"Augh!" she screamed as the tenacious muck sucked her deeper. Her knees were barely visible and her lovely silk dress was black with silt and rotten moss. Suddenly, a tiny sprout burst from the ground and curled its way upward, forming the thin trunk of a Highland tree. She lunged for it, but it remained just out of her reach. "Just a little bit closer," she gasped.

The tree, no larger than a poorly tended shrub, began to branch.

"Yes!" Kassandra cried as she managed to grasp one twig. She yanked with one hand, clawing and scraping the ground with the other, but the newborn branch snapped and she fell face-first onto the ground. "No!" she screamed as her upper torso began to sink and her knees were lost to view. She struggled frantically and her hands plunged deeply until even her elbows were buried.

Triu-cair leapt from her body and grabbed her flaming red tresses with his teeth. He yanked, but his strength was useless against the power of the bog.

She rocked, desperately trying to free herself, but within moments, only her head remained above ground.

Listen! Triu-cair screeched. *Stop fighting and listen.*

Kassandra paused, and heard hoofbeats echoing across the desolate moor.

The weasel jumped onto the tree and peered toward the horizon. *A legion,* he told her. *Twenty, maybe thirty horses. Coming directly this way. They will help you!*

"He must be leading them!" Kassandra cried. "Dagda! Dagda! Over here!"

The horses thundered closer and the ground shook

with the power of their strides. Soon the heaving breaths, the snapping leather and warrior battle cries flooded the landscape, drowning her pitiful calls for help. The spindly tree twitched, grew larger, stronger, but Kassandra craned her neck around it, still focused on the approaching horses.

Then, with a sudden surge, the tiny tree grew a thick trunk and the thin branches spread strong and wide. The horses galloped closer, their momentum gathering and accelerating. Triu-cair screeched and buried his head in Kassandra's hair and she stared at the stampede with horror.

"They aren't stopping," she whispered. "They will trample us."

The tree dipped, its steady branches encircling and sheltering her. The horses swept around her, each flashing hoof landing inches from her head. The massive creatures careened around her, oblivious to how close they were to the treacherous sinkhole.

Abruptly, one man reined in his steed, and the black horse reared over Kassandra's partially submerged head.

"Danu?" Cadedryn murmured.

The rest of the horses hurtled past until only he, Kassandra, Triu-cair and the tree remained.

Kassandra stared up at him, unsure for the first time. She hid among the branches, not certain she wanted him to see her.

Here is your man, Triu-cair told her silently. *Why do you not call out to him? He could pull you from the bog.*

Kassandra slowly extracted one hand and took hold of the sturdy branch. It felt solid and strong beneath her fingertips. "I have learned that some things are not as they seem," she replied.

The man on the horse pulled up his visor and reached into the thick tree. He plucked several berries from its flourishing branches and ate them. "I was starving," he said. "Thank you, mother earth—mother Danu—for providing me with nourishment."

"Thank you, strong Highland tree, for providing me with protection," Kassandra whispered, afraid to reach out to her dream friend. She did not know this man anymore. He was unpredictable. He was explosive and dangerous. She should forget him just like everyone advised.

His chest rippled with strength and his green eyes blazed with fervor as he scanned the horizon. The weapons on his saddle glinted with deadly meaning. She knew how he held them, how he used them. She knew his capacity to terrorize. She felt his heaving breath as he struggled against the weight of his shame.

She should look away. Leave him. Begin her life without him.

But she couldn't tear her gaze away.

Kassandra woke slowly and peered up at the ceiling in deep contemplation. What did her dream mean?

Turning on her side, she stared at her sleeping weasel, curled up in a ball at the bottom of the bed on a silken cushion. His lush tail twitched occasionally, indicating that he, too, dreamed.

She rose and looked out the window. The sun was about to set and thick, dark clouds hovering on the horizon were beginning to glow orange and pink. Wind blew through the garden below, causing the branches to sway. Behind her, Triu-cair stirred and offered a small cluck in greeting.

Kassandra glanced over at her friend. "I am terribly confused," she admitted. "I was so certain we were meant to wed . . . but perhaps I misinterpreted everything."

Triu-cair stretched his long, supple body, then scampered off the bed and over to his mistress.

"You are a naughty boy," she chided him as she bent down to scoop him into her arms. "If Kalial knew you were sleeping on the bed she would be very angry. She says you will frighten the ladies."

Triu-cair clucked again and gently nuzzled her face.

"What do you say to a secret ride? We could sneak out and go for a quick gallop with no one the wiser, just like we often do on the woodland ponies. You must be anxious for some fresh air and I need to clear my mind." Kassandra sighed and stroked Triu-cair's head. "I never expected my search to become so complicated." She rose and found her everyday clothes. "Tomorrow I will tell Kalial that I want to go home. Cadedryn is right: this is no place for me."

Triu-cair screeched with excitement and leapt from her arms to scamper to the door, then stared at it expectantly.

Kassandra giggled as she tried to run a brush through her thick red hair. "It feels wonderful not wearing that wig," she said. When Triu-cair squeaked in response, she waved to quiet him. "Shush! We don't want anyone to hear us, especially Kalial, and I don't want to bother dressing in my disguise for such a short ride." She looked out at the dark clouds. "It might rain," she commented. "I don't care if we get a bit wet. Do you?" Not expecting a reply, she walked to her clothing chest and rummaged to the bottom. "I will wear a hooded cape so we will not be recognized."

Dressing quickly, she pulled her hair back and tucked it under the hood, then surveyed herself in the polished metal propped on the vanity. "Not exactly the loveliest item," she said wryly, "but as long as it covers my hideous curls, I won't complain."

With Triu-cair balanced on her shoulder, she tiptoed out of her room and ran down the stairs and through the servants' door. Within moments, she managed to make her way along the edge of the courtyard and slip unseen into the stables. She quickly passed a number of stalls housing many fine horses until she reached the mare she had ridden previously. "Hello, Briana," she said softly, calling the mare by name. "It will take too much time to saddle up and the sun is almost completely set." She cast a disparaging look at the lady's saddle as she slid the bridle over the horse's head. "Besides, I abhor riding sidesaddle!" She led Briana over to a standing block and swiftly mounted astride.

For a moment she felt guilty. She had promised Kalial that she would behave like a lady. "Bah," she grumbled, shoving her misgivings away. "What harm will come to me from one simple jaunt? I will be departing soon anyway."

After adjusting her skirts so that her legs were fully covered, she rode out of the stable. Keeping to the deepest shadows, she snuck out of the courtyard and found a riding trail that led into the woods.

She squeezed her legs and the mare broke into a smooth canter. Although Briana was not as sturdy as a woodland pony, Kassandra found that her sensitive temperament made the ride more exciting. She laughed at the feel of the wind across her face and patted Briana reassuringly.

Triu-cair clung to Kassandra's shoulder and spread his lips in an imitation of a grin.

"Ready?" Kassandra asked both the mare and the weasel. Briana pricked her ears forward and the weasel wrapped his tail tightly around her neck. "Let's go!"

They surged forward, sailing along the path in blissful freedom. They easily leapt a small log that had fallen across the path and splashed through a meandering stream. The last rays of sunlight disappeared and a bluish haze guided their way.

"Faster!" Kassandra urged and the mare responded with a burst of speed. The billowing clouds darkened and a few drops of rain splashed Kassandra's face. "Faster! Faster!" she cried. "Just a bit farther!"

They careened down the path, their eyes adjusted to the deepening night. An owl hooted as they passed by and Kassandra laughed. She buried her face in the mare's mane as the rain began to fall in earnest. "Drat!" she grumbled as she pulled on the horse's reins, unwilling to risk the mare sliding on the slippery ground. Thunder reverberated in the distance and Kassandra mentally acknowledged it was time to head back to the castle. She patted the mare and slowed her to a trot, looking for a wide section of the path so they could turn around.

The trees huddled close, their wet branches brushing against her arms and legs and drenching her clothes. The sky blackened as clouds blocked even the moon, causing the once welcoming forest to become dark and dangerous.

The mare trembled, unable to see the ground or smell the path. She was a finely bred lady's mount, not a fearless woodland pony, and her muscles twitched nervously. She abruptly stopped as a blast of thunder shook the ground and she flicked her ears back and forth in agitation.

Kassandra wiped her face and attempted to see through the trees. "Come on, girl," she encouraged.

The mare shied sideways, crashing against a tree and bruising Kassandra's leg.

"Easy," Kassandra murmured, ignoring her leg as she attempted to soothe the animal.

Thunder rumbled again, much closer this time.

Briana whinnied and half reared.

"Over there." Kassandra squeezed her legs around the mare's girth. "There is a clearing just up ahead."

Triu-cair peeked his nose out from underneath Kassandra's hair and looked around warily. His sharp nails dug into Kassandra's neck as he clutched her tightly.

"Both of you must stay calm," Kassandra commanded. She clucked and bent over the mare's withers.

Briana stepped hesitantly forward, but her hoof landed on a twig, snapping it. She shied backward, almost unseating Kassandra, for her back was getting slippery as her nervous sweat mixed with the cold rain.

Kassandra clucked again, speaking softly and soothingly to the mare, when suddenly a bolt of lightning lit the sky.

The mare whinnied in terror and burst into a mindless gallop through the trees, breaking branches and stumbling over fallen debris.

"No!" Kassandra screamed. A heavy branch slapped her face, ripping her hood off and scratching her face and neck. She barely managed to stay mounted as Briana darted around another tree and crashed through a set of prickly bushes, but the weasel tumbled to the ground.

"Triu-cair!" Kassandra cried.

Thunder reverberated and the horse skidded to a stop, rearing high. Her long legs flailed in the air and her eyes rolled in terror.

"No!" Kassandra screamed again as she felt herself sliding backward.

The mare plunged to the ground, then surged forward as Kassandra scrambled to stay on her back. She gripped the mare's mane in desperation, but another lightning flash sent the mare careening in a new direction. The horse fell to her knees and Kassandra soared over her head, slamming headfirst into an old oak tree.

Chapter 7

Cadedryn cursed the thunder and lightning. He turned up the collar on his cape and hunched down, but the rain drenched his clothes and chilled his skin. His warhorse was tense but obedient, trained since youth to behave under strenuous conditions and despite loud noises.

"I wouldn't be out if it weren't for that blasted lass," Cadedryn grumbled. Kassandra's crestfallen face had made him feel guilty and he had taken a ride to relieve his tension. "I could be in the great hall, sipping warm ale and eating fresh food. It's all her fault."

A huge flash of lightning illuminated the thunderous clouds and Cadedryn peered around him with concern. He did not like being under the trees in such a storm. He spotted a clearing just ahead and guided his horse toward it.

Suddenly, he heard a woman scream, then the sound of a horse crashing madly through the trees in the other direction.

"What woman would be out in this?" he growled as he spurred his horse forward. He listened intently, hoping she would cry out for help again, but he heard nothing more. He frowned, becoming worried. "Miss?" he shouted above the downpour. "Miss? Are you hurt?"

An inhuman screech coming from the left raised the

hairs on the back of his neck. The screech came again and a shadow danced along the treetops. Cadedryn reined in and pulled out his sword. "Who goes there?" he called.

"Ohhhhh . . ." a woman moaned.

Cadedryn glanced over and spotted her huddled form. Her dress was torn and multiple scratches marred her freckled face. Her head rocked to the side, but her eyes remained closed.

"Ohhhhh," she moaned again.

Cadedryn dismounted and kneeled next to her, keeping a tight hold on his sword. "Miss?" He touched her neck. It was warm and a pulse beat strongly just beneath the surface. He tried to brush the hair from her visage, but the wet strands slipped from his grasp and he quickly gave up once he heard the inhuman screech once more, this time followed by a strange chattering.

Cadedryn peered up and gazed directly into a pair of glowing red eyes. Certain the creature was set to prey upon the hapless woman, he swung his sword at the beast, narrowly missing it.

The animal pressed flat against the branch, spun around and cocked his head. Then, taking care to circle widely around Cadedryn, he jumped from tree to tree, and scampered down a trunk to crouch by his mistress's side.

Seeing the creature hunkering next to the woman, Cadedryn clenched his teeth. A polecat. He flushed, annoyed that the small weasel had distracted him from looking after the injured woman. He sheathed his sword and angrily waved the creature away, then scooped up the semiconscious woman, faintly aware that the weasel only circled around and returned to stare at them both.

Another blast of lightning followed closely by the loud rumble of thunder made him hurry to his horse. "Miss, we are going to one of the crofters' huts just over that ridge. It is far closer than the castle and you need to get in front of a fire before you take a chill." As he swung up bearing the woman, the weasel scrambled onto the horse's rump, causing the horse to start in surprise. Cadedryn tried to brush the weasel aside, but the creature bared his teeth in warning, then slipped inside an open saddlebag. Giving up with a curse, Cadedryn switched his concentration to balancing the woman and guiding the horse.

Within a few minutes, Cadedryn located the cabin and ducked inside. His horse made its own way to the small shelter adjacent to the cabin, but the weasel boldly followed them indoors.

"I hope you don't soil my clothing," Cadedryn told the weasel as he peeled off his cape and flung it over a chair. The polecat bounded up into the rafters and found a comfortable place to lick himself dry, taking care to keep his mistress in sight.

Cadedryn laid the woman on the ground in front of the hearth and began building a fire to warm her. As soon as the flames caught, he turned to tend her.

His jaw dropped. In the torrential rain outside, he had not seen the color of her skin and hair. Now, in the flickering firelight, her bold red tresses looked like wild flames untamed by human hands and her suntouched skin glowed with vibrant health. Never had he seen such magnificent coloring or such lush curls. Highborn women were pale and carefully coiffed, appearing like elegant waifs drifting gracefully from room to room, whereas this woman exuded pulsing vitality.

He touched her fine facial features, stroking the line

of her brow and following the ridge of her jaw. He rubbed the pad of his thumb across a small indentation on her chin, then caressed the long line of her delicately exposed throat.

She was far too beautiful to be a peasant, yet her clothing was coarse and ill fitting. Who was she? Someone's bastard daughter? A by-blow of some irresponsible gentleman and some unfortunate beauty? And if so, why was she riding through the dark forest in a thunderstorm? "Are you fleeing some lecherous uncle or escaping a vicious husband?" he asked softly, feeling a kinship with the unconscious woman. He understood how you could feel so desolate and afraid that you had no thought to the consequences of your desperate actions. He had known such tormented nights after his parents' deaths. He had felt the need to ride recklessly through the night just to escape the gaiety of others around him.

He touched a damp curl. There were legends about red-haired witches and fire-breathing druids. Tales told over flickering campfires during long battle marches when men longed for some magic to transport them to another existence. Feminine magic . . . the kind that was filled with sighs of pleasure.

The kind of magic he needed right now.

Her eyes flickered and she groaned.

He wiped a piece of linen across her wet face and knelt beside her. "How are you feeling?" he murmured.

Kassandra's vision began to clear and she focused on his face. A sense of wonderment filled her. He had come for her. Cadedryn . . . Dagda, Celtic battle king . . . He, the man of her dreams, beside her and caring for her, just as she had always imagined. Their earlier argument forgotten, she smiled.

"Better . . . better now," she replied softly.

He wiped the rainwater from her brow and noted her blue eyes. The only other woman who had eyes as blue was Kassandra. He chuckled softly. In twenty-five years he had never seen such richly colored eyes, yet now he had met two women within a single day whose sparkling eyes contained more rich depth than anything he had ever seen. He had thought earlier that Kassandra's eyes reminded him of a deep Scottish loch, but even that paled in comparison. Splashed against golden skin and blazing tresses, this woman's eyes were beyond description.

She touched her head and closed her eyes in pain.

"You must have taken a nasty fall," he said, startled from his perusal by the evidence of her discomfort. He placed the cloth across her head. "You have a lump on your forehead," he informed her kindly.

Kassandra touched the spot and winced.

He brushed her hands away and gently cleaned her face. "Let me. Your hands are still too shaky. Trust me?" he teased.

Kassandra nodded. "Absolutely. I have always trusted you."

"You look like a drowned kitten in that soaking dress. A tiger-striped kitten. Are you cold?"

She nodded again and started to shiver.

His teasing look became more intent as he became aware of her breasts puckering under the wet fabric of her bodice. He stroked the linen over her neck and the area just below her throat. "Do you live nearby?" he asked.

"Two days' ride," she answered. "In a forest near the ocean." She leaned toward him, drawn to his heat, and his hands slipped behind her head, supporting her.

"Why are you here?" he asked, curious about her.

Her voice was husky, either rough from pain or accented as if from another place.

Kassandra pulled the cloth away and smiled. "You know why I am here," she replied, assuming he recognized her.

"Are you searching for someone? Someone to protect and care for you?"

Her smile broadened and her cheeks flushed with pleasure. Only hours before, she had been about to give up on uniting their souls, but now he was offering to love and protect her. She took a deep breath. He had been only surprised by her declarations, not offended. In his own way, she surmised, he was acting shy.

"Would you be my someone special?" she asked gently. "I've never wanted anyone as much as I want you."

He raised his eyebrows, surprised but excited by her boldness.

She touched his cheek, caressing the hard flesh with the tips of her fingers. She swept her touch outward, toward his earlobes, and brushed across them with the lightness of a butterfly.

He shuddered, desire blooming hard and fast. He snatched her hand and pulled it from his face while staring into her eyes. "You shouldn't do that," he whispered.

She tilted her head toward the fire and inhaled the scent of woodsmoke. "Do you like the forest?" she asked.

"If you are in it, I would like any forest," he answered, making her smile.

"The ocean?" she asked, trying to find out more about him. There was so much about her dream man that she did not know.

"Only if it is as blue as your eyes."

She turned to face him, a soft flutter awakening in her belly. Their gazes locked and a vibration passed between them, making them both draw shaky breaths. This was the part of the dream that was unfamiliar. Only a hint of this feeling had whispered through her dreams, yet it had inexorably drawn her across the hills and into his arms. Here she was. With him. Feeling him.

She brushed a lock of hair from his face, reveling in his impossibly long eyelashes. Such gorgeous eyelashes on such a hardened warrior. The flutter in her stomach broadened to envelope her thighs and ripple down the backs of her legs until her toes tingled.

He rose and put some distance between them, trying to stabilize his breathing. "Where is your family?" he asked, his voice deeper than usual as he tried to control his rising passion.

"Far away," Kassandra answered. She stood and walked up to him, her wet gown molding to her body.

"You have no one?" he asked as he closed his hands in a tight fist to keep from reaching for her.

"My sister."

"Your sister?"

"My half sister. We share a mother."

"Ahhhh," he whispered, believing he finally understood. In the light of the fire, he could see that not only her eyes looked like Kassandra's, but the lines of her face and the curve of her jaw were similar. Kassandra was pale and virginal. Although she had a temper, she was also a kind and gentle lady who dreamed of everlasting love. This woman, this tigress, was the opposite. She was bold and brilliant and he could feel her capacity for passion simmering beneath the surface.

Illegitimate sisters. One accepted into the fold of

her father's household, while the other was cast out, expected to survive on her own.

"I should return," the woman said as she looked around the small hut.

"Of course," Cadedryn answered as he draped his cape around her shoulders. "Does your sister, Kassandra, help you? Does she ensure that you are well provided for?"

Kassandra turned slowly and looked at him in perplexity. She shook her head, trying to decipher his strange comment.

His brows drew together in a frown and he pulled a pouch from his belt and withdrew several coins. "Take these. Purchase some warmer clothes and some hot soup at the tavern."

Kassandra fell back a step and drew his cape closer. The warmth she had felt at his considerate care was fading and a cold suspicion was intruding. "I cannot go to the tavern," she said.

"Is there someone there who will hurt you? Bother you? You are so lovely; it must be difficult to avoid those intent on taking advantage of you. If you'd like, you may use my name as your protector. While not all men like me, they all respect me and will not harm you if you are under my protection."

The blood pounded in Kassandra's ears and she was forced to turn away from him to shield the shock and pain filling her eyes. He did not know her! He had not rescued her because he knew they were life mates. He thought she was someone else!

"I am surprised Kassandra has not been kinder to you. She seems like a woman who would take greater care of others."

Kassandra choked on a sob. How was everything getting so muddled?

He stepped up behind her and placed his hands on her shoulders. "I would like to see you again," he said.

Kassandra lifted her chin and stared at the flickering flames, unaware of how they danced across her red tresses. "I am . . ." she whispered, about to tell him the truth, but the words died on her lips. If she told him she was Kassandra, how would she explain the elaborate ruse? Would Kalial be punished for her part in deceiving the court?

He turned her around and made her face him. "You are . . . ?"

His penetrating gaze bore into her, and she felt her legs begin to sway. He was her mate, even if he did not yet know it. She had come this far to find him, and she had no intention of letting him slip away. "I am honored," she finished. She glanced up at a noise coming from the rafters.

His gaze followed hers. "It is a pesky creature. Won't leave me alone."

She chuckled. " 'Tis my friend. I call him Triu-cair."

"You become more intriguing by the moment. Few ladies have pets and none has ever tamed a weasel."

Her gaze returned to his and her voice dropped to a murmur. "You don't want me to be a lady, do you?"

His breath caught. She knew nothing about him, not that his mother was a peasant or that his sole ambition was to regain his title. In fact, all she knew was that he was a man. He didn't want her to think about anything else. "No," he replied. "I've had my fill of ladies for the moment. I would rather spend some time with a woman."

She backed away, her heart speeding recklessly fast. "Tomorrow," she promised as she glanced outside at the diminishing rain. "I will meet you here tomorrow when the sun is at its peak."

He stepped forward, reaching for her. "Don't go yet. 'Tis still cold outside."

A slow smile spread across her lips and she released her hold on his cape, allowing it to slide to the floor. "I love the rain," she said huskily. She held her fingertips to her lips, then blew him a kiss. "Don't follow me," she whispered.

And before he could catch her, she and the weasel were gone.

Chapter 8

She ran through the rain, her heart thundering as loudly as the sky had only moments before. She felt his need and she wanted to give him everything, but he did not even know her real name.

She paused against a tree and spied her mare standing next to a thick bush, her reins caught amid the thorns. The mare's head swung toward her and she offered a nicker in greeting.

Kassandra nodded thankfully, and after regaining her breath, she managed to extricate the horse and check her over for injuries. Once assured that the animal was fine, Kassandra lifted Triu-cair to her shoulders, gripped Briana's mane and swung astride. The mare shied, but Kassandra's soothing voice encouraged her forward. "Easy, pretty mare. It is just the rain. The storm has passed." But inside, Kassandra battled her own tempest. Anger at Cadedryn's blindness waged with ecstasy at his capitulation. She could feel his interest and knew he would meet with her again—not as Lady Kassandra but as his tiger kitten.

A red-haired kitten. She pushed her hair out of her face and winced as she brushed against her bruised forehead.

Her limbs quivered as she recalled his intent gaze. Sister. He believed she was her own sister. How could she have let that happen? How could she have let him think she was two different people? Was it right? Should she have told him the truth? Or perhaps it was fate, a form of destiny forced upon one who fought its relentless drive toward fulfillment.

The mare flattened her ears and cantered through the trees while Kassandra's skirt snapped in the wind, barely concealing her bare legs. Triu-cair clung to Kassandra's red hair, chattering wildly at the foolishness of their careening flight through the darkness and scolding her for her recklessness.

"Look!" Kassandra cried, ignoring his comments as she spotted the glowing windows of the castle. She drew in the reins and peered through the rain. "Everyone will be inside," she said hopefully. "With luck, no one will see us." A flash of lightning flickered in the distance, followed by a quieter roll of thunder. Kassandra wiped the rain from her eyes and pushed her wet tresses away from her face once again. The storm was moving through. If she didn't get to the barn soon, the stableboys might come out and discover the missing mare.

She adjusted her dress as best she could and crouched low behind the mare's withers. "Fortune be with me," she prayed, and Triu-cair clucked in agreement. The mare cantered easily, her fear forgotten now that her warm stall was in sight.

As they reached the courtyard, Kassandra slowed Briana to a walk. She skirted the open areas, navigating the darkest shadows in an effort to remain hidden. Despite the barking hounds, she managed to reach the stable and ducked through the entrance.

Once inside, she slid down and led Briana to her stall. "You are fine and fleet," she told her, "but a bit of common sense would do you well." She patted the mare fondly, wiped her down and secured her gate as

Triu-cair prowled the straw mounds, searching for prey.

A sound made Kassandra gasp and she quickly ducked behind a pile of straw to avoid being seen.

"We are no longer youths," a woman whispered as two shadowy figures slipped inside the stable doors. "I must—"

"Just once more," a man replied as he pressed his body against hers. "Who will it harm? I have never forgotten the feel of your body beneath my own."

"Hush!" the woman admonished. "My situation has changed. I cannot risk everything for a moment of passion."

The man grew angry. "I have done much for you," he growled. "Have you forgotten what I did at your behest? I placed my soul in jeopardy!"

Triu-cair pushed his way through the straw pile and nudged against Kassandra's foot.

She emitted a tiny shriek of surprise. So intent was she on the mysterious couple's conversation, she had not seen her friend appear. She covered her face with her hand and squeezed her eyes closed, hoping the two would not come searching for her.

"I heard someone!" the woman said urgently. "We must go!"

There was a brief moment of silence, the sound of heavy breathing, then a pair of deep sighs.

"I will come to your room tonight," the man said. "You will leave the latch open to receive me."

"I—"

"No arguments. Now go. I will ensure that no one sees you cross the courtyard."

The woman's skirts rustled as she fled out of the stable, followed more slowly by the sound of a man's footsteps.

Kassandra remained still for several moments, then rose and peered carefully down the aisle. No one remained. "Come along, Triu-cair," she called under her breath as she slipped outside and raced toward the castle. "I have no interest in disturbing another's tryst!" She located the servants' side door, opened it and ducked inside.

Down the hall of the castle, she could hear someone playing a lute. In the great hall, the ladies and gentlemen of the court were dancing and laughing as they enjoyed the rich abundance of the king's banquet. She saw Lady Corine and her mother, Morgana, greeting each other near the front door, and Curtis bowing to a distinguished man she did not know. Kalial was sitting on the far side of the room, smiling at the antics of a court jester.

Sighing with relief that all the people who could possibly recognize her were occupied, Kassandra turned and tiptoed up the servants' staircase. A maid scurried past, too intent on carrying her platter to notice the redhead hovering in the shadows. Kassandra crept up to her floor, then assuring herself that no one would see her, she bolted down the hallway. Yanking open the door to her chamber, she ducked inside, slammed the door closed behind her, then leaned against the wooden slats and sighed with relief.

Triu-cair slid off her shoulders and curled into a ball on the bed, his bright eyes peering up at her with concern.

Her hands began to tremble and her jaw shivered. So much had happened. So much had changed. In one day, she had found her dream man, been rejected, seduced and then, in a cruel twist, rejected again.

Not to mention she had been witness to an unknown pair of arguing lovers.

She patted Triu-cair's head, then stripped off her dress and tossed it on the floor before collapsing on the bed in exhaustion. "Cadedryn did not know who I was," she whispered mournfully, the lovers temporarily forgotten. "He thinks I am two people."

Kassandra rolled onto her stomach and buried her head in the pillow, lying in torment until the sounds coming from the great hall died away as the revelers finally took to their beds. She tossed and turned, willing her body to sleep, but her mind remained stubbornly alert. Every inch of her body thrummed with sensations and her thighs ached with the echoes of innocent desire.

At last, she kicked the covers violently, then punched the pillow with surprising force.

Triu-cair squawked awake.

"I cannot meet him again," she abruptly declared as she stood and strode over to the vanity table and placed her hands on either side. "He has already declared that he will never bond with me. There is nothing I can do to change his mind, and seeing him again will only make my heart bleed. Before, I longed to link our spirits. Now I . . ." She started jamming pins into her hair to bind it against her head. "I don't know what I want." Her body tingled and she could not erase the feeling of his hands upon her shoulders. She did know what she wanted, and that it was much more than he was willing to give.

Triu-cair screeched and banged his tiny hands on the blankets as Kassandra lifted her black wig and jammed it in place. After spreading a quick layer of paste across her face, she retrieved a cape and slid Triu-cair into an inner pocket.

"I waited for him for ten years," she said as she flung some clothes in a bag and lugged it to the door.

She opened the portal and peered down the hallway. "I rejected all others because I wanted him, but he knows nothing of me. He is not waiting for me. Instead, his aspirations are focused on his rotten title," she told Triu-cair in a hushed voice.

She hefted her makeshift satchel and struggled down the passageway until she reached the stairs. She looked dubiously down the long flight, then at her bundle as she nudged it with her foot.

"I daresay, kicking your package down the stairs could result in some damage."

Kassandra spun around and stared at Curtis McCafferty. "What are you doing strolling about at this time of night?" she accused.

He sauntered closer and leaned against the wall with one leg crossed over the other. His clothes were rumpled and his boots were unlaced. "I could ask you the same question," he replied. "You appear to be a lady in distress."

Kassandra looked up and down the hall. Her cheeks flushed guiltily. "I'm leaving the castle," she said as she lifted her chin defiantly. "I don't like it here."

Curtis pushed away from the wall and gripped her bundle. "I'd rather be home as well," he replied agreeably. "Let me assist you. 'Tis a night of comings and goings. You are not the only one to have a sudden change in plans. Lady Morgana's husband left only hours after my father arrived."

"Aren't you concerned about me riding off in the middle of the night?" Kassandra asked. "Aren't you going to caution me and tell me to behave with more restraint?"

He lifted his eyebrows. "Is that what you want me to say?"

"I don't like Cadedryn Caenmore!" she answered

vehemently. "He is a blind, mealy badger with an insatiable desire to ruin everything and everyone!"

He chuckled. "Strong sentiments from someone who barely knows him." He lifted his hand to halt her interruption. "I know, I know. You have dreamed about him." He leaned close. "You should take care of what you say. There are those who would think poorly of a lass who foresees the future. They might brand you a gypsy—or worse, a witch."

Kassandra swallowed and self-consciously touched her wig, making sure her red hair was adequately covered. "I know," she said softly. "At times, I wish it were not so."

Curtis started down the steps with her bag. "Don't worry. I won't betray you. Tell me more about your dreams." His voice grew serious. "I want to know what you have seen."

Kassandra trailed after him, her stomach twisting into a tight knot. "I thought they were telling me that I should wed a certain man because he was always present. I thought it meant that we were destined to become joined."

"Destiny is never that simple," Curtis replied, a thread of disillusionment coloring his words. "My own father thought he knew his true destiny, but he was denied."

"What happened?"

"My father, David McCafferty, was madly in love with Lady Morgana."

"Corine's mother?"

"Aye. He believed destiny would bind them together for eternity, but he was terribly mistaken." Curtis reached the now quiet lower floor and walked over to a half-empty wine barrel. After putting down the bundle, he located a clean goblet, filled it with the fragrant draught, then handed it to Kassandra.

She glanced at the door and then at the cup.

"Give me a moment," he persuaded her. "I want to learn more about you." He motioned to the few servants finishing their tasks. "You should wait until everyone is asleep before you sneak out, or one of the servants will warn Lady Kalial."

Relenting, Kassandra took the cup and swallowed. The rich flavor rolled around her mouth and slid with velvet smoothness down her throat. A warm lassitude filled her and she took a deep breath.

"There," Curtis purred. "Come sit with me by the fire."

"What happened with your father and Lady Morgana?" Kassandra asked as she relaxed in one of the large chairs. "Does it have something to do with Cadedryn's family?"

Curtis's brow furrowed. "You see, there are four families that control our section of the Highlands: Caenmore, McCafferty, Fergus and Duncan. Morgana was born a Duncan. The king sought to bring the families together through marriage and thus avoid any feuding. He ordered a betrothal between Liam Caenmore and Morgana Duncan, believing that a union between her family and Caenmore's would more greatly benefit Scotland than one between her and the McCaffertys. At the time Laird Fergus was already married to his first wife."

Kassandra tilted her head after taking another sip. "But Liam did not marry Morgana?

"No, he wed a woman named Sarah."

Kassandra wrinkled her brow. "Then Morgana was free to wed McCafferty."

Curtis shrugged. "Yet they did not marry, for by then, it was too late. Fergus's wife died in childbirth and the king immediately wed Morgana to him. My heartbroken father wed the second daughter of a distant clan, but he never forgot Lady Morgana." Curtis rubbed his chin and looked into the fire's flames. "So you see, milady, destiny does not always follow a simple path. Liam married Sarah, thereby ruining Lady Morgana's chances of becoming a countess, which in turn, caused her to be wed to Lord Fergus, a man she grew to despise. Losing Morgana devastated my father and infuriated the king, and it was all done because Liam ignored the codes of conduct. If he had wed Morgana, all would be well." Curtis leaned back and closed his eyes. "Destiny as a means to finding happiness is a childish concept, fit for dreamers. Lust, power, greed . . . revenge . . . these emotions are what truly control life. You will never feel comfortable at court because you, just like Liam, do not adhere to these rules."

Kassandra covered her mouth to stifle her cry. His words were true. She had declared her love and been denied.

But there was one set of rules she was beginning to understand. Men of this society responded more to desire and need and less to love and emotion. Cadedryn had lusted after her body. She had seen the bold look in his eye and knew he had felt desire for her. No, not for her, for the tiger kitten. While rejecting love, he had embraced lust. He did not want eternal bliss; he wanted to regain the power of his earldom. She could not help him with his quest, but she had the ability to satisfy his other needs, thereby capturing his interest.

"Lust . . ." she repeated slowly. If she used lust to

gain his attention, she might have a chance to teach him new emotions. She had tried to force him to acknowledge their union, but he did not understand the forest ways. He was uncomfortable with her declarations because in his world, women did not approach men so boldly. They coaxed and cajoled, using a man's desire to their own advantage.

She was not in the forest now; she was in the Scottish court. She was being selfish and shortsighted to insist he come to understand her way. It was time to meld into his society and accept his customs. She would not talk of dreams, but would find other ways to engage his interest. Like being an illegitimate peasant with nowhere to go and no one to turn to but him.

Curtis looked at her through narrowed eyes. "What else have you seen in your dreams? Lady Corine said that you told Cadedryn you saw his father's murder."

Kassandra rose. "I thought I had," she murmured as a plan began to form in her mind.

"Who murdered him? I am Cadedryn's friend and should know if someone we trust has committed a terrible crime."

She shook her head. "I don't know."

Curtis sat forward and stared at her intently. "But you said you saw the murder."

Still preoccupied, she put her cup on the table and reached for her bundle. "I never saw the attacker's face," she answered. Then, her expression firming as her ideas coalesced, she faced him. "Lord Curtis, I've changed my mind. I am going to stay. I have some unfinished business to resolve. I *can* live by those rules, at least for the time being."

Curtis debated for one heartbeat, then smiled and rose to his feet. "Very well. Let me help you with your bag."

* * *

Later that night, after Cadedryn had returned to the castle and retired to his room, he stared at the smoldering flames in the fireplace. As the coals shimmered and glowed and the orange flickers shrank to tiny, halfhearted embers, he took several deep droughts of ale and leaned his head back against the chair.

He had forgotten to ask her name. Something about her had stirred his blood enough to make him forget even the most simple pleasantries. All he could remember was the feel of her silken skin, the color of her fantastic eyes and the glow of the firelight against her blazing hair.

Why hadn't he kissed her?

The intensity between them was shared. He had seen it in her gaze and felt it in her shoulders, which had trembled under his touch, yet he had restrained himself as if she were a highborn lass that required proper introductions and a lengthy courtship.

He kicked his heels up on a small trunk and tilted the chair on its back legs as he watched the flame's reflection dancing upon the ceiling. His mother had been a peasant. She had not known about the rules of etiquette demanded of the highborn class, and had not warned him of the perils of feminine wiles. She had died and he had been thrust into a household wherein his parentage was ridiculed and his lack of knowledge was mocked. The first woman he had courted had openly laughed in his face when he had asked her to accompany him to the archery field to practice together.

The chair legs fell back to the floor as he abruptly dropped his legs and buried his head in his hands, the shame of that day still fresh and painful. She had cruelly informed him that real ladies did not touch weapons and a true gentleman would offer to sit with her in the garden, not force her to traipse across a muddy field.

He had learned his lesson and had maintained a reserve around women ever since. They were complex and unpredictable as they often asked for what they did not want and merely hinted at what they did desire. He could not understand their subtleties and had gratefully retreated into a man's world.

Corine was no different than the others. Her eyes did not reflect her words and her fingers were cold and icy. He was well aware of her emotional indifference and fully accepted that her interest was solely based upon his prospects, not on any shared feelings between them.

But the tigress kitten was not a highborn lass. She was like him, displaced and shunned due to an accident of parentage. She would not require the intricate dance of courtship. Indeed, she might welcome his honest attention for the unabashed reason he offered it. He wanted to teach her the ways of love and share a few moments of pleasure.

Kassandra's words echoed in his mind. She had accused him of settling for Corine's cold bed and foregoing love's passion.

He lifted his face and smiled. He would have both his court-appointed bride and his lovely flame-haired temptress, and then he could forget Kassandra's wounded eyes and know that he had surpassed everyone's expectations.

The embers flickered dully, casting the room in an ominous orange glow as one by one they turned to black, yet still he sat in the chair, thinking about the two women he had just met. Kassandra, the guileless lady who helped servants and gushed about impossible

dreams of everlasting love, and his tigress, the sensuous half sister who rode her horse deep into the woods
on a stormy night and radiated life, vitality and
passion.

He rubbed his forehead, thinking back to the time
before his parents had died. He remembered now that
he used to have a recurring dream about a lovely blue-
eyed girl who played in a flower-strewn meadow. He
had forgotten about it until tonight.

He stood up, stripped off his clothes and lay down
on his bed. He was too old for dreams, he berated
himself as he forced the memories from his mind and
pulled a pillow over his head to block the last of the
firelight from his tired eyes. He was no longer a
dream-filled youth, longing for endless days of fun and
adventure. He was a master swordsman and the son
of an earl. He had obeyed the king, thus he deserved
to have his title reinstated. He must remain true to his
ambitions, not spend time revisiting old and forgotten
dreams. Not now. Not ever.

Chapter 9

The next day, the entire court was invited to attend a boar hunt. The ladies dressed in elegant gowns and the men sported long knives and throwing spears. Many groomsmen scurried about, trying to hold horses still while riders attempted to mount without mishap. It was a confusing, hectic scene and Kassandra watched from the sidelines with trepidation.

"Why are we going after a boar?" she asked Kalial once again.

Kalial looked at her with compassion, aware that the ritual hunt was unfathomable to her younger half sister. "The pig will be given to the villagers for their festival," she patiently explained. "It will not be wasted."

"But doesn't the king have enough in his herds to feed all his subjects?"

Kalial sighed, knowing she would not be able to justify the killing. "You do not have to ride the entire way," she offered. "Once we are underway, you may rein in and follow at a sedate pace. Most will think you are being ladylike and demure."

Grimacing, Kassandra led her mare to the mounting block. Her head itched and her face throbbed where it was bruised, but the paste adequately covered the discoloration and Kalial had not noticed the injury. Kassandra was thankful that Kalial appeared to believe her hesitancy was due solely to the brutal sport, but she was also nervous about how she was going to get away and meet Cadedryn at the crofter's hut.

Her heart thudded as she calculated how long it would take to make it to the hut, wash, change and be prepared to meet him. She should have said she would meet him at night. Trying to escape the crowd during the day might well prove difficult, although she noted Kalial's suggestion. Perhaps she could angle her mare away from the others with no one the wiser.

As she allowed a groom to help her mount the awkward sidesaddle, she carefully arranged her skirts and checked her wig. Raising her hand to her mantle, she confirmed that her coronet was firmly in place. Finally, she tugged on her riding gloves with her teeth, then blushed when one of the many milling young ladies looked at her with superior arrogance and lifted an arched brow at Kassandra's less-fashionable ensemble.

Sighing, Kassandra lifted her chin and plastered a smile on her face. It would do no good to say something rude. However, she couldn't resist grinning with amusement when the same lady toppled off the side of her horse when her gelding tripped over his own foot.

Soon King Malcolm arrived, followed by his English wife, Queen Margaret. They nodded to the hunt master and started out of the yard as their subjects vied for positions behind them. Two earls were in attendance, and they rode immediately behind the king. Next were the higher lairds and finally the lesser lords.

The king paused as he passed a man on a black stallion.

"Cadedryn," he acknowledged.

"Your Majesty," Cadedryn replied with a deep bow.

"You look much like your father."

Cadedryn's green eyes flashed, and his jaw tensed.

"I know you are an accomplished warrior, for I have seen your name mentioned in many reports from the battlefield. You have proven to be an asset to Scotland."

Cadedryn bowed again at the compliment and some of his tension eased.

"But your father offended the crown," the king continued. "I must have your assurance that you will not do the same."

Cadedryn's face tightened again and his eyes narrowed. "I will not fail you, Your Highness," he replied fervently.

The king nodded in appreciation. "How do you propose to erase his wrong?"

"I humbly request to complete his oath by wedding the daughter of William and Morgana Fergus."

"Lady Corine Fergus?"

"Aye, Your Majesty."

The king glanced at his wife, who smiled sagely. "The son and daughter," Queen Margaret mulled. " 'Tis an insightful resolution, and Lord Fergus ails. When he dies, the Fergus lands will need a strong hand. The marriage would prove beneficial to Scotland."

The king lifted his reins and urged his horse forward. "We will think upon the matter," he said dismissively. "You are an untitled man who merely maintains Aberdour Castle and its lands for the country. I could not allow you to wed one of our wealthiest, highborn maids. Ride at the back of the hunt, as your position dictates, although"—the king glanced over his shoulder—"you have my permission to break ranks once we are under way and ride in whatever position you can attain." The king glanced at the earls in attendance. "May the best man prevail."

Cadedryn clenched his fists as he watched the earls and lairds ride past. Several cast him disparaging looks, while others were blatantly hostile.

Kassandra held her mare to a slow walk as she saw Cadedryn struggle to contain his stallion. She could see the evidence of his white-knuckled fury as he was forced to wait until everyone passed him by. Compassion rippled through her as she saw how he tried to ignore the insulting stares, and she frowned when even Corine rode past with hardly a nod.

Kassandra clucked to her mare and moved closer to him, wanting to offer him comfort, but a knight intercepted her. "Milady, you should ride up with your mistress, Lady Kalial. May I lead your mare to her rightful place?" She caught Cadedryn's gaze as she stared at him over the knight's shoulder. His eyes were shadowed and the pulse pounded at his temple. He stared back at her, his expression cloaked and guarded as Curtis and David McCafferty joined him and tried to gain his attention

Kassandra shook her head, thinking quickly. "I fear that I have been instructed not to ride with someone to whom I have not been introduced." She cast about, as if searching for someone. "Ah," she said with satisfaction. "Caenmore. I know him."

The knight looked at Cadedryn with surprise. "Caenmore is a swordsman, not a lord, and he does not often converse with the ladies. I hardly think he would accept—"

"No matter, Sir Renton," Cadedryn interrupted as he allowed his stallion to prance forward. "I will assist the lady."

Curtis frowned and pointed to the other riders as they struck out across the meadow. "Cadedryn," he reminded his friend, "my father is here to ride with us, and the king all but gave you leave to outrace the others and join the lead. You cannot stay back and accompany a lass."

Renton touched his sword hilt to his forehead and bowed across the mane of his horse toward Kassandra, then spurred his horse to catch up with the other riders as Cadedryn shrugged his shoulders. "I will assist the lady," he repeated.

Curtis looked at his father in frustration, then at Kassandra with the beginnings of true anger. "You are distracting Cadedryn from what he must do. As I explained earlier, he must impress the king and gain a royal pardon."

"Do not chastise the miss," David interrupted. "Let her ride with Caenmore and let us enjoy a moment as father and son. It has been a long time since we spent time together without Cadedryn."

Curtis shook his head. "I want to ride with Cadedryn and reach the front of the pack so I'm present at the killing."

David frowned and flicked a jealous glance at Cadedryn, but said nothing more.

Kassandra's eyes widened and she raised a hand in defense. "I merely thought he needed someone to stand beside him. I did not mean to cause trouble."

Cadedryn answered her. "You did not disrupt anything. The McCaffertys were about to leave. I will catch up with them later."

Curtis drew a quick a breath at the abrupt dismissal. "Cadedryn," he declared. "This woman's interference must be stopped!"

"I will meet up with you this eve," Cadedryn insisted. "I have other business to attend at this moment."

Curtis yanked his horse around and spurred him,

causing the creature to explode into a gallop with a neigh of distress. David McCafferty bowed toward Kassandra, then sent his own horse trailing behind his son's.

As the dust settled, Cadedryn motioned for Kassandra to walk her horse next to his. "You do not need to ride beside me," he informed her. "I do not require your sponsorship. Despite what Curtis believes, the king will do as he wishes, and if he chooses to delay discussing the reinstatement of my title, neither I nor anyone else has the power to persuade him."

Kassandra shrugged and urged her horse to match strides with his. "I spoke the truth. It is inappropriate to ride with a stranger."

He grinned as his annoyance faded. "It was a kind thought," he acknowledged. "You are forever championing the unfortunate."

"Why would you consider yourself unfortunate?" Kassandra asked. "You are widely respected . . ."

"But not loved," he finished for her.

It was her turn to grin. "You denounce love. You cannot have it with some and reject it with others. If you are loved by one, you can be loved by all."

"And conversely, if you reject everyone, you must reject the one."

Kassandra rode in silence, considering his reply. "You have been cast out from your people," she said softly. "You have been rejected and thus you reject them."

Cadedryn's green gaze flicked over her face, noting the similarities to the woman he had met last night. He opened his mouth, about to ask about her illegitimate sister, but she suddenly reined in her mare and glanced back at the castle.

"I forgot something," she improvised, trying to find

a way to detach herself so that she could make her way to the hut before he did. "Go ahead and ride on. I will not be saddened to miss the hunt, but I encourage you to enjoy yourself."

"Do you find the hunt distasteful, or is it my company?" His voice was suddenly guarded and cold, and he leaned away from her as if he found her offensive.

Kassandra shook her head. "Not you. I admit I am not fond of the killing."

"The boar rarely suffers."

"Rarely?" She shuddered and turned away.

On impulse, he reached for the reins of her horse. "I will kill it for you. It will die a clean, painless death."

They stared at each other, each unsure of what to say, until Kassandra dropped her gaze and nodded. "Thank you. That would . . . I . . ." She turned away, embarrassed that she could not express herself. "Thank you," she mumbled.

Clucking to her horse, she turned her mare away and lifted her hand to wave good-bye.

Cadedryn watched her for a moment, an odd feeling rumbling at the pit of his stomach. Lady Kassandra was unusual, but her oddity made him feel strangely protective of her. People such as Lady Corine could say that Kassandra was uncultured and misplaced, but he found her refreshingly honest. She was the only woman he had ever met who reminded him of his mother.

The blast of a horn pulled him from his reverie and he sent his stallion galloping up the slope. He had promised to kill the boar, and he would not fail her.

Kassandra rode back to the castle yard and whistled to Triu-cair, who was up in the barn's hayloft, searching for his lunch. The weasel scampered down from his lofty perch and hastened to join her.

"Hurry," Kassandra grumbled as she looked up at the sun. It had taken much longer to return to the castle than she had anticipated, and she still needed to find the crofter's hut before Cadedryn arrived there. She turned and sent the mare trotting up the path she had traveled last night. Just as they entered the forest, she pulled up and allowed Triu-cair to scramble up her leg and sit in her lap before she continued on. Halfway up the winding road, she turned off the path and cut through the trees until she reached a beautiful, open ridge. If her sense of direction was correct, she could reach the hut in less time if she followed the ridge to the next line of trees. From there, she should be able to spot the cabin and enter far ahead of Cadedryn, provided the hunt was still in progress.

She leaned over and asked her mare to leap forward in a full gallop, welcoming the brief moment of freedom before she was forced to act on a daring plan that made her tremble with anxiety. The mare's hooves pounded the ground with reverberating force and she stretched her legs farther with each stride. The tall grasses whipped across the mare's chest and snagged on Kassandra's boots, and the wind whistled in their ears. All worries were swept behind her and only the glorious meadow lay ahead, when suddenly the mare stumbled.

Kassandra shrieked as she stared with horror at the vicious crossbow arrow protruding from Briana's shoulder.

A strand of trees rose in spindly formation to her right while a thicket of trees at the end of the ridge stood dense and forbidding—a perfect hiding place for someone intent on an ambush.

Another arrow streaked across the meadow and thudded into the mare's haunches. The mare reared in fury and pain as Kassandra scrambled to dismount and drag her to the relative safety of the thin trees. Triu-cair was flung to the ground and pressed himself flat as Kassandra shouted to the horse and tugged on the reins. "Come along, Briana!" she urged.

The rearing mare dropped to all fours and jumped forward, almost trampling Kassandra, but she leapt out of the mare's path and managed to position themselves between the trees and the source of the crossbow while calming the terrified beast.

A sudden sound coming from behind made Kassandra spin and she beheld a black stallion racing across the ridge toward them. Fearing that the other horse bore another attacker, she sprinted to the far side of the trees, but a third arrow whistled past her, only inches from her face. Trapped between the crossbow at the far side and the rapidly advancing stallion on the near side, Kassandra crouched low to the ground and released her mare's reins.

"Run," she whispered as she used a stick to strike the horse's hind legs. "Run!"

The mare bounded out of the strand of trees and careened through the grass and over the other side of the ridge, disappearing from sight.

A hooded person on horseback wielded a crossbow as he burst out of the forest and chased after the riderless horse, but as the pair was about to plunge down the other side, the cloaked face glanced toward the stand of trees.

Kassandra ducked her head and covered her face, trying to melt into the ground, but the attacker swung his horse toward her and lifted the crossbow once again. Knowing her assailant had spied her, Kassandra scrambled backward and picked up a sturdy branch to use in her defense. She swallowed, her hands trembling. Why was this person seeking to harm her? What had she done? Whom had she angered?

She lifted the branch and waved it toward the attacker, who halted several lengths from her and began stringing another arrow. Fear snaked through her heart as she stumbled backward, well aware that she could do little to defend herself. Suddenly, the black horse she had spied earlier barreled past her and raced directly toward the rider stringing the crossbow. With a gasp, Kassandra recognized Cadedryn's stallion. A flash of last night's dream flickered before her, and she cried out as she clung to the spindly tree.

"Take care!" she cried, deathly afraid that the attacker would release the arrow directly into Cadedryn's chest, but before the attacker could finish stringing the bow, Cadedryn closed the distance and pulled forth his sword. He swung the shimmering weapon over his head and swiped, dashing the crossbow to the dirt.

The attacker yanked on his horse's reins, trying to pull him around, but Cadedryn slammed into them both, knocking the horse off balance. The assailant tumbled to the ground, but rolled quickly to his feet and drew a sword.

Cadedryn leapt off his horse and faced him. "Remove your hood and fight with honor," he demanded as he brandished his weapon. "You attack a defenseless woman? Are ye' coward, or are ye' brave enough to fight a man?" he drawled as he lined up his sword with his assailant's head.

The attacker lunged forward, striking at Cadedryn's face, but he deflected the strike easily, then countered with a rapid assault. Swords flashing and steel clanging, the two engaged in a deadly battle, each determined to strike a fatal blow.

Cadedryn advanced quickly, pushing the attacker backward. His sword whistled through the air, slicing the black cape and drawing first blood. The assailant cried out and clutched his arm, but was forced to raise his sword once again as Cadedryn pressed his advantage.

Kassandra rose from her hiding place and stared at Cadedryn in stunned amazement. He was no longer the elegant jouster, nor was he the angry, shirtless fighter. This was a superb master, a swordsman who used his weapon as gracefully as a dancer. He wielded it as if it were an extension of his own body, like a hawk using his deadly talons.

The other man stumbled, falling to his knees. "Halt!" he cried as Cadedryn's sword touched his neck. "Mercy!"

Cadedryn paused. Then, his voice throbbing with anger, he said, "Show yourself. Only a coward attacks a lone woman and hides behind a hood."

The attacker bowed his neck and lifted his hands to his hood as if to untie it. Then, with the suddenness of a striking snake, he drew a throwing knife from behind his head and flung it at Kassandra, narrowly missing a fatal strike.

She screamed and collapsed to the ground just as the man scurried backward toward his horse and raised his hand as if to throw another missile.

Cadedryn leapt toward Kassandra and inserted himself protectively between her and the attacker, but the man did not throw another knife. Instead, he sprang atop his horse and yanked on the reins. Then, with a vicious kick, he sent the animal galloping up the slope.

Feeling an eerie sense of recognition, Cadedryn

took several running steps after the fleeing man. "Who hides behind the hood?" he shouted as he brandished his sword.

The man abruptly pulled his mount to a stop several lengths away from the couple and twisted around to face Cadedryn. "Someone who has heard of your disloyalty and will do anything to ensure that you do not follow down the path to ruin like your father," the man shouted back, his voice muffled and unrecognizable through the hood. He pointed to Kassandra. "Stay away from that woman, or hers will not be the only death the court must mourn."

"She had done nothing wrong!" Cadedryn answered angrily. "She is an innocent."

The man turned away. "Beware the illusion of innocence," he called as he cantered over the ridge and disappeared from view.

Cadedryn spun around and dropped to his knee beside Kassandra. "Are you hurt?" he said gruffly as he gripped her arm and pulled her close.

"My arm . . ." She twisted her shoulder and gazed at the torn sleeve of her dress.

Cadedryn touched her, sliding his fingers in the hole and exploring her flesh beneath. "No blood," he told her, his voice husky.

Kassandra's breath caught and she shivered. Tiny goose bumps spread from her shoulder and down her forearm, then across her abdomen.

His hand stilled.

She jerked back and drew the edges of the torn dress together. "He missed me," she stammered.

Cadedryn pulled away and helped her to her feet. "Poor aim," he replied, although his voice shook. Her skin was as soft as velvet and she smelled as fresh as

Highland flowers. "Why are you riding alone? You said you were returning to the castle."

Kassandra stepped away, and took several steadying breaths. She straightened her mantle and self-consciously stroked her black wig, which peeked from beneath the fabric.

Cadedryn waited for a response.

"I wanted a moment of solitude," she finally replied, unable to express a more plausible excuse. "What about you? Why did you leave the others?"

"I saw you through the trees," he answered, swinging back to face her. "You seem to land yourself in trouble no matter where you go."

Kassandra narrowed her gaze and placed her hands on her hips. "I only have difficulty when you are around."

"So the man was not attacking you before I arrived?"

She lowered her eyes and her hands fell to her sides. She scuffed her toe in the grass, then looked down the hillside. "My horse is injured. I pray she returned to the stables."

Without replying, Cadedryn walked over to his own horse and gathered the reins. "I will bring you to the castle," he said. "Perhaps you have learned your lesson. The rules of society are designed to protect women like you, thus you would do well to heed them."

"Your swordsmanship was impressive," she said after a long pause in which both of them struggled to hide their feelings. "Why do you think that man was trying to harm me?"

Cadedryn grunted. "I would not want to speculate upon his nefarious intentions, but thankfully, he was not highly skilled. He utilized ambush and trickery, not excellence. You are lucky his aim was not better."

Kassandra snatched a leaf from a branch dipping low beside her and sucked on the stem. "Where did you learn such prowess?"

"I'd rather not discuss my swordsmanship. 'Tis not a fit subject for a lady."

She punched him in the side.

"Ouch!" he yelled. "What was that for? I just saved you!"

"Do you know how pompous you sound?"

"I do not," he replied, truly affronted. "I was only protecting you from the dull details of training and warfare."

"Where did you get your sword? It looks unusual."

"That is another thing I don't want to talk about. A man's weapons are personal extensions of himself and are not suitable for casual conversation."

She lifted her hand to punch him again, but he caught her fist. "Not again," he cautioned her. "I may be fooled once, but never twice. Now come, I must bring you to the castle quickly for I have an appointment at noon."

Kassandra glanced at him with alarm. If she returned to the castle, she would be the one to miss their rendezvous, for she would be stranded with no sound mount. The sun was already high in the sky, and she doubted he would patiently await her arrival.

Her only other choice was to make *him* late. If he appeared well after the appointed hour, he would presume that his tiger kitten had given up waiting for him.

Kassandra walked very slowly over to Cadedryn and his horse as Cadedryn motioned impatiently to her. "You move as slow as a turtle," he grumbled as he looked up at the high sun.

Kassandra's stomach fluttered, but she kept her face bland. Her emotions rolled, churning with a mix of excitement at his obvious interest in the mysterious red-haired woman, and anger at his dismissal of her true self. She turned her back to the stallion and stared up at his face. A fine white scar ran from the corner of his eye to the edge of his jaw. How had she failed to notice it earlier? Nothing in her dreams had shown her such a scar. Fascinated, she reached out to stroke it with her fingertip.

He jumped back, his eyes blazing with surprise. "Milady!"

Kassandra flushed and looked away. "I'm sorry," she mumbled.

He twitched, and wiped his jawline to remove the sweet sensation of her caress. Without replying, he swung up on his stallion and reached down for her.

Kassandra glanced around, then looked up at him with trepidation. "Shouldn't you lead the horse while I ride? I don't want to travel too quickly."

"I have no intention of walking all the way back to the castle. Weren't you the lass who commented so derisively upon my horsemanship the first time we met? Are you now going to demonstrate your own inability to ride pillion?"

"I can ride any horse!" she retorted. " 'Tis not fear that makes me hesitate."

Cadedryn's mouth curved in a half smile. She was so easy to rouse and her defiance so predictable. "Any horse?" he questioned. "I doubt you know any more about a horse than how to decipher the head from the tail."

"I know you resemble more of the latter than the former," she snapped, her blue eyes flashing.

He laughed, his head thrown back and his body

relaxed. "Easy now, milady," he soothed. "Must we argue? Come ride with me, and perhaps we can carry on a polite conversation. I promise to keep a slow, steady pace."

A small smile broke upon her face as she acknowledged the ridiculousness of their argument. "I challenge you to name every marking possible on a horse," she teased.

He reached down and swung her up behind him. As she settled, he reined the stallion around and started down the slope. "You first," he replied.

Ten minutes later, he was laughing. Not a light, polite chuckle, but a deep-chested laugh that lifted the spirits and made his stomach ache. He twisted around and looked at her bright face and felt a sense of peace he could not recall feeling since the days before his parents' deaths. "How did you come up with that one?" he asked her.

" 'Tis the truth," she exclaimed. "I once heard one of the elders describe it. The white pony had a brown patch covering his ears and pole, appearing like a crown. She called it a coronet marking."

Cadedryn's gaze traveled up to her coronet, an elegant silver band woven with fine blue and lavender ribbons. It fastened in place a length of light blue silk, which covered all of her hair except one smooth black curl. "Your hair is quite dark," he stated, his tone abruptly serious. "Particularly with such light blue eyes." A ripple of awareness made him turn back around. A gentleman should not have unruly thoughts about virginal ladies of the court, especially not when he expected the red-haired woman who looked so similar to this one to be waiting for him just beyond the tree line. He shifted, trying to adjust his position in the saddle.

"Yes," she replied, her thoughts also straying to the

cabin. The horse stumbled, thrusting her against Cadedryn's warm back, and she was forced to wrap her arms around his waist to maintain her seat. She trembled, and as soon as the horse steadied, she pushed away from him and took a deep breath.

Cadedryn shivered as her breath whispered across his neck, then frowned with irritation at his reaction. He should not be responding to her this way. She was an innocent member of a well-respected family. He needed to concentrate on the tiger-colored lass waiting for him in the crofter's hut. She was the more appropriate recipient of his lustful thoughts. She was the type of woman who would understand such base emotions. "Try to sit up straight," he grumbled. "Your lack of balance is upsetting my stallion."

She glared at him, her back stiffening.

He frowned at her abrupt withdrawal. For a moment, he had relaxed and forgotten his intention to deposit her as quickly as possible before returning to the cabin. "I hope you have learned to take care. That attacker meant to kill you. Someone has linked our names together and thus placed you in jeopardy. Forget your dreams and forget me. I will cause you nothing but pain and I do not wish to be the cause of your distress. I advise you to stay close to the castle and find your pleasure in events that involve the entire court."

A wave of compassion flooded her. She could hear the buried loneliness in his voice. He needed her, even if he was not aware of his needs. "And how do you find your pleasure?" she asked gently.

"I do not concern myself with pleasure."

"Don't be foolish. Of course you do." She paused and smiled slyly behind his back. "What about women? You told me before that all men seek women for their satisfaction."

Cadedryn's chest tightened and he had to force himself to breathe evenly. Her husky voice reminded him of the woman from last night. His groin twitched and he shifted in the saddle to relieve his rising discomfort. "You should not be talking thus," he said, then clucked to the stallion and adjusted his breeches.

"You are the one who brought a man's desires to my attention."

"You pushed me too far and I said some things I should not have."

Kassandra leaned closer to him and clasped her arms around him, barely containing a laugh. "You suddenly seem tense. Perhaps you ought to relieve your stress," she said.

"I intend to," he grumbled as he tried to ease out of her tight hold.

"That is good," she answered as she laid her cheek against his back. "I hope you find *something* to do to relax. Life should not be burdened with such anxiety."

"Believe me," he commented dryly, "I have my amusements." Kassandra's statements were only fueling his desires and increasing his nervousness. He rose in his stirrups and stared at the sun through the trees. It was well past the time of his meeting with the tiger kitten.

His desire turned to irritation as they entered the castle courtyard and he pulled the horse to a standstill. He had killed the boar for her, yet she hadn't even asked how the hunt had ended. A boar hunt was nearly as dangerous as a bear hunt, and men were often wounded trying to prove their valor. "You should know that I brought down the boar. The kill was clean," he said to her, his voice clipped.

Kassandra blinked, surprised by his sudden coldness. Perhaps her taunting had affected him more than she had intended.

"I did not bring you a token," he informed her as he swung down and reached to assist her dismount. "I gave it to Lady Corine."

Kassandra shrugged. "Such a token would be distasteful to me."

He stared at her, his mind churning with confusion. He had told her about the token to stir her anger and make it easier to ride away from her, but she did not seem to care. He clenched his teeth, for if he was honest with himself, he had also wanted to see her jealous, and he could not explain why. Until yesterday, he had known his path, but this unusual woman was twisting him in knots and making him forget his intentions. If he was to maintain control and ensure her safety, he needed to distance himself from her.

"Who else knows about your earlier declarations? Who have you told that would seek to warn you away from me? Have you bothered anyone else with your ridiculous dreams? Declared deep and everlasting love with some other unfortunate knight who is now bent upon jealous revenge?"

Kassandra pulled away, her feelings deeply hurt. "My dreams are not fickle, nor are they ridiculous. Even your friend Curtis McCafferty had the decency to ask me about them."

Cadedryn stilled. "What did he ask?"

"He asked about your father's murder. At least he cares enough about you to ask if I can help bring your father's killer to justice."

Jealousy stabbed him and he glared at her. "Don't talk to him," he growled.

Kassandra lifted a brow mockingly. "Why not? He was kind to me."

"He is the one who ran into your caravan, yet you blamed me!"

Kassandra turned away. "You are being petty," she ridiculed.

He grabbed her shoulder and yanked her around to face him. "He did not kill the boar for you! He did not rescue you! Why do you speak so highly of him yet treat me with contempt?"

Kassandra's eyes widened. His face was twisted with agony and his eyes were nearly black with pain. Her heart thudded, and she felt his suffering deep within her soul. *Dagda*, she whispered silently. *I have never felt contempt for you. You are lost . . . so lost within this confusing world of kings and titles. Come with me. Live with me in the forest and leave the pain behind.*

He stared at her, braced for her anger, yet her eyes were soft with understanding. She touched his hand where he brutally clutched her shoulder, and he felt shivers ripple up and down his forearm. He abruptly released his grip and stepped away. "I am not fond of you," he growled. "Stay away from me."

"I am not the cause of your anger," she told him gently.

"But you are most certainly the source of my frustration," he answered angrily. "I must go. You have made me late." Then he swung back up on his stallion and galloped away.

Chapter 10

Cadedryn woke in a cold sweat. Moonlight shone through the open window and a cold breeze wafted across his damp temples. He flung off the covers and swung his bare feet to the floor, welcoming the cold stone, then buried his head in his hands and groaned.

He couldn't get Kassandra out of his mind. Even his dreams were filled with her. Who wanted to harm her and why?

He raked his fingers through his hair and rose to his feet. The sheet slid from his waist, exposing his naked body to the moonlight, but he hardly noticed. Instead, he strode to the window and gazed out at the numerous stars shimmering in the sky like sparks cascading from a blacksmith's forge.

In his dream she had turned her back on him, leaving him stranded alone on the top of a windswept mountain. He had reached out to her, but was too late. Her body had shimmered and swayed, drifting down the slope like mist evaporating under the blaze of the morning sun.

Kassandra.

No. It hadn't been Kassandra in his dream. It had been the other woman, the woman whose red hair and golden skin made his body taut with desire.

She had not been at the crofter's hut when he had finally arrived and he had felt her absence keenly.

After the disastrous ending with Kassandra, he had
wanted to find uncomplicated acceptance in her arms.
He had longed to taste her lips, hoping against all
hope that she would welcome his caresses and respond
with equal fervor.

Instead, he had returned to the castle and spent an
unpleasant evening trying to maintain a polite de-
meanor in front of the other lords and ladies dining
in the great hall. His foster father, David McCafferty,
had been sullen and rude, treating him as if he were
still a young squire. Lady Morgana had chosen to sit
next to David, reviving much talk about their previous
relationship. To cap off the evening, Corine had pointedly ignored him, expending her charms on Curtis,
who had appeared receptive to her attentions. Although Corine and Curtis had known each other from
childhood, their intimacy had grated on Cadedryn's
nerves. Even the king's public commendation on his
efforts in the boar hunt and subsequent invitation to
meet with him the following day had not completely
raised Cadedryn's spirits.

He rose from the bed and kicked a chair across the
chamber. He should feel exhilarated and flush with
victory. There was a good chance the king was considering forgiveness, yet all Cadedryn could think about
was Kassandra and her peasant half sister.

Perhaps Kassandra was right. He was focusing too
much upon his ambitions and not relieving his tensions
as a man should. Once he did, this distraction would
fade.

He picked up the chair and placed it carefully back
on its legs. His plans were almost complete; this was
not the time to lose his determination. He would find
the tigress woman and ask for her favors. Surely after

one night, he could get her out of his thoughts and concentrate on more important matters.

One floor below, a woman opened her door and her arms to her lover.

"Are you deliberately taunting me?" he questioned as he kicked the portal shut behind him. "Do you seek to turn my thoughts inside and out until I can no longer think clearly?"

"Is that what I do to you?" she murmured seductively as she trailed kisses along his throat.

"You did that just by sitting near me. I can smell your sweet perfume and it makes my heart quake with desire."

"Last night . . . you made me remember things I thought I had forgotten."

"Us."

"Aye," she confirmed. "Your touch reawakened me. I don't want to lose you again."

"I won't let that happen."

She pulled away and stared at him. "But I have obligations now. I must do what must be done."

He nodded, his gaze solemn. "I understand."

"Do you?"

"Yes."

"Will you help me?"

He gathered her back into his arms. "I always have and I always will. I know what you want, and I will get it for you."

She smiled and drew him forward, saying nothing more until the following dawn when she whispered good-bye as he slipped unobserved from her chambers.

*   *   *

After a long and restless night, Kassandra awoke to a sun-filled room and Kalial handing her a steaming cup of mint tea.

Kassandra sat up and took the cup with gratitude.

"How did you sleep?"

Kassandra frowned. Cadedryn had disturbed her all night. She had dreamed of his muscular arms and his powerful thighs. She had seen his penetrating gaze and felt the heat of his hands as he lifted her down from the stallion. It was unlike any dream she had had before, even more real than the dream that had sent her here. It was not a dream of the future, but one of the past. Each accidental touch, every shared gaze had been replayed in her mind and found its way into her restless night.

"Not very well," she admitted to her half sister. There had been more to her dream. It had contained a warning. Like a hovering bird of prey, a dark cloud had seeped through every scene, spreading its wings to enfold them in a dark and ominous embrace. It reminded her that she was here not only to find her mate, but also to help him, for the danger she had sensed was coming closer. Yesterday's attack upon herself had been a diversion. The true intended victim was Cadedryn. If she truly loved him, she must save him, regardless of whether he believed her or not.

Did she love him? She brought the tea to her lips. The refreshing scent cleared her mind and she looked at Kalial with a questioning gaze. "How did you know Ronin was the man for you?"

Kalial laughed. "I did not. I thought he was arrogant, high-handed and intrusive."

Kassandra tilted her head in curiosity. "You did not know? You could not feel him in your blood?"

"Oh, I felt him," she answered. "He made my stomach churn and set my senses spinning, but I did not have your gift of prophecy. It took me a long time before I understood my feelings."

Kassandra sighed and took another sip. "I know Cadedryn is my life mate, but I fear that our lives are too different. The things that we each believe are important are as dissimilar as the sun and the moon."

"The sun and the moon are partners. They need each other. You must find a common ground. If you are truly life mates, then your coming together should complete a whole just as the sun must follow the moon and the moon must follow the sun." Kalial fondly touched one of Kassandra's red curls. "You have been too intent on the culmination of your dreams. You must relax and let the fates guide you."

Kassandra grinned, aware that she had cautioned Cadedryn similarly. She ought to take her own advice and stop worrying so much.

"He is handsome," Kassandra said shyly.

Kalial nodded, her eyes sparkling with amusement.

Kassandra leaned forward and hugged her sister. "Thank you," she said. "You have helped a great deal!"

Kalial laughed as she extricated herself and helped Kassandra place the cup of tea safely on the window ledge. "Good. Now where is your little friend? I have not seen him this morn."

Kassandra gasped and looked around the room, realizing that, indeed, Triu-cair was conspicuously absent.

Kalial rose and went to the door. "Find him," she warned, "for if a servant does so first, your pet may come to harm."

Kassandra rapidly donned a light dress and hooded cape, not taking time to add her disguise. The sun had barely peeked over the horizon, and most of the court still slept. With luck, she would not be noticed.

Where are you? she asked silently as she trod lightly down the corridor and peeked into open rooms.

You are ignoring me, came the faint reply.

Kassandra spun around, trying to locate the source. *Come, Triu-cair. You can't do this. I have been distracted, but we are still friends.*

Friends help each other, Triu-cair answered.

Kassandra sighed in exasperation as she sensed that the weasel was up another flight of stairs. She raced up them, then paused in concern. This floor was much different from the one she and Kalial inhabited. Its rough, masculine aura sent shivers up her spine. *Come along, Triu-cair,* she called with a trace of desperation. *I cannot go up there!*

I won't come down.

"You beast!" she cried aloud, then clapped her hands over her mouth in dismay. *'Tis your own skin you place in jeopardy!*

When there was no answer, she climbed the steps as quietly as possible. *Triu-cair!*

Over here.

She saw a shadowy figure slip around the far corner of the hall. Was someone else traipsing the corridors at dawn? A sudden bump in one of the rooms made her gasp and she turned to face a closed door to her left. *Triu-cair! Are you safe?* she cried.

Help!

Kassandra's blood thrummed in panic and she ran toward the room, secrecy forgotten, her hood falling from her head. She flung the door open and dashed inside, and saw a man about to toss a blanket over her cornered friend. "Stop!" she shouted. "He is harmless!"

Cadedryn spun around and stared at her in shock just as she skidded to a stunned halt.

"You!" she cried.

"You!" he announced with satisfaction as he deftly shut the door behind her and slid the bolt home.

Kassandra glared at him. "How dare you attack my friend!"

Cadedryn leaned against the door and crossed his arms. "Your *friend*," he emphasized, "found his way up to my room and has done his best not to leave. Dare I wonder if you sent him to find me?"

Kassandra's mouth opened to deny his allegation when she suddenly changed her mind and turned on Triu-cair, casting him a withering look. "You did this a-purpose," she accused. "What was your intention?"

You want him. Here he is, Triu-cair replied boldly.

"I did this?" Cadedryn said softly as he trod closer and eyed her flushed face with interest.

"I . . ." Kassandra floundered, her breath stolen by the intensity of his gaze. She *did* want him. She could not deny the desire that coursed through her body. Her dreams spoke the truth. She wanted to feel his hands slide beneath her clothes and caress her heated flesh.

"I missed our appointment," he confessed. "But I regretted it sorely. Obviously, you felt similarly."

She nodded, at a loss for words.

He stroked her delicately freckled face with a fingertip and twisted a lock of her red hair around his finger. "Do I read your eyes correctly? Are you here because you want something from me?"

She couldn't breathe. She felt frozen, unable to respond with any measure of coherency. Her body trembled, ready for his caress. She could no more deny him than she could prevent the sun from rising. The sun and moon. Meant to be together.

He smiled, his lips spreading in a slow, sensual grin that sent ripples down her spine. "I am pleased you came. I was going to go looking for you, but you have beaten me to the task. I am impressed, tiger kitten. Tell me," he whispered seductively. "Are you an experienced kitten, or a curious one?"

She looked at him blankly, not certain what he was asking.

He lifted a brow, sensing the answer to his question in her silence. He rubbed his thumb across her lips, enchanted by the velvety softness. "I wanted to kiss you that night. Will you let me kiss you now?"

She sucked in her breath, feeling dizzy, and clung to his arm to steady herself. With her head tilted up to see him, she offered her mouth.

He chuckled and slid his finger between her lips, entering the moist cavern and groaning at her wet warmth. He brought his fingers to his mouth, tasting her. "I dreamed about you," he told her as his eyelids half closed and he gazed at her through twin slits of blazing heat.

She stumbled, weakened by his seductive assault. "And I you," she admitted; then she gripped his bare shoulders and pulled herself closer. "I want your kiss."

He groaned again and buried his face in her hair. He breathed in her scent, memorizing it. A heady sense of rightness filled him and he slid his hands behind her neck and angled her to receive him. But instead of devouring her, he merely brushed her lips with his, tantalizing them both.

"I want to teach you," he whispered.

"I want to learn," she moaned as the rest of the

world shrank and only his words and touch remained to bind her to earth.

He pushed the cape the rest of the way off her shoulders and let it rustle to the floor. "Your skin is more beautiful than the finest silk," he murmured as he caressed her arms with his open palms. He slowly turned her toward the window, pressing himself against her back. "Do you know how beautiful you are?"

Kassandra shivered as he moved her hair aside and kissed the back of her neck. "My hair," she whispered. "I don't like it."

He kissed the few tight curls that tickled her nape. " 'Tis wonderful," he told her. "Exotic and exciting."

She moaned and bent her head forward, granting him complete access.

"I want to make you proud of how you look and who you are," he murmured. "You should walk with your head held high."

Kassandra shuddered, aware that his words unknowingly reflected his own desires. She suddenly wanted to give him everything, too. She wanted him to have all that he thought he wanted, even if it meant losing him. She would do anything she could to help him gain his title. His loneliness broke her heart and made her ache with the need to make him whole.

She pushed down the neckline of her dress and bared her shoulder. As soon as she felt him tremble, she knew he needed this. He was too often concerned about everyone else. Right now, with her, he could forget everything and feel her love, even if that love was only expressed with her body.

Tugging harder, she pulled her dress off and let it join the cape upon the floor.

He drew in a quick breath, shocked by her nakedness, yet deeply aroused by her lack of inhibition.

"Close your eyes and let your body feel my touch," he said in her ear, breathing against the sensitive shell. "Think of each muscle as a separate part of you. Move each part of your body independently, letting it tell me what makes you respond. In this way, we will learn each other's caress."

Kassandra obediently closed her eyes.

"Now . . ." Cadedryn whispered. "Shift only the part of your body that enjoys my touch. Keep the rest of yourself still. Be like a candle, as your body flickers with the tiniest breath of wind but appears tall and silent when unaffected."

"Why a candle?" she asked breathlessly.

"How powerful is fire? How hot is passion? Your hair is like the brightest flame and I must be the kiln that tames your power."

Kassandra's eyes opened and she stared into Cadedryn's intent gaze as it was reflected in the window. A quiver began in the bottom of her abdomen as she pressed against his still clothed body.

He smiled and slowly shook his head. "Don't look at me. Feel me."

"You are still wearing your shirt," Kassandra replied.

"Do you want me to take it off?"

"Yes."

He pulled on the ties, then drew it over his head.

Kassandra sucked in her breath at the brush of his bare chest against her back. "Your flesh is so hard and cool."

"And you are soft and warm," he answered as he stroked her arm. "Move for me," he encouraged. "Tell me with your motions if you like my caress."

Kassandra lifted her arm awkwardly.

"Not like that. Move like a kitten who wants to be petted."

Kassandra inhaled, absorbing Cadedryn's scent as she closed her eyes again. She concentrated on releasing control of her body, on letting her muscles react with primitive need. She wanted to become one with him such that his needs became hers and her desires united them in an unending circle of love.

Cadedryn slid his fingers across Kassandra's back and she reacted by rolling one shoulder into his caress.

"Yes," he breathed in her ear. "Just like that." He ran a finger down the center of her bare back, then spread his hand wide to stroke her buttocks.

Kassandra arched her spine, then pressed against her tutor's hand.

"Move against me," he instructed. "Just enough to tell me you want me. Feel my hand. Taunt me. Make me desire you."

Kassandra wriggled her hind end.

"Slower. Think about caressing me without using your hands."

Kassandra gasped and started to pull away.

"Don't be shy. No one is here but you and I," Cadedryn reminded her as he watched Kassandra's skin shimmer in the window. Her nipples were hard and tight and the red thatch of hair concealing the juncture of her thighs was starting to glisten. He pulled Kassandra back against his swollen groin.

This time she moved with him. At first she was hesitant, but then she caught Cadedryn's rhythm and began to undulate. A deep need began to tingle in her core, and she emitted a soft moan.

Cadedryn's hands skated up her hips and traced along her abdomen, all the while continuing his rocking motion. He searched farther and wrapped his hands around Kassandra's breasts. "Don't use words . . . Let yourself feel us together . . . Give yourself to your man." His thumbs rubbed over Kassandra's nipples.

"Shushhh . . ." He sighed as her body relaxed against his and she became pliant with sensuality.

His heart thudded. It was as if she had been made just for him. Her body fit perfectly against his, and their natural rhythms beat together in beautiful synchrony. "I want to become lost within you."

"I will enfold you," she promised as she lifted her arms and wrapped them around his neck as her flame-colored tresses tumbled across her breasts and swept down to tickle her belly button.

Blood rushed through his veins and air swept through his lungs, making him dizzy. Her rising passion filled his senses and his own desire pulsed, making his hands shake. She was his sole focus—her shoulders, her arms, her slender legs . . . her proud breasts, her shimmering flesh. He wanted to arouse her to the point where she was dying for want of his touch.

His body coiled with need, ready to explode the moment she was ready.

"Say my name," he commanded. "Tell me that you want me and only me."

"Cadedryn," she breathed.

Cadedryn's pulse thundered and his member swelled further, its surging size becoming painful in his tight breeches.

Kassandra arched her body against his, her flesh rippling. She drew his head closer and, as she leaned back, she pressed her lips against his throat. His smell surrounded her—not just from his body, but from the very air. She felt his essence, the same energy she felt in her dreams.

"I can feel you," she whispered in awe. "As if we were meant to join . . ."

"I want to join with you. I want to be inside you and feel your heat surround me."

Fire swept through her, burning her. She heard his heavy breathing, felt his body tense as he pulled her hard against him.

"Open your thighs," he murmured, nudging them apart with his knee. "Wider."

Kassandra's nether cheeks brushed against Cadedryn's engorged rod and they both groaned. She lifted one bare foot and bent her leg around his, then slid her toe up and down, feeling his rough breeches. She explored the strong muscles with her toes, tracing and stroking the long lines.

He reached between her thighs and touched her core, shuddering at the wet evidence of her arousal. "Tell me," he gasped.

His voice sent ripples down Kassandra's spine and she flung her head back, sending her tresses flying.

Cadedryn became enfolded in her flames and his hands slid from her breasts to tangle in her hair. He grasped the mass at the base of her head and pulled her back even farther, forcing her chin up into the air. He kissed her exposed neck, then switched and suckled the other side.

"Tell me you want me," he growled.

"Yes! I want you!"

He spun her around and lifted her in his arms, carrying her swiftly to his bed, where he lay her down and stood over her. "Have mercy," he whispered. "You are beautiful." He untied his breeches and sank down beside her.

She turned to him, her arms open.

He lay atop her, his elbows bracing his weight while

he stared into her passion-filled eyes. The tip of his cock brushed against her and he closed his eyes, reveling in the sweetness of her silken skin. He shifted, pressing harder, and shuddered when her thighs opened to receive him.

She reached around and slid her hands up and down his back, feeling his tense muscles as he struggled to control himself. His power was immense yet he treated her with incredible tenderness. She arched, knowing that he needed still more from her and sensing that he was holding back for her. "I am yours," she whispered.

He thrust inside her, deeply, smoothly, his body shaking with passion.

She gasped at the pain. Her eyes opened wide and she pushed at his hips.

"Wait," he said, his forehead pressed against the bed.

She pushed again and this time his hips obeyed as he lifted a few inches off her, but instead of leaving her, he thrust back inside.

"Oh!" she cried, expecting the same pain, but this time pleasure filled her channel and she drew in a quick breath, suddenly wanting more. Clutching his shoulders, she pulled him closer and pressed thankful kisses across his chest.

As the bliss mounted, her eyes drifted shut. With each stroke, she held him closer and lifted her hips to meet his, then moaned with pleasure as his body rubbed against her.

He moved faster and faster, his neck clenched with the effort to keep a steady rhythm despite her tight grip. He smelled her passion rising and knew he had succeeded in awakening her from the depths of innocence. "Follow me," he groaned. "Follow me to the edge!"

She cried out, her need increasing until she felt a hunger so intense, it was as if she were starving for fulfillment. She tossed her head as sensations cascaded through her body. Swirling higher, her head spinning, she screamed as she became lost within the ever-increasing ripples of exquisite intensity.

He pounded against her, his control burned by the heat of her tight embrace. "Yes!" he shouted.

Kassandra's passion exploded—she felt as if every sense were set ablaze. Lights danced around her eyes and she could no longer think coherently. She became one with him, one with her lover. Her inner muscles clenched, held him with pulsing resistance; then her channel became drenched with ambrosia and became a loving, liquid embrace.

She felt faint . . . She felt her body floating into her familiar dream state, but the intense pleasure echoing throughout each part of her body forced her back, forced her to experience her ecstasy here. It was not a dream. This was real. This was Cadedryn's love.

Cadedryn shouted with satisfaction as he poured his seed deep into her, his essence claiming her as his. She was his woman, the other half of his soul. He wanted to merge deep within her, so deep he wouldn't ever have to open his eyes again and face the world that had betrayed him. He clutched her tight, desperate to make the pleasure last.

But it slowly faded and he was forced to breathe and confront reality.

He groaned and rolled off her and stared at the ceiling.

She shivered at the loss of his heat and curled up against him.

"Thank you," he whispered as he wrapped an arm around her and pulled her closer.

She stared at his face, watching the tension seep back into his jaw and seeing the skin around his eyes harden. Her heart ached with sorrow, knowing that her love had rescued him only for a moment and he was already sinking back into his cold loneliness.

But even one moment was worth everything she could give.

Chapter 11

When Kassandra snuck back to her room, she barely closed the door before Kalial opened it again and came in after her. "Where have you been? I have been waiting in my chamber to hear you return! 'Tis been well over an hour and Triu-cair came back long ago. What have you been doing?" She stared worriedly at Kassandra's flushed cheeks and swept a concerned gaze over her rumpled clothes.

Kassandra stared at Triu-cair in surprise, wondering how he had found his way back before she did. She furrowed her brow, aware that she had not been paying him much attention over the last hour, then walked over to a chair. She sat down with a thud, afraid her weakened legs would not support her much longer and hoping that her sister would not notice anything different about her. How could one moment with Cadedryn make her feel as if the world were suddenly brighter? The air suddenly fresher? She felt transformed and invigorated, but she ducked her head to hide her smile. It would not do to tell Kalial. Kassandra was not ready to explain what had happened, for she barely understood it herself. "I went for a walk," she mumbled as she tried to smooth her curls.

"A walk?" Kalial said angrily. "Without your disguise? You don't even have shoes on your feet! Are my warnings not clear enough? This is not Loch Ni-

dean! The people here would sooner burn you than
bend their stiff rules to accommodate your idiosyncra-
sies!" She paced the room in distress. "We must leave.
Immediately. I cannot risk your life for this ridiculous quest."

"No!" Kassandra cried, leaping to her feet. "Not
yet! He needs me."

"Needs you? He hardly grants you a passing
glance."

Kassandra ran to her half sister and clung to her
arm. "Please. Give me a few more days. I have to find
the danger that still threatens him."

"Kassandra," Kalial replied gently, taking her arms
and pushing her onto the bed. "Cadedryn Caenmore
has been summoned to the king's chamber."

"What does that mean?"

"That means the king may have granted clemency
to his family. If so, he will regain his title and become
Earl of Aberdour Castle. There is nothing he wants
more than that title, and he must wed a woman of
appropriate rank to maintain the king's favor."

"You mean Corine Fergus."

"Yes. I'm sorry."

Kassandra slid off the bed and slipped behind a pri-
vacy screen to change her clothes. Her eyes filled with
tears and she struggled not to let Kalial hear her distress. "I understand," she murmured, choking back
her sobs. "This is not proceeding exactly as I thought
it would, but I would still like a few more days. There
is something I must do. I know, because I dreamed
it. Something terrible is going to happen if I don't
stop it."

Kalial paced in front of the screen. "Do you know
what will cause it or when this event will take place?"

"Uh-uh."

"Do you even know if it is something that you *can* change? Some things are meant to be."

Kassandra peeked over the screen. "Like I am meant to be with him?"

Kalial looked at her in exasperation. "Will you never accept defeat?"

Kassandra shook her head and dropped back out of sight.

"Kassandra! Please take me seriously. You are a loving woman, with so much to offer. Maybe you were meant to find someone else and Cadedryn was but a catalyst. Once you experience passion, you will understand that your infatuation with Cadedryn is a childish game. Real love involves a physical connection that merges both the body and spirit."

Behind the screen, Kassandra touched her bruised thighs and grinned wryly. "I am sure I wouldn't know what you mean," she said.

"I want you to try to meet other gentlemen. Tomorrow night a group of traveling players will perform a drama. Will you come with me and consent to meet a few gentlemen?"

Kassandra wrapped herself in a dressing gown and came out from behind the screen. Seeing Kalial's implacable expression, she nodded her acceptance.

"Does that mean we will stay?"

"Only a few days more. A week at most," Kalial warned. "And you must stay vigilant about your disguise or we will depart sooner."

"Yes. I understand."

Kalial softened her tone. "I had one of my dresses altered to fit you. See?" She pointed to the open wardrobe.

A beautiful cream-colored gown covered with delicate blue stitching hung from the rod. Beside it was an elaborate silver headdress with a mantle of blue satin, cream lace and tiny silver flowers.

"It's lovely!" Kassandra gasped.

"It has a matching girdle of silver and blue satin. It will bring out your eyes and complement your coloring."

Kassandra's eyes sparkled as she enfolded Kalial in a huge hug. "Sister! You are so kind. Thank you for everything. I know you have risked much to bring me here."

Kalial patted her back and smiled. "If it sets your dreams to rest, then I will be satisfied. Now relax for a bit and then we will go down and join the others. Tomorrow you can wear the dress when you accompany me to the play."

After her sister left, Kassandra sat with Triu-cair and stroked his soft fur. *You tricked me today,* she chided in their private, unspoken language.

I'm a weasel. I am supposed to be crafty. Are you angry with me?

Kassandra smiled and stared at the sun as it spread ever-warmer rays across the Scottish fields. "No. But we may come to regret what happened this morning. How am I to leave, now that I have lain with him?"

Triu-cair offered no answer.

"I don't have much time left," Morgana whispered as she lifted a languid hand to her daughter's concerned face from the bed where she lay.

"Mother," Corine begged. "You must not say such things. You are strong and healthy!" She plumped a pillow and smoothed the blankets.

Morgana turned her head to the side and pressed her cheek against the pillow. " 'Tis my heart that aches," she replied.

Corine reached for a wet cloth and blotted it across

her mother's brow. Morgana often took sick when she wanted something, and Corine had learned long ago that the best way to soothe her temperamental mother at these times was to coddle her. "I am doing everything I can. Soon your disappointments will be avenged. I will wed Cadedryn Caenmore and become a countess."

Morgana smiled, her eyes glittering with vitality. "Good. That will make everything as it should be. You are an obedient child and I am proud of you. So lovely, too. You look just as I did when I was your age."

Corine smiled, inordinately pleased by the compliment. She had spent her entire life trying to please her mother, never fully succeeding. She was willing to do anything, even wed Cadedryn, if it would finally grant her the approval she desperately yearned to have. "Thank you, Mother. All will go according to plan."

Morgana pressed her hand to her forehead and closed her eyes. "If you believe that, you are a fool!" she snapped at her daughter. "Think of what happened to me. Stay alert and watch for any who seeks to befoul you." She opened her eyes and glared at Corine. "Don't let another woman trespass upon your man!"

Later that afternoon, dressed carefully in her disguise, Kassandra went to the stables to change the dressings on Briana's wounds. She cleaned the two crossbow puncture sites and applied a new poultice, then wiped a trickle of sweat from her forehead.

Briana nickered and butted her head against Kassandra's chest, then pricked her ears forward as Cadedryn entered the stable.

Kassandra swallowed her gasp of surprise. She spun around, desperate to hide her face until she could master her emotions.

"Lady Kassandra," he acknowledged. "I find you once again doing what a lady should not."

"I am merely tending my horse," she mumbled.

He leaned against the stall door and watched her as she finished spreading the poultice. He did not bother to tell her that ladies did not apply medicines, for he knew full well that she did not follow the rules. "Is she going to heal?' he asked.

"Yes. The arrows did not enter too deeply, for both hit her in the thick of the muscle."

He nodded, then fell silent as Kassandra wiped her hands on a towel and turned to face him. She looked him up and down and tilted her head to the side. "You are dressed most formally for the stables," she commented.

"I am not here to ride," he answered. "I just came from an audience with the king."

"Oh? And why did you stop at the stables? Shouldn't your steps have taken you to a public place to celebrate your good fortune?"

He chuckled and opened the door for her as she exited the stall. "I saw you in here and wanted to see what you were doing. As expected, you were showing kindness to another beast in distress."

She brushed by him and walked toward a tackle chest where her supplies were stowed.

He flinched at her accidental touch, and heat rushed through his body. He stood up straighter, shocked by his unprecedented reaction to Kassandra. His nostrils flared, and he smelled a womanly scent from her that instantly reminded him of his tiger kitten.

He cleared his throat and averted his gaze. His passions had already been assuaged today. He had no excuse for acting like a stud chasing a hapless, innocent mare. Lady Kassandra was a kind lass with fanciful delusions and did not deserve his lustful attentions.

"What did the king say?" Kassandra asked, turning toward him as soon as she was in the shadows. Even with her disguise in place, she feared that his penetrating gaze might see through her deception if she did not take care. She had only a few days to help him, but if he determined that she had deceived him, she would have an even harder time convincing him of any possible danger.

"I am to be an earl."

Kassandra lowered her head as the dark menace from her dream rippled through her mind. She sensed that the danger stalking him was coming nearer, and that regaining his title had only increased his risk. "Congratulations," she whispered, though her voice betrayed her misery.

He stepped up to her and lifted her chin with his finger. "You knew we would not wed. I told you I had plans already in place long before we met. If . . ." He paused, searching her gaze and fighting an odd sense of recognition. "If," he continued, "we had met before, or had things been different, I . . ."

She pulled away and shook her head. "Do not say it," she pleaded.

He ran a hand through his hair. "The king will announce my reinstatement at dinner tonight. I would like you to be there."

"Why? I do not care about titles and kingdoms. I care about kindness and love. I am concerned about the change of seasons and the fate of kits in the fox den."

"I'd like to dance with you."

She turned her back on him, sobs choking her throat. How could she deny him? If she did, he would hide behind a careless shrug and walk away, pretending he did not care. If she accepted his invitation, she would spend another unforgettable moment in his arms.

"Kassandra," he murmured. "Just one dance. As soon as I have completed my tasks here, I will have to return to my castle. Most likely, we will ever see each other again."

"Have you forgotten your father?" Kassandra cried. "Have you forgotten his murder?"

"I have not forgotten that he betrayed me, casting me out from the very place I called home." Cadedryn's voice rose. "I have not forgotten that his recklessness destroyed my family name and made me live a life of ridicule and contempt."

She spun around and glared at him. "Do you blame him for so much? Do you think his choice of bride was so terrible?"

Cadedryn stepped back and cloaked his expression. "My mother was a good woman, but she should not have become his bride. She should have been content to be his mistress."

They glared at each other, each furious that the other had broken their fragile truce.

Cadedryn opened his mouth to say more, but a sound at the entrance to the stables made him hesitate.

"Caenmore?" Curtis called out as he ducked inside. When he saw Kassandra, his expression became distrustful. "Are you still trying to persuade him to follow in his father's footsteps?" he accused. "You may be related to the McTavers, but you are a poor relation and no match for an earl. Begone and cease your prattle of dreams and destiny. You are not welcome here."

Stifling a cry, Kassandra fled, not hearing Cadedryn's angry words in her defense.

"Kassandra! Are you dressed?" Kalial called through the closed portal. "I am going down now."

Kassandra's eyes sprang open as she jerked awake. Her body trembled, but this time passion did not send shudders up her spine. It was fear. The danger was building, like a thundercloud rolling and tumbling in the distance, moving relentlessly closer. The black clouds formed faces, each melting into another. Liam . . . Sarah . . . Corine . . . Curtis . . . even Morgana and David. Beneath them all stood Cadedryn, his naked chest and haunted eyes bare to the elements. The storm had gathered above his head, its tumultuous anger about to erupt when Kalial's call had ripped her from the dream world and back into reality.

"I'm almost ready!" Kassandra gasped as she sprang to her feet. "I will be dressed shortly and will join you." As soon as she heard the receding footsteps she rubbed the paste onto her cheeks and blinked her eyes several times. Why couldn't she see the exact nature of the danger? Why was this dream so unclear?

Normally, she could see the future with easy clarity. But she could not understand this dream, and her failure was placing Cadedryn in danger.

If only she could get him to leave here. There was something—or someone—in this castle that threatened him. Here, evil wore a lovely smile and friends might prove to be one's greatest enemies.

Court was a complex and unnerving place, one with which she had no experience. So far, she had completely muddled her relationship with Cadedryn, confusing both him and herself with her multiple facades.

If only she could be herself.

She turned to face Triu-cair, but her longtime companion had no answers for her. "I cannot discard my disguises," she sighed. "He likes both Lady Kassandra and the tigress kitten for different reasons, and I enjoy spending time with him, even if it is not completely honest time."

She held out her hand, but Triu-cair skipped away.

Kassandra drew her breath in sharply. "Don't act as if what I am doing is wrong! You brought me to him! Besides, my dreams told me to find him, and I am only following my dreams, as I always have." She stared out the window, her eyes clouded with concern. "But in truth, I can no longer tell what is a dream and what is real," she said. "I thought I was meant to find Cadedryn and bring him home to Loch Nidean, but the fates have proven me wrong. He is following his own path, and it does not include me. Now I must complete my duty and protect him before I leave, yet I don't know from whence the danger comes."

She walked to her vanity and pulled the dirk from the drawer. It had led her here. Mayhap it had more to tell.

Triu-cair's tail twitched and he scampered closer to her. The white fringe under his chin quivered as he scrambled into her lap and touched her face with his tiny paw.

I do not have the answers, Kassandra told her friend silently, her eyes filling with tears once again.

Stop searching. Stop trying so hard. Let the days unfold and allow destiny to reveal itself.

Kassandra grimaced and replaced the dirk. *I want to be with him again*, she admitted.

Then forget the dreams. Be with him. Make a lifetime of memories together before you must return home.

Can I? she asked, her heart fluttering with excitement.

You are here. He is here.

She took a deep breath and nodded. She had only a few days left.

Dressing with care, she slipped the beautiful dress over her head and tied the laces in back. She carefully braided her hair, ensuring that all strands were completely restrained, and tucked it under the black wig. She then placed the blue satin mantle over her head and secured it with the silver circlet.

She examined herself in the polished metal. She looked cool, elegant and virginal, nothing like the naked siren of this morning.

She blew a kiss toward Triu-cair, then descended the stairs in search of Kalial, but Lady Corine accosted her before she made it to the bottom of the flight.

"Lady Kassandra!" Corine said. "May I have a word with you?"

Kassandra paused, her hand on the wall as she looked up the several steps to where Lady Corine was standing. Lady Corine's chambers were on the same floor as Kassandra's and it appeared they had chosen the same moment to join the festivities.

"Certainly," Kassandra replied.

Corine took a few more steps until she was only three steps above the younger woman. The added height made her tower over Kassandra. "I am displeased with you."

Kassandra stiffened.

"You should not dally with men who are not yours. Caenmore is mine, especially now that he is an earl. I warn you to stay away."

Yesterday, Kassandra might have fled at Corine's nasty rebuke, or she might have snapped back, presenting a false show of bravado. A week ago she would have stamped her foot and said that he was *her* dream man, *her* future husband, and Corine was the one encroaching. But today Kassandra was not feeling so bold, nor was she so certain of her own desires.

"Don't you care about anything other than his title?" Kassandra replied. "Can't you even pretend to love him? Or is your heart otherwise engaged?"

"What are you implying?" Corine hissed, her eyes wide with guilt.

Kassandra turned away and began descending the stairs.

Corine sprang after her. She gripped Kassandra's shoulder and spun her around. "Don't you dare turn your back on me! I will not tolerate such disrespect from you. I have a dowry of considerable wealth. I come from a highborn family and must marry to please them."

"Why Cadedryn?" Kassandra questioned. "I would think that your mother would despise the Caenmores after all she went through."

"She is the one who bade me pursue him. She should have become a countess then, and as soon as I marry Cadedryn, I will obtain the title. It is what she has always wanted and I will make sure she gets it."

Kassandra looked at her in surprise. "How would that please her? She will not be countess; you will."

Corine squeezed Kassandra's arm tighter. "Because losing Liam stripped her of the one thing she always wanted and thus denied her a lifetime of happiness. You have no idea what I live with, day after day, listening to her weep because of what Liam did. It is only right that I should receive the benefits of Cadedryn's riches as fair compensation for what his father did to my mother. My entire family will reap the rewards of our union."

Kassandra twitched out of Corine's vicious hold. "You're hurting me," she cried, stumbling down one step.

Corine followed her and shook her fist in Kassandra's face. "I will marry him and you will not interfere! I will have power and prestige beyond any other woman in this court other than the queen herself. You are nothing but a strange relative of the McTavers and should stay quietly in the background as your position dictates. I have already done much to make my mother happy, and I will not rest until I have wed Caenmore, so leave him to me!"

Kassandra backed away. "You are beside yourself, Lady Corine."

Corine leaned closer, her face twisted in an ugly snarl. "You accuse me of wanting his title, but you are as desperate as I to become a countess." She gripped Kassandra's hand and yanked it.

Kassandra's toes curled as she tried to maintain her balance. "I told you," she whispered. "I don't care for titles."

"You lie!" Corine hissed as she pushed against Kassandra's wrist, sending her teetering on the stair. "I can see it in your eyes!"

Kassandra gasped and flailed with her other hand, feeling herself start to fall. "No!" she cried.

"Oh my!" wailed someone from above. "The lady is falling!"

Corine grabbed Kassandra as if she were saving her, and pushed her against the wall. "You should take care, Lady Kassandra," she admonished loudly. "A fall that far could have been disastrous."

Kassandra pressed against the wall, cringing away from Lady Corine. As the other woman rushed down to check on her, Kassandra turned away from her nemesis, her emotions in turmoil. Nothing had prepared her for this place. She did not know how to deal with evil schemers and passionate interludes. She was lost and confused. For all that Corine was a terrible person, she was right about one thing. Kassandra was in no position to wed the new earl.

"I am unharmed," Kassandra reassured her concerned rescuer, although her voice trembled. "But if you would accompany me the rest of the way down?"

"Of course, dear. I will bring you straight to the table and get you some water. Come along."

Kassandra snuck one look at Corine's smugly victorious smile as she and her new companion walked carefully down to the main floor.

Chapter 12

David McCafferty noticed Lady Kassandra and an elderly matron enter the main hall, but his gaze slid past them to rest upon his son, Curtis. He frowned. Once again, Curtis was lounging with Cadedryn and ignoring his own father!

With a grumble of irritation, David stalked up to his son and gripped his arm.

Curtis turned with a start of surprise. "Father, how do you fare this eve?"

"I would fare better if I was granted a bit of your time. You are my only son and you have been gone for many years. You are all I have left," he complained. "Sit and spend some time with me."

"The king is going to announce Cadedryn's reinstatement," Curtis explained. "As his foster brother and close companion, I would like to be near him when the announcement is made. It will grant prestige to me and to our family name."

"Is your own name not enough for you?" David thundered.

Cadedryn stepped between them and placed a restraining hand upon his foster father's chest. "Milord, this is not the time to cause a scene. Your son is very proud of you and"—he glanced meaningfully at Curtis—"would greatly enjoy spending a few moments with his father."

Curtis looked back and forth between Cadedryn and David, then relented with a shrug. "You will save a seat on the bench for me at supper?" he asked Cadedryn.

"I will ensure that both of you are at my table," Cadedryn replied.

As they walked away, Cadedryn became aware of a woman standing behind him. As he turned to acknowledge her, Lady Morgana abruptly averted her gaze and acted disinterested.

"Lady Morgana," Cadedryn greeted her. "You are looking well. The last time we conversed, years ago, you and young Lady Corine were visiting the McCaffertys."

"Indeed," Lady Morgana responded. "Curtis and Corine were as close as a young boy and girl could be. But times change and youths grow. Now my Corine will be joined to you."

"I thank you for your sponsorship of our union. I know there are many hurts in your past, but I seek to absolve them."

Lady Morgana's eyes narrowed. "Do not think that I have forgiven you. I am only helping because my Corine deserves to have what was stolen from me."

Cadedryn lifted a brow. If things had been different, this woman would have been his mother. How would a child be shaped if his or her parent spouted such anger? Once he wed Corine, he would be living with such a woman.

Lady Morgana stalked away, leaving Cadedryn conspicuously alone. He tensed at the insult and attempted to ignore the snickers of the other highborn guests. God, he detested court! These people with their nasty remarks and withering stares . . . He couldn't wait to return to Aberdour Castle.

On the other side of the hall, Kassandra found a small bench along the wall where she was able to rest and sip her drink. Her face relaxed and her fear subsided. Kalial was correct. She was not meant for court life, for people like Corine confounded her. She had to remember that her goal was to save Cadedryn. Then she would return home to her peaceful forest and leave these people to their plotting.

Cadedryn caught her gaze from where he stood across the room, leaning against the wall, his green eyes hooded with an indefinable emotion. As she returned his look with a small smile, he grinned and raised his eyebrows several times.

Kassandra swallowed a laugh and averted her gaze. He was acting silly, probably hoping she would laugh aloud and embarrass herself. If he only knew the truth, he would be the one struggling to maintain his composure.

However, there was no way he knew that she was his tiger kitten. He had never even suspected that they were one and the same, thus he did not know how much her stomach fluttered or how her heart raced whenever he was near.

She took a deep draught of her drink, suddenly wishing it were ale.

"Why are you sitting all alone?" Cadedryn murmured as he stood over her a moment later. He noticed her ill-at-ease expression and cocked his head, intrigued. She was so beautiful . . . sensual even, and looked more like his tiger kitten than he had initially realized.

His cock twitched as he recalled the sensation of sliding inside the kitten's hot core. He coughed and rubbed the back of his neck, trying to erase the erotic images and focus on the innocent woman before him, but it was hard to say who fascinated him more. His tigress had laid siege to his physical needs, but Kassandra had managed to weasel her way into his heart.

He smiled down at her bent head, reminding himself that she was a sweet girl who, though eccentric, was becoming dear to him in a sisterly way. "I apologize for Curtis's angry words earlier. He was merely concerned about my welfare and did not know that we had reached an understanding."

"An understanding?"

"Indeed. I am fond of you and you are fond of me, but we have accepted that we can never marry."

Kassandra cast around quickly, searching for an escape.

He captured her hand and lifted it to his lips. "Are you the same lass who chastised me the other day? Now you act as if you'd rather I not talk to you. I thought you would appreciate my humble words of apology."

Kassandra tried to extract her hand, but he held it firmly. "Do not concern yourself with apologies," Kassandra replied as the butterflies in her belly rose to her head and made her feel dizzy. He must stop touching her! She yanked futilely at her hand, but he refused to release it. "I am content to be alone," she replied. "Go do . . . the things that earls do."

He sat down, still holding her hand. "I'm not feeling very much like an earl at the moment. I was waiting to see you in order to ensure that your feelings were not unduly damaged." He gazed at her intently as his thumb stroked her palm.

She finally yanked her hand free and turned slightly away from him. "Lord Curtis and Lady Corine are correct. It was a mistake to think we should join. We love different worlds. I want the fresh air and the scent of growing trees, whereas you like the dank closeness of a castle and the smell of gold." A flush darkened her cheeks as she remembered their last interlude. They both liked one thing, but she was not about to tell him that! Things were getting far more mixed up than she had ever expected when she started this impromptu charade.

Silence lengthened between them as both sat on the bench and looked out over the crowd. Cadedryn knew that her words had not been meant as an insult, though they sounded like one, and he quietly acknowledged that there was an element of truth to them. He turned back toward her and stared at her profile. The similarity of the two women was unnerving. The curve of their cheeks . . . the fullness of their lower lips. His stomach tightened at the memories of his tigress's body as he imagined what Kassandra's flesh would look like sprawled across a silken coverlet. "How many sisters do you have?" he asked abruptly.

"Three half sisters."

"You accept them? Your family allows such illegitimacy?"

Kassandra glared at him. "You do not understand my family circumstances and I suggest that we not pursue this conversation."

"I know one of your half sisters. I . . . I would feel dishonest if I did not let you know that she and I have spent some time together."

Kassandra gagged on her water, then pushed his hand away as he tried to help her. "My sister?" Kassandra sputtered. "You spent time with her, too?"

"I don't even know her name."

Kassandra blinked, then bit her lip as she realized

that he was not speaking of Kalial, but of herself as the tiger kitten. She giggled, then covered her mouth with her hand to contain her mirth.

"Many pardons," he murmured, disgruntled by her response. "I had not thought to tell you something amusing." He looked away once again, casting about for a subject she would appreciate. "You know quite a bit about horses. Do you know about their husbandry or their breeding?"

"Umm." She searched the crowd, seeking a distraction. "I know all about horses. I watched the forest ponies and learned how to combine the best traits of the stallion and the mare to create a better foal."

"I breed horses. I have their bloodlines sent from Aberdour and I tell my overseer which pairs to mate," he said.

She glanced at him. "You have some fine horses. I saw a few in the stables, and I like your stallion."

"They are tending to be a bit heavy in the croup."

Kassandra twisted toward him and frowned. "No, they aren't," she protested. "They are nicely shaped. Perhaps the fetlocks are a bit thick, however."

He grunted. "Their fetlocks are perfect."

She shook her head. "Not quite. They bulge a bit too much, indicating thicker bones in the joint, which predisposes them to injuries."

He pressed his lips together. "My overseer reports that one of my mares has such an injury."

"See? I'd wrap her legs whenever you ride her though forests or up the slopes. The support will help prevent that type of damage."

He watched her face brighten with animation and saw a hint of color on her pale cheeks. He wondered why she felt the need to wear such heavy creams.

"You were tending your mare yourself. What other unusual things do you have knowledge of?"

Kassandra glared at him. "Are you mocking me?"

"Not at all. I am truly interested."

She shrugged. "I know tracking."

"Tracking," he stated incredulously. "You mean, following man or beast through the woods?"

She started to get up, but he grasped her hand and held her still. "I am not teasing you. I am merely surprised. I have never heard of any woman who knows anything about tracking." He lowered his tone. "Not even my mother."

Kassandra paused. Pain threaded his voice and her heart ached at the longing his words unknowingly expressed. "Do you miss her?"

He stared into her blue eyes. They were kind eyes . . . caring eyes. They were youthfully innocent and clear of the insidious derision he saw in everyone else's gaze. "She was a peasant," he said, his voice turning harsh. He waited to see her eyes shift, to see them become distant with disgust.

"When did she die?" Kassandra asked, and this time she took *his* hand.

A lump rose in his throat. "Ten years ago. It was a terrible accident. She was sitting underneath an overhang, and a falling boulder crushed her. My father was devastated. He loved her too much."

"You cannot love someone too much," Kassandra argued.

"You can. It leaves you vulnerable to the pain of loss."

She let go of his hand and stared at her lap. She loved her Dagda with every pore of her body. Was it too much? Had she been blind to the truth and not allowed him his own way? "Perhaps you are right," she answered softly. "Perhaps my love for you made me selfish." She glanced up at him, her blue eyes filled with sorrow. She wanted to make him happy. If attaining the title and wedding Corine would make him happy, then so be it. But her heart cracked and pain washed through her. "I understand what it feels to give up a dream. The pain is immense."

"I did not think I could convince you so easily. Aren't you the one who argues about everything? Aren't you the same girl who swore we were destined to have an everlasting love? How can you forget me with such little effort?" He felt an odd sense of disappointment and an unexplainable rush of anger. "Your love must not have been as strong as you believed."

She stood up.

He stood with her. "I want to know," he said urgently. "Do you still love me?"

She faced him squarely. "Tell me the first thing that comes to your mind when I ask you a question. What is the most important thing in your life?"

"Reclaiming my earldom. What about you?"

She smiled sadly. "I don't know anymore."

Kassandra's words still echoed in Cadedryn's mind several hours later. He and Lady Corine sat at the first table next to the king and queen, and he should have been pleased with his position of respect. Instead, he kept glancing down the tables to where Kassandra sat, concerned about her forlorn face.

"You seem distracted," Lady Corine murmured. "You should be concentrating on the king. He is ready to publicly announce your good fortune, yet you act as if you'd rather be somewhere else!"

Cadedryn dragged his gaze away from Kassandra

and took a long swallow of ale. He had to keep focused on his task. Everything was coming together exactly as he wanted. Lady Corine was accepting his courtship and the king was granting him his rightful title. There was nothing else he needed.

Suddenly the king rose and lifted his hand for silence. "Today is a special day. Today we erase the past and start afresh." He gestured toward Cadedryn.

Cadedryn's heart began to pound as he rose slowly and faced the king.

"More than twenty years ago, our kingdom lost a good man when he chose to follow his heart and not his head. Liam Caenmore disgraced his name by shunning a respectable bride and wedding a peasant woman. Such actions are not allowed to those of highborn status. Leaders must always maintain their stoic strength and ignore their unruly passions. It was with deep regret that I was forced to strip Liam's title as a consequence of his irresponsibility. But I am not standing here today to recount that part of the tale. I am here to announce the restitution of the Caenmore family."

He paused, then stared directly at Cadedryn. "Cadedryn Caenmore, you have distinguished yourself in battle. You have shown yourself to be a strong and steadfast subject of the crown."

Everyone in the hall held his or her breath. Many leaned forward in rapt anticipation.

"In addition, the Highlands require a firm hand to maintain their loyalty. Since Liam died, the people living around Aberdour Castle have reduced their tithes and have shown a lack of respect, bordering on unrest." King Malcolm pulled forth a heavy broadsword and touched it to Cadedryn's shoulder. "I need a man to rule over the Aberdour lands and quell all disturbances, one who insists on appropriate respect and tithing. I need a man who demonstrates unflagging loyalty and who acts with the sole intention of contributing to the welfare of Scotland. Are you such a man?"

Cadedryn nodded. "I am, milord," he said solemnly.

The king smiled. "I hereby reinstate your familial title of earl, granting with it all the honor and responsibility it entails. Use your title wisely, knowing that I will watch you closely, for I will not tolerate any misuse of your power." He lifted the sword from Cadedryn's shoulder and replaced it in its scabbard. With a heavy sigh, he sat back down and motioned for Cadedryn to come forward.

"Thank you," Cadedryn said quietly as members of the court began whispering among themselves.

Malcolm took a long draught of ale, then wiped his face with the back of his hand. "I respected Liam," he said to Cadedryn privately. "He was a good friend. Even though I was forced to take his title from him, I left him to manage the castle and lands. If he had not consented to do so, I would have had a feudal war on my hands, as any of the lesser lords would have fought to gain possession of Aberdour. I was not going to let Liam's rash actions send my Highlands into civil unrest.

"Many wondered why I did not send Liam into exile," the king continued as he took another drink and rubbed his beard with his thumb and forefinger. "I knew that while Liam's heart went to Sarah, his soul still belonged to Scotland. His mistake was not in taking that woman to wife, but in doing so without my permission. I was greatly saddened to hear that in the end he took his own life."

Cadedryn's green eyes burned with conviction.

"Your Majesty," he declared loudly enough for others to hear, "I do not believe it was suicide."

Lady Corine's face drained of all color and she clutched the table edge, while Curtis half rose and shook his head warningly at Cadedryn from where he sat several feet down the long table. Next to him, Laird David McCafferty's face turned red with anger and he slammed his fist upon the table.

The king frowned at the McCaffertys, but turned aside briefly to listen to whispered words from his queen.

While he was distracted, Lady Corine leaned toward Cadedryn. "Put it all to rest so the king can forgive and forget," she insisted. "This is not the time or place to stir rumors better left unsaid. It does not matter what happened on a day so long ago. His manner of death is unimportant. The only thing you should care about is the fact that you are now an earl, and that soon the king will grant our betrothal."

Cadedryn stared at Corine with distaste. "Your single-minded determination to gain power is unbecoming," he stated.

"I am no different than you," she snapped back. "Don't accuse me of ambition when you have thought of nothing else since the day your father cast you aside."

Cadedryn drew a quick breath, stunned by Corine's vicious words but unable to refute them. He glanced toward the end of the table and caught Kassandra's concerned gaze.

She smiled at him encouragingly, unaware of the conversation between him and Corine, but seeming to sense his sudden discomfort.

Facing the king, he answered loudly enough for all to hear, "Your Majesty, I wish I could tell you that my father died a peaceful death, or even that he killed himself, following my mother into the other world, but I cannot. I believe that he was murdered, and that his murderer still walks free among us."

The king's brows drew together as he sat back and looked at Cadedryn. "This does not please us," he grumbled. "What proof do you have of this accusation and why have you never mentioned it before?"

"I did not think you cared to discuss his life much less his death."

"Tell me what you know," the king commanded.

"My father was found with an unusual knife wound in his chest. The only knife that would have created such a wound was his personal dirk, forged especially for him."

"He could have easily plunged the blade into his own heart," Malcolm replied. "A murderer would have stabbed him in the back and used his own knife. What you have said only proves that his death was a suicide."

"The knife was never found even though I myself cast it into the nearby bushes, suggesting that someone else was hiding nearby. I believe the act was done in order to make it look like a suicide."

The king leaned back and gazed at Cadedryn assessingly. "Do you know who committed such a dastardly act?"

"If I did, I would have taken my revenge years ago. Alas, I have no other information," he gritted between clenched teeth. "Like the mist, the killer came and went."

"Was it, perchance, a robbery gone afoul?"

"A full bag of coin on his person was left untouched."

Kassandra sucked in her breath, her eyes growing

wide. The memory of her dreams flickered through her mind and she began to shiver.

"The murderer must have the knife," the king mused.

Cadedryn swung his gaze to Kassandra. Green eyes bored into blue as he dared her to speak. "Not anymore," he replied quietly. "It must have become lost."

The king frowned. "Have you no other method by which to determine what occurred?"

For a heartbeat, Cadedryn said nothing, simply stared at Kassandra.

As if not of her own accord, she rose to her feet. Her breathing became erratic and spots danced in front of her eyes. She moaned and held up her hands as if to ward off an attacker. Dream visions filled her mind, crowding out reality. Mist rose around her as if she were deep in the woods once again and darkness drowned the rows of tables and quenched the hundred candles, leaving her alone and frightened despite the large crowd.

She saw an older man standing in the woods. He glanced over his shoulder at the sounds of another's footsteps and pulled his dirk free from his belt.

"Who goes there?" he demanded. Then his face relaxed and he lowered his knife, tossing it near his cape, which lay beneath a tree. "Ah . . . 'tis you." He nodded in greeting. Then suddenly pain burst through his body from where the knife plunged deep within his chest, and horror filled his voice. "You?" he gasped. "Why? Why now?" He fell to his knees, struggling to draw breath.

Kassandra felt the pain in her own heart. She felt her blood soak the ground as her life force drained away. Then, on the edge of consciousness, she saw someone racing through the trees . . . someone fast and light. The murderer.

She blinked. The vision was gone.

Cadedryn had turned away from her and was addressing the king with a shake of his head. "I am not prepared to discuss more in such public company," he said.

Curtis placed his palms flat on the table. "Cadedryn," he began, "this is not appropriate—" But the king waved him to silence.

"We will speak of it again at a later time. For now, we must enjoy our meal."

Cadedryn inclined his head.

The king motioned to everyone to resume eating. "I find that I am hungry," he said loudly. "Bring me some food while the play begins!"

Cadedryn glanced meaningfully at Kassandra to sit back down, then began tearing meat from a leg of mutton.

Kassandra slowly resumed her seat, her heart racing and her mind in chaos. Her dreams were crossing the sleep barrier and starting to come to her while she was awake. She shuddered and wrapped her arms around her shoulders. Premonitions about the future were fine. Even dream fantasies about her true love were acceptable. But these visions . . . visions of death and murder . . . they were far more intense.

She shook her head, clearing the fog that still clouded her thoughts. Perhaps it was the dirk. If she gave it to Cadedryn, maybe the visions would retreat and all would be back to how it was supposed to be. Mayhap that was what she had been sent here to do. She had to give him the knife so he could find the murderer.

But a shiver of trepidation snaked up her spine. The dirk gave evidence of a past murder. It said nothing of what was still to come.

Chapter 13

"Would you like to join the dance?" Cadedryn asked softly, his green eyes boring into hers. "The lines are forming."

She trembled, drawn to his magnetism, yet afraid to spend too much time in his presence.

"If you say no, I will assume you are afraid."

She rose. "I do not fear you."

"But I fear you," he replied, his expression serious.

"I . . . why . . ." She stammered, then took a steadying breath. "Why do you fear me?"

"What do you know about my father's death?"

She peered up at him, unnerved by his question as he pulled her into position and bowed, forcing her to curtsy in return. "I am not certain what I know," she whispered, aware of the other people in the dance. She tripped over Cadedryn's foot, trying to recall the intricate steps from a lesson Kalial had given her a year ago. At that time, the sisters had danced for enjoyment, but now Kassandra gave thanks for the knowledge. "My pardons," she muttered, concentrating on following the complicated dance pattern.

Cadedryn drew her hand to the right, sending her into a circular promenade. "You know something," he chided her. "You have the dirk."

"Why didn't you tell the king that I had it?" she asked.

He looked at her strangely. "You would have been placed under suspicion," he replied. "I was protecting you."

Kassandra's heart fluttered and she missed another step.

"I would rather you thank me," he said teasingly. "But if you promise not to tread upon my toes again, I will thank you."

They grinned at each other.

"I want to give it to you," she said.

"The dirk?"

"Yes."

"That means more to me than you know. Come take a ride with me soon," Cadedryn murmured. "You can bring me the knife and we can enjoy the warm sunshine."

She nodded shyly. "I would enjoy that very much."

"I would, too."

The dance ended and the men bowed as the ladies curtsied.

"I bid you good night," Cadedryn said as he led her to the edge of the dance floor.

"You are leaving?"

He looked around and grimaced. "I do not find these events pleasurable. There is a festival in town that will be more to my liking."

"Oh," Kassandra answered, crestfallen.

" 'Tis not you I seek to escape," he assured her. "I am simply uncomfortable spending long periods of time in such stuffy confines."

"I understand."

He nodded and bowed once again, then turned and strode for the door.

A festival, Kassandra mused. Suddenly her eyes lit up and she bit back a smile. She, too, would enjoy such an event! But she could not attend as Lady Kassandra. She would have to become the tiger kitten!

Kassandra eased her way out of the great hall, then dashed upstairs to her room. "Triu-cair!" she whispered. "I am in need of your weasel ways."

The polecat peeked out from underneath the bed. Kassandra clapped her hands with excitement. "We are going to a festival!"

Triu-cair wriggled his nose and scampered into the middle of the floor. She gripped the sides of her dress and spread the elegant skirts. "I must modify my clothes so I don't look like such a lady."

A sly grin stole across Triu-cair's face and he bounded to the door. *I know where to look*, he declared.

She laughed and opened it a crack, letting Triu-cair slide out into the hallway, then turned to divest herself of her mantle and wig. She shook her hair loose, then reached underneath her skirts to remove her slippers. Curling her bare toes with delight, Kassandra sat in front of the polished metal and scrubbed her face clean of the paste.

After several minutes, a scratch at her door made her spring to admit Triu-cair. She gasped as he lugged in a length of red satin. She snatched the fabric from Triu-cair's mouth and drew it into her room, terrified that someone would happen by before she could shut the door.

"Where did you find this?" she asked incredulously as she held the soft cloth to her cheek.

Hidden in a lady's room down the hall.

"Ladies are not supposed to wear red." Kassandra grinned. "No doubt the owner of this satin has some secrets she'd rather not share." Kassandra bit back a giggle and quickly began pinning the satin around her waist, then crisscrossing it over her bosom until she had transformed the elegant cream-colored gown into a flamboyant festival dress.

After making a matching cape for Triu-cair and setting him on her shoulder, she stood in front of the mirror and lifted her chin high. Tonight she was going to have fun. No dreams. No worries. Tonight she was going to concentrate on enjoying Cadedryn's company and exploring the fascinating customs of the Scottish populace.

Grinning, she pulled her hooded cape over her new dress and carefully covered her head. Then, with a quick glance along the hallway, she scampered down the stairs and escaped out a servants' side door.

Another woman also changed her clothes and prepared to sneak out of the castle. She donned a blue dress and covered her head with a veil. She placed a jeweled mask over her face and took a deep breath. She wanted to meet her lover, but her fingers trembled with anxiety. He had been her childhood sweetheart. The first and only male to touch her heart.

She had convinced herself that seeing him again would not affect her, but she had been terribly mistaken. His eyes had struck a chord deep inside her, and although she tried to resist, her passions had prevailed over her common sense.

He had asked her to meet him in the village, far away from prying eyes, and she had finally capitulated. She smiled grimly from beneath the heavy veil. This would be the last time. After tonight she would restrain herself.

It was a simple walk to the village, and before long, Kassandra had tossed her hood back and was humming under her breath. A tremor of excitement whispered through her. She had no doubt that she would find Cadedryn.

Although the night sky was dark, torches blazed along the earthen streets and rows upon rows of vendors lined the walkways as they set up their colorful carts and laid out tempting wares. People of all sorts were bustling to and fro as they finished their daily chores and prepared to take pleasure in the summertime festival.

Kassandra tried to avoid the crowd at first, certain her red tresses would generate snickering, but she soon realized that, other than a few appreciative whistles, the villagers accepted her as one of their own.

Triu-cair perched on her shoulder, thrilled to be out of the castle. *That smell! Baked biscuits!*

Kassandra cast him a swift, warning glance. *We have no funds, Triu-cair.*

Oranges! Sweetmeats!

"We are trying to find Cadedryn. All you seem interested in is food," she grumbled aloud.

Triu-cair whipped his tail over a baker's cart and curled it around a fresh bun. Within seconds, he had it in his mouth.

The baker cried out, but Kassandra quickly skipped through the crowd, laughing at the man's angry face while congratulating herself on a clever escape.

Suddenly a strong hand descended on her arm and spun her around.

She screamed, certain the baker had found her, when her lips were enveloped in a deep, sensuous kiss. She struggled briefly, vainly attempting to push the man aside, but he wrapped his arms around her waist and pulled her closer.

"I found you," he whispered in her ear.

"Cadedryn!" Kassandra gasped. "You frightened me!"

"You!" the baker shouted as he huffed toward the couple. "You stole my bun!"

Cadedryn flipped a coin at the man, then shook a finger at a contrite Triu-cair. "You, little friend, could have caused a bit of trouble."

"Indeed," Kassandra agreed, trying to pull the last of the bread from Triu-cair's grasp.

"Let him have it," Cadedryn said with a chuckle. "Spoils rightly taken are the property of the victor."

Kassandra laughed as she stared up at him. "You surprise me," she said softly.

His gaze swept her fancy red dress and his eyebrows rose. "And you never fail to surprise me. What interesting attire."

Kassandra's eyes narrowed. "You don't like it?"

Cadedryn's mind flicked back to his Lady Kassandra's lovely cream-colored evening gown. She had seemed angelic and nearly untouchable, whereas his tigress's clothing bespoke her availability in no uncertain terms.

"I like the dress," he replied softly. "And I am very fond of you in it." He pulled her into his arms and kissed her lips. "Tell me your name. I have never asked you your name, yet you seem to know mine."

Kassandra hesitated, casting about for an appropriate choice. She wanted it to start with the same sound so she wouldn't fail to respond when he called her. "Kaitlynn?" she answered, her voice rising as if in a question.

"Kaitlynn," he repeated, rolling the sound around in his mouth. He smiled and touched her hair. "Kaitlynn, the kitten."

Kassandra grinned as Triu-cair stood up on his hind

legs and balanced on her shoulder. "So, my tiger kitten, are you ready to have an eventful evening?" Cadedryn asked as he slid his arm around her waist and playfully swatted at the weasel, which leapt from her shoulder to his, then back again.

Kassandra skipped ahead, tossed her hair over her shoulder and batted her eyelashes. "I hear music!" she trilled, then spun down the street. "I can't wait to see what one does at a festival like this. I hope there is dancing, for I love to dance."

Cadedryn chuckled. She was such a captivating woman. Her mercurial personality was both fascinating and confusing. From hesitant virgin to laughing siren, she made him forget all the court intrigue and simply enjoy the evening.

Triu-cair stretched his tail out toward a keg of ale set up underneath a flickering torch. Clinging to Kassandra's dress with one foot, he angled the rest of his body underneath the spigot. With a flip of the toggle, he opened the keg and began drinking the dark amber fluid.

"Triu-cair!" Kassandra yelped as she attempted to drag him away.

"He's right. We should all have something to drink," Cadedryn commented. He paid the ale tapper, who grumbled at the quantity of spilled ale but handed two tankards to Cadedryn after wrestling the toggle away from the weasel.

"I don't care for ale," Kassandra grumbled, still annoyed with her pet.

"The second tankard is for your friend." Cadedryn laughed as he gave the ale to Triu-cair.

Triu-cair grabbed it with his tiny hands and plunged his head into the refreshment.

"You're encouraging him," Kassandra complained.

"And you," she whispered to Triu-cair, "should remember to behave!"

Cadedryn shrugged. "He's your pet and I find him—and you—interesting. Here." He handed her a wineskin from another vendor. "Is this more to your taste?"

Kassandra took a tiny sip and gagged, but when Cadedryn looked at her curiously, she forced a smile. "Ummm," she managed.

As if you are behaving, Triu-cair replied with a polecat grin. His sparkling eyes gleamed up at her as he licked his lips and hiccupped.

"You are the one who encouraged me," she hissed. "And I don't appreciate your drunken comments!"

"Are you talking to your friend?" Cadedryn asked as he motioned them forward.

"No!" Kassandra snapped, then tilted the wineskin to her lips for a long draught. The sour wine hit her stomach then raced through her veins and tickled her head. She clutched Cadedryn's arm, feeling slightly dizzy.

"Drink slowly," he cautioned. "That wine is strong."

Kassandra took another drink, unwilling to admit to the wine's powerful effect. Pleasant warmth spread through her and she leaned against Cadedryn. "Music," she reminded him while pointing ahead.

They turned the corner and entered a large square filled with villagers, farmers and an assortment of tradesmen. Some men from the castle strolled about with beautiful mistresses, and a few ladies wearing concealing masks watched from protected perches. In the center of the square was a cleared area for dancing with an adjacent stage containing several sweating musicians.

The musicians paused and wiped their faces, then prepared for a new song. Kassandra took another drink, no longer offended by the wine's sour taste. She tapped her foot and smiled giddily. "What fun!" she exclaimed, unaware that her voice was slurred. "It reminds me of the festivals at home!"

"Where is your home, kitten?"

She arched a brow and shrugged. "Let's not talk about such things. At least not tonight."

Triu-cair stood on her shoulder and imitated her actions, making onlookers laugh.

"Go!" Kassandra commanded, pointing to Cadedryn, whereupon the weasel leapt nimbly from her shoulder to his, and this time, stayed there.

"I said I found him interesting," Cadedryn exclaimed. "I did not say I wanted him!"

She giggled and stepped onto the dance square. Her hair swung in front of her face and she absently pushed it back, threading her fingers through her tresses in a languid, sensual motion. It felt good to be free of the wig and mantle. She shook her mane, then laughed as torchlight wavered in front of her eyes.

You're drunk! Triu-cair cautioned from his perch on Cadedryn's shoulder.

"I know!" she called out. "I like it!"

"You like what? The music?" Cadedryn asked.

She slanted her gaze at him and blew him a kiss.

His eyebrows lifted and he stepped back. Here was the tigress side of her again . . . the taunting, sensual temptress who seduced him with effortless ease. Her eyes, brilliantly blue eyes . . . so like Kassandra's. He shook his head. Forget Kassandra. She was a friend. She was a kind woman with some childlike qualities that made her special. Kassandra had the dirk and he needed it back, but their relationship would go no further. Here was his tigress, a woman warm and willing who desired nothing but mutual pleasure.

She twirled slowly, her hands in the air. She moved with innate grace as if she were a feather drifting on waves of music. Her fingers trailed through the air, caressing the wind. Even her lips parted in gentle relaxation. This woman was more than beautiful. She was stunning.

She arched her neck, baring it, then spun slowly in a circle. As her shoulder dipped, her dress slipped, revealing an inch of flesh.

Cadedryn stepped forward.

Seeing him, she wrapped her arms around her waist, then slid them up her body, her fingers spread upon her own back, until they wrapped around her head and were buried in the wealth of her hair. She shook her head, sending her hair tossing around her face, then trailed her fingers down her cheeks and over her bare throat.

He took another step closer.

She swayed back and forth to the beat of the music, her hips undulating and her shoulders rolling. Her sweetly seductive smile encouraged him.

He stepped onto the dance square and stopped, as if daring her to continue.

Her hands reached for him, near but not touching, stroking but not caressing. Weaving around him, she brushed her fingers scant inches from his body and the faint stir of her motions made his body quiver. His mind sharpened and he focused entirely on her. She was casting a spell upon him and he was helpless to resist her.

An old buried memory tickled his senses, of a red-haired girl laughing in a meadow filled with yellow daisies. The image flickered like a forgotten dream, then drifted away. He struggled to recapture it, but the girl was gone and in front of him was once again his dancing tigress.

She touched a finger to her lips, then spun in a circle and touched the fingertip to his mouth.

He grasped her hands, threaded his fingers between hers, and forced her arms behind her back. He joined her swaying motions, his hips grinding in pulse-pounding rhythm.

She arched against him, her breasts pressing against his hard chest. She bent toward his neck and suckled, then trailed her mouth up his throat to his ear.

"If you do much more of that, we will not stay at the festival much longer," he growled.

She smiled in satisfaction, aware that her actions had fully aroused him.

He spun her in a circle, lifting her legs in the air as she laughed and spread her arms wide, when suddenly they bumped into a woman who was attempting to skirt the dance floor.

"Excuse me," Cadedryn said as he let his tigress's feet touch the ground and he reached for the woman's blue-clad arm to steady her.

"Let go of me," the woman snapped.

Cadedryn started, then peered into the woman's eyes through the jeweled mask. "Lady Corine," he accused. "What are you doing here?"

Lady Corine gasped and yanked her arm free. She swept Cadedryn with a scathing look. " 'Tis not I who should be answering questions," she replied. "It appears that instead of staying at the dance and courting me, you have decided to dance attendance upon a woman of ill repute."

Kassandra gasped and ducked her head against Cadedryn's chest. The anger emanating from the woman washed the wine from her mind and filled it with trepidation. Why was Lady Corine here? She should be at the castle with the other gentry!

"I am enjoying the festival in the way that all men do," Cadedryn acknowledged smoothly, putting only a slight distance between him and his tigress. "You have not answered my question. What brings you here, dressed in a mask and veil?"

"I . . . I . . . I was seeking a special present for my mother," she stammered, casting about for an excuse that would ring true. "What is the horrendous creature on your shoulder?" she demanded.

Kassandra bristled, but kept her face hidden in Cadedryn's shirt. If Lady Corine recognized her, she would be ruined, and while her own reputation was not of great concern to her, if Kalial heard that she had cavorted in a red dress in the midst of a peasant festival, she would be furious. No matter what enjoyment it would give her to trade insults with Corine, she was not willing to upset Kalial to do so.

But how dare Corine call Triu-cair *horrendous*!

"And you feel you have a right to chastise me, madam?" he replied coldly.

"Indeed. I have every right, for we are to be betrothed."

His eyes narrowed. "The papers have not yet been drawn up."

She flicked her hand in dismissal. "I told you that as soon as you were assured your position in court, the king would give his acceptance. You know full well that uniting our lands is important to King Malcolm and partly the reason he has reinstated your title."

"My path to acquiring acceptance might have been

expedited by our possible union, but I regained my title through my own honor and valor."

She shrugged. "Nonetheless, it is time for us to proceed. It is inappropriate for you to cavort so publicly with such a woman so near to our announcement. It is highly insulting, especially considering your father's misbehavior."

Kassandra frowned as she felt Cadedryn flinch.

"Have your whore," Lady Corine finished in a waspish tone. "But keep her hidden away and remain discreet. I will not tolerate any rumors prior to our wedding."

"I will do as is appropriate," he answered coolly. "And I expect the same from you." He looked pointedly at her mask and veil, suspecting she had just come from a tryst of her own.

Corine's eyes narrowed. "I will accept you keeping a mistress, but I insist you stay away from that wench Kassandra. She is a disruptive chit who is not fit to share my table."

That made him angry. He pushed his tigress behind him and glared at Corine. "How dare you presume to tell me what I can and cannot do. Remember your place! If I avoid the woman it will be only because I choose to do so, not because you have ordered it! She is fair and kind, which is more than I can say for you."

Kassandra's heart slammed in her chest.

"So you *do* like her!" Corine accused. "Are you considering abandoning our plans and running off with Lady Kassandra?"

"Of course not! She is a young, uncultured distant relative of the McTavers who knows more about horses than clothing. She is totally unfit to be a countess, but what I decide to do on my own time will be my own affair."

Corine sniffed and turned away, quickly melting into the crowd.

Kassandra stumbled, her heart plummeting to the floor. Uncultured distant relative? Horses! Her rage rumbled and she shook with the effort to contain it. Unfit to be a countess!

Triu-cair screeched, aware of the rising anger about to explode in his mistress. He scrambled off Cadedryn's shoulder and scurried across the dance square to hide under the stage.

"You bastard!" Kassandra screamed as she slammed her fist into Cadedryn's back. Reputation be damned! He was despicable! She swung her fist and crashed it against his temple, then followed it up with a hefty kick to his shins.

Cadedryn shouted and grabbed his back, his head, then hopped back. The force of his tigress's attack was not only completely unexpected, it was also powerfully accurate. "What are you doing?" he asked in stunned bewilderment.

"You idiot!" she screamed and pummeled him again, her red hair flying, blinding her. She felt the satisfying thud as her right fist hit his chest, but her left missed him completely as he stepped nimbly away.

Not to be deterred, she started kicking and grinned with satisfaction when he yelped in pain.

"Whooo heee!" a man next to them shouted as he began to clap. "What a red-haired hellion!"

Kassandra gasped and ducked her head. Oh no! Her terrible temper! "Triu-cair!" she called as she picked up the hem of her dress and dashed across the dance square. The weasel scrambled out from under the stage and took a flying leap to land on her shoulder. *That way!* He pointed as he grabbed her hair like a pair of horse's reins. They raced through the crowd, darting in between revelers and leaping over benches. Behind them, Kassandra heard Cadedryn shouting for her to stop. She rounded the corner and leaned against the wall, gasping for breath. "That scoundrel!" she panted as she held her hand to her chest. "To think I was starting to regret my deception, wishing that he knew that Kassandra and his kitten were one and the same. He deserves everything I have done and more! Much, much more."

Triu-cair held his tiny paws over his eyes.

"Don't act shy," Kassandra grumbled. "If my best weapon against him is his own lust, then I shall not hesitate to use it. His only interests appear to be his ambition and his passion." Anger and excitement raced up her spine. "I cannot appeal to his ambition, but I can appeal to his lust, and I need to do something spectacular to punish him for his loathsome words. I've got to think up something extraordinary . . . something unexpected."

Triu-cair peeked out and looked at her with one incredulous eye.

Kassandra flicked her hair over her shoulder and shook out her skirts. She had hidden her true colors for too long.

She *was* a redhead, and that meant she had fire in her blood.

Chapter 14

The next afternoon Cadedryn found a note on his pillow.

Curtis walked in behind his friend. "Love letter?" he asked.

Cadedryn picked it up and turned it over, searching for a seal that would indicate the sender, but the wax was plain. He cracked it and quickly scanned the missive.

"Well?" Curtis asked. "Who is it from?"

"My tigress."

"Who?"

"My new mistress."

Curtis looked at him curiously. "I am pleased to hear that your interest in Lady Kassandra has faded, but I must caution you against starting a liaison at this sensitive time."

Cadedryn walked over to his chest, located a fur-trimmed cape and swung it over his shoulders. "My personal relationships have nothing to do with the king."

Curtis clenched his fists and glared at his friend. "Everything matters to the king."

Cadedryn raised an eyebrow. "I am surprised you find my affairs of such interest."

"You are ruining our plans!" Curtis shouted.

"*Our* plans?" Cadedryn asked pointedly.

"Your plans affect me," Curtis clarified, flushing a deep red. "I have received great honor by being your closest friend, now that you are an earl. Just like you, I want to assure my position in court."

"You can marry and elevate your status," Cadedryn pointed out.

Curtis shook his head. "I have no desire to wed. 'Tis you who must marry in order to more firmly establish your family."

Cadedryn opened the door and motioned for Curtis to precede him. "At this moment, I do not want to speak about marriage. My mistress requests my presence. I have to cut our visit short, for I am anxious to see her again."

Curtis reluctantly followed him. "Must be an exceptional wench."

Cadedryn smiled. "Quite exceptional. A flame-haired beauty."

"Red hair is a sign of inner demons and far cry from an appropriate choice for an earl. Your infatuation will subject Corine to ridicule."

Cadedryn spun around, glaring. "Corine?" he hissed. "Are you on such familiar terms with my intended that you call her by her given name? You are no longer children, thus such familiarity is forbidden." Cadedryn cocked his head and leaned forward. "I saw her in the village last night, dressed for a rendezvous. Could it have been you she was seeking?"

Curtis paled.

"Have you trespassed where you should not?" Cadedryn whispered.

Curtis thrust his chin forward and his eyes glittered with anger. "Such as your father did to mine? My father loved Lady Morgana, yet Liam stole her away, then flung her reputation and honor to the vultures before he ran off with *that peasant*."

"That peasant was my mother, and I warn you to hold your tongue!" Cadedryn shouted. "Answer me, Curtis. Have you renewed your relationship with Lady Corine?"

For a heartbeat, Curtis did not answer. Then his face smoothed and he smiled disarmingly. "What are we doing arguing about members of the fairer sex? I am here to help you achieve your goal, and I want nothing more than to see you and Lady Corine Fergus wed. My worries come from deep concern and respect, for your title is as important to me as it is to you. I do not want your lust ruining a decade of planning, for now is not the time to annoy the king. Will you please consider forgetting the red-haired woman, if only for the year? Then you can resume your liaison with discretion, or simply find another pretty face."

Cadedryn stared at Curtis warily.

Curtis patted him on the shoulder. " 'Tis not the time to have a disagreement. Our dreams are coming true."

Dreams. Cadedryn shifted away from Curtis and resumed walking through the hall. "We will not speak of this again," he warned. "I will do as I wish with my mistress. I have my reasons for enjoying this particular lass, but I will not jeopardize my position for anyone—not her, not even you. However, I fail to see how taking my pleasures could cause harm."

Curtis's eyes flickered with anger, but he ducked his head to shield his expression. Only after Cadedryn strode down the steps did he look up again with a snarl upon his lips. "You fool!" he hissed. "You are letting this woman disrupt everything we have worked so hard to achieve. How could you insult Corine after all I have sacrificed to give her to you?" He pressed his head with the palm of his hand, thinking hard. Finally, he lifted his gaze and stared at the soldiers milling around the courtyard. "I will not let you make the same mistake your father did, throwing everything away for a pair of pretty thighs. First you simper after Kassandra and now you pant after this mistress. I cannot allow it! My father bade me to protect Morgana's family over a decade ago, and I did everything I could, even befriending her young daughter and committing a mortal sin. Once again, I must see to it that no one hurts Morgana, or Corine—especially not another wench!"

Kassandra was hiding in the upper loft, awaiting Cadedryn's arrival with bated breath. She giggled, excited about the day. She intended to drive him crazy, and she was looking forward to the culmination of her plans.

She gasped and scrambled underneath some straw as Cadedryn's shadow crossed the threshold. She peered down through the slats and watched as he entered and glanced around, searching for her. Before long, he spotted another sealed note she had placed among some riding leathers.

Cadedryn picked up the note and examined the wax once again. Impatient, he ripped it open, then scanned it quickly. He frowned and reread it, then cursed loudly.

Kassandra held her hand to her mouth to stifle a giggle. This was working out exactly as she had planned!

Cadedryn shoved the missive into his inside shirt pocket. His tigress had worded the note almost exactly as the first, but it asked him to meet her behind the hounds' kennels. This time he walked more slowly, clearly confused but intrigued. He took care to peruse the people he passed, scanning their faces for a familiar visage.

Kassandra rolled on her back and laughed aloud. He was on a long treasure hunt, and she was the final prize! She flung a handful of hay in the air and closed her eyes as the yellowed stalks tickled her face and sprinkled her hair. How would he react when he found out she was playing a game with him?

Cadedryn circled the kennels, but saw no one. He looked inside the empty doghouses, but found nothing. Just as he was about to become discouraged, he spied a bit of lace peeking out from underneath a rock. He pulled it free and chuckled. It was lace plucked from a woman's undergarment.

He held it to his nose, breathing deeply. It was definitely hers. He nudged the rock with his boot, and grinned when he found another note. As he tucked the lace into his inner pocket, he scanned the newest set of instructions. *The tavern,* it read. *Find the next clue in an upstairs room in the village tavern.*

His groin stirred and his mind raced as he pictured what might be awaiting him in the tavern bed. Spinning on his heel, he cut through the garden and headed for the village.

"Hello, Cadedryn," a woman called out as he passed by.

The familiar voice caught him unawares, and he slid to a stop. Spinning around, he expected to see his tigress, but caught his breath when he saw the elegantly dressed Lady Kassandra sitting demurely on a garden bench.

"Milady," he acknowledged as he blinked several times in surprise.

"You seem startled," Kassandra said as she tilted her head slightly to the side and stroked a curl of her black wig that lay against her neck. "Is everything all right?"

"Of course. You simply surprised me." His piercing eyes scanned her pale features. His mistress's resemblance to Lady Kassandra was uncanny. Even the tone of her voice sounded similar, despite his tigress's husky accent. His heart pounded and he was torn between resuming his quest and sitting on the bench with her.

"Are you going somewhere?"

"Yes," he answered slowly. "I was supposed to meet someone in the village."

She inclined her head. "It must be important. You seem to be in a hurry."

"Yes," he repeated, then bowed and glanced up at her mischievous face. Was she up to something? "Are you waiting for someone?"

She wrinkled her nose in thought. "I suppose so."

"Your relative?"

She laughed. "Oh, definitely not Kalial!"

"A friend?"

"Ummm . . . no. Not a friend."

He frowned. "A gentleman?"

She gave a tiny shrug, and her blue eyes twinkled.

Jealousy raced through him and he took a quick stride toward her, then placed his hands on either side of the bench. "Have you had another dream?" he growled as he hovered over her, only inches from her face. "Have you changed your interest to another man? I suggest you leave the men of the court alone, for they are not the type you should wed. You said you wanted love and devotion, but men at court are interested only in money and power."

Kassandra leaned back and looked at him curiously. "You are no different," she reminded him.

"Exactly. Which is why I beg you to leave us alone. You should not be involved in twisted court politics." He touched her cheek. "You deserve more, milady."

Shivering under his caress, Kassandra nodded. "We leave soon," she whispered.

His heart cracked and he looked at her with confusion. Why were her words like a knife plunged into his gut? "Good," he forced himself to reply.

Kassandra looked away.

"Until our ride?" he reminded her.

She tilted her head and gazed directly into his murky green eyes. "Until we meet again," she said suggestively.

He gave her a funny look, then nodded and walked quickly away, missing Kassandra's wickedly gleaming eyes.

Cadedryn entered the village seeking his tigress while shaking off the unwelcome surge of jealousy about Lady Kassandra. How could two such entirely different women send him into such turmoil? It was uncanny and completely unnerving.

Turning down two streets, he located the tavern and ducked inside the shadowed entryway.

The tavern keeper hustled over. "Milord!"

"A room has been reserved in my name," Cadedryn informed him, then handed him a coin.

"Indeed! Upstairs and to the left. A lovely lady, indeed!"

Cadedryn took the stairs quickly, then strode to the

door the man had indicated. His heart thumping, he took a stabilizing breath, then flung the door open.

A long, red tapered candle burned on the table, its light barely illuminating the room. Cadedryn closed the door behind him and padded inside. The candle wavered, then burned brighter, shining on a pair of red stockings that lay draped over the bedsheet.

Cadedryn pivoted, searching the dark corners for his tigress, but to no avail. His heart thundered and blood rushed through his temples. Where was she? Why was she leading him on this merry chase? With slow, deliberate steps, he approached the bed, knowing he would find another letter.

This time he tore it open, his amusement beginning to change to ire. Enough was enough!

The market, it read. *The glove maker's stall.*

And at the bottom, a hint of encouragement . . . *getting close.*

He burned the missive in the candle flame, watching the white parchment blacken and curl as he debated his next move. He was not a puppy to be led by a string. She should not be taunting him thus. She should make herself available like a good, obedient mistress. But beneath his anger was a grudging salute. If she thought to get his full attention, she definitely had it.

He wound his way out of the tavern and navigated the streets, still littered with the remnants of last night's revelry. There were two markets in the village, one for the villagers where fruits, vegetables and common goods were sold. The other contained fancy items for the ladies of the castle and the visiting dignitaries. The Ladies' Market, as it was called, was known throughout the kingdom for its exceptional wares, for only master tradesmen were allowed to hawk their goods there.

Scottish wool from fine merino sheep was displayed in several stages of refinement from large bags, to cards, to spools and ultimately to final skeins of yarn or thread. There were metalworkers displaying tables of girdles, headbands and belts. Jewelers offered set and unset stones as well as a few elaborate examples of their commissioned work.

The streets of the Ladies' Market were filled with ladies and gentlemen casually strolling along the rows. A few men carried packages while many ladies fingered items of interest. As Cadedryn weaved through the throng to locate the glove makers, a cut garnet amulet caught his eye. The reddish color gleamed in the sunshine like a pair of cat eyes. As he looked closer, he saw that the piece had been skillfully shaped into the form of a cat.

"I'll take this," he said as he handed the jeweler several coins. "And the gold chain."

"Beautiful purchase, milord."

Cadedryn nodded. "Where are the glove makers?"

"Over there." The jeweler motioned. "Next row."

Cadedryn walked around to the last rows, but was flummoxed when he saw three stands. He was scanning the tabletops, searching for a note, when he was appalled to see Lady Kassandra once again. She was staring at him quizzically.

His face drained of color. Why was she here? What if she saw his missive and read it?

"Lord Caenmore," Kassandra said in a surprised tone. "Did your meeting end so quickly?" In her hand she held a pair of pink gloves that matched the silken mantle on her head.

Ignoring her question, he started to turn away, but

she stopped him by laying a bare hand on his arm. "Don't let me be a distraction. You were clearly searching for something or someone. Perhaps I can help? Are you looking for a pair of gloves for Lady Corine?"

Her touch was light, but it sent tiny shock waves over his skin. He took a deep breath, reminding himself that she was not his tigress. She was a prim virgin with a ludicrous dream of finding her true love in the one man who had no desire to love. He should not react to her with similar sexual interest just because her face was similar to his mistress's.

"No, not for Corine," he mumbled.

"No? Then for whom?" She lifted an arched eyebrow, secretly laughing at his obvious discomfort.

He flushed and quickly reversed his statement, aware that he had no other excuse for shopping in this aisle. "I mean, yes. I was looking for a present for her."

"Indeed! Well, then, what about these lovely white gloves with the silver buttons? No? Too youthful? How about this gray crocheted pair? No, too dowdy for her." Kassandra ran her fingers along the rows, reveling in Cadedryn's distress. This was so much fun! "Oh!" she cried as Cadedryn tried to move away. "What an awful color! Red! Why would anyone wear *red* gloves?"

Cadedryn froze and stared at the pair in Kassandra's hand. The corner of a white parchment peeked out from under the pearl buttons, and he swallowed, wanting to snatch the item from the lady's hands.

"Remove these immediately!" Kassandra called to the vendor. "You insult the good ladies of the court by displaying such vulgarity." She coughed to stifle her laugh at the look of horror on Cadedryn's face.

"Wait!" he said as the vendor reached for the offending articles. "Let me see them first."

"No," Kassandra replied as she tossed them over the table. "I insist that you find something more suitable for your lady. How about these?"

Cadedryn practically ripped the pair from the vendor's hands. "I will choose my own gifts," he grumbled. "Good day, milady." He tossed Lady Kassandra an angry glance and flung some coins at the seller.

Kassandra smiled at him. She opened her eyes wide and batted her eyelashes while offering a ladylike inclination of her head.

It was the gleeful glimmer in her eyes that made Cadedryn pause. He narrowed his gaze suspiciously. "Are you laughing at me?" he asked in a warning tone.

"Heavens no! What would I have to laugh about?" She turned her back to hide the quiver on her lips. If she didn't leave soon, she would give away her secret!

Cadedryn stared at her back, aware of the slender curve of her shoulders. Shoulders he wanted to shake!

"I have to be going," Kassandra mumbled as she hurried away. "Have a good day."

"And you as well," he replied without thinking, his mind spinning. Lady Kassandra was the most unpredictable creature he had ever encountered. From spitting hellion to teasing pixie, she was continuously portraying different sides of her perplexing personality.

He clenched his hands around the pair of gloves and heard the crinkle of paper. Abruptly reminded of his quest, he dropped his gaze from Lady Kassandra. His tigress was exciting and sexually interesting, and far more comprehensible. She had clear needs and desires, and she offered specific enticements. He wanted that certainty, that predictability. He nodded, convincing himself. But he had to force himself not to look after the retreating form of Lady Kassandra.

Chapter 15

The chapel bell tower. He caught his breath at the audacity of his tigress's next clue. How had she been able to sneak up into the bell tower and leave a piece of her under linens in a sanctuary? Or was she, perhaps, waiting for him there?

His groin twitched and he peered over the village rooftops toward the chapel spire. Could she be watching him right now? He shoved the gloves into his inner tunic, next to the other items he had collected along the way, and hurried out of the market. If she wasn't there, he was going to explode.

A street urchin sprang out from behind a pile of logs and clung to his leg.

Cadedryn was forced to an abrupt stop and shook his leg. "Go away, you pest!" he shouted, but before he could pull the urchin off, the boy scrambled away. Cadedryn stared after him, his brows drawn. The child had not asked for money, nor tried to steal anything.

Shrugging, Cadedryn resumed his quick stride, his gaze fixed on the spire on the far side of town. With his rapid pace, he would be there in minutes.

Suddenly, a flower cart barreled out of an alley and crashed directly in front of him. Cadedryn jumped back. "What idiocy is this!" he yelled when he saw the same urchin running away. This time he was considerably delayed as he was confronted with a wailing flower girl, who was alternately tearing at her hair and clasping her hands in distress.

Unable to bear her antics, Cadedryn gave her a coin and retreated a block to circle widely around the mound of broken debris, spilled dirt and wilting flowers.

His impatience soared and he mentally berated the street urchin for being such an annoyance, wondering at his motivation.

Up ahead, he spotted the chapel. Unlike the church at the castle, this sanctuary was still under construction, although the villagers were already using it for their services. It was made of gray stone and had a series of wide steps rising to its iron door. There were arched alcoves along the sides, some containing colored glass while others were still empty of adornment. The incomplete frontage should have made the place look forlorn. Instead, it seemed haphazardly welcoming, its jumbled outline gently inviting.

Cadedryn slowed his approach, noticing the urchin shadowing him. He spun around and glared at the boy. "What is your purpose?"

The boy slid to a stop several feet out of Cadedryn's reach. He shuffled his feet, then glanced up at the chapel bell tower and nodded, but as Cadedryn followed his gaze, the boy scampered off.

Far above, seated in the archway holding the iron bell, sat his elusive mistress.

The urchin forgotten, Cadedryn stared up at the flame-haired siren who had obsessed him. Her scent, her warmth . . . her brilliantly blue eyes were invading his thoughts and making him oblivious to all else.

The memory of her skin against his made him hot and he took a deep breath. She had led him on a merry chase, but he was ready to wrest back control.

Mounting the steps in one long leap, he yanked open the heavy doors as if they weighed nothing. His footsteps echoed on the stone floor. Rows of wooden pews hindered his progress and he had to skirt along the wall opposite the bell tower door. Growling with impatience, he cut through the pews, careful to avoid a series of small basins.

"Tiger kitten!" he called out.

A musical tinkling answered him and he peered upward, trying to locate the sound. He stopped short, stunned to see over a hundred bells strung along the length of the upper supports of the church. Sprawled along a wooden beam, holding a tiny bell, was Kaitlynn.

"Have I found my treasure?" he asked, his mouth curving into a smile. "Or are you going to force me to seek more bits of frippery?"

"Come on up," she purred. "Think you can catch me?" A wisp of wind rustled through the chimes, accenting the sensuous invitation.

He leapt onto the back of a pew, then jumped for a low crossbeam. After swinging for a moment, he pulled himself up and swung his legs over the beam, then turned and stared challengingly at his mistress. "Why are there chimes in the chapel?"

Kassandra smiled and ran her finger through a set of bells near her. "I heard that they each signify the wedding of a maid to her groom."

"Or mayhap the bedding of a bride by her husband," he murmured huskily.

She squealed and sprang to her feet, balancing with both arms outstretched. Casting a quick glance over her shoulder, she ran nimbly to the far side of the chapel roof.

Cadedryn rose more slowly, cautiously. " 'Tis a far

way down," he warned. "You should wait for me where you are."

She grinned and reached under her skirt. With a few tugs, she untied her petticoat and draped it over the beam. Pointing her bare toes, she wriggled them in his direction, then scampered to another beam and waved at him.

"If you have undertaken this ruse to make me forget your assault upon my person just yesterday, you have succeeded."

"More than forgetting, I want to make you remember."

He jumped to the beam on which she stood by leaping over the one in between. The vibration caused by his heavier weight sent the chimes tinkling.

She gasped and shrank back. "How did you do that?"

He stalked forward, his powerful frame pressing hers back along the narrow perch. "You sent me along a merry chase, but I intend to claim my prize."

She bumped against the stone wall, clutching the bell in her fist. She stared at him, her heart pounding with excitement. She had meant to arouse his slumbering passions, but now she trembled. He reminded her of a green-eyed McCat stalking its prey.

She glanced right and left, seeking another beam to race along, but he bore down upon her and trapped her with both hands on either side of her waist.

" 'Twas a fine game, tigress, but one I am about to finish."

Kassandra's heart throbbed as she stared into his blazing eyes. He was a firestorm and she had fanned him to life. She knew that, at this moment, he had forgotten his earldom. He had pushed aside his determination to regain his familial power. Right now he was balancing on the beam of a half-built chapel and chasing after a half-dressed tigress as a hundred chimes whispered encouragement.

She was his entire focus.

The knowledge made her breathless and she swayed, feeling faint.

He pushed against her full length, holding her upright, then shoved his knee between her thighs. "Open for me."

She shook her head. "I'll fall!"

"You came to me the other night, and now you entice me with an erotic game of cat and mouse." He reached between them, untied his breeches and pulled her skirt free. Nothing remained of her under linens, and he smiled in satisfaction at her vulnerability. "You are no longer in control," he informed her. "Obey me."

She nodded, her mouth dry.

"Wrap your legs around my waist."

She cast a quick glance down at the stone floor, very much aware of the precariousness of their footing so high above the ground.

Gripping a rafter with one hand, he smiled slyly. "You thought to outwit me? To outplay me?"

She yelped in surprise as he pulled one of her legs up with his free hand. Balancing on the other foot, she teetered. When his fingers touched her intimately, she felt like swooning. "Oh heavens!" she gasped. "I can't concentrate!"

"Then don't." His fingers swept over her swollen nub, then tickled her thigh, urging her to open wider.

She stared at him, knowing that if she let go of the wall, she would be completely dependent upon him. Only he could prevent them from crashing to the flagstones.

"Trust me."

She wrapped her arms around his neck and lifted her other leg. With both thighs wrapped around his strong body, she felt his shaft press against her. They both moaned, feeling an intense connection. Trust in each other. Passion with each other. Games fled and plans disappeared. As if they were truly in heaven and angels were caressing them with golden bells, she felt transported.

Holding the rafter with one hand and supporting her with his other hand wrapped around her back, he pushed partway into her. He groaned again as the sensitive tip of his penis burned with her heat. "I want you," he rumbled.

"I want you," she answered breathlessly, tightening her legs around his waist.

The chimes echoed in the high ramparts, merging their music with Cadedryn's and Kassandra's heavy breathing.

He shoved her back against the stone and pressed deeper inside. "Take me," he commanded. "Take all of me."

She arched her hips, mutely accepting him within her. She threaded her fingers through his hair, then dug her nails into his back and pulled him closer.

He responded by angling his hips and sliding deeper, measure by measure, until the long length of his shaft was enfolded in her pulsing sheath. He felt her insides clench and sudden moisture proved her excitement, exciting him in turn. He rotated, sliding the tip of his penis along her ribbed channel, hearing her responding gasp as he struggled to control his own responses.

"Yes!" she cried as she locked her ankles together. "More!"

"Slower," he demanded. "Take your time. Feel me."

She moaned and tossed her head back and forth, her ecstasy spiraling upward despite his caution. Her motions rocked the beam, sending the chimes jingling, drowning her passionate cries. "More! Now! I don't want to wait."

He swelled, his rod responding to her command as his passion mounted. Her moans echoed around him, reverberating in beautiful harmony like a church choir. The sounds guided him onward, and he stroked quicker and harder, forgetting his dangerous footing. He shifted to get more leverage and his foot slipped, sending a shower of dust far below.

She pulled him back, the weight of her body keeping him balanced until he regained a foothold, but neither paused in their motions. She scratched his back, urging him on, and her thighs quivered with a mixture of weakness and ascending passion. "Now!" she screamed. "Now!"

With two, quick strokes, he sent her tumbling over the edge of passion's precipice; then he leapt after her, his buttocks bunching, his arms rippling and his essence pouring deep within her.

Though they were frozen in ecstasy's grip, they felt as if they were falling. The wind swept over their sweaty faces and their arms quivered. The bells rang around them, reverberating off the high stone ceiling. Their minds swirled as if the world were spinning in huge circles around them and they were the only two people alive. For several, heart-stopping moments, their souls floated free.

Then a large bang startled them both back to reality.

Snapping their eyes open, they looked down below and beheld a village family entering the chapel.

"I be wantin' pink flowers on the altar and white bows on the pews," the young girl said to her mother. "And a set o' chimes bigger than any other!"

The mother nodded, but the father shook his head. "No flowers," he responded gruffly. "How do ya be thinkin' we can afford flowers?"

The girl's eyes filled with tears and she looked pleadingly at her mother.

"Harry," the mother said sharply. "What's be getting' into ya? 'Tis yur daughter's wedding day. Ya can get a few flowers for the lass!"

Kassandra and Cadedryn looked at each other in shock.

Kassandra slid her legs down and covered her mouth with her hand, taking care not to shake the beam and send the chimes tinkling. Still dizzy from her orgasm, she found it nearly impossible not to laugh aloud.

Cadedryn shook his head, although he, too, was finding it difficult to pull free of his kitten's inner embrace. He did not want this moment to end. He wanted to feel the connection of their bodies and the merging of their spirits.

Kassandra nudged him back one step and carefully smoothed her skirts, then reached to adjust his breeches.

He grimaced, his shaft still sensitive and eager for her touch, but when he caught her mischievous gaze, he smiled. "You minx," he mouthed. "What do we do now?" He shifted over to allow her a hand purchase, and a spray of dirt again trickled through the air.

"Fine!" the father grumbled. "But only a few. Two or three ought to do it."

"Just wait," Kassandra mouthed back. "They will be gone soon."

"Ten," the girl insisted as she brushed the dirt off her sleeve and glanced around.

"Five."

"Eight. Eight is a good number," the daughter cajoled, the dirt forgotten as she sensed her father giving in.

The father sighed in defeat. "Eight."

She squealed with delight and grabbed his hand. "What a wonderful father ya are! I'll show you where we will serve the feast." She began dragging her father forward as her mother smiled and followed. "I be wantin' a whole goose."

"What?" he shouted, but then the family exited through the side door and the rest of their plans became inaudible.

Cadedryn chuckled as he touched his tigress's nose. "You got us into this," he whispered. "How do you propose we get out?"

"We climb down," she replied tartly. "Kindly move back so I can retrieve my petticoat."

He shook his head. "I think we should leave it there and let the curator wonder at how it got up there. Maybe the lasses will start leaving petticoats instead of bells.

"No!" Kassandra gasped. "That would be . . . be . . ."

"Disrespectful? What do you think the curator would think if he found out that we had christened his chapel in our unique way?"

Unable to form an adequate response, Kassandra

searched for the safest way down. Tucking her skirt up into her waistband, she carefully lowered herself from one row of beams to the next until she reached the scaffolding bolted against the incomplete wall. Aware that he was following close behind, she scrambled to the ground and quickly adjusted her skirts.

He laughed and pulled her in for a kiss. "Now I know why I find you so unusual. No lady would have done what you just did."

Kassandra froze, her heart skidding to a stop. The pleasure of the moment fled as she was forced to remember her charade.

"Don't look so crestfallen," he said softly. "I like you as you are. Look, I bought you a present." He pulled out the garnet charm and held it out to her. "I want you to be my mistress. I want to give you a cottage and take care of you."

"A mistress? A woman seeking no commitment and wanting nothing but your cock and coin?" She snatched the necklace and bunched it in her fist, her blue eyes flashing. "Did you think I did this for want of funds?"

He stepped back, surprised by her vehemence. "I don't think of you as just a mistress. I am fond of you and look forward to spending time with you. There are many things I cannot explain to you, but suffice it to say, this is the best arrangement. It will serve everyone's needs."

Kassandra tossed her red hair, her temper rising. The rules Kalial had tried to instill in her dictated that she force her temper into submission, quash her normal response and try to act with ladylike maturity. But as the tiger kitten, she could be herself, a flame-haired hellion. She could act as wild and temperamental as she wished. And right now, she wanted to exact her revenge.

"I'm done with you," she growled. "No commitment? Just flesh and pleasure? Very well, then one day I might let you know if I desire to be with you again."

Cadedryn frowned and gripped her arm. He had opened his mouth to argue with her when the wedding planners reentered the chapel.

"Oh!" the daughter shrieked at her father. "Thank you!"

The father glanced with weary resignation at the couple standing in the pews. "Anything for me daughter." He sighed helplessly.

Kassandra took Cadedryn's momentary distraction to yank free of his grasp.

"Meet me tomorrow in the meadow beyond the crofter's hut," he commanded, although his voice sounded faintly desperate.

She blew him a kiss as she shrugged noncommittally, then strode out of the chapel, leaving him standing alone with no assurances and a wealth of unsatisfied needs.

Chapter 16

"She is driving me insane!" Cadedryn grumbled as he slammed his fist against the gate to the men's courtyard and kicked it open. As he and Curtis walked inside, Cadedryn shook his head. He couldn't think straight. He couldn't think of anything at all but her. She was like one of the magical druids that, once seen, were able to control one's mind and soul. Yet he couldn't decide which one of them was causing him more distress. Both Lady Kassandra and his tiger kitten were deliberately stirring his body and mind.

No, not Lady Kassandra. She was not to blame. She was too sweet to be knowingly churning his soul, but his tigress . . . Now, that woman was doing everything with forethought and planning.

He snorted as he picked up a sword and took a few practice swings. He and Kaitlynn were well matched. But, then, why did he constantly think about Kassandra?

"Who is driving you insane?" Curtis asked.

"The women. All of them," Cadedryn answered angrily.

"Lady Corine awaited your attentions today," his friend reminded him.

"I don't want her," Cadedryn whispered, then turned to his friend. "I don't know whom I should marry, but I don't want Corine. Kaitlynn is wild and exciting and . . . and . . ."

Curtis stared at his foster brother in horror. "She is only a lowborn girl with a pretty face. How can you even mention her and marriage in one breath? Everything you have ever wanted lies within your grasp!"

Cadedryn shrugged as he lunged at a stuffed burlap figure mounted on a stake. "Have I not labored under similar aspersions all my life? Have I not been called much worse?"

Curtis stepped in front of Cadedryn and gripped his shoulders. "You are about to erase all of that. Success is only months away! The king is pleased with you and has given you your title. With luck, his benevolence will wipe away any stigma previously associated with your family. That is your goal. After you wed Corine, all will be as it should have been. It is what my father, *your foster father*, wants. 'Tis what Lady Morgana wants, and the king has indicated his approval, as well. Marry Lady Corine. Wed her and put this flame-haired woman out of your mind!"

Cadedryn gently disengaged his friend's hands and leaned against his sword. "Curtis, you don't understand. It is not just her; it is both of them. When I am with either of them, I forget all this. It doesn't matter who I am or what name I am called. I feel renewed."

Curtis spun and slammed his fist against the wall. "No!" he shouted. "You can not do this! You cannot destroy everything! Your actions affect me, Lady Corine, and all who have supported you in this battle. Think of Lady Morgana and my father. Do our needs not matter to you?"

Cadedryn looked at Curtis. "Why is it so important to you?"

"*You* are important to me. My father took you in and treated you like one of his sons. Are you prepared to tell him that you want to throw it all away on some wench? Just like your father did?"

Cadedryn's eyes turned cold. "While I value your advice, my life is my own. 'Tis clear that we cannot speak of this matter." He slid his sword in its leather sheath. "I have an engagement to take a ride with Lady Kassandra. Perhaps she will understand my feelings, for she understands love. Let us forget our disagreement and remain friends."

Curtis clenched his teeth, his jaw ticking. He glared into Cadedryn's green eyes, trying to intimidate him with the force of his stare.

Cadedryn stared back, his gaze steady and sure.

Finally, Curtis lowered his eyes and mumbled assent. "Very well, Cadedryn. Friends as always."

Cadedryn grinned and slapped him on the back. "Good! I will see you later this eve."

Cadedryn was whistling when he approached the stable and saw Lady Kassandra already waiting for him. He had sent a note requesting her attendance and was inordinately pleased that she had agreed to meet him for the promised ride. She was dressed in a soft lavender gown, wearing a dark purple mantle clasped to her head with a silver coronet. Her thick black hair was visible beneath the soft fabric and her pale skin gleamed in the sunlight.

"Milady." He bowed. "You are prompt."

"And you are tardy," she replied.

"My apologies. Shall we ride in the forest or along the hills? I would like to spend some time with you without an audience," he said quietly. "Would you accept riding without a chaperone?"

"As long as you promise to act like a gentleman," she answered, her voice colored with wry sarcasm.

As Cadedryn swung up on his stallion, he looked at her with amusement. "Why are you annoyed with me today? Don't you have some kind thoughts for me?"

Kassandra looked ahead, avoiding his dancing gaze. "Not this morn."

"Yes, you do," he said softly. "I don't believe that you have forgotten your dreams. You tried to fool me the other night, but I think I have seen through your charade."

She harrumphed and mounted her mare sidesaddle with the assistance of a groom. "I doubt that," she grumbled.

"Don't you find it difficult to continue such animosity? It must be a struggle to maintain such sharp wit at my expense when your heart is kind and forgiving to all others."

"Hardly. You make an easy target."

He laughed and motioned for her to take the lead. "And you awoke with a burr in your side. Let us ride and allow the winds to clear your mind."

She rode out of the yard, spending some moments to ensure that her mare's injuries were not paining her too much for light exercise. After several minutes of silence, Kassandra relaxed and glanced behind her at Cadedryn. "You have not asked for the knife."

He shook his head to dispel his thoughts, temporarily distracted by the sway of Kassandra's hips on her mare. "Do you have it?"

She slowed her mount and pulled the dirk from her pocket. "Here. Now you can achieve all you want. You are an earl and you will soon have Lady Corine's hand in marriage. Then you will unite your lands and become one of the most powerful earls in the king-

dom. I . . . I hope that by returning the blade to you
I have helped. I know 'tis hard for you to understand,
but I searched for the owner of this knife because I
feared the outcome of one of my dreams. There are
powerful forces within this dirk . . . It came to me
from the other world and has brought us together, but
you are still in danger. I pray that this weapon will
protect you."

He took the engraved dirk and turned it over in
his hand. "Lady Kassandra," he said slowly, "I have
something to ask you."

"Indeed?"

He reached over and pulled her horse to a stop. His
gaze swept over her features. "You look so much like
each other," he said.

Kassandra's heart pounded and she held her breath.
Had he discovered the truth? "Like whom?" she
struggled to ask through a closed throat.

"Like your sister Kaitlynn. You are a lady, whereas
she is not. But you both have made me question my
ambitions."

Her face drained of all color and she swayed in
the saddle.

"I want to tell you, because you are the only person
who might understand me. You spoke of your dreams
and true love. You know what it is to feel such emotions. I need your help."

"My help?" she coughed. "How do you require
my help?"

"I no longer wish to marry Corine Fergus. You once
told me that a cold bedfellow would not compensate
for a lofty title, and I have begun to understand what
you meant."

The blood rushed back into her cheeks and Kassandra saw spots dancing in front of her eyes. Her lips trembled. Swallowing several times, she cast about for an answer.

"You have made me reevaluate my aspirations. All this struggling for recognition is pointless if I am unhappy."

Kassandra clucked to her horse, desperately sorting her emotions.

Cadedryn followed her. "What should I do?"

Kassandra glanced back. "Why ask me?"

"I need your advice."

She looked at him in stunned disbelief.

"You are the one who believes in following your heart. I thought you would understand."

"I cannot guide you."

He glared at her. "What game is this?" he said with a raised voice. "You pledged your everlasting devotion to me only days ago, and now you hesitate to take advantage of my indecision? I thought you would be ecstatic! Are you not going to demand that we wed? Are you not willing to ignore the consequences and declare your love?"

She bit her lip, her blue eyes shimmering with tears. "Cadedryn," she whispered. "I can't help you because I don't know what to do anymore. I don't want you to leave all that you desire just for an emotion that may wane. Love cannot be created from the mists of a hopeful dream. You told me that I was being childish and naive, and *you* were right. What do we really know about each other?"

"I know you are a good woman with a gentle soul. I feel I can trust you as I can trust no other."

Pain knifed through her as she remembered his words to his tigress. They had also spoken of trust up in the rafters of the church, yet now he spoke of it again to her. Her gaze narrowed. "Am I the only woman who is important to you?"

Cadedryn turned away, his stomach roiling with tension. He had such conflicting emotions. Kassandra was the type of woman he could feel close to, whereas Kaitlynn was the kind of woman that made him forget everything. One made him calm, while the other made his heart thunder. If only both women were merged into one . . .

Kassandra waited, hoping he would tell her the truth. If he did, she would relent. She would tell him the truth, in time, and explain why she had undertaken her dual identities. They would start anew and learn to love each other as she had originally hoped.

"Never mind," he muttered. "I am speaking out of turn. Forget my ramblings and let us enjoy the afternoon. You deserve much better than me, for I do not understand what I feel. I am full of contradictions."

Kassandra leaned forward. "Tell me," she replied urgently. "You said we should have trust between us."

Cadedryn flicked his hand in dismissal. "No. I do not want to hurt you." He released her horse's reins and clucked to his stallion.

Kassandra closed her eyes, willing away her tears. He was correct in one thing. She did understand love, but now she understood that love was not only about her emotions; it was also about caring for the other person's needs and desires. If she said that they should marry, he might agree, but in doing so, he would be abandoning the goals he held dear.

And whom would he be agreeing to wed? Lady Kassandra, the black-haired woman in disguise, or Kaitlynn, the flame-haired temptress who used her body to draw him close?

Both women were, in part, an illusion.

"Come," Cadedryn called out to her, unaware of her thoughts. "Forget what I said. Let us enjoy the pleasures of an afternoon ride and picnic, for I have a basket of cheese and wine that the kitchen servants packed for us and I do not want it to go to waste."

Kassandra nodded hesitantly.

He smiled. "Don't look so anxious. I am the one who should be tied in knots, not you. A man unsure of his path is like a ship adrift without a rudder. I need your calming influence to remind me to stay the course."

They rode in silence, following the same path that led to the crofter's hut before angling off in a new direction. Sunshine trickled through the trees and laid flickering patterns of gold upon the forest floor. Up ahead, an open meadow shimmered with yellow tansy and purple heather and undulating rows of fragrant green grasses. Even the birds trilled joyous songs of summertime happiness.

Kassandra ignored it all. Butterflies danced in the pit of her stomach and her palms became damp with sweat. A new emotion began to simmer to the surface. She felt jealous.

Jealous of Kaitlynn.

Why hadn't he told her the truth about the other woman? Why was he hiding his thoughts and actions? Was he fonder of the tiger kitten than of the lady? Did he not feel the same depth of attraction to the lady as he did to Kaitlynn?

"Is something bothering you?" Cadedryn asked as he pulled his horse to a stop and dismounted. He looped the reins over a branch and held his hands up to assist her descent.

"No," Kassandra replied sharply as she jumped to

the ground on her own and twitched her skirts in irritation.

He raised an eyebrow and offered his elbow to help her navigate a large log.

"I don't need your help," she snapped. "I am perfectly able to climb over a log on my own. Is that our destination?" she asked as she pointed through the trees toward the open meadow.

He laughed. "Do you reserve this brand of affection solely for me?"

She couldn't stop from curling her lips in a faint smile. "I am being rather rude, aren't I?"

"Just a tad."

They exited the shimmering shadows and stepped out into the bright sunshine. He touched the wrinkle between her brows and cocked his head in inquiry. "Won't you forgive me? You said that you will be leaving soon. Let us separate on good terms."

She smiled.

"Here." He found a smooth area free of rocks, then unfolded the blanket covering the picnic basket and snapped it open. "Sit, rest and relax. We will eat cheese, drink wine and say our good-byes." He clasped his hands to his heart and acted as if he were swooning with despair.

She couldn't help it. She giggled.

He raised his brows several times, then swept her a flourishing bow. "Milady?"

"You can be surprisingly amusing," she relented as she sat down. "Every now and then I see a glimpse of your humor."

"What are friends for but to amuse and entertain each other?"

"Friends?"

He touched her cheek, noticing a small freckle peeking through the layers of heavy cream. "Aye. Good friends." He stared at the freckle as a slight frown furrowed his brow.

She sighed and leaned back on her hands. He was right. All this deception had been exhausting. What harm would it cause if they simply relaxed for the afternoon and enjoyed the sunshine?

He shook his head to clear his stray thoughts, then began unpacking the basket.

Several hours and many cups of wine later, the two lay in the grass and stared up at the billowing clouds floating across the blue expanse. "I am not fond of court," Kassandra admitted. "I much prefer the beauty of the forest or the magic of the meadow. All the primping required for the castle functions is simply dull and useless."

He turned and faced her. "You stun me, Lady Kassandra. You are always dressed so finely and you wear such formal attire, even here far away from everyone. If you dislike it, why do you still wear your mantle?"

Kassandra touched the sides of her face where her silken hairpiece covered her wig. "I don't like my hair."

He looked closer at a black ringlet dangling from her temple. This close, he could see how coarse it was. Her words reveberated in his head, echoing another woman's lament. Kaitlynn didn't like her hair either. How odd these women could be.

He returned his gaze to the sky. "Your hair does not matter to me," he said. "And anyone who grows to love you will not care about its color or texture." He took her hand in his and held his scarred hand up to the sunshine. "I, too, have physical attributes I dislike. You initially recognized me because of the scar that runs across my hand. Once a lass told me it was the ugliest scar she had ever seen."

With her other hand, Kassandra traced the scar from his finger to his wrist.

An unexpected shiver rippled through him at her gentle touch. His hand twitched, and he had to force his body not to react to her caress. Her hands were as warm as his tigress's and her fingers stroked him with similar sensuality. He took a deep breath to steady his suddenly pounding heart.

As he tried unobtrusively to disengage their fingers, Kassandra held his grasp.

"What happened? How did you receive such a devastating injury?" she asked.

"If you truly had dreams about me, you would already know," he teased. Her thigh felt warm near his and he shifted away, mildly uncomfortable with the sensation.

Kassandra let go of his hand, then rolled to her side and rose on one elbow. She stared down at him, her face serious. "Do you really want me to answer you?"

Her blue eyes glimmered with reflected sunlight and her long lashes framed her eyes with rich, auburn highlights. Enchanted, he gently touched the eyelash tips. "The sun's glow makes your eyelashes red," he murmured.

She blinked quickly and ducked her head, plunging her face in shadow. "I do know how you injured your hand. At least, I used to think I did. But I am beginning to understand less and less of what I thought I knew."

He chuckled and reached behind her for a long strand of grass, which he placed between his teeth. "That, my dear, happens to us all."

She smiled and lay back down with her eyes closed

as she conjured up her dream. She remembered the forest and the moonlight. She recalled the clang of sword against sword and the tang of blood. Pushing her thoughts further, she envisioned Cadedryn's scar and let it fill her mind. She saw a new courtyard. A younger, angrier Cadedryn and an image hovering behind him. "Your father . . ." she began. "It has something to do with your father."

The smile on his lips faded and he stared at her profile.

"You were so angry after the death of your father. You could not get the memory of his blood out of your thoughts. You struggled constantly against someone . . . another boy. He resented you and you distrusted him. One day he ambushed you from behind the shelter of a large oak tree. He attacked you with his sword and sliced your hand all the way up to your shoulder. The blood . . . so much blood . . . you exploded with rage. You drew your sword and lunged for him, wanting to kill him."

He shivered with fear. How did she know details he had never shared with anyone? To prophecy was akin to witchcraft.

"The boy is now a man and he is connected to your father's death. Am I right?" she asked hesitantly, seeing the shock in his eyes.

"No," he replied harshly. "That boy did slice my hand a year later to the day of my father's death, but he is not the one who murdered my father. I know because when I pinned him to the ground that day, he begged for my mercy. We swore everlasting kinship and from that moment forward we have never wavered in our loyalty to each other. If he knew something about my father's death, he would have told me."

She shook her head. "I felt the malevolent spirit of your father's murderer. I know he is involved."

Cadedryn rose and stood over her, his enjoyment in the afternoon quickly vanishing. "You are wrong, Kassandra. Please do not talk like this. If others heard you, you would be in grave danger. The time of the druids and the soothsayers is long past. We live in a Christian society that decries such abilities."

She stood up as well and stared at him with fervent intensity. "Please hear me, for you may still be in danger. I see a man in my vision. He is tall, with dark hair and brown eyes. He is a strong warrior and as experienced in warfare as you."

"Kassandra!" Cadedryn said sharply, his fury evident. What she had described about his injury had been far too close to the truth, making her warning seem all too real. He reached for her and yanked her next to him. "Stop! Your dreams will frighten people. 'Tis time you kept them to yourself. My injury had nothing to do with my father's murder. Curtis McCafferty and I fought, and his blade slipped. He never meant to maim me. It was a mere accident between two boys and I forgave him that same day."

Kassandra lowered her gaze in confusion. "I was so sure . . ."

"So you see, your vision is once again misguided. There was no malevolent spirit to blame, simply unsteady footing and a pair of untrained youths."

Kassandra's mind spun crazily as she tried to reconcile this new information with her dream. "It must be someone else . . ." she whispered. "Someone who is connected to him . . ." She looked up, fear making her eyes wide.

He grunted and began retrieving the picnic items. "You are the one in danger. 'Twas you who was attacked, not I." He paused and looked at her with a flicker of sorrow. "You are an enigma, Lady Kassandra. Just as I think we are becoming friends and I am enjoying your company, you start spouting these dire prophecies. I have no desire to hear about them again. Do I make myself clear? No more dreams."

Kassandra struggled to clear her mind of the swirling images. She shook her head. It didn't make sense, but then, nothing was making sense. "I fear for you." She touched the dirk he had sheathed in his belt. "Keep this near, for it came to me through my dreams so that I could bring it back to you. You must use it well, for it is blessed with your guardian spirit. It contains magic."

"Stop! Nothing more!" he threatened.

"Do you know the meaning of my name?" Kassandra whispered.

He stepped back and glared at her.

"Kassandra tried to warn her people of danger, but no one believed her. She perished because of their arrogance." She rose and composed her face. "But I will not perish, nor will I let your ignorance triumph. Listen to my words of warning."

"I am not in danger. No one benefits from my death."

Kassandra turned away. "As no one benefited from your father's? Did that stop his murder? Mayhap fortune is not the motive for your family's tribulations. There are other, more compelling reasons—lust, jealousy, revenge. You are in grave danger."

As she strode away from him, he felt his stomach roll. Her words were so final. "From what?" he shouted after her.

She turned back and stared at him. "From someone. Someone close to you."

He rubbed his temples. "I do not know what parts of your dreams are real, but will it please you if I promise to listen and watch?" It did not matter what he thought of her notions. She was convinced that her dreams were true, and she spoke only because she cared.

She smiled and nodded. "Yes," she said softly, then turned and disappeared into the woods toward her horse.

He quickly packed the picnic items and followed her back to the horses. They rode in mutual uneasy silence until they reached the courtyard.

"Kassandra," he whispered as he handed her down for the final time.

She touched his lips with her finger. "Don't speak," she cautioned. "I have done what I came to do. You are warned. You have your knife." Her eyes glowed and she gave him a quick, impulsive hug. "Good-bye," she murmured. "I am going to leave tomorrow."

"Tomorrow?"

"Aye. There is nothing else for me to do here. Kalial will be relieved."

"We will not see each other again?" he asked.

"No."

He stared at her, his heart frozen, caught in an unfamiliar spasm of pain. It could not be. How could he wake up each morning knowing he would not talk to her that day? He thought briefly about Kaitlynn. Her beauty took him to pinnacles of desire he had never known existed, but she was not the one he wanted.

As Kassandra walked rapidly away, he noticed a strand of red hair clinging to his vest. His gaze snapped up and he stared after her, noting the sway of her hips and the golden hue to her arms, so unlike the pasty whiteness of her cheeks.

She had a freckle.

Black-haired women rarely had freckles.

His heart began to hammer. They looked so much alike . . . No. It could not be. He shook his head in denial and spun away, his emotions in turmoil.

Chapter. 17

"I am leaving for Aberdour Castle tomorrow," Cadedryn informed Curtis as he packed his saddlebags and organized his heavier trunks. They were in Cadedryn's room, but Cadedryn was feeling edgy and uncomfortable with his friend's hovering presence.

Cadedryn had achieved his goal of regaining his title. Now with Kassandra leaving and his decision not to pursue Lady Corine firming, he saw no reason to remain. Besides, after Kassandra's warnings, he felt that he could not trust anyone. It was time he returned to the familiarity of his own castle and regrouped.

"How could you?" Curtis accused. "Everything is so close to coming together just as we wished. Lady Corine . . . the king . . . your name and reputation . . . Why would you leave court at this crucial moment? Have you heard nothing of what I have said over the last two days? Is it that woman?"

Cadedryn peered out the window, his heart in chaos. Was he truly ready to throw everything away? "It is not just for her," he murmured. "I need time to reevaluate my plans. I'm seeing things . . . feeling things I don't understand. I have not been to Aberdour in years and the castle needs my presence, especially now that I am her earl. I am going to wait to decide upon my bride until after I have had some time to sort out my thoughts."

"Are you blind to the truth?" Curtis replied, his voice turning ugly. "Marrying Corine is critical to completing our plans and erasing your father's disgrace."

"Does it matter? I do not want to marry her. The king gave me my title without demanding I join our lands. Corine and I have no love for each other. It would not serve either of us to spend our lives in an unsatisfying union."

"You are making the same mistake your father made! How could you be such a fool?"

Cadedryn's eyes flared with anger and he spun to face his friend. "How could you have done this?" he shouted as he raised his scarred hand. "Why did you hate me so much when I came to your household?"

"I felt guilty!" Curtis shouted back.

"About what?"

Curtis slumped against the door. "About things I had done, feelings I had. But that is past us now. You know I am sorry. I didn't mean to cut you so deeply. It was an accident."

"Was it? Or did you intend to harm me, perhaps even to kill me? What about my father? Do you know something about his death you have withheld from me?"

"Why would you even think such a thing? Did one of *them* tell you that? Lady Kassandra? *Your tigress mistress?*"

Cadedryn laughed, but the humor did not reach his eyes. "It does not matter who suggested the thought. Swear to me that there is no basis of truth. Swear that you mean me no harm and that you are hiding nothing from me." He pulled his sword and pressed it against his friend's neck. His eyes narrowed and he gazed steadily into Curtis's terrified face.

"Of course I swear!" Curtis shouted. "My family took you in and my father treated you like a son. He treated you better than he treated his own flesh and blood. He even arranged for a marriage between you and my childhood companion!"

"Does that make you angry? Resentful? That a boy of mixed parentage will have greater power and glory than you? That I will marry Corine?" There was a long pause as Cadedryn stared at Curtis's angry face; then he dropped his sword and stepped away. "I apologize, foster brother," he said calmly. "I would have been angry as well. You have endured much."

Curtis flushed. "You should marry her. Until you do, the past will forever haunt us all."

"It will no longer haunt me," Cadedryn replied. "Perhaps you are the one who must learn to let the past rest."

Curtis turned away. "You are still leaving," he stated as he kicked one of Cadedryn's trunks.

"Aye."

"When?"

"Tonight."

Curtis took a deep breath. "You are right. It is time for me to realize that you have changed your mind, and no matter what I say, I will not be able to convince you otherwise."

"Do you care for Corine?" Cadedryn asked. "Is that why you are so concerned about her marriage?"

Curtis swallowed uncomfortably.

Cadedryn placed both hands on Curtis's shoulders. "Then ask for her yourself. Do not repeat *your* father's mistake and lose the woman you want."

Curtis nodded, then pointed at the dirk tucked in Cadedryn's belt. "That is your father's knife?"

Cadedryn drew it out and touched the engravings. "Lady Kassandra returned it to me."

"May I see it?"

Cadedryn handed the dirk over and resumed packing.

"Did she say more about Liam's murder?"

"Not enough to assist me," Cadedryn replied evasively as he checked his belongings once more.

" 'Tis a beautiful piece," Curtis said, returning it.

Cadedryn nodded, wrapped it in oilskin and placed it in his weapons trunk. As he withdrew his hand, a cold shadow brushed over Cadedryn's heart. Kassandra had warned him to keep the knife close, but did it really matter? What could one knife mean? He had others that were more serviceable which he always wore on his person when he traveled. The dirk was merely a piece of pounded steel, important only for memories of his father. There was no possibility of it being imbued with the spirit of a guardian.

Nonetheless, he shivered as he closed the trunk.

An hour later, as Cadedryn was directing the removal of his trunks and arranging for a convoy to bring them to his castle, his foster father knocked on his door.

"Enter," Cadedryn called out, then smiled in greeting as he beheld David McCafferty. "Laird," he acknowledged.

"Earl," David replied with a smile.

The men grinned at each other.

"You have come a long way since the day I came to take you to foster with me," David said as he leaned against the doorjamb.

"You gave me many skills. Because of your fostering, I learned to hone my swordsmanship and use it to benefit Scotland."

David nodded. "Curtis tells me that you are leaving for Aberdour."

"Aye."

"You should stay here. The king will not be pleased that you are abandoning court so quickly."

"The king wants me to settle any unrest in the Highlands. I cannot do that from here."

David sighed. "Is that your real reason?" he questioned.

Cadedryn turned toward a guard who was waiting for instructions. "Take my weapons trunk down to the stable where my wagon is being packed. Secure it well."

"Aye, milord."

David watched the guard descend with the trunk balanced on his shoulder, then looked penetratingly at his foster son.

"I have conflicting thoughts," Cadedryn admitted.

"I advise you to think carefully upon your decisions. Leaving court is unwise. Corine Fergus, and consequently her mother, will suffer insult."

"Nothing has been formalized, but I certainly have no intention of distressing either of the ladies. I simply need time to sort out my feelings and decide upon the best course of action to ensure my and Scotland's health and happiness."

David shrugged. "You will do as you wish, for you are no longer a youth whom I can mold or guide."

The easy friendliness on David's face shifted, revealing a hint of his anger, but before Cadedryn could comment, a sound outside the window made both men look down to the courtyard. The soldier with Cadedryn's chest was struggling to lift it into the wagon.

Lord Curtis was walking by and stopped to assist the man. He fiddled with the strap that held the trunk closed, tightened it, then appeared satisfied. The guard thanked him and Curtis strolled away as the soldier proceeded to secure the other trunks.

Cadedryn turned away from the window and placed a hand upon David's shoulder. "You are always welcome at Aberdour. Please come often to visit. No matter what happens."

The older man smiled. "Indeed, I will," he replied, but an undertone of harshness made his words sound more like a threat than a promise.

Late that night, well past the time when most of the castle inhabitants had fallen into a deep sleep, Kassandra tossed and turned, her dream full of angry faces and gleaming knives. The shadows shifted and elongated, then warped and twisted until she felt herself overtaken by their flickering shapes.

It was her forest, but as she struggled to push the murky shadows aside, everything began to change. She knew she was dreaming, but the colors became as vibrant as they were in the daytime. She could smell the pungent scent of pine needles and the musky smell of a meandering badger. Even the sounds of the birds became sharp. Instead of muted, echoing, and warbling tones, they turned crisp and vibrant.

Kassandra spun around, searching for affirmation that she was in a dream. Triu-cair stood beside her, his face tense. "This is a dream, isn't it?" she asked him.

Yes. But it is merging with real life. He scurried onto her shoulder. *I'm afraid.*

"You are never afraid. You have always protected me. You have guided me through the mists and never faltered. How can you be afraid?"

Triu-cair shivered and clung closer to her. *Look.*

Up ahead, in a meadow, they saw one man and one woman standing back to back. Kassandra squinted, trying to make out their identities. She gasped. "It's me! Me and Cadedryn!" She lifted her skirts and ran forward, but the ground underneath her feet became treacherous with muck and mud, slowing her progress. She struggled to get free, succeeding in alternately yanking her feet free of the bog only to again get stuck with the very next step.

Someone is coming!

Kassandra paused and peered ahead. A hooded person was stalking through the forest, a knife clasped in his hand. This was no shadowy figure, but someone real, someone who intended to kill Cadedryn. The threat was no longer ephemeral . . . It was leaping from her dream and preparing to strike. "Danger!" Kassandra screamed.

Cadedryn frowned and looked around, oblivious to the warning. Unarmed, he appeared to be searching for something. Behind him, the other Kassandra seemed equally unaware. Her red tresses flowed down her back in a rippling cascade and she held a bouquet of flowers in her left hand.

"Take heed!" Kassandra screamed as she saw a second hooded figure approach from the other side of the meadow. It was no longer clear whether it was a man or a woman, nor which of the two unsuspecting people was the intended victim. Suddenly there were dozens of hooded figures, and Kassandra was forced to crouch down to avoid attracting their attention. "There is danger everywhere," she cried in distress. "Everywhere! Everywhere! It is coming closer. It is coming now!"

Crash, crash!

A castle loomed in the distance, but dense fog blanketed the ground around it. Armed men on horseback thundered closer, their swords held high. One swung at Cadedryn's neck, narrowly missing him.

Kassandra screamed.

Crash, crash, crash. "Kassandra! Wake up!"

Kassandra's eyes snapped open.

"Kassandra! You are dreaming!"

Her gaze swung to the closed door and she recognized Kalial's frantic voice. Triu-cair cowered at the end of the bed, his red-rimmed eyes flicking back and forth in extreme agitation.

"I'm awake," Kassandra whispered. "It was a dream."

"Kassandra! Open the door!"

"I'm awake," she called out, louder this time.

"Thank the saints. Now open the door and let me in. You were screaming so loudly, I heard you in my room."

Kassandra swung out of bed and padded to the door. As soon as she opened it, Kalial swept her up in a hug. "You poor thing. I had hoped that these dreams would fade if you found the man you sought, but it appears that they are becoming more powerful. What happened? What is going to happen?"

Kassandra felt tears fall from her eyes and she started to shake. "It was terrible," she whimpered. "So much evil . . . so much vengeance."

"Against whom? Against you?"

"No . . ." She frowned as she remembered her other self in the dream. "Maybe. I don't think so." Her head jerked up. "Cadedryn! He is in danger! They are going to kill him."

"Where is he? If the danger is imminent, you must tell him."

Kassandra leapt from the bed and began yanking
on her clothes. "He is traveling to a castle . . . a huge
castle, nearly twice as large as yours . . . It must be
his castle."

"Did he tell you he was leaving?"

"No, but I know it. Kalial, my sister, I must go to
him. I must save him."

"But—"

Kassandra pulled on her cape. "This is what I was
meant to do. Don't worry about me. I will be safe.
Tell Ronin that I went back to the forest, or anything
you must so that he does not blame you for letting
me go."

"You must go now? When will you be back?"

Kassandra looked at her sister. "I don't know when
I will return, but I do know that I have not succeeded
in saving him. He will die tonight. I can sense it."

Kalial clasped her hands on either side of Kassandra's frightened face. "Very well. Go to him. Save
your man."

Chapter 18

Wearing peasant garb and balancing Triu-cair on her shoulder, Kassandra snuck through the castle and entered the dark stable. Several horses shuffled their feet and one kicked his stall as Kassandra raced down the aisle toward where Cadedryn kept his favorite stallion. She shuddered as she beheld the empty stall. He had done as she had suspected. He had left the castle.

Her anxiety soared.

Kassandra placed Triu-cair on the ground and he scampered to a pile of rags Cadedryn had used to wipe down his horse. The weasel sniffed the rags, then stood up on his hind legs.

Fresh. He left not long ago, he told her.

"Follow them," Kassandra instructed as she led Briana out of another stall farther down the aisle. Slipping only a bridle over her head, Kassandra gripped the horse's mane and swung herself astride.

Triu-cair scurried out of the building and began racing through the courtyard as Kassandra rode close behind. He kept his nose near the ground, well able to track Cadedryn's unique scent even in the dark.

Soon they cleared the castle courtyard and entered the surrounding forest. Kassandra glanced back, her heart pounding. The moon was shadowed behind clouds and a cold breeze sent shivering chills up and down her arms.

Someone is following us, Triu-cair said as he paused and peered through the dark.

"No. I made sure we were not seen," Kassandra hissed. "Besides, 'tis Cadedryn who is in danger, not us." She clucked for Briana to move forward, and after a nervous sidestep, the mare complied. Triu-cair resumed sniffing the ground, and they soon found themselves on a small narrow road that wound its way northward toward the Highlands.

A thin trail of mist snaked through the trees. Kassandra shivered and drew her cloak closer. "I am not dreaming," she muttered, but she rubbed her eyes. The moon glowed through a break in the clouds, filtering through the trees with an eerie blue light.

Her breath caught and she began to feel lightheaded. Everything was so familiar . . . She felt as if she had been here before. "Stop," she said aloud to herself. "I have ridden alone at night many times. There is nothing to fear. Once I reach Cadedryn, I will warn him and all will be well." She pushed her cape off her shoulders and shook her red curls free, comforted by the familiar cloak of her own hair.

A shadowy motion to her right made her gasp and she hauled on the mare's reins, causing the hapless creature to skid to a stop. "Who goes there?" she called out as she stared intently at the shadow. A light breeze whistled through the trees, and the shadows shifted again, revealing a spindly bush waving back and forth in the wind.

Kassandra let out her breath and covered her mouth with her hand. "This is a forest like any other," she whispered to herself. "Pretend it is Loch Nidean."

A clang of sword against sword echoed through the forest.

Kassandra screamed, then pummeled her mare's sides and sent her galloping forward. "Cadedryn!"

The clash of steel came again and again, faster and faster as the combatants struggled for supremacy. Kassandra burst around a bend in the road and beheld Cadedryn backed against a boulder by three hooded attackers.

Her abrupt arrival caused all to pause and stare at her in shocked surprise.

"Run, Kaitlynn!" Cadedryn shouted as he saw her tresses glowing in the moonlight, but Kassandra ignored him, leapt from her mare and raced forward. His shock escalated as he recognized Lady Kassandra's mare. "Run!" he bellowed.

Suddenly one of the attackers spun toward her and swung, coming within inches of delivering a lethal blow to her midsection.

Kassandra snatched a handful of dirt from the ground and flung it in her attacker's face, then rapidly sidestepped his flailing arms while he howled with pain as sand and debris blinded him.

She grabbed the man's sword and heaved it into the bushes, then spun back to face the others.

Cadedryn was pulling his sword from another man, who fell to his knees while clutching the gaping wound in his belly. For a brief moment, Kassandra smiled, thinking that victory was theirs, when suddenly Cadedryn gasped and stepped backward, his hand gripping a blade protruding from his chest.

He opened his mouth, but nothing came forth. He took several short gasps, then fell back against the boulder. He stared at her stunned face and a flicker of regret whispered across his eyes; then he slumped to the ground and fell to his side, his eyes closed against the excruciating pain.

Kassandra dashed past the remaining attacker, oblivious to the risk of her own safety, and fell to her knees next to Cadedryn. She gripped his shoulders and shook him. "No!" she screamed. "I warned you! I warned you that they would come after you! How could this happen?" She twisted and looked up at the man who had thrown the dirk. "Why? Why do you seek to harm him?"

The hooded attacker stepped forward and pressed his sword against her chest. "You ruined everything," he accused. "You, too, should die. I tried to warn you that day in the meadow, but you ignored my threat. Now you both will suffer the consequences of your stubbornness."

Triu-cair scrambled up the side of the boulder, then squealed from high above their heads.

The man jerked back and peered around in alarm.

Kassandra huddled against Cadedryn.

Cadedryn gripped her shoulder, trying to rise, but she gently pushed him back. "Stay still," she whispered.

"Come," the attacker commanded his men. "We must depart. Let the whore be found with his lifeless body. 'Twill make for fewer questions."

Her temper raged to life. She sprang up, her fingers curled into sharp weapons.

The man kicked her, sending her smashing against the rock.

He stood over her and laughed. "You can do nothing to stop me," he gloated as he lifted his sword to deliver a final blow to Cadedryn's groaning body.

"Hurry!" one of the injured attackers cried. "I hear horses. Someone followed her."

The man paused with his blade lifted.

Cadedryn again struggled to sit up, but collapsed against the ground.

The injured man grabbed the leader and spun him around by the shoulder, then shoved him toward the horses. "We cannot be seen near the earl's body. The whore is not worth our lives. We will be accused of murdering him and will see no mercy. Come. Let the man suffer a long death for your thrown blade sunk deep in his chest and he will not survive. We must ride!"

The attacker nodded and cruelly kicked Cadedryn's side, sending him rolling onto his back. He then picked up his wounded comrade and flung him over the saddle of one of the horses. With one final glance at the flame-haired woman and the wounded man, they galloped off, leaving Kassandra and Cadedryn alone in the road.

Kassandra took several deep breaths and gripped a tree for support as her legs threatened to crumple. Triu-cair sprang from the boulder and scrambled over to Cadedryn.

He still lives. Barely.

"Blessed Mother Earth!" Kassandra cried as she yanked the engraved dirk from his chest and beheld the jagged wound. Seeing his pale brow, she cradled him against her bosom and stroked his once vibrant face with trembling fingers. She had to save him. It was her destiny.

She looked up at the moon. "I call upon you, great spirits of the forest . . . Heal this man." She pressed her palm flat against his wound, feeling his blood drench her hand. " 'Tis not his time to leave you, Mother Earth," she cried.

Cadedryn groaned and his eyes flickered open.

"Tigress . . . ride away . . . or you will be accused . . ." he whispered, his voice so faint she could hardly hear him. "Could be bandits . . . or worse."

Ignoring him, she lifted her free hand and swept the air over his head. "Great spirits of the sky," she intoned, "Dagda needs your strength."

Wind whistled through the woods, tossing leaves and snapping twigs as it increased in strength and swirled around the couple.

"Heal him!" Kassandra commanded. A piece of bark tumbled against her knees and Kassandra grasped it. She recognized it as bark from a willow tree. A healing tree. She held it against his wound, then ripped a strip of cloth from her skirts and tied it tightly around both the bark and his chest.

Cadedryn squinted, trying to still his spinning world. "Kassandra? Is that you?"

She touched her lips to his forehead. "Danu, mother of the gods, will take care of you. Rest and let her power infuse you."

Cadedryn touched her face in wonderment.

Kassandra's head snapped up as fear rushed up her spine. She heard a new set of horses thundering up the road. The wind died in an instant, leaving behind an unnatural stillness in which the horse's hooves reverberated louder and louder, coming ever closer.

Hurry! Triu-cair urged. *We do not know if the riders are friend or foe!*

Kassandra laid Cadedryn down and ran around the boulder in search of his horse. She found the stallion standing just off the road, his saddlebags loaded and ready for travel.

"Come! Come!" she coaxed and she pulled the horse forward. The stallion resisted, tossing his head. Kassandra snapped the reins. "I will take none of this.

Come!" After one final head toss, the stallion relented and obediently followed her.

After scrambling back to Cadedryn's weakened body, she forced him to his feet. Placing one of his boots in the stirrup, she shoved until he managed to swing his other leg around and slumped atop his stallion. He swayed, barely conscious.

They are only moments away. We have no time to spare! Triu-cair cried as he bounded up on her shoulder just before she leapt atop her mare's back and grabbed the stallion's reins.

She nodded, then without a backward glance, she led Cadedryn's horse out of the clearing and escaped into the mist-shrouded forest.

He woke slowly, his senses coming to life one at a time. First he heard the crackling fire and the faint sounds of nighttime animals. After several moments, he could smell the smoke and burning wood as well as a pot of simmering meat-laden stew. Then he became aware of pain in his chest and the roughness of the saddle blanket beneath his head.

He slowly opened his eyes.

She sat across the fire from him, her red hair highlighted by the glowing embers. She was sleeping against a tree, her face relaxed in gentle repose. Her features were beautiful, even with the thin film of grime caused by her recent travails. His lovely tigress.

The fire flickered low, casting her hair in shadow. He stared, trying to understand what his eyes were telling him. Not his tiger kitten. Lady Kassandra.

He spotted her weasel perched on a low branch, also sleeping soundly. The camp was orderly, its location well chosen, the horses tethered near a small stream and the various foodstuffs strung high in the tree branches where foraging animals could not scavenge. How did Kassandra—or Kaitlynn—know so much about surviving in the wilderness?

When his gaze returned to her, her eyes were open and she was looking back at him.

"Who are you?" he asked.

She sat upright and picked up a length of coarse linen lying beside her. Without speaking, she drew it over her head, tucked her hair underneath and smoothed her features.

Cadedryn felt his heart stop. "Lady Kassandra . . ." He struggled to sit up and glared at her. "Where is my tigress?"

She pulled her scarf off and shook out her hair. "I am right here," she replied, watching him warily.

He glared at her, his anger rising. He had suspected . . . but had ignored his own senses, not believing that either one of them would deceive him. His breathing increased and blood rushed to his head. "How dare you," he snarled as he struggled to take even breaths. "You deliberately tricked me. You played me for a fool. For what reason? I was falling in love with you."

"With me?" she taunted, then replaced her scarf and assumed a gentle expression. "Or me?" She yanked off the cloth and sprang to her feet, shaking her finger at him. "You played yourself! You were the one who could not see what was right before your eyes! You were the one unable to feel with your heart. I told you who I was. I told you I was your soul mate, yet you rejected me. You warned me about men"— she held her hand up to stop his interruption—"but I had hoped that you would prove your own words wrong. I had hoped you would reject my facade and see my true identity."

He tried to sit up, then gasped with pain and fell back. "You speak in twisted words. You play a game to trick me into loving you, then damn me for doing just that. What kind of warped plot have you created?"

"If you had listened to me in the first place, none of this would have happened!" she shouted.

"Listened to you? What? Do you mean about your dreams? For God's sake, woman, you didn't know me. We were strangers to each other! You have the audacity to accuse me of not recognizing you, but you don't understand the first thing about love and devotion!"

"Well, I don't love you anymore!"

"And I don't love you!"

They glared at each other, the flames between them burning hotter than the fire flickering at their feet. Kassandra wanted to pummel him with her bare hands and make him beg for forgiveness, while Cadedryn held his clenched fists at his sides so as not to grab her by the shoulders and shake her.

"Is that final?" he growled.

"Completely," she snapped back.

"Then why are you here? Why are *we* here?"

"You were so pigheaded, you refused to see the danger. Without me, you would be dead."

"If you were a few steps closer, *you* would be dead," he growled, then took several calming breaths. He felt a warm trickle of blood from his chest and he touched it, remembering his wound. He frowned, recalling something else. The wind. The moon. A sense of immense peace. A name tickled his mind . . . Dan . . . Danielle? No.

"And I didn't even like pretending to be your tigress," Kassandra added, angry enough to try to hurt him, even if her words were not true.

His gaze narrowed. "This was all for revenge, wasn't it?" he accused.

A superior smile spread across Kassandra's face. "Not initially. It was an accident at first, but revenge did cross my thoughts. You swore that you could never love me, but then you found yourself panting after my skirts. I have a temper and I don't let anyone beat me at anything. You crossed swords with me the first day we met and challenged me every day thereafter. You deserved everything you got."

His green eyes glittered with anger. Hurt and betrayal surged through him. She had toyed with his heart with callous disregard. He had spent nights in emotional turmoil just because he could not understand his attraction to two women and feeling inordinately guilty because he was beginning to care for both of them.

He had rejected Corine because of this woman, because he had begun to experience the closeness that was possible with a woman he could grow to love and cherish. He rose slowly to his feet, clutching his wound. Oddly enough, he did not feel nearly as weak as he expected, and the bleeding had already slowed. "You sent me spinning with your devious playacting. That day in the market . . . you were taunting me." He took several slow, deliberate steps until he was standing in front of her.

She rose, her blue eyes glimmering with wary caution.

He grasped her arm in a strong grip. "You think you have accomplished the ultimate revenge? You think you have played with me and will skip away the victor? Do you expect to leave me now? Guess what I can do, Lady Tiger? I can keep you. Whether you like it or not you are coming with me all the way to Aberdour Castle."

Chapter 19

"What?" she shrieked, trying to yank out of his hold. "Are you crazed? I saved you because I honor all living creatures, even ones as aggravating as you, but I will not go all the way to your castle! Now that you are awake, I am leaving."

"Who attacked me?" he asked as he reached over her head and pulled down one of the ropes that was wrapped around a tree branch.

"Huh?" Kassandra shook her head in confusion. "You can't change the subject like that." She looked up to see what he was doing, then yelped in surprise when he grasped her free hand.

He laughed as he deftly looped the rope around Kassandra's wrist and tied it tight. "Don't act so stupefied. I may not have seen the danger until it was too late, but you seem to know events before they occur. I believe that I was attacked because I decided not to marry Corine. That obviously upset someone enough to attempt murder, and you are my only clue as to whom."

"Let me go!" Kassandra shouted, yanking away from him and twisting her hand as she tried to slip free. "This is preposterous! I don't know who it was; I only know it was the same man who attacked me on the ridge."

"You said that we were meant to be together. Why protest now?"

"I said we should be wed, not that you should kidnap me!" Kassandra snapped.

He chuckled, pleased to turn the tables on her. "Well, it seems that your other dreams have come true. Perhaps I was mistaken in rejecting your proposal. Mayhap, we *should* wed."

"No!"

"No? Ever since we met, you have done everything possible to convince me that we ought to. Are you now telling me that your dreams are false?"

She frowned.

"Decide, yes or no. Should I heed your dreams or not?"

"Yes . . . but no, not like this."

Looking into her wounded eyes, he shrugged, then tied the other end of the rope to the belt around his waist. "Forgive me if I don't know exactly what to say at this moment." He swayed in place, his energy fading. The wound had affected him more than he had initially thought. "All I know is that I want you right here where I can see you." He paused, then stared into the fire. "It was Curtis, wasn't it?" he asked, deep sorrow clouding his voice. "Our vow of brotherly loyalty was a farce from its inception."

Kassandra shook her head. "No. It was not him."

Cadedryn grunted. "Stop churning everything into a muddled mess," he begged. "At our picnic, you accused him. You said that the man who sliced my hand was connected to my father's murder."

Kassandra winced at Cadedryn's tighter grip as he tried to remain standing. "Curtis was not on the road tonight," she insisted. "He did not throw the knife."

Reaching across a log, she picked up the dirk and showed it to him.

He glanced at it, then stared at it in shock. "My father's dirk!"

"This is the blade I pulled from your chest, the very blade I cautioned you to keep near. Once again, you ignored my warnings."

Cadedryn shook his head. "It cannot be. I placed that knife in my trunk. It couldn't have been in the hands of my attacker . . ."

Kassandra yanked on the rope as she placed her hands on her hips. "I gave it to you and told you it held your guardian spirit. Why did you leave it where someone could steal it?" She shook her fist at him. "You are a fool!"

"That proves it was Curtis. I saw him near my trunks."

"It was not Lord Curtis," Kassandra grumbled as she tapped her foot. "It was someone older, but I suppose that, once again, you won't listen to me."

He stared at her, thoroughly confused. Her warnings had been true. Her belief that someone wanted to kill him was right. Her conviction that the knife was important had proved correct. And she had dreamed they would fall in love with each other.

A slow grin stole across his face. "I will listen to you," he said huskily, this time not teasing her, but speaking with conviction. "And because I am beginning to believe you, I am going to keep you nearby. 'Tis not the knife, but *you* who are my guardian angel." He touched her face and ran his hand down her cheek. "You knew we were destined to find each other. You saved me."

"It was my duty," she harrumphed.

He smiled with one corner of his mouth. "Your duty? You have done everything the last several days because of your duty? You lay with me out of duty?"

She looked away. "Yes," she forced herself to say. "I am bound by the rules of my society to help others. I knew you were in danger and I had to find a way to gain your trust."

"You came because you wanted to find your life mate," he chided her softly. "You wanted me."

"Stop!" Kassandra cried as she pulled back against her tether. "That part of my dream was . . . was . . . was misinterpreted! I misunderstood the meaning!"

"I am going to marry you," he informed her. "Besides, simply coming to my rescue and being alone with me in the middle of the night places you in a compromising position. We must marry."

"But I am telling you that the dream was wrong," she pleaded. "I don't want you like this. We will be miserable."

"Except in bed. We are quite compatible in that area."

She gasped and flushed a deep, becoming red. "How dare you say that to a lady."

He chuckled. "You cannot play that card on me. You threw away whatever protection that title afforded when you sought to seduce me."

"You beast! You bastard! I will not marry you. I don't want to marry you now. Let me go!" She began plucking at the knot on her wrist.

His grin faded and he grew pale. He felt his bandage again, then lifted bloody fingers to the firelight. He fell back against a tree and groaned.

Kassandra took an involuntary step forward.

"Help me . . ." he whispered.

Kassandra gripped his other shoulder and lowered

him to the ground. "You should not be arguing with me," she scolded him.

His hand shot out and captured hers in a vicelike grip. "You must bring me to my castle or I will surely die. You did something for me earlier . . . something magical. Would you leave me to perish after saving me?"

She froze, her gaze captured within his.

Cadedryn touched the line on her temple where her hair started. So soft. "I will untie you if you promise to stay with me. At least until we reach the castle."

She shook her head. "I must return to my homeland."

He slid down to the ground as he released her, his eyes growing cold and unrelenting. "I just discovered that the woman I thought I cared for was nothing more than a lie. The woman I thought was my friend was secretly plotting against me. And someone is seeking to murder me. I have no more patience. Tomorrow we will go to Aberdour. Together."

The next morning dawned wet and dreary. Cadedryn rolled to his side as the last vestiges of his dream rippled through his mind. He smiled, his eyes still closed, as he felt Kassandra's wet lips caress his own.

"Ummmm," he moaned. "I knew you would capitulate."

She kissed him again, this time stroking his lips with her soft tongue.

He reached for her, intent upon deepening the kiss, when he was startled by a loud shriek. His eyes snapped open and he beheld Triu-cair standing nose to nose with him. The weasel's small, pointed tongue flicked out and he licked Cadedryn once again.

"What!" Cadedryn thundered as he struggled to sit

up. Triu-cair scurried backward as Cadedryn wiped the back of his hand across his lips in disgust. "You beast," he grumbled as he glared at the offending creature. "You licked me! I should have sliced you in twain the first time I saw you."

Triu-cair sat back on his haunches, his lips spread in what appeared to be a grin. His beady gaze swung upward and he shrieked again.

Filled with sudden suspicion, Cadedryn followed his gaze and looked up into the tree branches.

Kassandra. Lounging on the branch like a tiger kitten, dangling a rope betwixt two fingers.

Cadedryn reached for his belt, already knowing what he would find.

"Did you really think that you could keep me by using this?" Kassandra purred, indicating the twisted twine. She negligently tossed it aside and propped her chin on her hand.

"How did you get free?" Cadedryn asked as he rose to his feet. " 'Twas the method by which we bind prisoners. No one has escaped before."

"You don't know anything about me," Kassandra answered. "Take care, that pinecone is about to fall—"

"Ouch!" Cadedryn glared at a pinecone that plunked upon his head, then tumbled to the ground.

Kassandra giggled. "I guess I should have told you sooner."

"You could not have known it would fall. You threw it, you little brat."

"Just as I cannot possibly know that you will trip over a root in a few moments when you go to relieve yourself."

Cadedryn scanned the ground, taking note of a web of tangled roots to his right. Grinning, he walked to the left and began unlacing his breeches. Glancing over his shoulder, he called out to her, "You cannot intimidate me with your prophecies. I—umph!" He stumbled over a buried root and fell to one knee.

This time Kassandra wrapped her arms around the tree branch and laughed uproariously.

Cadedryn rose to his feet, his eyes flashing with ire. "You dare mock me?" He reached for a branch and swung himself up into the tree.

Kassandra gasped. "Your wound!"

"Feels fine. But you know that, don't you?"

She scuttled backward, her glee tempered by wary nervousness. "I don't know everything. Just the things that appear in my visions."

"Can you read thoughts?" He balanced along the branch, edging closer like a predator about to pounce on its prey.

She shook her head.

"Are you sure? Take a guess."

"You are angry?"

"Very good." He leapt forward, his hand swiping through empty air just as she dropped to the ground.

She peered up at him, her eyes dancing with merriment.

He looked down, his gaze intent. "And now?" he asked.

"Frustrated?"

He swung down, his feet landing firmly on the ground. "What is about to happen now?"

She tensed as a shiver tickled the back of her neck. "I'm not sure . . ."

"Come now," he responded huskily. "No predictions? Can't you tell what I am about to say or do?"

"I told you, it doesn't work that way."

He stalked forward as she nervously backed away.

"I am going to make love to you. Soon. And I am going to make you pant for more."

Her eyes grew wide. She swallowed as the tickle turned into a full shiver that swept her from head to toe. If he touched her, she would surrender. She would be at his mercy. "I am leaving," she warned him.

"No, you are not." He knelt on the ground and held his fingers out toward Triu-cair. "Come here, little beast. You and your mistress are two of a kind." He glanced at Kassandra's guarded expression. "I am coming to realize that there is much more to you than I ever suspected. Much more." He stroked Triu-cair's head as the polecat arched his back and flicked his tail in appreciation. "Are you from Scotland?"

"Yes, of course!"

He lifted Triu-cair and cuddled him against his chest. "Where does your family live?"

Kassandra's gaze dropped as she searched for an answer. "I live with Kalial," she attempted.

Cadedryn shook his head. "No, you don't."

"I mean that I live nearby."

"Really? Where?"

Kassandra huffed. "I am not saying anything else."

He smiled, his eyes glimmering with mischief. He bent down and picked up the rope Kassandra had tossed aside. "Nothing else? Well, I suppose we have a long time for explanations."

Kassandra flicked her hair over her shoulder and cocked her hand on her hip. "May I remind you, I am leaving? I did what I was supposed to do. I found you and saved you. I have no other reason to stay."

"Yet here you stand. You could have left in the middle of the night."

"I wanted to see your expression when you awoke to find me unbound."

"Did you enjoy my moment of discomfort?"

"Immensely!"

"I doubt you enjoyed it as much as I am going to enjoy yours."

Kassandra glared at him. "What are you blathering about?"

Cadedryn shrugged and turned his back on her as he walked toward the tethered horses. He tightened his stallion's girth and checked his saddlebags.

Kassandra trailed after him. "Aren't you going to try to detain me?"

"Nope."

Kassandra frowned, then proceeded to bridle her own mare. "I suppose we should say good-bye."

"I doubt it," he replied as he tied the rope to his saddle.

She drew her brows together in frustration.

He turned and leaned against his horse, watching her confusion with barely suppressed amusement.

"Why not?" Kassandra demanded.

"Because you are going to stay with me and we are going to Aberdour."

"Why do you suppose that?" Kassandra questioned sarcastically.

Cadedryn slapped his stallion's rump and the horse bounded several feet away before stopping. Triu-cair squealed with delight from his perch atop the saddle.

"Triu-cair!" Kassandra called. "Come here this instant!"

Nope.

Kassandra's jaw dropped and she glared at her friend in disbelief. "What?" she shouted.

I can't. I'm tied to his horse.

Kassandra spun to face Cadedryn. "You kidnapped him!" she screamed. "You stole my weasel!"

"You'll get him back just as soon as we reach Aberdour."

Her temper flared. She launched herself at Cade-dryn, knocking him to the ground, punching and kicking him with all her strength.

"My wound!" he shouted.

"I won't fall for that again. You—"

He rolled on top of her. "I am not lying. You opened my injury again. I'm bleeding."

She bucked and twisted, trying to get out from under him. Jerking her leg, she kicked the back of his head.

"Augh! You little fireball!" He shuffled back and sat on her legs, then pinned her arms above her head. "Stop. You're scaring Triu-cair."

Kassandra spit on his face.

He stared at her in shock. Shifting her wrists to one hand, he wiped away the spittle, then looked at his hand. "That was not a ladylike thing to do." He looked at her furious face in wonder. "Who are you? Are you the lady or the mistress?"

Kassandra slid her gaze away, embarrassed.

He touched her smooth cheek, tracing the fine freckles. "So beautiful . . ." He rubbed her lips with his thumb. "Sensuous . . ." He thrust his hand into her hair and kneaded the back of her head. "I told you I was going to make love to you. You are so wild . . . yet I have seen you as cool and composed as the queen herself. Who is the real you? Lady Kassandra or Kaitlynn the tigress? Only a woman with honor and courage would have saved me from certain death last night, but how could that same woman attack a wounded man and spit upon him?"

Her eyes widened as tears welled up. She tried to turn away, but he held her fast.

"Are you crying? Why? Shame? Anger? What emotions are roiling inside your complex heart?"

"I don't want you to marry me if you don't love me . . ." she whimpered.

He leaned closer and kissed her tears. "How could I learn to love you when you never let me know your true self?"

She wrinkled her brow, as close to a shrug as she could manage with him sitting on her.

He brushed his lips across hers.

She jerked her head away.

He nuzzled her neck and inhaled deeply. She smelled of feminine sweat and wood smoke, but underneath the forest scents was something uniquely her own. Rich . . . musky . . . erotic. "I understand your anger. I should have known the truth. I saw your facial similarities but never reconciled the two into one mysterious and enigmatic person. Forgive my blindness."

"Stop kissing me," she demanded, uncomfortably aroused by his breath against her neck.

"Why did you cover your hair?"

"I told you before. I don't like it. It's red."

He rocked back and looked at her angry eyes. "Red? Is that your only reason?"

She slid her gaze away, suddenly aware of how ridiculous she sounded. How could she explain that she was hiding not only her hair color, but also herself? She was ill-tempered. She was too unrestrained. Ladies like her half sister, Kalial, had mellow hair color and gentle dispositions. "I can't explain it to you," she mumbled.

He buried his nose in her tresses and found the curved shell of her ear. He nibbled it, luxuriating in the trembles in her body he aroused with his subtle ministrations. She might try to be Lady Kassandra, but her body still reacted like his tiger kitten.

"I told you to stop!"

Ignoring her, he shifted his hips against hers, seeking her moist warmth. The rough fabric of her peasant gown rubbed abrasively against his breeches, and as the cloth massaged his groin, it brought him to full erection.

She wriggled, trying to avoid feeling him. Her breath shortened and her heart began racing. In desperation, she curled her toes and clenched her fists in an effort to ignore his motions.

"You want me," he said. "Why are you fighting it?"

"I only want you to let me go."

He rocked harder, changing position so that his cock nudged the sweet juncture between her thighs. He grinned at her involuntary gasp of pleasure. The ache in his chest receded as his mind focused on his hips. He rocked faster, hearing the rasp of their clothing almost as loudly as their panting breaths. His need for her skyrocketed and what had started as a taunt became a pressing desire.

"You want me," he accused. "Admit it."

She flung her head back and forth. "No," she groaned, but her hips tilted upward, seeking closer contact, and the huskiness in her voice betrayed her.

He released her hands and slid his down her arms, tracing the sensitive inner surface of her wrist and forearm. His pleasure built as her body arched in response, and his motions became more forceful and erratic as he neared his climax.

She writhed beneath him, opening her legs and bending her knees as she lifted her hips off the ground. Her dress bunched between them and she tossed and turned, trying to be free of the restrictive clothing. Her inner muscles rippled, longing to be filled, and wet heat flooded her sanctum.

"Yes," she gasped. "I do want you! Now!"

He bucked against her, his hard shaft encased by his tight clothes and her dress cushioning his brusque motions. Like rough hands sliding up and down, rubbing his tip and wrapping him in a calloused grip, his clothes encased him and pushed him to ecstasy. He groaned and his hips jerked; then he paused with his eyes tightly closed as proof of his climax rippled down his shaft and dampened his breeches.

Kassandra twitched, yearning for his hips. "Don't stop," she begged, but he sighed and rolled off her, exhausted and replete. "Cadedryn!" she called sharply, her center still pulsing with need.

He turned his head and looked at her, his expression triumphant. "You cannot resist me."

Passion was replaced by fury and Kassandra struggled to her feet. "You did that on purpose," she accused.

"Hmm."

"You found your pleasure yet left me wanting!"

"Mmm-hmm. Just a little reminder that you must stay with me if want to be fulfilled."

Her eyes narrowed and she shook her skirts down. "You are a beast. I will punish you for that!"

He rolled to his side and pressed his hand over his bleeding wound, the pain resurfacing. "The score is not even close to being even."

Chapter 20

It took several days of riding through the lowland forests before they reached the edge of the Highlands. Throughout their journey, Cadedryn remained alert, listening for sounds of pursuit and ensuring that their passage was well hidden. Once he thought he saw Curtis's horse, but it was immediately lost to view and he never saw it again.

As the days passed, he was astounded time and again by Kassandra's forestry skills. She was able to locate sources of water and find edible plants with an innate ability that far surpassed his own, and she seemed to know where there were rabbits or deer long before he could spot them.

Never once did she complain about the dirt or lack of comfortable bedding, and he sensed an aura of peace around her he had not felt at court. Was this the real Kassandra? This woman with a torn dress and wild red hair who rode astride her mare without benefit of a saddle? This woman who cooked over a fire and readily ate with her fingers . . . who strode barefoot through the forest with easy, relaxed grace as she hummed with the songbirds. Could she be the true melding of Lady Kassandra and Tiger Kaitlynn?

She had not mentioned leaving again, but her gaze often drifted toward her pet and her eyes flickered as if she were talking to him. If she had begged him for

Triu-cair's return, he would have relented. He could not force Kassandra to stay if she truly wanted to go. But she did not ask, and he did not offer. Instead, they rode in unspoken harmony, working together and quietly learning about each other.

Soon they crossed the Highland moors and entered Caenmore lands. Despite being pleased that they were nearing Aberdour, Cadedryn shifted uncomfortably in his saddle.

"Does the wound still plague you?" Kassandra asked.

He shrugged.

"I found some comfrey last night," she offered. "If you apply it to your injury, the pain will diminish."

"Your knowledge of medicine is much appreciated," he said once they paused and Kassandra applied the comforting poultice. "The wounds on your mare healed well. Where did you learn such skills?"

"From the people of my village," she answered as she glanced at him from under her lashes.

"Ah." He looked at her curiously, wishing she would offer him more details of her childhood.

Kassandra lifted her chin. "I know more than simple remedies." She pointed to a willow tree on the far hill. "The bark from that tree would also help your pain. I know plants that relieve constipation or diarrhea, that can induce vomiting and quiet one's stomach. I know how to set bones, stitch wounds and even deliver a baby."

"You must have been a fascinating child. I'd like to know more."

"You would not find it interesting," she hedged.

He stared at her closed face, aware that she was hiding things from him. He debated about pushing her to reveal the truth, but remained silent. When she felt ready, she would tell him. Until then, he must be content to wait.

"I have never seen a woman ride astride without a saddle. Do you find it comfortable?"

Her brows lifted. "Would *you* rather ride sidesaddle?"

He laughed and shook his head. "I see your point. The sidesaddle must feel rather precarious."

She shook her hair back, her expression challenging him. "Does it make you uneasy? To see a woman ride with skill equal to your own?"

"A bit. My mother never sought to excel in the masculine arts as you seem to do. She doted upon my father, always supporting and praising him."

"So my skills disturb you?"

"Not at all. They intrigue me."

Kassandra ducked her head and smiled shyly. It felt good to hear him say kind words to her. Her stomach fluttered. "Did you enjoy your childhood?"

"Definitely, but when everything was suddenly thrust into chaos after my parents' deaths, I became angry. First, my mother died, and then my father sent me from the only home I had ever known. I was devastated. I could not understand or forgive his actions, especially when he was killed before we could come to terms. It was far easier to concentrate on regaining my title."

"Yet despite your suspicions you did not pursue his murderer."

"Grief clouded my judgment and anger superceded my sense of loss. I let everyone convince me that he had committed suicide. I spoke of my suspicions only to the one man I called friend."

"Curtis McCafferty."

"Aye."

They crested a hill and Cadedryn pointed to one corner of the far horizon. "That is the land Morgana's father owned. A large portion was given to Laird Fergus as a dower gift, the same portion my father would have received had he married her." He turned and pointed to another corner. "That is Fergus land. He has no sons. If I wed Corine, I will own it all upon Laird Fergus's death, including Morgana's dower properties."

"What happens if you die?"

Cadedryn's gaze swung back to her. "If I die before I wed, Aberdour will go to whichever laird captures her, for I have no other living kin. There will be civil unrest as many fight for her lands, which is exactly what the king seeks to avoid."

"If you die after you have wed?"

"If we have no children, then the property and title will go to the man who marries my widow."

Kassandra stared at Cadedryn's tense face and shuddered.

"Come. We are near my castle," he said as he started his stallion up the last part of the hill. As they crested the peak, he pointed across a vast valley to a massive, gray stone structure with a series of seven outlying defensive towers and two moats. The partial ruins of an older keep lay nearby, giving evidence to the many generations the Caenmores had lived on this land. Even from this distance, the iron-tipped ledges and sheer walls of the castle looked intimidating and powerful.

"Aberdour Castle," Cadedryn announced. "My home."

Acres of untilled land rolled from the base of the castle, punctuated by huts with small gardens. Many of the homes looked unkempt and forlorn, and even the sheep herds appeared straggly. Several peasants stood at their front doors, watching Cadedryn and Kassandra pass. Cadedryn's eyes narrowed in anger.

" 'Twas not like this when my father ruled the land," he grumbled. "The fields were rich and the herds flourished. The peasants have grown lazy. 'Tis no wonder the tithes have decreased. I should have come home sooner."

Kassandra's inner trepidation built as they rode over the moor and approached the castle. For the first time in days, she felt self-conscious about her hair, and she awkwardly smoothed the strands away from her face as she attempted to restrain the wayward curls.

Triu-cair peeked his nose out from underneath Cadedryn's tunic. *I smell food rotting in the storage shed.*

"Most of the lambs are singletons," Kassandra added.

Cadedryn glanced at her with a lift of his brow. "You know about singletons?"

"Yes, the sheep birth rate. They are delivering singletons instead of twins."

Cadedryn nodded grimly. "More evidence of inefficiency and poor management. Robert, my overseer, has been writing to me about his concerns, but I thought he had exaggerated. Now I see that he did not."

Kassandra winced, feeling Cadedryn's anger. She impulsively reached over and squeezed his thigh. "Now that you are here, everything will be as it should. A home needs its master."

He glanced at her hand, then at her. "And its mistress," he replied softly.

Kassandra jerked her hand away. "Do you love me?"

His gaze swept her face, tracing the slope of her cheek and flicking over the freckles that dusted her nose. Love her? He needed her. She knew things that others did not. She had skills that were uniquely her own. He wanted to cherish and protect her. She made him feel more alive than he had felt in years. But love? "I want to marry you," he said. "I don't understand your sudden resistance. You found me. You proposed to me. Don't you want to be a countess?"

She kicked her mare and sent her galloping toward the castle, too annoyed to answer him.

A few moments later, Kassandra pulled her mare to a stop and waited for Cadedryn to catch up with her. She stared uneasily at the castle that loomed ahead. It was larger than any she had ever seen. Her half sister's castle looked like an elegant cottage compared to Aberdour, and even the king's court was small in comparison to this Highland stronghold.

She took a deep breath, her gaze darting to the numerous arrow holes and high watchtowers. Over a hundred men manned the military sites, each bristling with shiny, well-maintained weapons and black and red tabards with shimmering silver stitching. No one welcomed their arrival. Instead, the armored faces of the Caenmore soldiers displayed unrelenting menace.

At the end of the bridge, a large iron studded gate slid upward on well-oiled chains and the inner courtyard was revealed. A double row of mounted guards rode over the first bridge and raised their lances to bar Cadedryn and Kassandra's passage.

Cadedryn sat tall in his saddle and stared at the first guard. "Robert McDuff," he acknowledged. "It has been ten years since I saw you. You must be well over fifty summers now, but you look the same as you did when I was just a youth."

The guard peered across the second bridge, his jaw going slack. "Young Cadedryn?"

Cadedryn smiled. "The Earl of Aberdour, at your service." Cadedryn bowed slightly. "I have returned home. I trust I am welcome."

"Earl?" Robert McDuff broke ranks and trotted his horse up to Cadedryn's stallion. He searched Cadedryn's face after glancing only briefly at Kassandra. "Your father's title?"

"Has been restored," Cadedryn finished. He looked at the well-trained men and well-tended moat with pleasure. "I see that your missives spoke true. You have upheld the family honor in managing the castle. My father would be pleased."

"I was devoted to Liam, God rest his soul, and I am, in turn, your faithful servant, but the peasants have been less dedicated. They are afraid to work the land as they used to, fearing that their fields and herds will be raided by neighboring clans. Perhaps now that you are home, the raids will cease and the fields will be safe." He spun his horse around and stood in his stirrups. "Sound the horns! The earl had returned! Make way. Make way!"

The guards lowered their lances and shifted to the edge of the bridge as a young page raced up a steep flight of steps and carried the message of Cadedryn's arrival to the other soldiers.

Soon the trumpets blared and men at every level of the fortress pounded the hilts of their swords against the heavy stone, sending a reverberating welcome that could be heard for miles.

Cadedryn and Kassandra rode the rest of the way into the courtyard, flanked by Robert and the double row of guards.

A rotund, gray-haired woman ran forward and

squealed with delight. "Cadedryn! You have returned home! We knew you had been to court and have been waiting to hear the news, but a messenger has yet to arrive this fortnight!"

"Moxie, my old nursemaid and now the castle keeper," Cadedryn explained to Kassandra as he smiled and swung off his stallion. "Moxie, meet Lady Kassandra." Handing his horse's reins to a groomsman, he helped Kassandra down from her mare, then took her hand and held it high. "Lady Kassandra, the next countess of Aberdour!"

Many of the servants who had made their way to the courtyard shuffled and averted their eyes, while others stared at Kassandra with stunned disbelief. Even the soldiers twitched in obvious surprise. Her unusual riding style, her dirty clothes and her flaming tresses made her seem an unlikely countess.

Moxie glanced behind them, searching for Kassandra's entourage, and Kassandra blushed in shame when Moxie determined that no one else accompanied her lord and his lady. Suddenly, a huge smile split Moxie's face and she reached to enfold Kassandra in a motherly embrace. "How wonderful!" she exclaimed. "Anyone who loves my young Cadedryn and is loved by him in return will be welcome in this home, just as I welcomed Liam's bride, Sarah. I will bring you to your rooms immediately and you can freshen up so you may be properly introduced to the staff."

Kassandra struggled to pull free and took a quick step backward. "No," she replied sharply. "You misunderstand. I have not agreed to marry the earl. I accompanied Cadedryn to Aberdour only because he stole my pet, Triu-cair."

Moxie looked at Cadedryn. "But dear," she murmured, "you are traveling without a chaperone."

"I don't care!" Kassandra cried. "I am tired of all these rules! I just want to go home."

"Lady Kassandra is tired," Cadedryn explained to the shocked audience. "I am certain you will all forgive her outburst."

As the servants nodded, Kassandra swung her fist at Cadedryn's head.

He ducked and quickly wrapped his arms around her. "An amazing woman," Cadedryn explained aloud. "So brave and daring. You can understand why I have chosen her to become my countess." His face remained firm as he ignored Kassandra's gasp of outrage. "Please bring milady to her rooms and send a messenger to my chamber immediately. I have several missives that must go out today." He gently pushed Kassandra toward Moxie, then untied Triucair's leash from the saddle and cradled the weasel in his arms.

Moxie looked back and forth between the two people. Lady Kassandra stood with her arms akimbo and Cadedryn's green eyes were kind but unrelenting. Taking pity on the young lady, Moxie stepped forward and gently took her arm. "Come with me, milady. The day is well over half past. The best you can do is get cleaned up and rested. Then we can sort everything out. Perhaps you can discuss these matters with him later."

"Just for the night," Kassandra finally stammered. "I will stay only one night."

Cadedryn smiled noncommittally and motioned for Kassandra to precede him into the castle.

Feeling unsure of herself, Kassandra entered the vast hall, followed by Moxie, then more distantly by Cadedryn and Robert, who were speaking together in lowered tones.

Once inside, she stumbled to a halt. The great hall

was twice as large as any room she had ever seen. Enormous tapestries depicting Caenmore history draped the walls. A long table spanning half the distance from wall to wall had carved edges and heavy sloping legs, which ended in rounded feet, and there were fifteen matching chairs arranged along each side.

Moxie put a comforting hand on Kassandra's shoulder. "The late Caenmore and his wife were fond of artisans. They welcomed masters in every trade and spent their time beautifying the castle."

"But Cadedryn's mother was a peasant. These things are . . . exquisite!"

"Not just a peasant. An artist. Liam appreciated fine things. He met Sarah when he commissioned her father, Mr. Douglas Tate, to carve an end chair for his dining table. He was so enamored of the master's daughter, he commissioned another and another and another, just to see Sarah again." Moxie waved at the collection of chairs. "Each took Mr. Tate a sennight to complete, and the late earl insisted that he and his daughter reside in the castle during that time. It was a long and sweet courtship between two people destined to find each other. True love."

Kassandra walked forward and stroked the sloping lines of a chair. It was as smooth as satin and glimmered with a rich gloss. "Beautiful," she breathed. "Each one is a masterpiece."

Moxie nodded. "When Liam asked Sarah to marry him, Douglas Tate made the great table as a wedding gift. It took him a year to complete."

Kassandra walked slowly over to the tapestries. "These are incredible."

"They tell the tale of Cadedryn's ancestors. One day you will be woven into Caenmore history."

Kassandra turned to face Moxie. "He does not love

me. He wanted his title and lands. His offer to marry me was based upon his need for my protection."

Moxie laughed. "Your protection? Forgive me, milady, but he is a seasoned warrior and you are but a little lass. I doubt he asked for your hand out of necessity. Do you love him?"

Kassandra sighed. Did she? She dreamed of him. Her heart raced when he was near. She wanted to see him happy and satisfied. "I think so," she murmured. "I always knew we were destined to find each other."

Moxie shook her head. "No, dear. Love is not something you *think* you feel. You know it. Perhaps the reason he has not said that he loves you is because he is not certain you love him."

Moxie led Kassandra up the stairs, then down the length of the hallway to the last room. As she opened the door, Kassandra gasped. The enormous room contained three carved wardrobes and an elegant canopy bed as well as a small table and chairs. But the most astonishing feature of the room was the huge stone fireplace that filled the entire far wall.

"It is so big!" Kassandra cried as she stepped into the room. She walked up to the mantel and touched the carved stones.

"This was Sarah's favorite room. Liam had it designed just for her, and had the stone imported from a faraway place. Sarah loved to sit in front of the fire and tell stories to Cadedryn." Moxie blinked her eyes several times to stop her tears. "We all miss her."

Kassandra looked at her with compassion. "I am sorry for your loss."

"Cadedryn was hurt the most. He lost his mother and his father." She cleared her throat and stepped back in order to shut the door. "Well, if you need

anything, I will be pleased to assist. In the meantime,
a bath will be sent up to you, and feel free to search
the wardrobes for suitable clothing. Yours looks a bit
worse for the wear. Sarah was small, like you. Some
of her clothes might fit you."

"Thank you."

Moxie cast her a happy, grateful smile. "No, *thank
you*. I am so pleased to see Lord Cadedryn again,
especially now that he has a bride of his own. Perhaps
soon the halls will echo with the sounds of another
youngster."

Cadedryn stood in a room built off to the side of
the great room, stroking Triu-cair's silky fur. The weasel had adapted well to his makeshift leash and had
bounded along after Cadedryn as he entered the
room, then leapt into his arms. The polecat's presence
was comforting and Cadedryn smiled as he looked
around. Liam had spent much of his time here reading
tally sheets and instructing his overseers. It was also
where he had shown Cadedryn a Bible filled with elegant pictures and rows upon rows of finely penned
scripture.

Cadedryn placed Triu-cair on the floor, then walked
to the desk where the Bible was stored. Locating the
drawer, he pulled it out and opened the book's front
cover, then ran his finger down the names and dates.
The last read *Liam and Sarah, birth of son Cadedryn
1051.* He looked at the entry with sadness. His father
had been too devastated to enter the date of Sarah's
death.

Unease rippled through him. The room was forlorn,
empty of the sounds he had taken for granted as a
child. His father's booming voice . . . his mother's

tinkling laugh. Now the emptiness yawned around him, transforming the sanctuary into a cold and unwelcoming cavern.

As he closed the book, he noticed a slip of paper peeking out from between the pages. Curious, he withdrew the letter and opened it. The words were faded and the paper was yellow and brittle. Cadedryn squinted, trying to make out the words. It was addressed to his father. *Liam*, it read, *I . . . Sarah's death. I warn you, more will . . . Take care . . . You and your son . . . If you want to save him . . . foster. . . . family . . . murder.*

There was no signature at the bottom.

Cadedryn slowly refolded the letter and replaced it between the pages of the Bible. Something *had* happened to his father. Liam had been warned and then been advised to send his only son to foster for protection. Cadedryn had not been cast aside because his father no longer wanted him. Liam had been trying to save him.

There are things you do not know, his father had said to him that final day. Had Liam received the letter that very morning? Was that why he had been in the meadow, screaming at the injustice of it all? Had the missing words in the letter been kind or cruel? Had the letter been a warning . . . or a threat?

He intended to find out, and Kassandra was going to help him.

Cadedryn extracted a quill and trimmed it with a penknife, then found an inkwell tucked into another drawer. After carefully opening the Bible's cover, he dipped the quill and wrote in the missing entry. *Sarah and Liam Caenmore, death 1066.*

He paused, his quill hovering over the page. Triucair scrambled up on top of the desk and rose on his hind legs. "Soon," Cadedryn promised as he lowered the quill and sanded the words. "Soon we will find out who harmed my family and put the murderer to rest. Then, provided I can convince Kassandra, I will write your mistress's name beside mine."

Triu-cair sniffed the quill and batted it between his paws.

Cadedryn closed the Bible and placed it back in the drawer. He extracted a piece of paper and, after wrestling the quill back from Triu-cair's nimble paws, he prepared to write two letters.

One he addressed to Ronin McTaver, making polite inquires about the health of Kassandra's family and assuring Ronin and Kalial that Kassandra was in safe hands. Kassandra had been continually vague about her home, and he needed more details before he could proceed with their betrothal, including how to formally request her hand and how to appropriately compensate her family for her loss through marriage.

He addressed the other letter to the king. This one was brief. It indicated his appreciation for the return of his title and reiterated his loyalty to the crown. He also added that he had chosen a bride, and due to unusual circumstances, would like special permission to wed her.

Cadedryn sealed the letters, then rose and walked to the window. They would go out by messenger tomorrow.

He would spend tonight trying to convince Kassandra to stay.

Chapter 21

Later that evening they graced the dinner table in silence, waiting for the next course. Cadedryn sat at the head of the table with Kassandra directly to his right. An elaborately engraved candelabra holding four candles illuminated their end of the table, creating a sense of intimacy in the great hall.

"The table and chairs are beautiful," Kassandra mentioned as she took a sip of her soup. "Moxie told me that your grandfather made them." She was wearing a midnight-blue velvet gown shot with long rows of green ribbon that had belonged to Cadedryn's mother. Although out of date, the dress was in perfect condition and fit her well.

"Yes," he answered as he looked up from his wine goblet. "He enjoyed working with his hands, and encouraged Sarah to do the same. My mother learned how to engrave metal and created many exquisite pieces of jewelry."

The gown suited Kassandra. Unlike the pale pastels she usually wore, the dark blue made her eyes even more brilliant. Did she have any idea how beautiful she was? She acted nothing like Lady Corine, who preened frequently and always posed to highlight her best features. Kassandra's motions were brisk yet graceful, much like a young girl who had not yet discovered her inner passion even though he knew differently. His groin tightened as his gaze swept her unbound tresses. "I love your hair," he murmured.

She brushed it back self-consciously. "I asked Moxie for a mantle, but she said Sarah never wore one."

"I'm pleased she was unable to honor your request."

Kassandra averted her eyes. "My hair makes me look too heathen."

He grinned. "Perhaps that is what I like about it."

"Who made the candleholder?" Kassandra asked, diverting the conversation.

"I did. I want you to wear your hair down and unfettered always."

Her eyebrows lifted in surprise. "You made it? You work metal, too?"

"I used to. Will you do that? Wear your hair free for me?"

"This is beautiful. It takes much skill to do such intricate work."

"I made that as a boy. It is a crude piece compared to my later work."

"Later work?"

He stared at her. The candlelight flickered across her face, bringing out the red and gold of her hair. Her eyelashes were like burnished copper and the light freckles dusting her nose brought depth and character to her perfect features. He wanted her. Now. Forever.

"Cadedryn!" she said sharply as she covered her mouth. "Why are you staring at me? Do I have something caught in my teeth?"

He dragged his gaze away and motioned to a servant for a refill of wine. "You didn't answer my request about your hair."

"You didn't answer *my question* about your work."

He drained the goblet and peered at her over the rim. "Why must I surrender first?" he murmured softly, almost as if he were speaking to himself.

Her brows drew together and she looked at him curiously, suddenly aware of a new tension in the air. His hooded expression revealed little. "I told you that I am uncomfortable about my hair color. It makes me look like a . . . like a . . ."

"Like a fire faery, dancing in a blazing hearth."

She sat back, nonplussed. "You sound like a bard."

"Am I less a warrior because I can compliment a woman with flowery words?"

Her mouth opened, but she couldn't speak. She finally shook her head.

"I am sending a missive to your family, informing them of your whereabouts. Can I convince you to stay until we hear back from them?"

"What does it matter? The sooner I leave, the easier it will be."

Cadedryn cast about for another excuse. He did not want to tell her about the second letter. "I need your help, Kassandra. I must find my father's murderer and so far, you have provided my only clue. Won't you be kind and help me? Give me a fortnight. How can a few weeks of your time compare to bringing a villain to justice?"

She looked across the candles at his intent expression. He needed her. Despite her efforts to convince herself otherwise, they were connected. They were linked, soul to soul. He had hurt her and rejected her, but she had also hurt him by toying with his emotions. Even if she was convinced that they could not wed, she could fulfill her obligations and stay near him until the danger was resolved. If she did not, her dreams would plague her and guilt would haunt her.

She trembled as she lowered her gaze, unable to admit even to herself that she wanted to stay.

"If you need me, I will help you," Kassandra murmured.

"Then why don't we drop our guard and be true to ourselves? There is no one in this castle to impress, nor anyone within these walls who cares what clothes we wear or what color your hair is. Wear your tresses down and cease being self-conscious. Let us relax and enjoy each other's company."

"What about you?"

"I will show you my metalwork."

It was her turn to notice the candlelight flickering over his hardened features, softening the harsh lines and making him seem almost vulnerable. Who was he? A swordsman who enjoyed women only for pleasure? A politician who manipulated marriages and fortunes? A poet? A lover?

"Come." He stood up, sliding the chair back and reaching immediately for hers. "It has been ten years since I entered the forge."

She stood more slowly, aware of the dinner yet to be completed. "The servants . . ."

"Forget the rules. Let us do as we want for a short while. Soon enough we will be forced to make decisions. Is it so terrible to interrupt a meal?"

Her heart fluttered and her breathing quickened.

"For tonight, forget that the sun rises every morn and the winter comes every year. Shall we not live for the moment and defy convention?"

She smiled, a glimmer of mischievousness making its way into her blue eyes.

He smiled back and stroked her red curls. "Any woman who could come boldly to my room in order to exact revenge must have a bit of wildness in her heart. It does not take a soothsayer to decipher your true soul."

She trembled at his caress while his words touched her deep inside. She had spent years trying to deny her impulsiveness and a lifetime trying to temper her wildness. "My dreams set me apart from everyone. My family tries to understand, but even they do not quite comprehend me. I often feel very . . ."

"Alone? Is that why you clung to your dream mate so tightly? Is that why you sought to find me?"

"Perhaps. Yes."

"This is not a dream, and I am flesh and blood. I understand you."

"Do you believe in my dreams?"

His voice dropped to a husky whisper. "Yes."

She stepped into his arms and laid her head against his chest.

"Will you leave your hair uncovered for me?"

"Yes. I will," she whispered.

He took her hand, laced his fingers with hers and led her outside into the moonlight. The massive court-yard was deserted, although one could see torches flickering in the manned sentinel towers at each corner. He walked her past the stables and led her to the far side of the courtyard to a large stone building that stood next to a flowing fountain of spring water.

A heavy double door blocked their way. Cadedryn lifted a key from a nail on the wall and unlocked the door. "I left orders for no one to enter the forge. It will not be clean. Would you rather wait until morning?"

She shook her head and grabbed a torch and flint from the wall.

He grinned, his heart lighter than it had been in

years. He struck the flint and lit the torch for her, then pushed open the left door.

It groaned as it scraped inward, revealing a dark, cavernous workroom that echoed with memories of fire and metal.

"When I worked here," he said as he brushed cobwebs out of their way, "I imagined a fire faery watching over my shoulder, keeping me safe."

She lifted the torch and stared into his eyes.

"I did not tell you everything," he said quietly. "I believe your dreams because I dreamed of you, too, only I had forgotten. Seeing you sleep next to the campfire as we rode here reminded me of my buried memories." He touched her face. "We belong together."

She shook her head in confusion.

"As a youth, I felt a flame-haired female watching over me, protecting and soothing me. I did not recognize your face, Kassandra, but I know you have been with me for a very long time. Somewhere along the way, I lost my path. You were sent here to help me find it again. My mother would have liked you."

She swallowed, tears thickening her throat and filling her eyes. "Show me this place you loved," she whispered.

He strode through the room, lighting two more torches, then placing hers in a holder beside the door.

As the torches flickered to life, the room was transformed. Rows upon rows of finely worked swords lined the walls, three and four thick in some places, each different in some unique way. Short swords with corded handles, long swords with elegant engravings, even broadswords with jeweled hilts filled the space. Some swords were blackened while others shimmered with a polished sheen and still others were inlaid with copper, silver or gold. It was an armory of supreme craftsmanship, unlike anything Kassandra had ever seen.

"Who made all these?"

"I did. At least, most of them. A few are examples from foreign masters."

"It takes years to learn this craft. Years of intense dedication."

He walked over to a blackened long sword and lifted it to the torchlight. Although the center was black, the double-sharp edge was shiny. A beautiful engraving down the length of the sword reminded her of something. She stepped over and peered at it. "The dirk!" she exclaimed. "It is the same pattern as on the dirk."

"My mother taught me how to work metal from the moment I was able to hold a tool. When I was seven, my father hired a sword master to design a special sword for him, and when the master saw my interest, he let me practice my craft on his template swords. I soon tired of decorating and demanded to learn how to forge the swords themselves. Over the years, I honed my craft, ever improving on my workmanship."

"These are superb. Artistry is in your blood."

"So is war. While creating swords, I also learned how to use them. It made me into the swordsman I am, allowing me to defend Scotland from her enemies. My father told me that demonstrating my loyalty through swordsmanship could provide my best chance to regain the title. At the time, I did not care about titles, but after his death, I had nothing else. The fight to reclaim my title gave me purpose and direction."

Flashing back to the time she had seen him fight, Kassandra smiled. "You were superb the day on the ridge when you saved me, but you frightened me the time in the fighting yard. I had never seen men fight so brutally. Not at all like the men from my home."

He lifted a lock of her hair with his sword. "I wanted you to see the true man you so recklessly set your eyes upon."

She closed her eyes and inhaled, smelling the dust and cobwebs, but also smelling the tang of metal and the smoke of a long-dead fire.

He touched her closed lids, stroking her long eyelashes as they cast shadows across her cheeks. "But you are an enigma to me. You push and pull me . . . draw me closer, then thrust me afar. Your body aches for me, your dreams conjure me. But your mind rejects me. How is this possible?"

"Why did you really bring me to Aberdour?" she questioned softly, her breath held.

"To give us time."

"Time for what?"

He leaned forward and replaced his fingertips with his lips. Her flesh was warm and he could taste faint moisture at the corner of her eye.

"To figure out what we feel for each other. Time to be with you."

"With me?"

"Without distractions." He kissed her under the curve of her jaw, lifting her chin with a gentle nudge of his nose. "Without games."

As she started to reply, he covered her mouth with his.

She quivered, her emotions tangled by the sweetness of his words and the pain in her heart.

He licked her lower lip and threaded his fingers through the hair at the back of her neck.

Her thoughts fragmented, became unformed and

disjointed. No games. No hidden motives. She arched her back and pressed closer to his warmth. She did not want him to stop. This was her dream—no, this was real.

He lifted her around her waist, just holding her, his head buried in her breasts. He inhaled deeply, feeling the cloak of her hair draped around his head. "I never thought I would feel happy again," he whispered. "Not after my mother died and my father cast me aside. But you bring everything back to life. I know that the tigress is only part of you, but that part brought me out of the grave, while the other part of you, the lady, made me look at my life with new eyes. You forced me to reevaluate my goals."

She wrapped his shoulders in her arms and rested her face atop his head.

He swung around and placed her on a wooden table charred with numerous blackened scars. She braced her hands behind her, her fingers sensing the hours he had spent working on the hardened surface.

Using his forearm, he brushed the dust from the table. Several tools clattered to the stone floor and the torchlight flickered as years of neglect were swept away. "I want to see your hair splayed across my workbench . . . I want your life to infuse my forge with new flames."

His gaze bored into hers. Her breath quickened. Without conscious thought, she reached for him, sliding her hands beneath his shirt. He felt hot, his skin burning with an internal fire while the air around them remained cool.

He pushed her up, sliding her along the wood as he laid her back. He towered over her, briefly blocking her view of the ceiling as he straddled her, but as he rocked back, she gasped. Along the ceiling were racks of more swords, long and thin with glittering edges.

She was surrounded by finely honed steel. Beside her in rows upon the walls, beneath her in piles of discarded shards, above her in shimmering racks like spikes held in place by magical hands. But she felt no fear. Like him, the weapons were elegant yet strong. This was where he felt comfortable. She sensed that this was where he wanted to make love to her, to forge a bond between them that was stronger than the metal he loved.

Steel and fire. The torchlight danced around them as if it wanted to come alive and join the two humans on the table, to leap into her wild tresses and sparkle through her shimmering eyes. Like their souls, one full of fire, the other as hard as a blade, the room reflected and enhanced them, allowing them to merge together like a pool of red-hot liquid metal.

Kassandra gripped his shirt and struggled to untie it. Her blood burned with desire. She wanted him, wanted to feel his sword buried within her. When the cords knotted, she shifted her attention to his breeches, but her fingers shook so badly, she could not untie them either.

"The fire faery protects you still," she growled in frustration as the pulse in her neck thrummed.

"Perhaps she is jealous," he chuckled, but he reached for something tucked into the waistband of his breeches. Finding it, he held out a small, beautifully formed dirk.

She took it and held it to his chest. "The dirk that led me to you," she murmured. "You trust me with a knife as sharp as this?"

"Would you cut me with a blade my mother engraved?"

She plucked the cord of his shirt away from his chest and sliced it. The dirk slid through the twisted threads with a faint whisper and his shirt gaped open at the hollow of his throat.

A thrill raced through Kassandra. There was something wild in the heart of the steel and it transmitted vibrations to her palm. Her blue eyes opened wide and she stared at him.

He stared back.

"You want to use it," he told her.

She shivered.

"Which one are you tonight? The lady Kassandra or the wild tigress? Do you dare?"

She shook her head. "I am who I want to be . . . where I want to be. With you." She slid the sharp blade through another cord, relishing the sound of it cutting and the feel of his muscles twitching. More of his chest was revealed and she touched the tip of the dirk to his skin. "You are at my mercy," she whispered.

He still straddled her, his large, heavily muscled body towering over her small prostrate form. He could crush her, overpower her, kill her with one blow. "Yes," he replied quietly. "I am completely at your mercy."

Chapter 22

She smiled, her lips curving slowly as her cheeks flushed with heat. Using the dirk, she sliced down his linen shirt until it lay open. Underneath, his hard flesh shimmered with a fine coating of sweat, reflecting the orange torchlight. Twin nipples rose small and hard amid a swirl of black hair.

She switched her attention to his breeches, reveling in his swift intake of breath as she lowered the knife. Using the tip, she plucked the cords loose, then cut them free of the lace holes one by one.

As she concentrated, her breath bathed him in moist warmth and his erection swelled larger. As the cord strings sprang apart, his rod strained to be free, pushing dangerously close to the razor-sharp blade. Then suddenly, as Kassandra's hands swept downward and she cut the breechcloth, his cock jutted forth as strong and proud as any sword.

He gripped her wrist, then gently but firmly lifted it over her head and pinned it to the table.

"You do not trust me," she taunted him.

"No. Your anger is too easily aroused and your temper is too tumultuous, for you are a red-haired seductress."

She licked her lips, oddly pleased by his words.

His gaze dropped instantly to her mouth.

She saw his shift of attention, and licked her lips again, this time more slowly.

"You have a beautiful mouth. Full, red lips. A dark freckle at the right corner." His hips twitched.

She looked at his cock, so close to her mouth and so tantalizing. Lifting her head a little, she flicked her tongue out and faintly touched the tip.

He sucked in his breath and jerked back, but she lifted her knees and braced him.

Slanting a daring look up through her lashes, she peeked her tongue out once more, this time tasting a salty substance that made her taste buds blaze to life. "Let me," she begged. "You said we could do as we wished."

His eyes darkened to deep forest green and his expression sharpened to chiseled alertness. He tilted his hips forward, his actions still wary.

Pushing him closer with her knees, she shifted his body close to her mouth. The head glimmered with tight, translucent skin and the shaft strained toward her, ignoring its master's hesitancy. Kassandra swirled her tongue over the tip. It pulsed in reaction and a bead of white liquid trickled forth.

Kassandra licked again, fascinated by the reactions she caused, then lifted her head higher and wrapped her lips around him.

They both gasped as they felt simultaneous rushes of heat. His head dropped back as his resistance melted away and he gave in to the incredible sensation of her mouth around him. Her tongue explored and stroked, making his mind shake as his body bucked in pleasure. Her mouth was heaven and he wanted to live deep within her cavern forever. He felt his ecstasy rising, ready to explode.

But he abruptly pulled free, pushed her knees apart

and lay flush upon her. "Not yet." He slid down her body, spreading her legs and rapidly untying her skirts. His hands were more steady than hers, and the strings quickly fell apart. He yanked her skirts aside and rapidly removed her underclothes, laying her bare to his gaze and open to his touch.

He kissed her inner thigh, tickling her in a sensuous, delicious way.

She drew in a quick breath and tried to clench her legs together, embarrassed about her own reactions.

"You kissed me," he growled. "I get to kiss you."

Her thigh muscles relaxed slightly, and she let him push her knees apart, but she bit her lip anxiously.

He kissed her other thigh, then suckled gently.

Thrills raced up and down her legs and her toes curled. Her head fell back and her hair tumbled down the far side of the table as she braced her elbows on the black-scarred surface.

His mouth moved closer and he breathed against her dark red curls, stimulating the center hidden within.

Her hips twitched and fierce longing ripped through her. Her hesitancy disappeared as desire raged and suddenly she wanted his kisses, wanted to feel his heated mouth against her. She opened her legs farther, splaying herself for him, for his pleasure and for hers.

His tongue found its way to her and his first taste of her beautiful womanhood almost sent him over the precipice. He groaned, feeling closer to her than he had ever believed possible. She smelled like rich musk and tasted like ambrosia. He licked again, the sensitive buds upon his tongue finding the central rose, tasting the delicate petals and relishing her quivering responses.

He slid his hands underneath her buttocks and lifted

her higher. She was pliant to his ministrations, yet panting with pleasure, held still by need yet shaking with uncontrolled reaction. He buried his face deeper, merging with her, licking and tasting faster and faster as she screamed with delight. The intensity escalated, soared and swirled around them. His own pleasure burst forth, risen by the beauty of her response, by the knowledge that he was able to do this to her.

"Now!" she screamed and he slid off the end of the table, planted his feet and dragged her to the edge with him in one smooth motion. Without pausing, he plunged his cock into her drenched core and slammed into her.

She screamed again, calling his name as she gripped the sides of the table and encouraged his fierce attack. "Harder, harder!" she shouted as her inner sanctum clenched and pulsed, caught in the throes of a long unending climax. "Join me!"

He pumped thrice more, then shouted his own release deep within her, his spear shaking with powerful contractions, pouring his soul deep within her womb.

Her legs fell open. . . . Her toes relaxed. She took a deep breath, then released it in an exhausted rush as he collapsed on top of her. His weight lay across her, his head pillowed between her breasts, heavy but welcome. He, too, breathed deeply as if he had finished racing across the Highlands and only now had reached his safe haven.

Their combined heat slowly cooled, and the night breeze snaking in through the open doorway chilled their flesh despite the flickering torchlight. Cadedryn stirred, then rose off her and reached on the ground for her discarded skirts. He draped them over her, closed his own breeches as best as he could, then lifted her into his arms.

Kassandra snuggled against his chest, her lids shut in drowsy surrender. "Where are you taking me now?" she murmured.

He stepped out into the moonlight and made his way across the courtyard without the benefit of a torch. He knew the way; he had traveled it often. Entering the great hall, he ignored the startled looks of the staff and wound his way up the stairs, past the chamber where Kassandra had changed, and strode with her in his arms until he reached the master bedchamber. Kicking open the door, he paused. This was his parents' room. This was the place of their love, the place where he had been conceived. He looked down upon Kassandra's drowsy face.

"Here," he finally answered in a whisper. "Where you belong."

She woke slowly, aware of streams of sunshine and the aroma of hot cider. Her eyes still closed, she stirred, smiling at Triu-cair's faint chatter and the maid's irritated exclamation, but her eyes snapped open when she heard Cadedryn's low voice.

"Leave the platter," he said to the maid. "The lady still sleeps."

As the door closed, Kassandra sat up and glared at him. "Why am I in your room?" she queried. "I chose the chamber with the great mantel. The maid will—"

"The maid will say nothing."

"I shouldn't be here! My reputation—"

"No one here cares about your reputation. You promised me a fortnight." He looked at her angry face and raised an eyebrow. Her tousled hair cascaded around her shoulders in a fetching mess. He was too happy to argue with her, and he mentally vowed to ignore her furious face and make her happy as well.

"I did not promise to sleep in your bed."

He shrugged and handed her a cup of cider. "Very well. You are not obligated to sleep here."

She frowned, taken aback by his easy capitulation. She pushed a lock of hair behind her ear as her mind sought a suitable reply. How was she to argue a point he did not disagree with? She looked around the room and wriggled her toes. The bed was quite comfortable. "What if I decide I want to sleep here?" she challenged.

He shrugged again and turned slightly to the side, hiding a secret smile. "As you wish."

Her fist clenched. This was getting complicated! "Without you," she added snidely.

"I prefer my old room. All my belongings are still there. Feel free to utilize this chamber at your will." Smoothing his face, he sat on the chair next to the bed, tore a piece off a steaming pastry and popped it in his mouth. "Would you like to see my stables?" he asked.

Their debate forgotten, Kassandra's face lit up. "Yes!" she cried. "And your hay storage and the grain bins and—"

He held up his hand and laughed. "I meant the horses. Most people are interested in the horseflesh, not the husbandry."

She grinned self-consciously.

His laugh faded and he stared in awe at her lovely blue eyes. How could one woman be so beautiful? Last night, in the moonlight, she had glowed, and in the forge, she had burned. Now she fairly sparkled with infectious enthusiasm. "To be frank, I am not certain about the hay and grain, and I know little about the pastures. I have focused my attention on controlling the breeding and understand the bloodlines.''

She shook her head dismissively. "Breeding is only part of the horse. You must also manage their environment in order to produce a truly outstanding animal.''

He bowed his head. "I am honored to learn from you. 'Tis clear that my lands need help. Shall we spend some time exploring? I'd like my people to know that I have come home to help them.''

She smiled and pointed to a wrap hanging at the end of the bed as she slipped one bare leg out from under the covers. "Could you please hand me that?"

Cadedryn's eyes flared. "I have seen you as you are.''

Kassandra flushed and pulled her leg back under the blanket. "Not in the daylight. Not like this.''

"Like this?''

She sighed in exasperation. "If you won't hand it over, please leave so I may dress." Then, to Kassandra's horror, Triu-cair bounded onto Cadedryn's lap and snatched the rest of the pastry from the table. "Stop him!" she shouted, the covers slipping from her shoulders to her waist.

Cadedryn leaned back as he chewed his own pastry, trying not to react to the sight of her pink nipples. "If you want it back," he informed her, "you must catch him. He's your weasel.''

"Augh!" she cried as she watched Triu-cair nibble the delicious treat. The weasel grinned at her and lifted his lips in a version of a smile. "You thief!" She slid a quick glance at Cadedryn, who appeared uninterested in her plight, then she leapt naked from the bed, snatched the wrap and tackled her weasel.

The two tumbled and rolled, a mass of screeching and scrambling, until a ruffled and empty-handed weasel dashed to the other side of the room and Kassandra sat triumphant and unclothed in the center of the chamber.

Cadedryn's brow lifted again. "Where is the pastry?" he asked in amusement.

Kassandra opened her mouth, showing a glimpse of the half-chewed prize, then swallowed with obvious relish. "No one does me ill and survives my wrath," she announced haughtily.

Cadedryn's face stilled and he turned to look out the window as unwelcome thoughts invaded his mind. He understood her statement all too well, for he had lived by it all his life. Unfortunately, someone *had* done ill to him, and had most definitely avoided *his* wrath. Whoever had murdered his father had unfinished business with him.

But today was not a day for retribution. Today he wanted to enjoy life and learn everything he could about Kassandra.

At the top of the far hillside, two people sat on horseback and surveyed Aberdour Castle. Both were displeased with what they saw.

"I thought you killed him," the woman hissed furiously. "Why are the flags announcing the earl's presence flying upon the ramparts?"

The man clenched his fists and glared down the valley. "He arrived yesterday, accompanied by that woman. He should have died! I saw the blade plunge into his chest. How could he have survived? That woman," he spat. "She is the cause. She saved him. Everything is her fault."

His companion turned and stroked his snarling face.

Her expression smoothed into softer, more comforting lines. "What are you going to do about him? About her?"

"It was foolish to attack him as I did. Now he is warned. He will be more vigilant."

"He has no idea what we plan. He knows nothing."

"He will suspect. First his mother and father, then the attack on Kassandra and now him. He is highly intelligent. The coincidences will not go unnoticed." The man's face became contemplative and he scratched his chin. "We must use his own thoughts and feelings against him."

The woman turned away and looked over the sunlit castle. Nowhere in Scotland had she ever seen such a magnificent fortress, yet few had ventured to visit since the Caenmore family had fallen into disgrace. She smiled with satisfaction. A few words whispered here . . . a rumor repeated there . . . For all those years, it had been a simple task to keep Cadedryn isolated from society. After such work, he should have been easy pickings—a cowed, insecure man who desperately sought approval from anyone. He should have been thankful to marry a woman such as Corine.

"He was falling in with our plans perfectly until Kassandra arrived," she murmured. "Why is such an odd child able to sway his mind? She must be using some trick we haven't yet discovered. I heard tell that she dreamed about him and had visions about Liam's death."

The man turned to face her. "Dreams?"

"Dreams of the past. Dreams of the future. Mayhap even the power to change events."

"Did she dream of us? Does she know who killed Liam?"

The woman frowned in irritation. "Of course not.

No one can truly see what is not in front of them. It is a gypsy trick, and one we should use to our advantage. What do you think the populace would feel if they knew their new earl harbored a fey witch in their midst?"

The man sat back on his horse and stared at her with admiration. "You are a clever woman, my love. 'Tis why I could not let you go."

She smiled, her lips twisting in a cruel smile.

Chapter 23

Cadedryn and Kassandra raced through the old ruins, then far across the open field, each bent low over their steeds as they urged the heaving beasts faster and faster. With powerful bounds, the horses soared over a tinkling stream and plunged through acres of waist-high grasses until they finally pulled up beneath the spreading branches of a red maple tree.

Kassandra laughed and leapt off her mare, collapsing to the ground. Triu-cair squealed and jumped down, his eyes tearing from the wind. He scampered up the tree and began searching for grubs.

Cadedryn swung down more slowly and took a moment to pull the saddles off the horses and hobble them before he joined Kassandra in the cool shade. "No woman should be able to ride like that," he informed her. "Not only is it obscene to see you with your beautiful thighs spread around a horse's muscled flesh, but it is highly inappropriate for a woman to beat a man in a horse race."

Kassandra stretched her arms over her head, wove her fingers together and cracked her knuckles. "You wanted to get to know me better," she said, giggling. "I am highly competitive and utterly ruthless."

He sat next to her with one leg bent and the other stretched straight. He plucked a long stem of grass and put it between his teeth. "You were right," he finally commented. "I had no idea that mare of mine was so fast. She looks too fragile for speed."

"Wrapping her legs gave her the extra support she needed," Kassandra replied. "Horse breeders have focused on strength and power because they primarily breed for war, but if you want speed, you should concentrate on lightness and agility."

"Based on your summation, a woman should always outrace a man."

Kassandra glanced up, assessing his words. "Are you challenging me again?"

He laughed and grabbed her hand before she could spring into action. "Not at all. If I concede the race, can we rest a moment?"

She relaxed and swept him with a sensual look. "Rest?"

He leaned over and brushed her lips with his. "There is one thing for which a woman needs a man."

She smiled and closed her eyes. Lifting her arms, she wrapped them around his shoulders and drew him closer.

He kissed her more deeply, taking his time to explore her mouth and feel her responses. She in turn nibbled his lips, leisurely enjoying the special closeness of the afternoon as they kissed under the leaves of the great maple.

After some time, he rolled onto his back and pulled her across his chest. He held her close, rubbing her back as she took deep, relaxed breaths. "What do you want in the next ten years?" he asked her as he nuzzled her curls.

She rested her ear against his chest and listened to the steady beat of his heart. "I never thought about that," she admitted. "I spent my time concerned about the present. The farthest ahead I planned was to find you."

"What did you think would happen once you found and married your dream man?"

She tilted her head and rested her chin on his chest. "I'm not sure."

He grinned.

"Is that silly?" she asked.

"I'm not sure I would call it silly," he answered. "But I certainly would call it shortsighted."

"What about you? What did you think would happen once you married Corine?"

He closed his eyes and pushed her head back down. "Not fair," he grumbled.

She laughed and cuddled closer. "Now what are we going to do?"

"Nothing. Absolutely nothing at this moment."

She pulled back and sat up.

He opened one eye and looked at her warily.

"Why?" she asked seriously.

He was quiet for a moment, but then, when she thought he was not going to reply, he answered her so softly she had to strain to understand his words. "Because I don't know what to do."

Her eyes clouded and she looked at him thoughtfully. He closed his eyes again and feigned sleep, but she could feel the tension in his body. She had not thought of him as the one who was confused. He had always seemed so driven and self-assured. Could he have been as lost as she? She lay back down and wrapped her arm tightly around his waist. "I'll help you," she whispered. "We'll help each other."

He squeezed her back, some of his tension easing.

*   *   *

She slept with him that night.

They lay together in the master bed, entwined in each other's arms. Gently caressing each other's backs, they faced one another, alternately laughing and speaking quietly, and at other times saying nothing at all.

He traced the curve of her jaw and brushed his lips across her forehead while she tickled his earlobe and nuzzled his neck. It was a time of exploration, and both proceeded with languid hands, finding wonderment at the other's sensitive areas.

Kassandra sighed as Cadedryn touched behind her knees and moaned as his fingers trailed along the backs of her thighs, while Cadedryn groaned in appreciation when Kassandra discovered the ridges of his abdomen, kissing and blowing softly over them.

"You are a dream," he murmured to her.

"You are *my* dream," she answered.

Rolling her around so that her back nestled against his chest, he tucked her head on his arm and pressed his lips against her hair. "What would you say if I told you I love you?"

"Love me?"

"I love you."

"You do not believe in such tender emotions. You said that you never wanted to fall in love."

Silence stretched between them, but it was a comfortable, companionable silence in which he smiled. "I believe in it now. I want to love and protect you."

She grinned. "It is I who must protect you."

"Shall we protect each other?"

"Very well."

He turned her around. "So . . . do you love me?"

She stared up at his green eyes, her stomach doing flip-flops. She felt giddy and unbelievably happy. "I do. I do love you."

"I want us to be together forever."

Her heart caught. "It is not that simple," she said softly. "You are an earl and I . . ." She pulled away and looked at him with a serious gaze. "I come from a place called Loch Nidean. Kalial is my half sister. We share a mother but both have unknown fathers, as is the tradition in our family. I live in the woods and sleep among the ferns. I play with bunnies and squirrels. I am not anything like Lady Corine. I will not make a good countess for you."

"You will be a perfect countess."

"I don't think you understand."

"I do understand. You are not a sheltered lass, raised by a strict family to be meek and mild. You are unusual."

"Exactly."

"Do you think this revelation surprises me?"

She drew her brows together. "Doesn't it bother you?"

"That you do not come from a traditional family?" he asked. "No. My father married a peasant because he loved her. I want to marry you, and I do not care from whence you came, as long as we can live and love together." He drew her leg in between his and crooked his arm to pull her closer.

"I have dreams," she reminded him. "Dreams of the future."

"Ummm," he murmured as he kissed her ear.

"I ride astride and hate to wear shoes!"

"Umm-hummm. Do you want children?"

"Yes."

"Good. So do I."

"I have red hair!"

Cadedryn took a deep breath as he shook his head. "Kassandra, there is nothing you can say that will change my mind. I love you for who you are, red hair and all. I want to see your forest and I'd like to meet your family. I need to know only one thing. Will you marry me?"

Silence spread through the bedchamber. In the distance, a horse whinnied and an owl hooted. Kassandra sighed and snuggled closer. "Yes," she whispered. "I will marry you."

Deep in the night, Kassandra sat up, her palms damp with sweat and her heart pounding. She had dreamed of Liam's death, but this time she had seen the murderer's face. She struggled to hold on to the image, to fix it in her memory, but the person's visage melted back into the shadows, becoming obscured within a blue mist.

Kassandra slipped silently out of bed and stood staring out the window. It had been within her grasp. She had seen the malevolent spirit, but now her mind was stubbornly blank. She knew without a doubt, however, that the man who had attacked both Cadedryn and herself was linked to the person who had killed Liam.

Yet she couldn't recall the person's face. Tears of frustration trickled down her cheeks.

The danger was not past. It was coming closer.

And she felt helpless to stop it.

Several days later Kassandra and Cadedryn sat in the great hall, laughing at the bizarre antics of Triu-cair. The weasel was chasing a clever little mouse all around the hall, a mouse that had been able to elude capture for well over an hour. Just as Triu-cair pounced on the small creature, a horn announcing someone's imminent arrival reverberated through the room and the mouse was able to scamper away.

Cadedryn rose and motioned for Robert to open the door. "Who comes?" he asked.

Robert stepped outside for a brief moment, then returned. "It appears to be Lord Curtis. And the ladies Fergus, as well as Laird McCafferty."

Cadedryn's expression tensed, and he reached for Kassandra's hand. "Raise the gates."

"Cadedryn . . ." Kassandra murmured. "I am nervous. I had a dream last night."

"Don't worry," he replied. "Everything will be fine." But he released her hand and began pacing.

Within moments, they heard the clatter of several hooves, then the strident voice of a female demanding immediate entrance.

"Open the door," Cadedryn commanded and Robert once again swung the heavy door wide.

Lady Corine, Lady Morgana and Laird McCafferty swept in, followed more slowly by Lord Curtis and an elderly man Cadedryn did not recognize. "Good afternoon," Cadedryn said, distrust clouding his voice. "What brings all of you to Aberdour?"

Curtis flicked his gaze toward Kassandra. "May we speak in private?"

"Anything you have to say can be said in front of my intended," Cadedryn replied.

Curtis pushed the elderly man forward. "This man is an old shepherd who once lived in the meadows above Aberdour. He knows something about your father's death."

Cadedryn looked warily at the gray-haired man. "What information do you have?" Behind him, he felt Kassandra's start of surprise and heard her intake of breath.

"I saw a lass kill your father that day in the forest," the man said in a thick brogue. "I was walkin' through the trees and saw him fall to his knees. A young woman had stabbed him in the chest and her hands were covered in blood." He looked around the room. "A woman in red, like her." He pointed toward Kassandra.

"How do you know this?" Cadedryn demanded as he gripped the man's shirt and pulled him close to his chest. "What purpose do you have in speaking now? What is the real truth? Who paid you to lie?"

"I not be lying, nor hiding the truth!" the man cried as he attempted to pull out of Cadedryn's vicelike grip. "At least, not now. Someone did pay me to keep quiet, but 'twas ten years ago. He said I should not be telling anyone what I saw, or I'd be lying at the bottom of a loch. Then a few days ago, a messenger came to me sayin' that 'twas time to come forward, so I made me way to court and asked for ya. When the servant found that you had already left, he brought me to Lord Curtis."

"When he told me that the woman wore red," Curtis said, "I suspected that he had mistaken a red cape for red hair. It was my father that told me he suspected that Lady Kassandra and your red-haired mistress were one and the same." Curtis looked at Kassandra and swept her with an angry glare. "I tried to catch up with you that night and followed you for several days, but you seemed to melt into the trees. I finally returned to court to tell Father, who insisted all of us come to Aberdour in order to save you from Kassandra's deceitful clutches. We have already sent for the bishop. She should die for her crime."

"The man speaks falsely," Cadedryn declared as he flung the elderly man to the ground. "Kassandra would no more kill my father than I would."

"He tells the truth!" Curtis shouted back. "Why do

you insist on remaining blind? Kassandra has bedeviled you from the start, befouling all our plans!"

"You speak as a fool. Kassandra would have been a mere child. How could she have overpowered a man such as my father?"

"How do you know how old she truly is? Perhaps she is six and ten or perhaps she is six and twenty. Women have ways of changing their appearance. You cannot trust her!"

"She has done nothing. She is innocent. I would place my entire reputation—my title and my lands—upon that conviction."

Curtis looked at him curiously. "You love her that much? Enough to risk everything?" he asked, but before Cadedryn could answer, Laird McCafferty shoved his son aside.

"You must not allow that wench to foil your ambitions, Cadedryn. Marry Corine. She is the woman you were always meant to wed. Forget Kassandra. She is guilty and will soon be dead. Your union with Corine will bring everything back to its proper place. I, as your foster father, demand it!"

Kassandra gasped and pressed a hand to her mouth. Her heart raced and memories of her dreams sped through her mind. Swords . . . blood . . . a red cape.

"Cadedryn," Lady Morgana interjected. "If you don't believe him, I brought something that is sure to convince you. Here is a letter you should read." Her gaze slid slyly toward Kassandra. "Read this before you say anything more in Kassandra's defense." She handed Cadedryn a folded parchment.

Cadedryn frowned, recognizing the penmanship from the letter he had found earlier in the Bible. He opened it, scanned the missive, then sat heavily on a chair. The color in his face drained and his eyes began to glitter with suppressed emotion.

"What does it say?" Kassandra asked as she came forward.

"Stay back!" Cadedryn shouted, leaping to his feet. Kassandra froze.

He paced to the other side of the room and shoved the letter inside his tunic. Silence filled the hall as he stared at Kassandra's confused face. His chest rose and fell as he drew several breaths. Then his gaze shifted and he looked at Robert and his expression hardened with resolve. "Take her away," he commanded. "I do not want to see her again."

"Cadedryn? What does the letter say?" Kassandra asked.

"It is about you, Kassandra. It . . . it proves your guilt."

"No! You know that is not true!"

"The words have convinced me not to defend you anymore. Good-bye, Kassandra."

"I was nowhere near Aberdour when Liam died," Kassandra pleaded. "I am the one who encouraged you to delve into the past and seek answers to his death. You know me. You love me!" She reached toward Cadedryn, but he flinched away.

"Witchery!" Morgana exclaimed. "You flew through your dreams and stabbed him flush in the heart, then took your enchanted weapon back home with you."

"Robert," Cadedryn called sharply. "Take her to the cell in the old keep and guard her well, then hand her over to the bishop when he arrives. I want nothing more to do with her."

"Cadedryn!" Kassandra cried as Robert began dragging her from the room. "Cadedryn! How could you believe them?"

"Burn her!" Lady Morgana screamed. "She is a witch, seeking to enchant an earl of Scotland! She must die for her crimes against the Caenmore family!"

A small russet creature streaked down the stairs and launched itself at Lady Morgana.

She shrieked and fell back, flailing her arms.

"Triu-cair!" Kassandra gasped as she ripped her arm out of Robert's hold and snatched her friend off the wailing woman.

Morgana touched her bloodied face and looked at her red hands in horror. "She controls beasts!" the lady screeched. "The animal has been possessed and does her dastardly will!"

" 'Tis only a weasel," Kassandra snapped back. "There is no witchery! Your fears rule your mind." She swung around and glared at Cadedryn. "And you! You are not fit to be my friend much less my husband! Marry Lady Corine. Wed her and forget me, for as soon as I exit this hall, I will have forgotten you!"

Cadedryn clenched his hands, his own anger surging. "Have you so little faith in my judgment?"

"If your judgment tells you to throw me to the wolves, then no, I don't believe in you!"

"My word is my honor," he growled, hoping she would understand and believe him.

Her blue eyes shimmered with unshed tears, but she held her chin high. "I despise you! You said you loved me and that you would protect me. Keep your love! Keep it, for I want no part of it! Your words are meaningless and without honor."

His face devoid of expression, Cadedryn turned on his heel and left the hall.

As the door swung shut behind Robert and Kassandra and the echoes of Cadedryn's footsteps receded, the old man rose from where he had been cast and peered fearfully at the remaining people in the room.

"Did I say whot you wanted me ta say, milaird? Will you promise to leave my family alone?"

Morgana unclasped a bracelet from around her wrist and tossed it at the man as Laird McCafferty clapped him on the back. "Yes," he answered. "You did splendidly, but you will have to tell the bishop as well, so don't go far."

The man nodded, then fled outside, slamming the great hall door behind him.

Corine looked at her mother with dawning suspicion. "Did you bribe him?" she asked. "Did you force him to accuse Kassandra?"

Morgana shrugged. "What does it matter? He did see someone wearing a red cape kill Liam; that much is true. Kassandra has red hair and is a thorn in my existence. Why not use his tale to my advantage?"

Curtis frowned. "I brought him here because I thought he had knowledge of Liam's death. I have no wish to accuse an innocent woman."

"She is not innocent," David grumbled. "Why are you being so obstinate? You are as stubborn as Cadedryn. Kassandra must be eliminated so that we can complete our plans, just as we needed to get rid of Sarah."

"What are you saying?" Curtis demanded. "Did Kassandra kill Liam or not?"

"Of course not!" Morgana answered. "Do you think a child like that would have the skill and daring to commit murder? That would take someone with inordinate abilities and special attributes." She smiled and lifted her chin proudly.

"Father!" Curtis cried.

"Mother!" Corine exclaimed. "You can't mean that! Did you kill Liam?"

"I did what I needed to do in order to ensure my daughter's happiness," Morgana replied. "You, my dear Corine, *will* become Countess of Aberdour."

Corine and Curtis gasped and looked at each other across the room. "I never wanted to be countess," Corine whispered. "That was *your* dream."

"And Curtis will own Aberdour and all of its vast properties," David McCafferty added, ignoring Corine.

"I will not gain Aberdour, not unless . . ." Curtis stared in horror at his father.

"It will be as Morgana and I planned from the beginning, since before either of you were born. Liam should have wed Morgana. Then we intended upon arranging his death, thereby leaving Morgana widowed. I would have been the perfect choice for her second husband. It was a wonderful scheme. She would have her title, and I would obtain all the properties." McCafferty pounded his fist against the table. "But that bitch Sarah ruined our plans! She deserved to die!"

Curtis fell back, his eyes wide with shock. "Why Liam? Why kill him, too?"

"Isn't that obvious?" Morgana replied. "David would raise Cadedryn and help him regain his title. Then he would arrange Cadedryn's marriage to my daughter, only Cadedryn's life after his wedding would be unexpectedly short, just like his mother's and father's." Morgana caressed David's cheek. "After Corine had finished mourning the loss of her *beloved* husband, she would wed Curtis McCafferty. My daughter and David's son. It was a perfect plan. We would be able to control half of the Highlands and a child of my blood would become Countess of Aberdour!"

Morgana squeezed her daughter's arm in a painful grip. "Don't look so stricken, Corine. I know you want Curtis. You have been sneaking behind my back, spreading your legs for him like a cat in heat, thinking I knew nothing about your whoring ways. Did you really think I would be oblivious to what was happening? Did you think I didn't orchestrate the entire affair?"

"Mother!" Corine wailed again. "If you always knew, why did you force us to hide our feelings?"

Morgana slapped her across the face. "Silence!" she shouted. "You will marry Cadedryn. Then you will kill him. Only after he is dead will I allow you to wed your rutting stud. You should be on your knees, thanking me for everything I have done for you."

Curtis leapt forward to defend Corine, but David shoved him against the wall, pinning him to the gray stone. "Lay no hand upon Morgana," he cautioned. "She speaks the truth. Cadedryn must die. His father destroyed my happiness and ruined Morgana's only chance at becoming a countess. 'Tis good that you like Corine, for 'twill make your marriage easier. You, too, should be pleased. Why do you think I let you spend so much time together when you were children? Soon you can pound your cock deep inside her anytime you want."

Curtis stared at Corine, his entire body trembling. "Did you know? Did you plan this with your mother? Did you use my love for your own revenge?"

Corine shook her head, then buried her head in her hands and sobbed louder.

David abruptly released Curtis and turned to gather

Morgana in an embrace. "I love you, Morgana," he whispered. "Have I made you happy?"

Morgana smiled, her eyes sparkling with pleasure. She placed a kiss upon his lips. "Aye. And once I see that red-haired witch burning at the stake, I will be even happier. Will you do that for me?"

"I'll do anything for you."

Chapter 24

Kassandra sat on her prison cell's stone bench and stared up at the shaft of light that announced the rising dawn. Dust motes danced on unseen currents, drifting then suddenly spinning in crazy circles before spiraling out of sight. Although her body remained perfectly still, her muscles were coiled into tight, painful knots and her knuckles were white with fiercely contained tension.

She rose in agitation and pressed her cheek against the cold bars over the cell's single window. The night had passed, a night of terrifying dreams. She peered through the bars at the heavy stones forming the outer wall of Aberdour Castle and her gaze was drawn inexorably to the high window of the master chamber.

How could she have been so wrong about Cadedryn?

A tear slipped out, but she dashed it away. She would shed no more tears over him. She would spend no more nights dreaming of him.

Robert opened the cell and placed a washbasin and pile of folded clothes on the mattress. " 'Tis time to change," he told Kassandra. "Moxie provided a clean dress and sewed a mantle for you. She is concerned about how you are faring and knew you preferred to cover your head."

Kassandra caught her breath and touched the clothes. "That is kind," she replied softly. "What about Cadedryn? Is he concerned? Does he send anything?"

Robert shook his head.

Kassandra's gaze hardened and she picked up the mantle. "We were never destined to be together. I feel like such a fool. I was wrong all along."

"He asked me to guard you. He must care for you."

"Perhaps he cares only to ensure my demise."

Robert shook his head again. "He has not left his room. I heard him pacing all night."

"He let them accuse me of murder. He vowed to protect me yet quailed at the first test. I do not want him." She tossed the mantle at Robert with a flare of defiance. "I will not wear it," she declared. "I will not hide. I want Cadedryn to see my face when the flames envelop me!"

Robert frowned and tried to hand back the mantle. "Wear it," he pleaded. "Your hair is sure to frighten the bishop and he will more likely convict you."

Kassandra stroked a lock of her hair, then twirled it around her finger. "I once feared people's ignorance. I hid my hair so that strangers would not look at me askance, but why should I be the one to hide? If people can see only with their eyes clouded by superstition and not listen to truth spoken by one pure of deed, then I sorrow for them."

A knock on the door startled them both. "The bishop calls for the accused to come forth!" a crier announced.

"Already?" Robert asked as he flung open the door. "He has already arrived?"

The crier looked at Kassandra's flaming tresses and shuddered. "The trial will commence immediately, by order of King Malcolm."

Kassandra paled. How had events come to this?

                        *   *   *

Up in the master chamber, Cadedryn smashed his fist against the table, then pounded his head against the stone wall until white spots danced across his vision.

How could he have failed her? He opened the letter Morgana had handed him and read it again, even though he knew the words by heart. *You can let the court decide or we will slay her right now. It is your choice.*

He inhaled deeply, his blood pounding through his temples. He loved her more and more with every breath he took. He ached to enfold her in his embrace, to tell her that he would do anything for her, even sacrifice his home and title, if only it gave them more time to love each other.

Yet they had threatened to kill her then and there. Otherwise, she would be charged with murder and ordered to be burned at the stake, but at least that would buy him some time. His only chance to save her life was to prove her innocence by bringing the real killer to justice, and he had to do so without involving anyone else whose life could be unjustly threatened.

He prayed only that in the process of saving her body, he did not lose her heart.

Making a swift decision, he left the bedchamber and strode down to the great hall, then out to the courtyard, where he called for his stallion. Within moments, he was thundering over the moat and toward the village.

Curtis solemnly watched Cadedryn race toward the village church. "Do you think he rides to defend her?"

he asked Corine. They stood in a guest chamber where they had spent a terrible night arguing. Corine was deeply devoted to her mother, and Curtis was shaken to the core by his father's revelations. Both Cadedryn and Corine had been raised to worship land and power and had faithfully pursued their ambitions. Now they had the opportunity to gain more than they had ever hoped to achieve. All they had to do was accept their parents' plans and do as they were instructed.

Corine rose and stood beside him. "No. He wouldn't dare cross my mother. Morgana will have anything she desires, one way or another. Everyone fears her wrath. Besides, if Cadedryn does speak in Kassandra's defense, my mother will accuse her of sorcery and say it proves that she is a witch. There is no other possibility. One way or another, by tomorrow Kassandra will be dead."

Curtis turned and placed two hands upon Corine's shoulders. "You wrote to me several years ago and asked me to convince Cadedryn to request your hand in marriage. I did what you asked. Like my father, I will do anything for the woman I love. So tell me, do you still want to marry him?"

Corine gazed into her lover's eyes. She could be like her mother. She could twist this man around her finger and force him to do immoral deeds.

A sense of power rippled through her. She could control Curtis. She could be a countess and become immensely rich and influential. She would be even more powerful than Morgana herself.

All she had to do was say yes.

Arriving only moments before the wagon bearing Kassandra rolled down the village street, Cadedryn swung from his stallion and raced inside the church. He knelt respectfully before the bishop. "Your Excellency," he greeted.

"Laird Caenmore," the bishop acknowledged.

"I wish to speak with you privately."

"Is it important?" the bishop inquired. "A trial is about to begin."

"Aye. 'Tis of great importance. Something the king will be anxious to hear."

"Very well." The bishop rose and motioned for Cadedryn to follow him behind a curtain that cloaked the back of the dais. "What is so urgent that you must speak of it now?"

Cadedryn withdrew the letter Morgana had handed him, as well as the faded letter he had found in the Bible. He handed them both to the bishop. "I believe this first letter was a warning to my father, given to him in the days before his murder. It is written in the same hand as this other note, a note that was given to me yesterday by Lady Morgana."

"The penmanship appears similar," the bishop agreed. He read the letters, then frowned. "This is disturbing."

"In addition, there is a witness who says he saw a woman kill my father. He states that the woman was in red. He pointed to Kassandra because she has red hair."

"Why has this witness not come forward before now?"

"Perhaps he was threatened, but unless the person who threatens him is imprisoned, he will most likely deny such a claim."

"Why discuss this with me in private? Why not bring it to the floor during the trial?"

"I have been a loyal subject of the crown and have

served her faithfully for many years. I intend to do so for many more, but I must ask a great favor. We must pretend to convict Kassandra."

The bishop frowned deeper.

"If we convince Morgana that I have been suitably cowed and that Kassandra is no longer a risk, we can draw her out and see who else is involved in her plot. I . . ." Cadedryn paused and clenched his fist. "I do not know if Curtis McCafferty and Lady Corine are equally guilty. I am not even sure of Laird McCafferty."

"I do not like making a mockery of my court."

"Of course not, Your Excellency. I wish only to delay the true trial. 'Twill all be in the interest of justice. If Kassandra is guilty, the verdict will stand. If she is not, then this will be our best chance at discovering the true conspirators."

"King Malcolm advised me to listen well to your statements. He thinks highly of you. I will do as you say, but I will not allow my ultimate decision to be swayed by anything other than what I see and hear."

Cadedryn smiled. "As it should be. Thank you."

They both heard the crowd's sudden surge in noise and knew that Kassandra had arrived. Taking a deep breath, Cadedryn ducked out from behind the curtain and stood next to the altar. Soon the doors opened and men poured in, filling the pews until the latecomers were forced to stand at the back of the church. No women were allowed in the church while it was being used as a courtroom, for females were expressly forbidden in a court of law.

Laird McCafferty elbowed his way to the front, dragging the elderly gentleman behind him. "Give way! I have the witness!"

The bishop straightened his robes, then slowly

emerged from behind the altar and ascended the steps. He turned and faced the milling crowd. Raising his hand for silence, he looked toward the door. "Bring the accused forward to face justice!"

The door swung open and a shaft of brilliant sunlight shot across the church floor. For a moment there was nothing but dazzling sunshine, then what appeared to be an angel floated through the glow, her crimson halo shimmering around her head in radiant glory. Then the angel walked through the light and stepped into the shadowed aisle.

Not an angel. Kassandra. Kassandra with beautiful scarlet curls that cascaded down her back in magnificent splendor.

Cadedryn's heart thundered and he nearly fell to his knees as she was led forward to face the bishop.

"Kassandra," he whispered.

She turned, startled by his appearance. She gasped and the color drained from her face. "Why are you here? Do you come to gloat over my fate? Can you not leave me to endure this ordeal with a remnant of my pride?"

He stepped forward and grasped her hands. "All is not as it seems," he murmured, but she turned away from him and faced the front of the church.

The bishop held up his staff. "Hand the prisoner over to me," he commanded.

Kassandra shivered with dread, her legs suddenly too weak to move.

"Have no fear," Cadedryn whispered as he gently pushed her toward the bishop.

Kassandra glared at him over her shoulder, then pulled free of his hold.

"Who charges this woman?"

"I do!" Laird McCafferty bellowed. "She is a witch,

with the power of the devil in her blood. She flies through the night, slaying those whom she dislikes. She killed Liam Caenmore, then kept his knife to preen over her deed. She is a witch and a murderer and should burn!"

"Lady Kassandra, answer the charges," the bishop extolled.

She turned to face the bishop and pressed her lips together in defiance.

He turned to Cadedryn. "Do you have evidence against this woman? Do you have knowledge of her unnatural powers?"

"She says she has dreams," Cadedryn said, forcing the condemning words out of his constricted throat.

Kassandra sucked in her breath, her eyes filling with tears. "Cadedryn?" she asked. "You *do* seek my death! What did that letter say to so completely convince you of my guilt?"

He swallowed and turned away from her stricken gaze. "Kassandra came to court to find me and then set out to seduce me with trickery. I was to marry Lady Corine, but Lady Kassandra tried to stop me. I have seen the truth. I will wed Lady Corine and unite our families as they should have been united long ago." Stepping closer to the altar, he looked directly at Laird McCafferty. "I have broken her spell. I have been freed of her enchantment and I denounce her magical powers."

McCafferty smiled as he crossed his arms and nodded. "Good. As your foster father, I am pleased that you have come to your senses." He turned toward the bishop. "I have a witness who further proves Lady Kassandra's guilt." He pushed the elderly man forward.

The man looked at Cadedryn, his eyes filled with

sorrow. "I saw a woman in red kill Liam Caenmore," he repeated. Then, as McCafferty nudged him to point at Kassandra, he flung himself prostrate in front of the bishop. "I can say no more!"

McCafferty's face turned purple with rage, but Cadedryn swiftly gripped the elderly man's shoulder, picked him up and flung him at Robert. "Take this man away. We do not need his testimony."

"Have you anything to say in your defense?" the bishop questioned as he peered down his nose at Kassandra.

Hurt, pain, anger and fury all raged within her heart. Spots of black and white danced in front of her eyes and her head spun in dizzying circles. She gasped, trying to draw air into her suddenly frozen lungs, but her chest would not obey. Blood pounded between her ears and shuddered through her heart. She didn't know what to do—she wanted to scream; she wanted to shout. She wanted to take a sword and send it plunging into Cadedryn's cold heart. "Why?" she panted. "Why do this? I thought we loved one another. I thought we . . ." She blinked rapidly, trying to keep everything in focus.

Cadedryn clenched his teeth so hard, he felt his jaw would crack. He did love her! He loved her with all his heart, but she could not know the truth—not yet. He could not risk her life just to see her beautiful blue eyes look at him with sweet emotion. It was better that she hated him. It would make her stronger, better able to endure the night before he could prove her innocence.

Her red hair blew against her face from a breeze sweeping through the church entrance. A dove flapped through the door and fluttered up into the rafters, then sat and cooed down at them. Cadedryn looked up, remembering when they had romped in the high reaches of the half-built church. Aye, she had seduced him, but not with magic. She had captured his heart, but not with stealth. She was his soul mate, his true destiny, but he could not claim her.

"We are nothing," he said coldly. "You always knew that I placed my title above all else. If I marry Corine, I will have everything I always wanted." *Except you. I want you.*

She closed her eyes against the pain. Sobs welled up in her throat but died before they could erupt. It was as if everything within her rose up in a hailstorm of anger, then suddenly, inexplicably, drained away. She became a void. The pain disappeared. There was no more love. No more passion. Anger and humiliation drifted with the breeze. There was nothing left within her . . . nothing left to feel.

"She is guilty!" the bishop declared as the men rose in a thunder of stomps and catcalls. A few—those who had known her at the castle—looked away, but others shouted obscenities at her as they pounded the pews.

She opened her eyes and nodded. Turning from the table and followed by Cadedryn, the bishop, Laird McCafferty and Robert, she walked down the aisle, through the frenzied men, and exited the church.

A hail of rotten garbage pummeled them, and Cadedryn was forced to fall back, although he glanced meaningfully at Robert. "Stand by," he commanded. "Guard her well."

Robert nodded, but Kassandra lifted a blank gaze and stared past his shoulder.

Cadedryn wanted to reach for her and tell her that everything would be all right. His thighs twitched with the need to protect her from the flying debris and his lips quivered with the desire to tell her how much he loved her.

The bishop stepped out of the church and held up his hand for silence. "Prepare the bonfire for tomorrow. We will set the witch aflame as soon as the sun breaks over the morning horizon."

A chorus of angry voices greeted his delay, but the bishop ignored them. He motioned to Robert to take her away and turned to nod at Cadedryn.

Cadedryn nodded back. He had one night. One night to prove Kassandra's innocence.

Chapter 25

That evening, well after Kassandra had been returned to her cell and the moon had risen high in the night sky, there was a soft knock on the servants' door that led to the kitchens from the great hall. "Enter," Cadedryn said as he opened the door a crack and motioned for the bishop to slide inside.

"I hope you have good reason to ask me to enter from the kitchens," he warned.

"Yes. I want you to observe unobtrusively. Please stand behind the screen in the great hall and listen with open ears."

The bishop paused. "I will not hear what you want me to hear, nor say what you tell me to say. I am beholden only to God. Your position and title mean nothing to me."

Cadedryn smiled. "Then we have much in common. Please." He motioned to the screen.

As the bishop stepped behind the screen, there was a knock on the main door.

Taking a deep breath, Cadedryn opened it to his expected visitors. "Lady Morgana and Laird McCafferty. Lord Curtis. Lady Corine. Thank you for coming. The servants have prepared a meal for us and laid it on the table so that we may feast in private."

Lady Morgana sauntered inside the hall, her face smugly victorious. "A feast?" she asked. "Cause for celebration? I presume you wish to formalize your and Corine's betrothal? I must tell you that Lord Fergus has already agreed to the arrangement I drew up. I happen to have the dower papers with me."

"I want to ask you a question," Cadedryn said. "And I want you to answer truthfully."

"Of course," Morgana smiled. "I have always been honest."

"I don't believe that, but I want your honesty now. If you are true, then I will give you everything you have ever wanted. I will marry your daughter and give her my name and my castle."

She looked at him through wary eyes. "What do you want to know?" she asked carefully.

"Who murdered my father?"

"Why, Kassandra of course! The bishop just convicted her."

"The truth. If you do not tell me, I will not marry Corine."

Lady Morgana gasped. "You *must* marry Corine! You have to!"

Curtis stepped forward. "Cadedryn—"

Cadedryn looked at his friend. "You want me to marry the woman you love?"

The two men exchanged looks. After ten years of battling side by side, they knew each other better than most brothers. "Do you remember that day by the tree?" Curtis replied.

"Yes, I do," Cadedryn answered.

"Those words were true. I wanted you to marry Corine because I thought it was the best union for both you and her. But"—he stepped over toward Corine and gathered her hand in his—"I would not wish it now. I love Corine, and I want to marry her. Not for land or for gain, but because I want to wake up every morning and see her beautiful smile."

"Curtis!" McCafferty shouted. "How dare you say such things? That is not the plan! Cadedryn must wed Corine."

Cadedryn glared at McCafferty and Morgana. "For decades, you and Morgana have been carrying on a clandestine affair. When did it change from fresh love to twisted desperation? Was it when Morgana told you that she wanted a title more than she wanted you? Did your heart turn cold and brittle as you watched the woman you love pine after something you could never give her? Didn't you tremble with rage? Yet you still chased after her, even when she married Lord Fergus. You panted after her like a puppy trailing behind his mother. You didn't plan any of this, did you? You were nothing but a pawn in Morgana's devious plot."

"You fool!" McCafferty shouted. "You know nothing! *I* devised the plan to murder you and then wed our children! *I* am the one who told Morgana there was still a way to claim her title. I am even the one who killed Sarah so Liam would fear for your life and send you to me for fostering. *I planned everything!*"

Morgana took two quick strides and slapped McCafferty's face. "How dare you say that! *I* killed Liam. Me, a woman, killing a great big man like Liam Caenmore!" She spun and looked proudly at Cadedryn. "David was afraid to kill him, but I was not. I knew I could get close to Liam and plunge a dirk deep into his heart, for he would never suspect a woman was capable of murder. Even after I sent Liam that note, he did not suspect me."

"The plot is over, Morgana," Cadedryn told her, his

voice hard and emotionless. "You killed my father. You must be brought to justice."

"Liam deserved it! He destroyed everything! I should have been a countess! You understand. You have struggled to become an earl, ignoring everything that worked to turn you astray. You even denied your love for Kassandra because you wanted your title!"

Cadedryn stared at her flushed face, seeing the greed that had rotted her soul. "You are correct, milady. I was once as blind as you, but I thank God I learned that love is far more precious than any title." He walked to the screen and pulled it aside, revealing the bishop.

Morgana paled and abruptly sat down on a chair.

"You have lost, milady, laird. You lost your lover," Cadedryn said sadly. "And now your freedom. You both will go to prison for what you have done."

Morgana flung herself at McCafferty. "David!" she screamed. "Stop him! Make him marry Corine! He is ruining everything just like his father did!"

"I will force you to marry her!" McCafferty shouted as he flung the table over and lunged after Cadedryn.

Cadedryn stepped backward and pulled his sword free. "Don't be a fool, McCafferty. I am a far superior swordsman. 'Twas you in the meadow, wasn't it? You were the coward that attacked a defenseless woman. Did you also attack me that night on the deserted road? Another act by a desperate man."

"You succeed at everything, don't you? Even my son is more loyal to you than to me!" He swung his sword wildly at Cadedryn's head. "This time *I* will win."

"Father!" Curtis cried. "Stop this. 'Tis over!"

Cadedryn ducked and easily parried the thrust.

"Lower your weapon. The bishop is watching. Confess and we will not add this attack to your crimes."

"I want to see your blood on the ground!" McCafferty vaulted over the table and lunged again. "I want you to die knowing that I won!"

"Won? There was no contest."

"But you get everything, don't you?" McCafferty snarled as he slammed his sword against the table. "You get Kassandra and your title! No one let me have anything I wanted!"

"You could have had everything," Cadedryn countered. "You could have had the woman you love and a place to call home. 'Twas your greed and lust for power that kept you two apart."

McCafferty lifted his sword and advanced, his face twisted with rage.

Corine screamed as Curtis pulled his own sword.

Cadedryn backed away, his blade held in wary defense. He motioned for Curtis to stay back and hold Corine. "This is my fight," he murmured.

McCafferty swung his sword over his head and pointed it at Cadedryn. "You and all those you love will die. You can't stop it now. Kassandra has already been convicted."

Cadedryn lowered his sword and shook his head. "No, Laird McCafferty. She will live. She will become my wife." He turned away in disgust. "Now that the bishop knows the truth, she will be set free." Out of the corner of his eye he saw McCafferty move, but before he could react, a knife whistled past his head. He gasped, and leaned down to pick up the knife that clattered to the floor. "You seek to murder me with a knife to my back?" he cried as he brandished the blade.

"You are like Liam!" McCafferty screamed as he rushed to attack. "You have everything! A castle, a title, wealth and love! Now you have *her* and Curtis!" He picked up the candelabra and flung it at Cadedryn's head.

Cadedryn ducked, then raised his sword once again in defense.

McCafferty faced Cadedryn. "Your blood will cleanse me!" He bounded forward, his sword aimed at Cadedryn's heart.

Cadedryn parried.

The two locked, face-to-face, sword against sword. Cadedryn stared at McCafferty, seeing the insane glint in his eyes. "David," he pleaded. "I do not want to kill you . . ."

McCafferty pushed him back and disengaged their swords, then lunged forward again.

Cadedryn moved quickly, trying to deflect the blade, but the swords slipped along each other, sliding with increasing speed, producing the terrible screech of metal against metal, until suddenly Cadedryn's blade slid into McCafferty's chest.

The laird's eyes grew wide and he stared at Cadedryn in surprise. He dropped his sword and stumbled back, then clutched the blade's hilt where it protruded. "Cadedryn?" he asked in wonder. He turned and faced Morgana. "Darling?"

Cadedryn stepped forward and yanked the sword free, his eyes clouded with sorrow. "I'm sorry," he murmured. "Despite it all, you were my foster father. I did not want to hurt you."

McCafferty fell to his knees. His face underwent changes as if he were seeing things that were not there. He reached out, struggling to grasp something just out of his reach, but his hands fell to his sides, empty and bereft. Blood poured from his wound, drenching the floorboards. He swayed, then collapsed into his own pool of blood.

"Morgana loved . . . the title more," McCafferty cried, his voice growing weak.

The bishop kneeled next to him. "That is not love," he said quietly. "Love is what you will feel when God forgives you." He made the sign of the cross over David's dying body, then rose and stepped back.

McCafferty blinked. His lips turned in a slight smile and his facial muscles relaxed. Then he was gone.

"How could you?" Morgana screamed as she lunged at Cadedryn and pummeled him with her fists. "How could you do this? I want my title!"

Cadedryn tried to grasp her hand, but she flailed wildly. Her hand snagged on the engraved dirk in Cadedryn's belt and she yanked it free.

"This is it," she said, her voice rising even higher. "This is the knife I used to murder Liam. How did that sorceress get it?" She held it pressed against her breast, then looked at McCafferty's body. Her face crumpled. "I cannot live without you, David. You are all I have left!" she cried, then plunged the dirk into her own chest.

"Stop!" Cadedryn shouted as he jumped forward, but the blade had already found its mark and blood poured forth. Cadedryn frantically pulled the blade free and tried to stop the flow, but Morgana pushed him weakly away. "Leave me," she whispered. "I want to be with him . . ."

Corine screamed again, struggling against Curtis's firm hold. "No!" she wailed. "Mother!"

The bishop pulled Cadedryn back, then made the sign of the cross over Morgana'a head, but his eyes were filled with sorrow. "She has taken her own life. Not even I can save her soul now."

Cadedryn stared in shock at Morgana's lifeless body.

"I will tell the king what I heard and will pronounce Lady Kassandra innocent. But the details of this night will not be made public. There are too many important families affected by this tragedy. 'Tis better that all is laid to rest."

Corine buried her face against Curtis's chest. "Marry me," she begged. "Marry me now so that we can forget today and live the rest of our lives looking toward the future. I don't want to think about any of this again. I just want to feel your love surround and enfold me."

Curtis nodded, then gently assisted Corine to a chair. He walked over to Cadedryn and clasped his hand.

"I did not intend to kill your father," Cadedryn told him.

"I understand. 'Twas in self-defense."

They both nodded. Their bond of loyalty had been tested and proved true. "Corine is the one you love. Let us not make the same mistakes as our fathers. Marry her," Cadedryn urged.

Curtis nodded. "I intend to."

Suddenly, the door to the great hall burst open and Robert raced in, his normally stoic face twisted with anxiety. "She's gone!" he cried.

"Who's gone?" Cadedryn asked.

"Kassandra! She has escaped!"

Chapter 26

Earlier that night, Kassandra had drifted awake from the depths of a mist-filled dream. She woke slowly, aware that something was different. Something had changed.

She rolled over and stared out the window at the full moon. Cadedryn had betrayed her. He had abandoned their love in favor of his ambition. By tossing her aside, he would fulfill every one of his desires. He would wed a Fergus woman. He would curry the king's favor and have his title. His life would be as he wanted it: secure, sedate and predictable. Powerful.

Would he be lonely? Would he yearn for her in the cold nights? Would he remember the beautiful afternoon they had spent together under the maple tree? To him, it would be only a stray memory of a time before. He would forget her face and her touch. He would forget her dreams.

But she would never forget.

A sound coming from outside made her sit up. A few people from the village had shouted outside her window for hours, even dancing and reveling in their glee. They welcomed her punishment for they feared magic with deeply imbedded superstitions. Her half sister had warned her about such people. She had told Kassandra of their unwillingness to understand or accept others of a different nature. She had feared for Kassandra's safety among the populace.

Kassandra had not completely believed Kalial. She had been naive and trusting, thinking that Cadedryn and his people would come to understand her. Come to love her.

The sound came again and she rose to face the disturbance. For the first time in months, her dreams had been peaceful and serene. She should have felt relaxed, assured that Cadedryn was finally safe, but a new fear clutched her heart. She did not want to die.

The sound came yet again and Kassandra peered through the bars. Her lips turned upward in a bittersweet grin as she beheld Triu-cair peeking over the ledge.

"Triu-cair!" she whispered. "Why are you here? It is too dangerous. You must go back. Go back to Loch Nidean."

Triu-cair held a small key in his jaws and it clanged against the bars as the weasel wriggled through the window. *Do you want to get out?*

Kassandra took the key and stared at it in surprise. "How did you get this?"

I'm a polecat. Triu-cair grinned. *I stole it from Robert's belt while he went to the garderobe.*

Kassandra turned and tiptoed to the door, which led directly to the courtyard, and pressed her ear to the wood. Robert had said nothing to her after her sentencing, their earlier camaraderie lost after the bishop's condemning words. Now Kassandra listened to his footsteps as he paced back and forth outside her cell. Since the few villagers who had harassed her were gone, his steps were leisurely, passing far to the right before swinging just as far to the left. Judging from the time it took him to return, he might not even see or hear her if she timed her departure right.

Kassandra clenched the key in her hand. Some recess of her mind had hoped that Cadedryn would come for her. She had foolishly prayed that this was a dream and he would fling open the door and declare it time to awaken. But he had not come.

If she didn't try to escape now, she would be dead by tomorrow morning.

Taking care to move quietly, she placed the key in the lock and opened it with a loud click. She froze, her heart beating madly, certain that Robert would hear her, but his steps continued unabated. Sighing with relief, she pushed the door open a crack and slipped out.

A satchel lay conspicuously near to the door, presumably filled with bread and cheese for tomorrow's final meal. She hesitated only briefly before taking it and slinging it over her shoulder.

Triu-cair scurried around the corner and leapt upon her shoulder. He pointed his nose toward Robert's horse tethered to a tree. It was a fine-boned gelding with a wise brow, clearly built for endurance. A full bedroll and set of travel bags hung off the saddle and the bridle was already placed upon his head.

Kassandra glanced at the dark castle rising high in the moonlight behind her. A lifetime was ending. To leave now would be to admit she had been wrong. Her dreams . . . Cadedryn . . . all were over.

To her left, she saw a tall pile of logs, her funeral pyre. Soon the moon would sink and the sun would rise. Then they would come for her.

She looked up at Cadedryn's window, her heart splintering into thousands of tiny fragments. Despite everything, she still loved him.

We must go.

She nodded, hearing Robert turn on his heel and commence his pacing back toward her. She took a deep breath, then raced on light feet toward the gelding. He welcomed her with a soft nicker, which Kassandra quickly muffled. After tying up her skirts, she gripped the cantle and swung up on his back. She reined him around and took one last look at Cadedryn's window. For a brief second she hesitated. Her heart skipped a beat.

Then she set the gelding cantering down the hill away from Aberdour Castle.

Kassandra galloped through the valley, then to the top of the far hillside. At the peak, she spun to face the castle. Anger warred with her pain. Her heart felt heavy and sluggish, as if her blood no longer wanted to beat through her veins. Without Cadedryn, life held no joy. Each day stretched before her full of sadness and despair.

She dashed a tear from her cheek. She must not wallow in self-pity. He had betrayed her. She had stayed true, protecting him even at the risk of her own life, but he had failed her. She would find her own way to the coast. She knew east from west and would journey using the stars and moon. If she kept off the roads and traveled only by night, she could find her way without any assistance.

Suddenly the hairs on the back of her neck rose as she became aware of a rider coming across the double moat. Not so soon! How could they have already discovered her escape? She should have had until morning!

She spun her gelding around and kicked his sides, sending him racing across the moor. She glanced over her shoulder, hoping to see the horse and rider turn toward the village, but instead, they headed toward her and began galloping hard. She gasped in terror, stunned at the horse and rider's intense burst of speed.

"Run!" she shouted to her gelding as she pushed him to greater effort. She was a fearless competitor who rarely lost a race. This time, she *could* not lose. Leaning across her gelding's neck, she bent into the wind, her brilliant hair tangling with the horse's mane and tears of anger blinding her vision. Why chase her? Why not let her go back from whence she had come?

Triu-cair clung to her clothes as the threesome swept through the grasses and headed toward the shelter of the forest. "Run!" she cried again, as she heard the other horse gaining upon them. "We can lose them in the trees!"

They thundered down the valley, the gelding losing the race stride for stride. Kassandra pummeled his sides and flung her hands high upon his neck, giving him every bit of encouragement, but the other horse surged past them, then angled abruptly, cutting them off.

The gelding skidded to a stop, tossing his head in the air and whinnying. His tail swished and he pinned his ears flat against his head, then reared, striking with his front hooves. The other horse sprang upward, rising on his hind legs and crashing his powerful chest into the gelding's shoulder, forcing the gelding back onto his four legs and blocking his ability to run toward the forest.

Kassandra screamed, hauling on the gelding's reins, intent upon running him in the other direction, but her pursuer reached across and ripped the reins from her hands.

"Cease!" he shouted. "You will kill us both!"

Kassandra's head snapped up and she glared at the man. "Cadedryn! Why do you pursue me? Do you hate me so much?"

"No, I—"

She kicked his shin, then leapt from her horse and started running on foot toward the trees.

"Kassandra!" Cadedryn shouted as he jumped from his stallion and gave chase. "Stop for one moment!"

Tears streamed down her face as she ran. "I hate you," she cried, stumbling briefly before regaining her stride. "You betrayed me."

He ran after her. "Let me explain—"

She spun around and reached for a rock, flinging it at his head. "I want no explanations!" she wailed. "You did not defend me. You are a spineless, ambition-driven bastard who crumbles under the first test of our love. I hate you!"

He ducked the rock and warily approached her, his hands outstretched. "I love you," he replied softly. "I never abandoned you."

"Yes, you did! In the great hall, you let them take me without so much as a word in my defense. You stood in court and denounced everything about me!"

"They threatened to kill you, Kassandra. Speaking aloud would only have sealed your fate more firmly, and I knew that if we did not expose Morgana and David's plot, we would never be free of their malevolence."

"You believed the awful things they said about me."

He took another step closer, pleading with her to listen. "Never. I never would believe that your heart was anything but pure."

Kassandra wiped away her tears, her eyes narrowed in doubt. "In the church, in front of the bishop, you branded me a witch. You told him about my dreams."

"I had to. I had to make Morgana and David think that they had won so their defenses would be down and they would admit to their deeds. It was not sufficient that I believe you; I needed the bishop to know that you were innocent. And now David and Morgana have admitted their guilt. Both lie dead, David by my hand, Morgana by her own."

Kassandra crumpled to the ground, burying her head in her hands. "You want me gone so you can wed Corine."

He kneeled next to her, gathering her in his embrace. "No. Corine is going to marry Curtis. And I want to spend the rest of my life with you."

"I am not who you want," Kassandra cried, trying to push his arms away. "You want some highborn woman with mild manners and . . . and who knows how to embroider!"

"I want you," he answered, holding her firmly. "I want someone who can ride across the moor in the starlight. A woman who is as beautiful across a campfire as she is across an elegant table. I want someone who loves me so deeply that she dreams about me. I want you, Kassandra."

She stared into his eyes as Cadedryn remained on one knee in front of her. "I know it has been a long night and you have been sorely tested, but I ask you, do you still dream of me?"

Kassandra hesitated. She stared at his face bathed in moonlight. Triu-cair's warm body pressed against her legs, but he offered her no words of wisdom. It was her choice. She had completed her duty. Cadedryn was safe. She was safe. She could go home and try to forget everything.

But Cadedryn knew not only the color of her hair, but also the truth about her life. There were no more secrets between them, no more plots swirling this way and that. She could ride away and return to the safety of her forest, or she could stay with him, in this land that didn't always make sense to her.

And she could love him. She smiled.

He smiled back.

"You are my dream. We are meant to be together," she murmured, touching his cheek.

"Then you will stay with me? You will marry me?"

"What of your title?"

"I wrote to the king when we first arrived and just recently received word back. He has already agreed to our marriage. He is pleased that I support the union of Curtis McCafferty and Corine Fergus and have formed an unbreakable alliance with both of them. For now, the Highlands are secure. But even if it were not true and the king had refused my petition, I would still marry you."

"And risk losing your title?"

"You are far more important to me."

She kneeled with him and brushed her lips across his. "For the second time, yes," she whispered. "I will marry you."

Epilogue

A thin strand of fog snaked through the trees and encircled his feet, then spread along the ground in an ever-thickening blanket. His heart began to race as he recognized the fog of his dreams. Kassandra had led him here. She had reached across the boundaries of sleep to find him, just as he now hungered to find her.

He blinked, not sure what to do. "Kassandra?" he asked hesitantly. He sensed a vibration coming from the trees, but as he tried to walk forward, the mist tickled his calves, holding him back. He struggled to keep his footing, suddenly aware that she was toying with him.

He gripped a tree branch and peered through the mist. He felt her. He knew she watched him.

You cannot come here. Strangers are forbidden.

"I am not a stranger," he called out. "I am . . ." He paused as his brows drew together and he fell to his knees in confusion. "What am I?" he questioned the forest. "Am I a laird? Am I a swordsman? An earl?" He stroked the trunk of a tree in a sensual caress. "A lover?"

Who are you? Who do you want to be?

"I am Dagda, and I have come to claim my Danu." He rose and stepped boldly into the forest, striding through the thick mist and pushing aside the heavy branches until he beheld her smiling face.

He gathered her in his arms as his heart raced and blood rushed through his body. "It's you," he whispered. "I found you! You knew all along, but I had to learn."

"Why have you come?" Kassandra questioned as she clung to his wide shoulders.

He held her in front of him and looked at her with his deep green eyes. "Because I love you."

She stared at him as the dream mist wrapped them in a loving embrace. She touched his face, her fingers trembling with longing. "I want you . . ."

"We are meant to be together. You know that deep in your soul. You have dreamed it and now I have dreamed it. Let me love you, now and forever."

"I cannot leave my forest. You cannot leave your castle."

"I will come to your forest in my dreams if you live with me in my castle while we are awake. You complete my kingdom. You are my countess. We must love each other. My father knew the truth. He saw the way. He loved my mother and found happiness within her arms. I once thought he was the fool, but now I know he showed me the path. You are my heart. I love you. I want to be with you."

"I love you. I have always loved you. We are soul mates, bound together by ties that transcend time and place."

Cadedryn looked up at the weasel perched upon a tree branch, grinning down at them. Cadedryn nodded, then beheld the red-haired babe held within Kassandra's arms. He pulled them both close, and buried his face in Kassandra's flame-colored tresses.

The mist swept around them, carrying them deep into the dream world. Although their sleeping bodies lay resting in the master bedchamber of Aberdour, their souls floated free. The moon shone through the window, calm and serene, but within their mutual dream, the stars flickered like thousands of dancing fire faeries.

Danu and Dagda. Mother earth and her battle king.

Kassandra and Cadedryn, the Earl and Countess of Aberdour.

The steamy novels of
Sasha Lord

Under a Wild Sky
0-451-21028-X

Ronin, a battered warrior, seeks refuge from his
enemies in a secluded wood, only to be attacked by forest
men. But when Ronin takes the men's leader captive, he soon
learns that this young man he's holding prisoner is actually a
beautiful woman whose passion for life and love
matches his own.

In a Wild Wood
0-451-21029-8

When Matalia seizes Brogan trespassing in her family's
forest, they begin an adventure that will endanger their
lives—and they discover a passion that will
challenge their hearts.

Across a Wild Sea
0-451-21387-4

When a violent storm casts Xanthier ashore, Alannah gives in
to an untamed desire. And a promise made in the heat of passion transforms their lives forever.

Beyond the Wild Wind
0-451-21785-3

Wildly impetuous Istabelle O'Bannon, the daring captain of a
sailing ship, is desperate to reclaim a precious treasure—and
she trusts only one man to help her.